The Śūraṅgama Sūtra

The Śūraṅgama Sūtra
(Leng Yen Ching)

Chinese Rendering by
Master Paramiti of
Central North India at Chih Chih Monastery,
Canton, China, AD 705

Commentary (abridged) by
Ch'an Master Han Shan (1546-1623)

Translated by
Charles Luk
(Upāsaka Lu K'uan Yu)

Dev Publishers & Distributors
New Delhi

Published by
Dev Publishers & Distributors
Second Floor, Prakashdeep,
22, Delhi Medical Association Road,
Darya Ganj, New Delhi – 110 002

www.devbooks.co.in

ISBN: 978-93-87496-72-9

Printed in India.

Respectfully dedicated to Mr. and Mrs. Carroll Aikins who are fervent Canadian Buddhists and whose very valuable and generous support has made possible my presentation of this important sermon which, according to the Buddha, will be the first sūtra to disappear in this Dharma ending age.

Contents

Preface xv

I The Noumenon in the Tathāgata Store 1

Ānanda's Weakness—the Reason for this Sermon 1

Meditative Study of All as Void (Śamatha) 2

Wiping Out the Five Aggregates and Eight Consciousnesses to Expose the Unreality of Ego 3

Probing into the false mind to wipe out the first two aggregates and first five consciousnesses 3

Refuting the false mind to eliminate the third aggregate and expose the unreality of the sixth consciousness 9

Revealing the Bright Samādhi 10

Origin of Inversion 11

Actual Inversion 12

The Inverted Mind 12

Probe into the false mind 12

Thinking is unreal 12

The sixth consciousness is empty 13

The seventh consciousness is unreal 14

Refuting all inversion 15

The Inverted Perception 15

A bright light to reveal the One Reality 15

Returning perception to Mind 16

Inverted Men 18

The worldling's inverted views 18

The Hinayanist's inverted views 18

The heretics' inverted view of annihilation 20

The inverted behaviour 22

Delusion and Enlightenment are of the same source 23

Refuting the false perception to eliminate the fourth aggregate and reveal the non-existence of the seventh consciousness 25

Wiping Out the Unreal 25

The Non-Existence of Discriminative Perception 25

Ānanda's wrong view 25
Unreality of illusory causes 25
Falseness of both sense organs and consciousness 26
All phenomena returnable to causes are unreal 26
Borrowing the Essence of Perception to Pick Out Causal Externals 27
Setting up the essence of perception 27
Picking out causal externals 27
The nature of perception 28
The (Underlying) Nature of Perception is not the Essence of Perception 28
The capacity of perception 28
Picking out causal objects 29
The essence of perception 29
The Essence of Perception Mistaken for Externals 30
Refuting this misconception 30
True perception 30
Wiping Out the Capacity of Perception to Reveal the True Mind 30
The capacity of seeing 30
Breaking up the capacity of seeing 31
Revealing the Real 31
Removing the essence of perception to wipe out the fifth aggregate and eighth consciousness 32
Eradicating Attachment to the Ego to Reveal the One Reality 32
Rooting out Ānanda's misconception of objects BEING and NOT BEING perception 33
Misconception of objects BEING perception 33
Misconception of objects NOT BEING perception 33
Mañjuśrī's Helpful Interposition 34
Wiping Out Alaya's Self-Evidencing to Reveal One Reality 36
Ānanda's Discrimination 36
Wiping Out Ānanda's Discrimination 36
Rooting out the self as such 36
Eliminating cause and condition 37
Revealing the essential Bodhi 37
Brushing away wrong assumptions 37
Eliminating the Essence of pPerception to Reveal the Inceptive Enlightenment 38
Wiping Out Ānanda's Discrimination 38
Revealing the Inceptive Bodhi 38

Revealing the unreality of the two realms to expose the non-existence of Dharma (things) 40
Individual Karma 40
Collective Karma 41
Revealing the Independent Basic Bodhi to Expose the Unfettered Absoluteness (Bhūtatathatā) 43
Wiping Out All Traces of the False to Enter the Abstruse to Reveal the Bhūtatathatā 43
Direct Pointing to the One Mind 44
Fusing Myriads of Things into the Absolute to Reveal the Identity of Phenomenon with Noumenon 45
Fusing the Five Aggregates 45
The First Aggregate Rūpa 45
The Second Aggregate Vedanā 46
The Third Aggregate Sañjñā 46
The Fourth Aggregate Saṁskāra 47
The Fifth Aggregate Vijñāna 47
Fusing the Six Entrances 47
Entrance Through the Eyes 47
Entrance Through the Ears 48
Entrance Through the Nose 49
Entrance Through the Tongue 49
Entrance Through the Body 50
Entrance Through the Intellect 50
Fusing the Twelve Āyatana (Six Sense Organs and Data) 51
Eyes and Form 51
Ears and Sound 51
Nose and Smell 52
Tongue and Taste 52
Body and Touch 53
Intellect and Dharmā 53
Fusing the Eighteen Fields or Realms of the Senses 54
The Field of Sight-Perception 54
The Field of Sound-Perception 54
The Field of Smell-Perception 55
The Field of Taste-Perception 56
The Field of Touch-Perception 56
The Field of the Sixth Consciousness 57
Fusing the Seven Elements into the Absolute to Reveal the Free Intermingling of Phenomenon and Noumenon 58
Exposing Faulty Differentiation 59
Pointing to the One Source 59

Instruction on the Seven Elements 59

The element of earth 59

The element of fire 60

The element of water 61

The element of wind 62

The element of space 62

The element of perception 63

The element of consciousness 65

Ānanda's Understanding Expressed in His Gāthā 66

II The Phenomenon in the Tathāgata Store 68

The Meditative Study of All as Unreal (Samāpatti) 68

The One Mind Being the Source of Both Delusion and Enlightenment 68

A Probe into the Disciple's Understanding of Noumenon and Phenomenon to Reveal the Rise of Illusions 69

The Real Missed by Cognizance of the False 70

The Three Finer Conditions of Unenlightenment 70

The Six Coarser Conditions of Unenlightenment 71

The Law of Continuity 71

Continuity of the (physical) universe 71

Continuity of living beings 72

Continuity of karmic retribution 73

The Uncreated and Unending 74

The Unhindered Intermingling of Noumenon and Phenomenon 74

Expounding the Common Source of Delusion and Enlightenment to Sum up the Intermingling of Noumenon and Phenomenon 75

III The Tathāgata Store Containing Both Noumenon and Phenomenon 77

Meditative Study of the Mean (Dhyāna) 77

Elimination of 'is' to reveal the True Mind 77

Elimination of 'is not' to reveal the True Mind 77

Simultaneous elimination of 'is' and 'is not' to reveal the Absolute Mind 78

The One Mind, Sudden Awakening and Realization 78

IV Self-Enlightenment 83

Objects Contemplated in Meditative Studies 83

Practice of Meditation for Self-Enlightenment 83

The subjective mind in the meditation 84

The objective phenomena in the meditation 84
The point of departure 86
Looking into the roots of kleśa to find the sense organ suitable for meditation 86
Expedient Instruction on the One Mind 91
Main Instruction on the Three Meditative Studies of the One Mind 93
How to Untie the Six Knots 96
Meditation on the six sense data 98
Meditation on the five sense organs 100
Meditation on the six consciousnesses 102
Meditation on the seven elements 105
Meditation on the organ of hearing 109
Mañjuśrī's Gāthā Teaching the Appropriate Method for Human Beings 116

V The Enlightenment of Others 124
Discipline and Its Three Decisive Steps, Śīla, Dhyāna and Prajñā 124
Prohibition against carnality 124
Prohibition against killing 125
Prohibition against stealing 126
Prohibition against lying 128

VI Bodhisattva Development into Buddhahood 130
The Tathāgata Store from Which Arise Both Saṁsāra and Nirvāna 130
The Origin of Living Beings and the World 131
The Inverted Cause of the Existence of Living Beings 131
The Inverted Cause of the Existence of the World 131
The Twelve Types of Transformation 131
The Twelve Groups of Living Beings 132
Transmutation of Saṁsāra into Nirvāṇa 134
The Three Gradual Steps to Wipe Out Saṁsāra 134
Progressive Advance in Bodhisattva Development 136
The Stage of Dry Wisdom 136
The Ten Stages of Bodhisattva Faith 136
The Ten Practical Stages of Bodhisattva Wisdom 137
The Ten Lines of Bodhisattva Action 138
The Ten Acts of Dedication 139
The Four Additional Harnessing Stages 140
The Ten Highest Stages of Bodhisattva Attainment 141
The Universal Enlightenment 142

The Absolute (or Wonderful) Enlightenment 142
The Title of This Sūtra 142
VII The Six Planes of Existence Caused by Unenlightenment 144
The Six States of Living Beings in Saṁsāra 144
The realm of devas 146
The realm of seers and spirits 146
The realm of human beings 146
The realm of animals 146
The realm of hungry ghosts 146
The realm of hells 147
The Ten Causes and Six Effects in the Realm of Hells 147
The Ten Karmic Causes of the Realm of Hells 147
The habit of sexual desire 147
The habit of craving 147
The habit of arrogance 148
The habit of anger 148
The habit of deceitfulness 148
The habit of lying 148
The habit of resentment 149
The habit of wrong views 149
The habit of unfairness 149
The habit of disputation 150
The Six Retributive Effects in the Realm of Hells 150
Retributive effects of wrong seeing 150
Retributive effects of wrong hearing 150
Retributive effects of wrong smelling 151
Retributive effects of wrong tasting 151
Retributive effects of wrong touching 151
Retributive effects of wrong thinking 152
Degrees of Perversity in Relation to Suffering in the Hells 152
The Ten Categories in the Realm of Hungry Ghosts 153
The Ten Categories of Animals (Birds, etc.) 154
The Ten Categories in the Realm of Human Beings 155
The Ten Categories in the Realm of Seers 156
The Realm of the Gods 157
The Six Heavens of the Realm of Desire 157
The Four Regions of the Dhyāna Heavens of the Realm of Form 158
The first region of the three dhyāna heavens 158
The second region of the three dhyāna heavens 158
The third region of the three dhyāna heavens 159

The fourth region of the four dhyāna heavens 159
The five heavens from which there is no return 160
The Four Heavens of the Formless Realm of Pure Spirit 161
The state of the Great Arhat 161
The four heavens beyond form 161
The Anagamin stage 162
The Four Classes in the Realm of Titans 162

VIII Warning to Practisers: The Fifty False States Caused by the Five Aggregates 165
States of Māra Caused by the Five Aggregates 165
The Ten States Affected by Rūpa 165
The Ten States Affected by Vedanā 169
The Ten States Affected by Sañjñā 173
The Ten States Affected by Saṁskāra 181
The Ten States Affected by Vijñāna 189
The Falsehood of the Five Aggregates 195
Falseness of rūpa 195
Falseness of vedanā 195
Falseness of sañjñā 196
Falseness of saṁskāra 196
Falseness of vijñāna 196
Glossary 199
Index 209

Preface

We take refuge in the Buddha,
We take refuge in the Dharma,
We take refuge in the Sangha,
We take refuge in the Triple Gem within ourselves.

This important sermon contains the essence of the Buddha's teaching and, as foretold by Him, will be the first sūtra to disappear in the Dharma ending age. It reveals the law of causality relating to both delusion and enlightenment and teaches the methods of practice and realization to destroy for ever the roots of birth and death. It aims at breaking up ālaya, the store consciousness, whose three characteristics are: self-evidencing, perception and form, by means of the three meditative studies of noumenon which is immaterial, of phenomenon which is unreal and of the 'Mean' which is inclusive of both, and leads to the all-embracing Śūraṅgama samādhi which is the gateway to Perfect Enlightenment and reveals the nature of the Tathāgata store of One Reality.

In the practice of the Śūraṅgama samādhi to wipe out the store consciousness, we should know that the latter has been under delusion for a very long time and that it is very difficult to transmute it into the Great Mirror Wisdom. Hence the Buddha uses two of its characteristics, *perception* and *form*, to explain the falseness of both so that we can relinquish our attachment to them and break its first characteristic, self-evidencing. The illusion of *form* which includes the body and mind made of the five aggregates and the visible world is tackled first by returning each of its aspects to where it arises to prove its unreality. Then the illusion of *perception* is wiped out by revealing its essence, or ālaya, which like a second moon is also an illusory creation. Hence the Buddha says: 'When seeing (perceives) seeing, seeing is not seeing (for) seeing strays from seeing; seeing cannot reach it,' which Han Shan ably interprets thus: 'When the absolute seeing perceives the essence of seeing, the former is not the latter which still differs from it; how then can false seeing reach that absolute seeing?' Absolute seeing is likened to the real moon in the sky; the essence of seeing to a second moon seen by bad eyes; and false seeing to the moon's reflection in water. In other words, the true moon stands for basic Enlightenment; the second moon for ālaya, or the essence of seeing which is close to the true moon; and the moon in water for perception, an illusion which is very far from the real moon. As to ālaya which is the unenlightened aspect of the self-nature, we cannot lightly dismiss it as non-existent, and this is why the Buddha avoids mentioning it for, as He says in His gāthā:

'Old habits flow like torrents in
Ālaya's subtle consciousness.
Since the real yet unreal can create confusion
I have refrained from revealing it to you.'

In answer to Ānanda's request for instruction on the three meditative studies (śamatha, sāmapatti and dhyāna), the Buddha reveals the light of Śūraṅgama samādhi from the host position of the all-embracing One Mind in its state of passionless imperturbability. Readers should not regard this revelation as some kind of miracle which cannot be proved by science and which should be dismissed as nonsense. We have mentioned in our previous book, *The Secrets of Chinese Meditation*,[1] that all serious students of the Dharma experience this state of brightness as soon as they succeed in stilling their minds in the practice of dhyāna.

This absolute Mind as revealed by the Buddha, has three great characteristics: greatness of its essence or substance, called Dharmakāya; greatness of its attributes or manifestations, perfect in wisdom and mercy, called Sambhogakāya; and the greatness of its functions, perfectly converting all living beings to the right Path, called Nirmāṇakāya.

Instead of cognizing the True Mind, we cling to the illusory body and mind made of the five aggregates as an ego, with sense data in the surrounding world as its objective field of activity. This *coarse* attachment to ego and things (dharmā) arises from *discrimination* and pertains to both the sixth and seventh consciousnesses. The *subtle* attachment to ego and Dharma is *inborn* for it arises from the seventh consciousness clinging to ālaya's perception as an *inner ego* and its realization of sainthood as *Dharma*. Only after wiping out both *discriminative* and *inborn* attachments can we reach the source of the One Mind and attain Enlightenment. Hence the three meditative studies which aim at destroying both coarse and subtle clingings.

It is much easier to relinquish the discriminative clinging than the inborn attachment and few practisers succeed in overcoming the latter; hence Han Shan says: 'This pass is the most difficult one to get through

[1] Rider, London.

and only one or two percent of practisers can succeed in negotiating it.' (See *The Secrets of Chinese Meditation*, p. 58, Rider and Co.) Here is the great difference between the Buddha Dharma and the teachings of other religions in the Orient.

The inborn attachment to an ego can be cut off only after one has reached the seventh stage of Bodhisattva development whereas the inborn clinging to Dharma still remains in and above the eighth stage, for the seventh consciousness has its unclean and clean characteristics. The unclean one is wiped out in the seventh stage when the name of store consciousness is dropped and replaced by that of pure consciousness which can now be transmuted into the Absolute. However the seventh consciousness still remains and clings to the Absolute as the object aimed at; this is the subtle attachment to Dharma. Hence the Buddha says: 'The idea that Bodhi Mind is created after the samsaric mind has been annihilated pertains to saṁsāra' (see p. 99), for this clinging to the Absolute that can be attained also implies the duality of subject and object, that is attachment to Dharma. Only after this last attachment has been cut off can Enlightenment be realized. These two coarse and subtle attachments do not go beyond the Eighth Consciousness and its created five aggregates, the breaking up of which is the aim of the teaching in this sūtra.

This sermon deals with basic Ignorance caused by the first dim thought of self-awareness as subject and its counterpart, dull emptiness, as object. The dimness so created by mind's separateness is called Primordial Darkness by non-Buddhist philosophers in the East and is the origin of creation according to the Buddha 's teaching which then explains the three subtle causes of unenlightenment: basic ignorance, subject and object, and its six coarse conditions: knowledge, responsiveness, attachment, assigning names to objects, karmic activity and suffering. These six conditions result in the manifestation of different forms, such as the world and living beings in the store consciousness. Here begins the law of continuity: that of the physical world resting on the four wheels of wind, water, metal and space which spring from the illusion thus created; that of living beings of the four types of birth; and that of karmic retribution caused by carnality, killing and stealing, the three cardinal conditions of birth and death.

The Buddha orders the twenty-five enlightened ones in the assembly to disclose the various means by which they have attained enlightenment so that others can learn something from them. After their statements of their realization by means of the six sense data, six sense organs, six consciousnesses and seven elements of fire, earth, water, wind, space, consciousness and perception, the World Honoured One asks Mañjūśrī for his opinion on these twenty-five methods. Mañjūśri praises Avalokiteśvara Bodhisattva for the latter's method by means of the organ of hearing which is the most suitable for human beings.

The Buddha then teaches the assembly the Śūraṅgama mantra and rituals for avoiding all obstructions on the Path to Enlightenment. We have not presented this section of the sūtra partly because the Chinese transliteration of the mantra is corrupt so that an English transliteration would be misleading, and partly because of lack of space. Moreover, the average Western student of Buddhism seems to have little faith in mantras and rituals which should not be published lest they create unnecessary disbelief and confusion and so compromise the beauty of this profound sūtra.

The Buddha goes on to explain why living beings are caught in the net of saṁsāra through the twelve types of birth and how to escape by practising the fifty-five gradual stages of Bodhisattva development to realize Complete Enlightenment. As asked by Ānanda, He described the realms of hells, the ten realms each of hungry ghosts, animals, human beings and seers; the six deva realms of desire, the eighteen deva realms of form, the four deva realms beyond form and the four realms of titans.

Before the meeting ends, the Buddha warns the assembly against fifty mental states caused by the five aggregates which hinder the practice of Dharma. These states should be recognized by all students in their meditation and cases are known of those having visions of Buddhas and Bodhisattvas who by clinging to them, fell into heresy and thereby returned to saṁsāra.

This translation is based on the explanation and commentary written by Master Han Shan of the Ming dynasty after his own enlightenment. The original Chinese text is a forest of vertical columns and is not divided, as in our presentation, into chapters with headings and sub-headings which the master added for the benefit of students. After this important sūtra reached China it was read and studied by all great masters before and after their major awakening, and was widely expounded and commented on in all well-known monasteries throughout the country. According to the late master Hsu Yun, it should be studied carefully until it is well understood by students of Mahāyāna and Ch'an before they begin their spiritual training.

In spite of our desire long ago to present this sūtra to sincere students in the West, we hesitated to do so because it is very profound and is beyond the comprehension of materialistic commentators and blasphemers who are inclined to seize every opportunity to criticize and vilify the holy Teaching thereby misleading the reading public and causing embarrassment and even loss of money to well-meaning publishers. A European book reviewer recently took the unnecessary trouble to question our competence to translate sūtras in sanskrit without appreciating that we have only Chinese sūtras in our country so that all our translations are from Chinese texts.

We are, however, indebted to our two Canadian readers, Mr. and Mrs. Carroll Aikins, who have studied and practised Mahāyāna and Ch'an for some thirty-five years and who, when hearing of our hesitation during their visit to Hongkong in 1963, immediately offered to purchase a thousand copies of our translation for free distribution. They told us that it was worth spending money to spread the Buddha Dharma, and we can find no words to express our thanks and gratitude for their encouragement and valuable support in this Dharma ending age.

All brackets are mine and are added to make the sūtra and commentary more clear and intelligible to sincere students of the Dharma in the West. Only part of Han Shan's commentary has been translated and is presented in the form of footnotes.

Upāsaka Lu K'uan Yü (Charles Luk)

Hongkong

I

The Noumenon in the Tathāgata Store

Thus have I heard. Once the Buddha stayed in the Jetavana vihāra near Śravāsti with twelve hundred and fifty bhikṣus, (most of whom) were great arhats who had crossed the stream of transmigration. They upheld His teaching firmly, could leap over all realms of existence and had achieved the respect-inspiring deportment which was held in great esteem throughout the country. They followed the Buddha to turn the Wheel of the Law and were qualified to hand down His Dharma. Being self-disciplined, they set a good example in the three worlds in which they appeared in countless transformation bodies to deliver living beings and to save future generations from defilement. They were led by Śāriputra the Wise, Mahā-Maudgalyāyana, Mahā-Kauṣṭhila, Pūrṇamaitrāyaṇīputra, Subhūti and Upaniṣad.

There were also countless pratyeka-buddhas who (since they had conquered their old habits) had nothing more to learn, (yet) came to the Buddha's vihāra determined to seek (ultimate) Truth.

Now the summer retreat had just finished when the bhikṣus took stock of their errors and mistakes and when the Bodhisattvas from the ten directions, determined to wipe out their remaining doubts and suspicions, reverently awaited the Teaching in their search for its esoteric meaning. And so the Tathāgata arranged His seat and sat with crossed legs to proclaim the profound (Doctrine). Such a Dharma feast to purify the assembly had never taken place before and His melodious voice was heard in the ten quarters. Led by Mañjūśrī, a number of Bodhisattvas as countless as sand grains in the Ganges, had come to the holy place.

Meanwhile, King Prasenajit who was keeping the anniversary of his father's death by offering vegetarian food to him, came personally to invite the Tathāgata to the inner palace for a royal feast of best and rarest delicacies, to which he also invited the great Bodhisattvas in the assembly. In the city the elders and devotees also offered food to members of the Order and reverently waited for the Buddha's arrival.

Ānanda's Weakness —The Reason for This Sermon

Commanded by the Buddha, Mañjūśrī took the Bodhisattvas and arhats to the royal feast. Ānanda, however, had not come back from a distant engagement, and so was not among the invited. He was returning to the vihāra alone without his superior or teacher, and bowl in hand went begging from door to door in a nearby town. He intended to call first on a donor who had not given food to the monks that day, regardless of whether or not he was virtuous, a noble or an outcast. In his practice of universal compassion, he did not especially choose a poor man as his patron. He wanted to help all living beings earn countless merits, for he had seen the Buddha scold Subhūti and Mahākāśyapa who, though being arhats, could not realize universal mind (when begging for food). He very much admired His teaching which had eliminated all his doubts and suspicions in this respect.

So when he reached the town's gate, he walked slowly adjusting his mien to the rules of discipline. As he went begging for food, he came to a house of prostitution where Mātaṅgī, (a low caste woman) succeeded, by means of Kapila magic, in drawing him close to her sensual body on the mat, so that he was on the point of breaking the rules of pure living. But the Buddha was aware of all this and, after the royal feast, He returned to the vihāra with the king, princes and elders who wished to hear about the essentials of the Dharma. He then sent out from the top of His head a bright and triumphant multicoloured light within which appeared a transformation Buddha seated, with crossed legs, on a thousand-petalled lotus. The Buddha then repeated the transcendental mantra and ordered Mañjūśrī to use it to overcome the magic and to bring Ānanda with Mātaṅgī to the vihāra.[1]

Meditative Study of All as Void (Śamatha)

When Ānanda saw the Buddha, he prostrated himself at His feet, weeping bitterly and saying that, since the time without beginning, though he had heard much about the Dharma, he still could not acquire the transcendental power of the Tao. Earnestly he asked the Buddha to teach the preliminary expedients in the practice of śamatha, samāpatti and dhyāna[2] which led to the enlightenment of all Buddhas in the ten directions.

---

[1] Ānanda's weakness was the reason why the Buddha gave this important sermon. For sensuality is the main cause of our transmigration in saṁsāra and can be removed only by Wisdom. Hence Mañjuśrī, the symbol of wisdom, was ordered to use the Dhāraṇī of the Great Samādhi to save both Ānanda and Mātangī. The radiant light shining from the top of the Buddha's head revealed this bright samādhi which alone can ensure the attainment of Enlightenment and without which living beings cannot escape from the wheel of birth and death. And so Ānanda asked for instruction on the practice of śamatha, samāpatti and dhyāna for the realization of Great Samādhi.

[2] Śamatha is the meditative study of all as void or immaterial, samāpatti is the meditative study of all as unreal, transitory or temporal and dhyāna is the meditative study of the Mean as inclusive of both.

There was also present a great number of Bodhisattvas, as countless as sand grains in the Ganges, and great arhats and pratyeka-buddhas who had come wishing to hear about the Dharma. They all waited silently and reverently for the holy Teaching.

Wiping Out the Five Aggregates and Eight Consciousnesses to Expose the Unreality of Ego

Probing into the false mind to wipe out the first two aggregates and first five consciousnesses

The Buddha said to Ānanda: 'You and I are close relatives. Tell me what you saw in the assembly when you made up your mind to give up all worldly feelings of affection and love (to follow me)?'

Ānanda replied: 'I saw the thirty-two excellent characteristics and the shining crystal-like form of the Buddha's body. I thought that all this could not be the result of desire and love, for desire creates foul and fetid impurities like pus and blood which mingle and cannot produce the wondrous brightness of His golden hued body, in admiration of which I shaved my head to follow Him.'

The Buddha said: 'Ānanda and all of you should know that living beings, since the time without beginning, have been subject continuously to birth and death because they do not know the permanent True Mind whose substance is, by nature, pure and bright. They have relied on false thinking which is not Reality so that the wheel of samsāra turns. Now if you wish to study the unsurpassed Supreme Bodhi to realize this bright nature, you should answer my questions straightforwardly. All Buddhas in the ten directions trod the same path to escape from birth and death because of their straightforward minds, with the same straightforwardness of mind and speech from start to finish without a trace of crookedness.

'Ānanda, when you developed that mind because of the Buddha's thirty-two excellent characteristics, tell me what saw and loved them.'

Ānanda replied: 'World Honoured One, my love came from the use of my mind, my eyes seeing and my mind admiring them, so that it was set on relinquishing birth and death.'

The Buddha continued: 'As you just said, your love was caused by your mind and eyes but if you do not know where your mind and eyes really are, you will never be able to destroy delusion. For instance, when the country is invaded by bandits, the king, before sending his soldiers to destroy them, should first know where they are. That which causes you to transmigrate without interruption comes from defects in your mind and eyes. Now tell me where your mind and eyes are.'

Ānanda replied: 'World Honoured One, all living beings born in the world through the ten types of birth hold that this knowing mind is in the body. As I look at the lotus-blue eyes of the Buddha, I see that they are on His face. Hence my understanding that my eyes are on my face whereas my knowing mind is in my body.

The Buddha asked: 'Now as you sit in this hall, where do you see Jetavana park?'

Ānanda replied: 'World Honoured One, this great hall is in Jetavana park which is, therefore, outside the hall.'

The Buddha asked: What do you see first in this hall?'

Ānanda replied: 'World Honoured One, in this hall, I see first the Tathāgata, then the assembly, and only when looking outside do I see the park.'

The Buddha asked: 'When you see the park, what causes you to do so?'

Ānanda replied: 'It is because the doors and windows are open that I, though sitting in this hall, see the park outside.'

The Buddha then extended His golden hued arm and touched Ānanda's head with His hand, saying: 'There is a samādhi called the all-embracing Supreme Śūraṅgama, a gateway through which all Buddhas in the ten directions attained to the wondrous Majestic Path. Ānanda, listen now attentively.'

Ānanda prostrated himself at the Buddha's feet and knelt to receive the holy instruction.

The Buddha said: 'If you (are right) that, while sitting in this hall, you see the park outside through open doors and windows it would be possible for someone sitting here to see only things outside without seeing the Buddha (within).'

Ānanda replied: 'One cannot see the grove and stream outside without seeing the Buddha (here).'

(The Buddha said:) 'Ānanda, it is the same with you; (if your mind is not deluded), it will be clear about all this. However, if your knowing mind was really in your body, you should first be clear about everything inside it. You should, therefore, see everything in your body before seeing things outside it; even if you cannot see your heart, liver, spleen, and stomach, at least you should be clear about your growing nails and hair, about that which moves along your nerves and the pulsing of your veins. Why are you not clear about all this? If you do not see things within, how can you see those outside? Therefore, your contention that your knowing mind is inside your body is groundless.'

Ānanda bowed and said: 'After hearing the Buddha's Dharma-voice, I now understand that my mind is really outside my body. For instance a lamp should light up everything in a room before the courtyard outside through the open door. If I do not see what is in my body but see things outside it, this is like a lamp placed outside a room which cannot light what is in it. This being so clear that there can be no doubt, am I still wrong about what the Buddha means?'

The Buddha said: 'All the bhikṣus followed me to Śrāvastī to beg for food and have now returned to Jetavana park. I have taken my meal but as one bhikṣu is still eating, is the whole community well-fed?'

Āṅanda replied: 'No, World Honoured One, though they are arhats, they have not the same body or life span then how can one by eating cause all the others to satisfy their hunger?'

The Buddha said: 'If your knowing mind is outside your body, the two are separate. Thus when your mmd knows something, your body should not feel it and when your body feels something, your mind should not be aware of it. Now as I show you my hand, when your eyes see it, does your mind discern it?'

Ānanda replied: 'Yes. World Honoured One, my mind discerns it.'

The Buddha said: 'If so, how can your mind be outside your body? Therefore, your contention that your knowing and discerning mind is outside your body is groundless.'

Ānanda said: 'World Honoured One, as you have said, if my mind does not see what is in my body, it is not within it, and if my body and mind know each other, they are not separate and my mmd is, therefore, not outside my body. Now after thinking about this, I know where my mind is.'

The Buddha asked: 'Where is it?'

Ānanda replied: 'Since my knowing mind does not see what is in my body but can see things outside, I think it is hidden in my sense organ. For instance, if one covers one's eyes with a crystal bowl, the latter does not obstruct this sense organ which simply follows the (faculty of) seeing to distinguish all things seen. Thus if my knowing mind does not see what is in (my body), it is because it is in the sense organ, and if it sees clearly what is outside without being obstructed, it is because it is hidden in that organ.'

The Buddha asked: 'As you just said, the mind is hidden in the same way that the eyes are covered by the crystal bowl: now when one so covers them and sees the mountain and river, does one also see the bowl?'

Ānanda replied: 'Yes, World Honoured One, one also sees the bowl.'

The Buddha said: 'If your mind is like the crystal bowl, when you see the mountain and river, why do you not see your own eyes? If you do they should be outside and should not follow your faculty of seeing. If they cannot be seen, how can you say that this knowing mind is hidden in the sense organ, like the (eyes) covered by the crystal bowl? Therefore, your contention that the knowing mind is hidden in the sense organ is groundless.'

Ānanda asked: 'World Honoured One, I now think of the bowels concealed in the body and of the apertures on its surface. Therefore, where there is concealment there is darkness and where there are openings there is light. As I am now before the Buddha, I open my eyes and see clearly and this is called outward seeing, and when I close them, I see (only) darkness and this is called inward seeing. What does the Buddha think of this?'

The Buddha said: 'When you close your eyes and see darkness, is this darkness opposite to your eyes or not? If it is, it is in front of them, then how can this be inward seeing ? Even if there is really such inward seeing, when you sit in a dark room without the light of the sun, moon or a lamp, this darkness should also be in your bowels. If it is not opposite to your eyes, how can there be any seeing? Now let us forget (your so-called) outward seeing and assume that there is inward seeing, then when you close your eyes and see only darkness, which you call seeing what is in your body, why when you open them and see clearly, do you not see your face? If you do not, there is no such inward seeing. Now assuming that you can see your face, your knowing mind and organ of sight should be in the air, and then how can there be inward seeing? If they were in the air, they should not belong to your body, and the Buddha who now sees your face, should be your body as well. Thus when your eyes see something, your body should have no feeling. If you insist that both body and mind have separate feelings, there should be two separate perceptions and then your body should (one day) become two Buddhas. Therefore, your contention that to see darkness is inward seeing is groundless.'

Ānanda said: 'I have always heard the Buddha when teaching monks, nuns and male and female devotees say: "When the mind stirs all sorts of things are created and then all kinds of mind appear." I now think that the substance of (my) thinking is the nature of mind which arises when it unites with externals and which is neither within nor without nor m between.'

The Buddha said: 'You have just said that because phenomena are created, all kinds of mind appear when uniting with them. So this mind has no substance and cannot unite with anything. If that which has no substance can unite with externals, this is union of the nineteenth realm of sense with the seventh sense datum.[3] This is sheer nonsense. If the mind has substance, when your hand grasps your body, does your mind feeling

[3] No such union can occur because there are only eighteen realms of sense and six sense data.

this (touch) come from within or without? If from within, you should see what is in your body and if from without, you should see your face.

Ānanda said: 'It is the eyes that see and the mind that knows is not the eyes: to say that it sees is wrong.'

The Buddha said: 'If the eyes can see, when you are in a room, do you see the door (outside)?[4] Those who are dead and still have eyes, should see things; if they still see, how can they be dead? Ānanda, if your knowing mind has substance, is that substance single or manifold? As it is in your body, does it spread to every part of it or not? If it is one substance, when you grasp a limb, all four should feel that they are grasped; if so there would be no grasping (of any particular limb). If there is, the contention of a single substance does not hold good. If it is a manifold substance there should be many persons; then which substance is yours? If it spreads to every part of your body, this is the same as in the previous case of grasping. If it does not spread, then when you touch your head and foot at the same time, while your head feels that it is touched, your foot should not, but this is not so. Therefore, your contention that the mind arises where there is union with externals is groundless.'

Ānanda said: 'World Honoured One, I have heard the Buddha discuss Reality with other sons of the King of the Law (i.e. Bodhisattvas); He also said that the mind is neither within nor without. I now deduce that if the mind is in the body, it does not see anything within and if it is outside, they both cease to feel each other. To say that it is within is wrong for it does not know anything in the body. To say that it is within is wrong for it does not know anything in the body. To say that it is without is also faulty since body and mind can perceive each other. As they do so and since nothing is seen in the body, the mind should be between the two (i.e. the inside and outside).'

The Buddha said: "If your conception of a mind "in between" is correct, it implies a position for it. Now according to your inference, where is this intermediate position? Do you mean that it is (in or on) the body? If it is on the surface of the body, it cannot be in its center, and the conception of a mind in the center is no different from that of a mind in the body (which was refuted earlier). (Moreover) is its position manifest or not? If it is not, it does not exist. If it is, it is not fixed. Why? For instance, if a stake is driven into the ground to mark a center, when seen from the east it is in the west and when seen from the south it is in the north. As this stake can only lead to confusion, so is (your conception of) a mind in between completely chaotic.'

[4] A reference to Ananda's previous contention that the mind is in the body (i.e. the room) and the eyes are apertures on its surface (i.e. the outside doors).

Ānanda said: 'The intermediate position that I mentioned is not these two. As the World Honoured One has said, the eyes and form are causes from which sight-perception arises. While the eyes can distinguish, form does not follow anything and perception lies between them; hence the mind arises.'

The Buddha said: 'If the mind lies between sense organs and sense data, does it include both or not? If it does, its substance and what is outside will be mixed up together, and since the mind perceives while its objects do not, two opposites will be set up; then how can there be an intermediate (position)? If it is not inclusive, (that is if it is independent of the sense organs and sense data), being neither the knower (subject) nor the known (object), it has no substance; then what is this intermediate? Therefore, your contention that it is in between is groundless.'

Ānanda said: 'World Honoured One, previously when I saw the Buddha, with His four chief disciples, Mahā-Maudgalyāyana, Subhūti, Pūrṇamaitrāyaṇīputra and Śāriputra, turn the Wheel of the Law, He always said that the nature of the knowing and discriminating mind is neither within nor without nor between the two, exists nowhere and clings to nothing, hence it is called mind. Is that which does not cling to things called mind?'

The Buddha replied: 'You just said that the nature of the knowing and discriminating mind exists nowhere. Now in this world, all things in the air, in water and on the ground, including those that fly and walk, make the existing whole. By that which does not cling to anything, do you mean that it exists or not? If it "is not," it is just the hair of a tortoise or the horn of a hare, then how can there be (this extra) non-clinging? If it "is" it cannot be said not to exist. That which "is not" is simply non-existent and that which "is" should have a position; then how can there be no clinging?[5] Therefore, your contention that that which does not cling to anything is the knowing mind is groundless.'[6]

---

[5] The very idea of existence implies a dwelling place, hence its clinging. Therefore, both 'is' and 'is not' are a dualism which has no room in the True Mind.

[6] The absolute One Reality is the Eternal Mind which is beyond birth and death and is the common source of both Buddhas and living beings. Man, because of his basic ignorance caused, since the time without beginning, by the first thought which screened his True Mind, became subject to birth and death. Thus both the permanent and impermanent united to transform (that True Mind) into the store consciousness (ālaya vijñāna), the root of saṁsara. This ālaya consciousness has three characteristics: a karmic one which is basic ignorance resulting from *self-evidencing*, a changing one which turns fundamental wisdom into false *perception*, the root of the first seven consciousnesses; and its expression in appearance, or *form*. Because of basic ignorance, the spiritual, bright, and nirvanic Absolute Voidness was changed into dull and deluded emptiness. Hence, Mañjuśrī said (in his gāthā later on): 'Thus in delusion there appeared one-sided emptiness.' Within this

Refuting the false mind to eliminate the third aggregate and expose the unreality of the sixth consciousness

Thereupon Ānanda rose from his seat, uncovered his right shoulder, knelt upon his right knee, reverently joined the palms of his hands and said to the Buddha: 'I am the Tathāgata's youngest cousin and because of His

---

dull emptiness, ignorance gradually crystallized and turned into illusory Form made of four elements, resulting in a world created within the void. Hence Mañjuśrī continued: 'In which an imaginary world arbitrarily was built.' When false Perception confronted Form, a very small portion of this Form was gradually grasped as being self-possessed, and being supported by wrong perception, mind and form united and grasped at this dim (little) form as an Ego, thereby creating a living being made of five aggregates. Hence Mañjuśrī continued: 'Steadying itself the thinking process made the continents - While the (illusory) knower became a living being.' This is the origin of a living being. Ever after, this living being grasped at his body and mind as his Ego. How then can he now recognize his (essential) boundless True Mind? So in delusion, he thinks that his mind is in his body. Since Ānanda clung to a mind within his body, he mistook this (illusory) mind for True Mind; hence he saw only the Buddha's excellent characteristics which he admired but failed to realize that neither body nor mind exist. As he relied on the five aggregates, he divided them wrongly into six sense organs with corresponding sense data. He further clung to the tour elements that produced five sense data as his Ego's fields of activities, thereby (fretting) six consciousnesses and indulging in discriminations, illusions and karmic acts.

This was the origin of the cycle of births and deaths caused by attachment to body and mind as an Ego. This strong attachment hardened as aeons succeeded one another and can now be broken only by a powerful samādhi. For this reason, the Buddha before proclaiming this samādhi, asked Ānanda where his mind and eyes actually were. The mind which Ānanda thought to be in the body showed the place held by the bandits where the king should send his soldiers to destroy them. Since Ānanda always treasured his Ego, he would suffer shock and alarm if it was suddenly crushed. In order to calm him, the Buddha put His hand on the disciple's head, reassuring him that there was a samādhi called the all-embracing Supreme Śūrangama, a gateway through which all Buddhas had reached the profound Majestic Path.

From this point until He spoke later of two kinds of Basic Inversion, the Buddha aimed to wipe out the duality of Ego and things (dharmā) thereby revealing the fundamentally enlightened True Mind with the aid of the transcendental power of that Great Samādhi.

To break up the illusory Ego made of five aggregates which all living beings hold as existing, Ānanda was pressed in turn to point out the seven different places in which he thought the mind could be found. Actually, the first two aggregates rūpa (form and matter) and vedanā (reception, sensation and feeling) were destroyed for previously the four elements had been grasped as having an Ego, with the idea of there being a mind in the body; this is body as an abode of mind. As Ānanda failed to locate his mind in his body, he turned to a position outside it but could not find his mind there either. So after seeking vainly in seven different positions, the conclusion was that rūpa was non-existent and that vedanā was equally false. Careful reading of the text on the mind's so called seven positions shows the wiping out primarily of the illusion of rūpa and incidentally of vedanā. And, as dealt with later in the text, the other three aggregates sanjñā (conception or discerning), saṁskāra (discrimination) and vijñāna (consciousness) were gradually eliminated. Readers should attend to all this in order to understand this profound Teaching.

great affection, I have been allowed to be His disciple, but I have presumed on His compassion. And so although I have heard much of His preaching. I have failed to avoid the worldly and have been unable to overcome the magic which has turned me round, causing me to visit a house of prostitution. All this is because I failed to reach the region of Reality. May the World Honoured One be compassionate enough to teach us the Path of Śamatha for the benefit of those lacking faith and holding perverted views.' After saying this, he prostrated himself with knees, elbows and head on the ground. Then he stood up in reverent silence, with the whole assembly keenly awaiting the Teaching.

Revealing the Bright Samādhi

By the Buddha's transcendental power, all sorts of rays of light, as brilliant as hundreds and thousands of suns, shone from His forehead, illuminating all the Buddha-lands which shook with six kinds of quake. Thus a number of worlds, uncountable as the dust, appeared simultaneously and (by the same power) united into a single world wherein each of the great Bodhisattvas, while staying in his own realm, brought his palms together to listen to the Dharma.[7]

---

[7] This Light revealed the whole substance of the Great Samādhi. Since Ānanda had failed to awaken to the unreality of mind and body, he again asked for the Teaching on the Path of Śamatha (on the meditative study of the Void). He did not realize that the Buddha had first mentioned this Great Samādhi and then pressed Him hard about the mind's positions for the sole purpose of urging him instantly to awaken to the non-existence of the four elements and the falseness of the five aggregates, so that the substance of Samādhi appeared in full on the spot.

Had Ānanda been sharp rooted, he could have cast away all illusions, the meeting would have been dismissed and the Śūrangama assembly would have then come to an end. However, he was deluded and the Buddha was obliged to use expedients to awaken him. For his delusion was due to his grasping at illusory birth and death which he mistook for reality. Hence His teaching in the following text on the two basic inversions to root out the third aggregate sañjñā.

As the Buddha was about to explain these inversions, He sent out from His forehead rays of light to reveal what Lin Chi called 'the true man of no fixed position who, from his forehead, sends out the light that shakes the world.' (See Ch'an and Zen Teaching, Second Series, p. 110. Rider.) However, because of self-deception, people do not recognize this man of no fixed position in spite of his daily activities and are separated from him by screens and obstructions put up by their wrong thinking which divides (their individed whole) into six sense organs and sense data. Now the Buddha-Light (which is inherent in all of us) shone on the realms of the sense organs, sense data and consciousness which are identical with Reality (the underlying principle from which they spring). This is why the text mentions the appearance of Buddhas in their lands suddenly revealed in this Light which destroyed the darkness of ignorance. Hence the six kinds of quake to overthrow the six sense organs and sense data and so remove their obstructions, so that all the worlds

Origin of Inversion

The Buddha said: 'Since the time without beginning, all living beings have given rise to all sorts of inversion because of the karmic seed (of ignorance) which is like the akṣa shrub.[8] This is why seekers of the Truth fail to realize Supreme Enlightenment but achieve only (the states of) śrāvakas, pratyeka-buddas, heretics, devas and demons, solely because they do not know the two basic inversions, thereby practising wrongly like those who cannot get food by cooking sand in spite of the passing of aeons as countless as the dust. What are these two basic inversions? Ānanda, the first is the basic root of birth and death caused, since the time without beginning, by the wrong use of a clinging mind which people mistake for their own nature, and the second is their attachment to causal conditions (which screen) the basically bright essence of consciousness which is the fundamentally pure and clean substance of Nirvanic Enlightenment. Thus they ignore this basic brightness and so transmigrate through (illusory) realms of existence without realizing the futility of their (wrong) practice.[9]

---

could become one. This is Reality *shining* on darkness and performing *its function* (see Ch'an and Zen Teaching, Second Series, p. 102) of dissipating it at once, thus enabling all serious practisers to climb without effort the Transcendental Path. Hence countless Bodhisattvas appeared in this Light seated in their own places, and bringing their palms together to listen to the Buddha's teaching on the Great Samādhi.

By means of its Light, the Buddha revealed the whole substance of the Samādhi. In the following chapters, the Teaching merely reveals this state of Brightness, and if it is understood, there will be no need to study the Buddha Dharma. Because Ānanda was not awakened to it, the Buddha was obliged to make further revelations one after the other. In answer to Ānanda's renewed request for instruction on śamatha, the Buddha began his (further) Teaching by showing this Brightness.

[8] The akṣa seed is threefold and so illustrates the simultaneous character of illusion, action and suffering.

[9] The Buddha, before teaching the Great Samādhi, revealed the root cause of birth and death by declaring that since the time without beginning all living beings had given rise to all sorts of inversion because of their karmic delusion about Basic and Fertilized Ignorance. This (twofold) ignorance causes all sorts of karmic seeds which produce the bitter fruits of delusion, action and suffering, and so are likened to the threefold akṣa seeds. This illusion can only be broken up by the Great Samādhi which was pointed out first. Seekers of the Truth cannot realize Supreme Enlightenment but are misled by delusion into other ways simply because they cannot distinguish two basic roots: first, the root cause of birth and death which is the discriminating mind which they mistake for their self-nature; and second, the fundamentally pure and clean substance of Nirvanic Enlightenment realized by all past Buddhas, that is the Essence of their Consciousness which is basically bright but can give rise to causal conditions. By clinging to these (illusory) conditions, they ignore the basic brightness and suffer aimlessly from birth and death. This Essence of Consciousness is the substance of the Eighth Consciousness which is basically bright and is the wonderful

Actual Inversion

The Inverted Mind

Probe into the false mind

Ānanda, as you have enquired about the Śamatha Gateway through which to escape from birth and death I must ask you a question.' The Buddha then held up His golden hued arm and bent His fingers, saying; 'Ānanda, do you see this!' Ānanda replied: 'Yes.' The Buddha asked: 'What do you see?' Ānanda replied: 'I see the Buddha raise His arm and bend His fingers, showing a shining fist that dazzles my mind and eyes.' The Buddha asked: How do you see it?' Ānanda replied: 'I and all those here use the eyes to see it.' The Buddha asked. 'You say that I bend my fingers to show a shining fist that dazzles your mind and eyes; now tell me, as you see my fist, what is that mind which perceives its brightness? Ānanda replied: 'As the Tathāgata asks about the mind and since I am using my own to search for it exhaustively, I conclude that that which searches is my mind.'

Thinking is unreal

The Buddha said: 'Hey! Ānanda, this is not your mind.' Ānanda stared with astonishment, brought his two palms together, rose from his seat and asked: 'If this is not my mind, what is it?' The Buddha replied: 'Ānanda, this is your false thinking which arises from external objects, deludes your true nature and deceives you into mistaking, since the time without beginning, a thief for your own son, thereby losing (sight of) that which is basically permanent; hence the round of birth and death.[10]

---

shining True Mind of Basic Enlightenment. Since all living beings fail to realize this wondrous Bright Mind, it is (screened by delusion and) transformed into the Essence of Consciousness which leads to wrong thinking. Therefore, the Buddha aimed first to root out this false thinking and then the Essence of Consciousness so that the basically enlightened True Mind could manifest through the Great Samādhi. Hence His revelation of Samādhi before wiping out false thinking. The following text deals with the elimination of falsehood to expose Reality with His teaching on Śamatha, the Path to Reality; that which was to be wiped out was precisely these two (basic) inversions.

[10] This eliminated the false mind to expose the first inversion. Before wiping out this false mind, the Buddha spoke of the Path of Śamatha because His aim was now to reveal the substance of the Great Samādhi, Śamatha is meditative study of the void. As the pure and clean True Mind of the Tathāgata store (or the Absolute in the midst of delusion caused by the passions and desires), is fundamentally devoid of a single (foreign) thing (dharma) it should be the object of this meditation on the void. Beside this meditation on substance, there is no other method, but due to the false mind and false thinking caused by defiling causes, the True Mind is hidden and does not appear. Now if (illusory) mind and seeing are eliminated, all causal conditions cease to exist and the True Mind will manifest. Cognizance

The sixth consciousness is empty

Ānanda said: 'I am the Buddha's beloved youngest cousin whose mind so admired Him that I left home to serve and make offerings to the Tathāgata and to all Buddhas and enlightened teachers in lands as countless as sand grains in the Ganges. If I am determined to do all difficult Dharma duties, it is because I use this mind, and even if I now slander the Dharma, causing my excellent qualities to weaken for ever, it is also because of this mind. If it was not mind, I would have no mind and would be like the earth or a log for nothing exists beyond what I feel and know. Why does the Buddha now say that it is not mind? This frightens me and also this assembly and not one of us here can avoid being doubtful and suspicious about it. Will you be so compassionate as to enlighten us?'

From His lion seat the Buddha in order to teach Ānanda and the assembly so that they could all achieve the Patient Endurance of the Uncreate (Anutpattika-dharma-kṣānti), held out His hand to touch Ānanda's head, saying: 'The Tathāgata has always said that all phenomena are manifestations of mind and that all causes and effects including (all things from) the world to its dust, take shape (solely) because of the mind. Ānanda, if we look at all the worlds and all existing (things) including even grass and leaves, and investigate their roots, they are all made of matter and have qualities, and even the empty void has its name and appearance; then how

---

of all causal creations as having no nature of their own are the state of True Mind. Hence the Buddha's answers, based on the substance of the Samādhi of the Absolute, to Ānanda's questions arising from his false mind and false seeing that discriminated between causal conditions. And so He had to break the false mind before teaching the Path of Śamatha.

When the Buddha first asked Ānanda why he left home, the disciple replied that it was because his eyes saw and his mind loved His excellent physical characteristics. The Buddha declared: 'That which causes you to transmigrate ceaselessly is the fault of that mind and those eyes.' This shows their falseness. Then Ānanda looked in vain for his mind in seven different positions, and though the mind was searched for, the body was also found not to be its dwelling place, so that unreality of the body was shown.

The Buddha, replying to Ānanda's renewed inquiry about the Samādhi gateway, skilfully eliminated first the false mind and then the false seeing. Therefore, he held up His fist and asked Ānanda: "As your eyes see my fist, what is your mind?' to point out the non-existence of the false mind. As the disciple said that that which searched for his mind was the mind itself, without knowing that he wrongly mistook the mind that discriminates in saṁsāra for the real one, the Buddha shouted: 'Hey! This is not your mind.' This shout was like a previous vajra-sword that cut off (Ānanda's) discriminating mind, but unfortunately he was not awakened. So he stared with astonishment and asked: 'If this is not my mind, what is it?' The Buddha replied that it was only false thinking arising from external objects, that is the discriminating Sixth Consciousness which derived from an accumulation of Consciousness actually screened his true nature and should not have been regarded as real. Since he recognized that false mind and disregarded his permanent True Mind, he was caught on the turning wheel of birth and death.

can the pure and clean profound Bright Mind which is the (underlying) nature of every (discriminating) mind be without its own substance? If you grasp firmly the knowledge which comes from your discrimination between feeling and seeing as your true mind, it should have its own nature independent of all (sense data such as) form, smell, taste and touch. As you now listen to my sermon on the Dharma, you differentiate because you hear my voice.'

The seventh consciousness is unreal

'Even if you (succeed in) putting an end to all seeing, hearing, feeling and knowing, and so preserve inner quiet, the shadow of (your) differentiation of things (dharmā) still remains. I do not want you to hold that this is not mind, but you should examine it carefully and minutely: that which continues to possess discerning nature even in the absence of sense data is really your mind; (on the other hand) if this discerning nature ceases with sense data, this is merely the shadow of (your) differentiation of them, for they are not permanent and when they cease to exist, so does this (so-called) mind, like the hair of a tortoise and the horns of a hare. If your Dharmakāya can so easily cease to be, who will then practise and realize the patient endurance of the Uncreate?'

After hearing this, Ānanda and all those present were completely bewildered.[11]

---

[11] Ānanda used to rely on his Sixth Consciousness, that is his clinging mind which he mistook for his True Mind. As he was scolded by the Buddha (for self-conceit), he was completely bewildered and thought that if he had no mind, he would be like earth or a log. The Buddha, out of compassion for the whole assembly, taught them how to develop non-creating mind; He extended His hand to touch Ānanda's head to reassure him and to wipe out his perplexity, saying: 'Why do you think that you are without a mind and are like a lifeless thing?.I have always said that all phenomena are manifestations of the mind and that all worldly causes and effects, either direct or indirect, take shape because of the mind. This is True Mind; why do not you waken to it? All phenomena in the world, as well as the smallest things, are (made of) matter and have qualities, and even the empty void has its name and appearance; then how can the wondrous pure and clean Bright Mind which is the underlying nature of all mental states, have no substance? Instead of understanding the substance of True Mind, you grasp firmly at your false thinking that discriminates (aimlessly) about True Mind; is this not inversion? If it was True Mind, it should have a nature of its own even after all sense data have ceased to exist. Since it is no more when there are no sense data, is it not false? As you listen to my sermon on the Dharma, you differentiate solely because of my voice, but when I stop speaking, this mind of yours will cease to exist. This is the differentiating mind which arises when you hear my causal voice; this is your (discriminating) Sixth Consciousness which vanishes when sense data disappear.' This wiped out the third aggregate, sañjñā, to expose the unreality of the Sixth Consciousness.

In the last paragraph of the text, the unreality of the Seventh Consciousness is exposed. It is not only the discriminating Sixth Consciousness which is false but 'If you put an end

Refuting all inversion

The Buddha said: 'Practising students, even after they have realized the nine successive states of dhyāna,[12] still cannot step out of the stream of transmigration and so fail to become Arhats, because they cling to this samsaric false thinking which they mistake for Reality. This is why, though you have heard much (of my Dharma), you have failed to win the holy fruit.[13]

The Inverted Perception

After hearing this, Ānanda, in bitter tears, prostrated himself with his head, knees and elbows on the ground, knelt and brought his two palms together, saying: 'After I left home to follow the Buddha, I merely relied on His transcendental power and always thought that I could dispense with practice since He would bestow samādhi upon me. I did not know that He could not be my substitute and so lost (sight of) my fundamental Mind. This is why, though I joined the Order, my mind was unable to enter the Tao. I was like a destitute son running away from his father. I only realize now that, in spite of much listening (to the Dharma), if I do not practise it, I shall come to nothing as if I had not heard it, like a man who cannot satisfy his hunger by merely speaking of food. World Honoured One, I am caught by the two hindrances because I do not know the (real) nature of the still and permanent Mind. May the Tathāgata be compassionate enough fully to reveal to me that wondrous Bright Mind and so open my Tao eye.

A bright light to reveal the One Reality

Thereupon the Tathāgata, from the sauvastika on His chest, sent out a radiant multi-coloured precious Light which illuminated the Buddha

---

to all seeing, hearing, feeling and knowing to stop using all six senses and so preserve your inner quiet, there is still the shadow of (your) differentiation of things.' This is the Seventh Consciousness which grasps at the innermost self as an ego and which is the organ of the Sixth Consciousness; it is precisely the root of birth and death, so 'How can you hold it as Reality?' The Buddha was about to expose the falseness of the fourth aggregate, saṁskāra, and so wipe out the Seventh Consciousness, so He said: 'I do not want you to hold that it is not mind; what I want you to know is that false thinking is not True Mind; you should examine carefully and minutely this: that which has its independent substance when sense data cease to exist is your True Mind, but that which vanishes with sense data is (simply) non-existent, like the hair of a tortoise and the horns of a hare, in which case your Dharmakāya should also be subject to destruction, and if so, who will practise and realize the patient endurance of the Uncreate?'

[12] The states of dhyāna in the four dhyāna heavens, the four heavens beyond form and the heaven beyond sensation and thought.

[13] The Buddha had now wiped out false thinking: in the following text he removed false seeing (perception) as well.

lands in the ten directions as countless as the dust and which, after shining on the heads of all Buddhas everywhere, veered to Ānanda and the assembly. The Buddha then said to Ānanda: 'I now hoist the banner of Great Dharma so that you and all living beings in the ten directions can realize the pure and bright Mind of your profound and subtle Nature and so win the Eye that is pure and clear.'[14]

Returning perception to Mind[15]

'Ānanda, a moment ago you said that you saw my shining; tell me, how did its brightness come about, what caused it to take the form of a fist and with what did you see it?'

Ānanda replied: 'The Buddha's golden hued body is like a precious hill and manifests (the state of) purity and cleanness, so that the fist shone. It was really my eyes that saw Him bend the fingers and form a fist which was shown to all of us.'

---

[14] This eliminated the disciple's false seeing. Ānanda had heard the Buddha's teaching and had believed that the discriminating mind vanished as soon as all causal sense data ceased to exist and so realized that it was not True Mind. Therefore, his previous seeing of the Buddha was false. Hence he asked Him to reveal the wondrous Bright Mind so as to open his Tao eye which alone could put an end to his false seeing. This inverted perception was due to his inner Sixth Consciousness clinging to his outer body as an Ego, and was precisely his attachment to the dual reality of Ego and dharma; this discriminative attachment to the duality of Ego and dharma is called *discriminative perception* (as opposed to inborn or natural perception). Now the organ of his Sixth Consciousness, that is his Seventh Consciousness, clung to the characteristic *Perception* of the inner Eighth Consciousness as an Ego and was his inborn grasping at the duality of Ego and dharma. It is called one's *Inborn Perception*. Since sense organ and consciousness depend on each other, this is the field of wrong thinking; hence the two hindrances that caught Ānanda.

Before teaching the elimination of falsehood, the Buddha sent out, from the sauvastika on His chest, a radiant multi-coloured Light to stress that wrong thinking was originally the great Wisdom-light of the True Mind in the Tathāgata store which, under delusion, turned into false thinking, and so transformed this Wisdom-light into false seeing. This Light illuminated all the ten directions to show its manifestion. As this Brightness is self-possessed by both the saintly and the worldly, it first shone on the heads of the Buddhas and then reached Ānanda and the whole assembly. He who seeks the True Mind and True Perception should only cognize this Brightness which, under delusion, turns into false thinking and seeing. Now to change the latter into the fundamental Brightness which is self-possessed, it is only necessary to change the false into the true. He who awakens to this True Light achieves instantly the wondrous pure Bright Mind and realizes the Eye that is pure and clean, so that his mind and perception become true. This was the Great Dharma banner set up by the Buddha.

[15] This is the secret of Ch'an Transmission according to which *Function* should be returned to *Substance* for realization of mind and perception of self-nature. Readers are urged to pay particular attention to the profound meanings of these two idoms, *Substance* and *Function*, in their ch'an training.

The Buddha said: 'In truth wise people should be awakened by examples and analogies. Ānanda, if I had no hand I would have no fist and if you had no eyes, you would have no (faculty of) seeing. Is there any connection between your organ of sight and my fist?'

Ānanda replied: 'Yes, World Honoured One. If I had no eyes, I would have no (faculty of) seeing; so there is an analogy between my organ of sight and the Buddha's fist.'

The Buddha said: Your reasoning is incorrect. For instance, a handless man has no fist, but a man without eyes still has his (faculty of) seeing. When you meet a blind man and ask him what he sees, he will tell you there is nothing but darkness in front of him. Therefore, though things may be screened from view the (faculty of) seeing continues.'

Ānanda said: If a blind man sees nothing but darkness before him, how can this be called seeing?'

The Buddha asked: 'Is there any difference between the darkness seen by a blind man in front of him and that seen by a man who is not blind when he is in a dark room?'

(Ānanda replied); World Honoured One, there is no difference.

The Buddha said: 'Ānanda, when a blind man who used to see only darkness suddenly recovers his sight and sees every thing clearly, if you say that it is his eyes which see, then when a man who saw darkness in a dark room suddenly lights a lamp which enables him to see what is there, you should say that it is the lamp that sees. If a lamp can see things, it should have (the faculty of) seeing and should not be called a lamp; if it really sees, it has no relation to you. Therefore, you should know that while the lamp can reveal form, seeing comes from the eyes but not from the lamp. Likewise, while your eyes can reveal form, the nature of seeing comes from the mind but not from the eyes.'[16]

---

[16] The Buddha, before exposing the unreality of indiscriminative seeing, held up His fist to probe Ānanda. The disciple, being still in the Hinayāna stage, knew nothing of Ālaya's three characteristics (self-evidencing, perception and form), for he knew only the six consciousnesses and used to hold on to sense organs and sense perceptions, so that he relied on the eyes that 'can see' without realizing that this seeing originated in the mind. As the Buddha was about to teach him how to return this seeing to the mind, He held up His fist, asking: 'What do you use to see this?' Ānanda replied that he used his eyes to see the fist, for he still held that seeing derived from them. So the Buddha compared His fist with the disciple's eyes, asking: 'If I had no hands, there would be no fist, but if you had no eyes, would you have no (faculty of) seeing?' He then spoke of a blind man who saw only darkness, but had he really no (faculty of) seeing? Since the darkness seen by the blind man is the same as that seen by another who is not blind while sitting in a dark room, it follows that seeing does not come from the eyes. When the blind man recovers his sight and sees things, if this can be called the eyes' seeing, then when a man in a dark room suddenly lights a lamp, this should be called the lamp's seeing. This makes no sense for the lamp can only reveal objects but seeing belongs to the man. Therefore, the organ of sight can only reveal form but the nature of this seeing belongs to the mind and not to the eyes. This is returning perception to mind.

Inverted Men

Although Ānanda and the assembly had heard these words, they remained speechless. As they did not awaken to the Teaching, they brought their palms together and waited for the Buddha's further instruction with their minds set on hearing it.[17]

The worlding's inverted views

The Buddha then held up His shining hand, straightened. His fingers to give (further) instruction to Ānanda and the assembly and asked: 'After I attained Enlightenment (Bodhi), I went to Mṛgadāva park where I told Ājñāta-kauṇdinya and his group of five bhikṣus as well as you monks, nuns and devotees, that all living beings failed to realize Enlightenment and became Arhats because they were misled by foreign dust which created delusion and distress (by entering their minds). What at that time caused you to awaken so that you can now win the holy fruit?'

Ājñāta-kauṇḍinya then rose from his seat and replied to the Buddha: 'I am now a senior in the assembly in which I am the only one who has acquired the art of interpreting because I had awakened to (the meaning of) the expression "foreign dust," so that I won the (holy) fruit. World Honoured One (foreign dust) is like a guest who stops at an inn where he passes the night or eats something and then packs and continues his journey because he cannot stay longer. As to the host of the inn, he has nowhere to go. My deduction is that one who does not stay is a guest and one who stays is a host. Consequently, a thing is "foreign" when it does not stay. Again, when the sun rises in a clear sky and its light enters (the house) through an opening, the dust is seen to dance in the ray of light whereas the empty space does not move. I deduce that that which is still is the void and that which moves is the dust. Consequently, a thing is "dust" when it moves.'

The Buddha said: 'Correct.'

The Hinayanist's inverted views

The Buddha then bent, straightened and rebent his fingers and asked Ānanda: 'What did you see?' Ānanda replied: 'I saw the Buddha open and close His fist.' The Buddha asked: 'You say that you saw my fist open and close; was it my fist or your seeing that opened and closed?' Ānanda replied: 'As the Buddha's fist opened and closed, I saw that it and not

---

[17] Ānanda used to lean on the false mind for support. The Buddha, after showing the falseness of the first two aggregates, rūpa and vedanā taught him to return the seeing to the mind. The disciple was thrown off balance and, not knowing what to say, was speechless. He was still uncertain and awaited His further preaching.

the nature of my seeing did so by itself.' The Buddha asked: 'Which one moved and which was still?' Ānanda replied: 'The Buddha's hand was not still; as to the nature of my seeing which was already beyond the state of stillness, it could not move.' The Buddha said: 'Correct.'

Thereupon the Buddha sent out from His palm a radiant ray of light to Ānanda's right, and the disciple turned to look at it. Then He sent out another ray to Ānanda's left and the disciple turned to look at it. The Buddha then asked: 'Why did your head move?' Ānanda replied: 'I saw the Buddha send out radiant rays of light to my right and left, I turned to look at them and so my head moved.' (The Buddha said:) 'As you turn to the right and left to see the Buddha-light, is it your head or your seeing that moves?' (Ānanda replied:) 'World Honoured One, it is my head that turns; as to my seeing which is already beyond (the state of) stillness, how can it move?' The Buddha said: 'Correct.'[18]

The Buddha then declared to the assembly: 'So every worldly man knows that what moves is dust and that he who does not stay is a guest. You have seen Ānanda whose head moved of itself whereas his seeing was unmoved. You have also seen my fist which opened and closed of itself whereas his seeing neither expanded nor contracted. Why do you still regard the moving as your body and surroundings, and so, from beginning to end, allow your thoughts to rise and fall without interruption, thereby losing (sight of) your true nature and indulging in backward actions? By missing the (True) Mind of your nature and by mistaking (illusory) objects for your Selves, you allow yourselves to be caught in the wheel (of saṁsāra) thereby forcing yourselves to pass through transmigrations.[19]

---

[18] The Buddha wiped out both the worldly view of permanence and the Hinayanist view of impermanence which have no room in the Absolute which is beyond both illusory states.

[19] The Buddha reprimanded both worldlings and Hinayanists for their inverted views to eliminate both the worldly and saintly states. If people in this world already know that the moving is 'dust,' it is clear that saṁsāra is impermanent, but why do they still regard it as (real and) lasting? If Hinayanists know that the head moves whereas the nature of seeing is unmoved, it is very clear that the latter is really lasting, but why do they still regard it as impermanent? The Buddha meant: 'Since you now know what is and is not permanent; why do you still hold that what moves are your bodies, and (external) objects?' These two rebuttals implied the Buddha's idea of eliminating both the false and the real. He meant that if this body and all objects (outside) it were impermanent, why did worldly men regard them as permanent? Thus He reprimanded all worldly men. If this very body and all things (external to it) were really permanent, for 'the non-existent body of illusion is Dharmakāya,' then why did the Hinayanists hold that they were impermanent? Thus He reprimanded the Hinayanists.

These discriminations result in the continuous rise and fall of endless thoughts while the True Nature is overlooked. This is why people indulge in backward actions and lose (sight of) the self-possessed Nature of Mind. 'For you have recognized (external) objects

The heretics' inverted view of annihilation

After Ānanda and the whole assembly had heard the Buddha's words, their bodies and minds became calm and composed. They thought that, since the time without beginning, they had lost (sight of) their own minds by wrongly clinging to the shadows of their differentiated causal conditions and that they had only now awakened to all this, like a (hungry) baby who had not suckled for some time and suddenly saw its loving mother. They brought their palms together to thank the Buddha and wished to hear His teaching on the dual states of reality and unreality, existence and non-existence and mortality and immortality of body and mind.

King Prasenajit then rose and said to the Buddha: 'Before I received the Buddha's instruction, I met (Kakuda) Kātyāyana and (Sañjaya) Vairātīputra who both said that when the body died, its annihilation was called Nirvāṇa. Although I have now met the Buddha, I am still not clear about this. All those here who are still in the stream of transmigration wish to know how to realize that mind and prove that it is beyond birth and death.[20]

The Buddha said to King Prasenajit: 'Great King, I now ask you about your body of flesh and blood: is it permanent and indestructible like a diamond, or does it change and decay?'

(The king replied:) 'My body will decay and finally be destroyed.'

The Buddha asked: 'Great King, you have not yet died, how do you know that your body will be destroyed?'

The king replied: 'World Honoured One, though my impermanent, changing and decaying body is not yet dead, I observe that it changes and decays without a moment's pause and is bound to "go out" like a fire that gradually burns out and will be reduced to naught.'

---

as your Self and are caught in the midst of wrong actions so that you turn the wheel of birth and death.' (In other words to root out the worldly man's 'is' and the Hinayanist's 'is not' to reveal the 'Mean' which includes both existence and non-existence.)

[20] The Buddha had sent out a ray of light to teach Ānanda that the unchanging was there with the moving body and objects. So we know that (the state of) birth and death also comprises that which is beyond both. Ānanda now understood this and wanted the Buddha to teach him what was and was not real and true, and what were birth and death and what were not, so as to draw a clear line between reality and unreality in order to remove his remaining doubts. But he had not yet put his wish into words.

In the past King Prasenajit had followed heretical teachers. Kakuda Kātyāyana taught the doctrine of (simultaneous) existence and non-existence, and Sañjaya Vairātīputra, that of naturalism. Though there were many heretical sects in India, their doctrines did not go beyond the two wrong views of permanence and annihilation which the king had studied, so that he clung to the idea of annihilation even after he had met the Buddha. As he had now heard Him teach that the Mind is beyond birth and death, he was not clear about it and asked for elucidation.

The Buddha asked: 'Yes, Great King, you are old now but how do you look compared to when you were a child?'

The king replied: 'World Honoured One, when I was a child, my skin glowed and when I grew up, I was full of vigour, but now I age and weaken, I grow thin and my spirits are dull, my hair is white and my face wrinkled so that I know I shall not live much longer; there is no comparison between now and when I was full of vitality.'

The Buddha said: 'Great King, your appearance should not decline.'

The king replied: 'World Honoured One, it has been changing all the time too imperceptibly for me to notice it. With the constant change of seasons, I have become what I am now. Why? Because when I was twenty, though still young, I already looked older than when I was ten, while at thirty I was older still. As I am now sixty-two, I am older than at fifty when I was stronger. World Honoured One, I notice this imperceptible change in every decade, but when I look into it closely, (I see that) it has occurred not only yearly, monthly and daily, but in each moment of thought. That is why I know that my body is destined to final destruction.'

The Buddha said: 'Great King, you observe this ceaseless change and know that you will die, but do you know that when you do, there is that which is in your body and does not die?'

The king brought his two palms together and said: 'I really do not know.'

The Buddha continued: 'I will now show you the (self-) nature which is beyond birth and death. Great King, how old were you when you first saw the Ganges?'

The King replied: "When I was three my mother took me to worship the deva Jīva. As we crossed the river, I knew it was the Ganges.'

The Buddha asked: 'Great King, as you just said, you were older at twenty than at ten; and until you were sixty, as days, months and years succeeded one another, your (body) changed in every moment of thought. When you saw the Ganges at three, was its water (the same as it was) when you were thirteen?'

The king replied: 'It was the same when I was three and thirteen, and still is now that I am sixty-two.'

The Buddha said: 'As you now notice your white hair and wrinkled face, there must be many more wrinkles than when you were a child. Today when you see the Ganges, do you notice that your seeing is "old" now while it was "young" then?'

The king replied: 'It has always been the same, World Honoured One.'

The Buddha said: 'Great King, though your face is wrinkled, the nature of this essence of your seeing is not. Therefore, that which is wrinkled changes and that which is free from wrinkles is unchanging. The changing is subject to destruction whereas the unchanging fundamentally is beyond birth and death; how can it be subject to your birth and death? Why do you bring out Maskari Gośālīputra's (wrong) teaching on total annihilation at the end of this life?'

Upon hearing this, the king realized that after death, there will be (no annihilation but) life again in other transmigrations. He and the whole assembly were happy and enthusiastic at the Teaching which they had never heard before.[21]

The inverted behaviour

After hearing this, Ānanda rose from his seat, prostrated himself before the Buddha, brought his two palms together and knelt saying: 'World Honoured One, if both seeing and hearing are beyond birth and death, why has the Buddha said that we have lost (sight of) our True Nature and so acted in an inverted manner? Will you be compassionate enough to enlighten us and so wash off our defiling dust?'

Thereupon the Buddha lowered His golden hued arm with the fingers pointing downward and asked Ānanda: 'As you now see my hand, is it in a correct or inverted (position)?'

Ānanda replied: 'All worldly men regard this as inverted but I myself do not know which position is correct or inverted.'

The Buddha asked: 'If they hold that it is inverted, which position do they consider to be upright?'

---

[21] This eliminates the heretical idea of annihilation (at the end of this life). Ānanda wanted the Buddha to reveal the permanent nature of his (ephemeral) body and mind. Since this was a most difficult thing to explain, He used King Prasenajit's query to expound it.

Not only did the king overlook the identity of birth and death with the permanent (nature from which they spring) but he also clung to the wrong view that annihilation would follow death. Had he known that death was (only illusory and) fundamentally unreal, he would have realized that it was the same with birth; thus he would have understood the profound meaning of True Permanence. It was very difficult for him to be clear about this imperishable nature at the end of (each illusory) life, but it could be demonstrated with the aid of his body and mind.

Therefore, the Buddha asked the king whether his body was changing and decaying or was permanent and imperishable like an indestructible diamond. If his body was closely examined, it was really changing in every moment of thought and was, therefore, impermanent, for from his childhood to his prime and old age, it had altered gradually and was bound to decay and come to an end. This is the birth and death of the impermanent body and mind in which the (self-) nature is really permanent. But how can it be realized? And so the Buddha asked him about his seeing the Ganges to prove its nature, which was the same in spite of the gradual change of his physical appearance from his childhood up to then. This proved that that which changed was subject to destruction whereas that which did not was his True Nature.

Ānanda replied: 'If the Buddha holds up His hand pointing to the sky, it will be upright.'

The Buddha then held up His hand and said: 'If worldly men so discriminate between an upright and inverted hand, they will in the same way differentiate between your body and the Buddha's pure and clean Dharmakāya and will say that the Tathāgata's body is completely enlightened whereas yours is upside down. If you look closely into your body and the Buddha's, where is this so called inversion?"

After hearing this, Ānanda and the assembly were bewildered and gazed fixedly at the Buddha without knowing whether their bodies and minds were really inverted.

Delusion and Enlightenment are of the same source

The Buddha was moved with compassion and, out of pity for Ānanda and the assembly, said in His voice as steady as the ocean-tide:[22] 'Virtuous men, I have always declared that Form and Mind and all causes arising therefrom, all mental conditions and all causal phenomena are but manifestations of the mind. Your bodies and minds are just appearances within the wonderful, bright and pure Profound Mind. Why do you stray from the precious, bright and subtle nature of fundamentally Enlightened Mind and so recognize delusion within enlightenment?'[23]

---

[22] Ocean-tide voice is the unfailing response to the needs of men, like the ocean-tide which never fails to rise and fall.

[23] Ānanda had now heard the Buddha use the seeing of the Ganges to reveal that which was beyond birth and death in the midst of changing conditions. He thought that when he spoke before of seeing the Buddha's fist, that was also the nature of his seeing which proved that he had not lost (sight of) his true nature. Why did the Buddha agree with the king and disagree with him? This proved that Ānanda had failed to know where his inversion really was.

And so the Buddha held down His hand which was in a natural position which worldly men mistook for being inverted. This illustrated precisely the body and its conditions in the true state of permanence which the disciple rejected and from which he strayed. Such is the inverted view held by Hinayanists and heretics. His hand was then held upright but was (in reality) inverted which worldly me regarded as right; this is the impermanent state of birth and death which they called permanent. Such is the inverted view of worldly men.

The Buddha said the arm was His and fundamentally was neither right nor wrong, but the mere change of its position gave rise to discrimination. This was precisely the wrong way in which deluded people looked at things. The Buddha's Dharmakāya and your body are just the same but if you discriminate between them, you will call His an enlightened body and yours an inverted one. The Buddha's aim was to urge Ānanda to look through the physical body to realize the spiritual Dharmakāya. Hence He asked Ānanda: 'Look closely into your body and the Buddha's and tell me where the so-called inversion lies.'

Since Ānanda and those present failed in this because of their delusion, they were bewildered and did not realize where the inversion really lay. The Buddha took compassion on them and said: 'I have always declared that form and mind and all causes arising there-

'(Mind's) dimness creates (dull) emptiness and both, in the darkness, unite with it to become form. The mingling of form with false thinking causes the latter to take the shape of a body, stirred by accumulated causes within and drawn to externals without. Such inner disturbance is mistaken for the nature of mind, hence the false view of a mind dwelling in the physical body and the failure to realize that this body as well as external mountains, rivers, space and the great earth are but phenomena within the wondrous bright True Mind. Like an ignorant man who overlooks on the great ocean but grasps at a floating bubble and regards it as the whole body of water in its immense expanse, you are doubly deluded amongst the deluded. This is exactly the same delusion as when I hold my hand down; and so the Tathāgata says that you are the most pitiable people.'[24]

---

from, all mental conditions and all causal phenomena are but appearances in the (True) Mind.' *Form*, (the aggregate rūpa) comprises the five physical organs and their six modes of sense (e.g. ear and sound, etc.). *Mind* comprises the last four of the five aggregates and the eighth consciousness. All *causes* are sense organs and sense data. *Mental conditions* are the fifty-one mental ideas and *causal phenomena* comprise body, the world and the myriad things that constitute man's surroundings.

Thus you should know that your body and mind are just things that appear in your wonderful, bright and pure Profound Mind. Why do you recognize only your illusory body and mind thereby losing sight of the precious, bright and subtle nature of your fundamental Enlightened Mind and so recognize delusion within Enlightenment? For fundamentally you were not deluded but merely lost sight of Reality by wrongly clinging to unreality, hence your delusion in the midst of Enlightenment. This is exactly where your inversion lies.

[24] The Buddha said that all things were but manifestations of the mind, but being apprehensive that those present could not understand this, He traced inversion back to its origin to reveal the same source of both Ignorance and Enlightenment in order to root out the false mind and false seeing.

In the pure and clean True Mind of the One Reality, there was fundamentally neither body and mind nor outer world, but it was stirred and screened by a single thought, thereby transforming the all-embracing Absolute Void into dull emptiness, hence the words: 'Dimness creates dull emptiness.' Then ignorance thickened in this relative voidness and crystallized into illusory form made of four elements, hence the words: 'Both dimness and emptiness unite with the darkness to become form.' As the True Mind was screened by delusion, the fundamental bright wisdom was changed into wrong perception which confronted illusory form, and, as time passed slowly, it united with some small portion of the four elements, thereby taking the illusory shape of body and mind, made of five aggregates; hence: 'The mingling of form with false thinking causes the latter to take the shape of a body.' Because this illusory body was grasped, the self-possessed True Nature was overlooked, hence the recognition of 'inner disturbance by stirring accumulated causes' as the nature of the self-mind. After losing (sight of) the boundless True Mind, the illusory body and mind were grasped, and mind was wrongly thought to be in the body. Hence the failure to realize that this body as well as outer mountains, rivers, space and the great earth were but phenomena appearing in the wonderful bright True Mind. This is like rejecting the great ocean to recognize one of its bubbles; this already showed one delusion, and if a

Refuting the false perception to eliminate, the fourth aggregate and reveal the non-existence of the seventh consciousness

Wiping Out the Unreal

The Non-Existence of Discriminative Perception

Ānanda's wrong view

Ānanda was moved to tears by the Buddha's compassion and profound Teaching, brought his two palms together and said: 'After hearing the Buddha's wonderful Dharma. I have realized that the wondrous Bright Mind is fundamentally perfect, so that I always dwell in my Mind-ground. But if my awakening has been due to the Buddha's preaching, I have (really) used my causal mind to hear it with reverence, thereby merely realizing that mind. I dare not pretend that it is the fundamental Mind-ground. Will you be compassionate enough to enlighten me so as to remove, my (remaining) doubts so that I can return to the Supreme Tao?'[25]

Unreality of illusory causes

The Buddha said: "You are still using your clinging mind to listen to the Dharma; since, however, this Dharma is also causal, you fail to realize the Dharma-nature. This is like a man pointing a finger at the moon to show it to others who should follow the direction of the finger to look at

---

bubble was mistaken for the whole body of water, this was another delusion. Thus you are doubly deluded. Such inversion does not differ from that caused by my lowering an arm. Hence the Buddha declared that Ānanda and those present were the most pitiable people.

The Buddha by His revelation of two basic inversions (page 13) had now rooted out the third aggregate saññā and the first six consciousnesses in His dealing with the first basic inversion.

[25] Ānanda's statement showed his second basic inversion. (See p. 13.) Hitherto he had recognized his discriminating mind as the true one. As the Buddha now disclosed the profound, bright, all-embracing True Mind about which he had not previously heard, he was moved to tears, but his comprehension by means of illusory mind of the Teaching did not mean his experiential awakening to True Mind. Therefore, he dared not pretend that he had really wakened to the fundamental Mind-ground and asked the Buddha to remove his doubt on this point.

Although the ancients had unshaken faith in their self-minds, they could not attain real awakening until they had settled their doubts about their self-minds. But in Ānanda's case his discriminating about the Buddha's voice with his causal or samsaric mind (prevented) his enlightenment. As (his faith) still depended upon his intellect or Sixth Consciousness he still accepted illusory causes and so missed Reality.

the moon. If they look at the finger and mistake it for the moon, they lose (sight of) both the moon and the finger. Why? Because the bright moon is actually pointed at; they both lose sight of the finger and fail to distinguish between (the states of) brightness and darkness. Why? Because they mistake the finger for the bright moon and are not clear about brightness and darkness.

'Likewise, if you mistake your (intellect which) hears my preaching voice for your (true mind), the latter's discerning nature should be independent of that differentiated voice. For instance, when a traveller spends the night at an inn, he does so for a time and then leaves, not staying there for ever: as to the inn-keeper, he has nowhere else to go for he owns the inn. It is the same with your mind.

Falseness of both sense organs and consciousness

'If it is your True Mind, it has nowhere to go. Then why in the absence of speech has it no discerning nature of its own? This discriminating (intellect) does not arise only when I speak, but also when you discern my appearance; it has no discerning nature of its own when there is no form. (It is not True Mind) even when you reach the state in which all discrimination ceases, a state that is neither form nor Voidness, which the heretics call Primordial Darkness.[26]

All phenomena returnable to causes are unreal

'If that which has no discerning nature of its own ceases to exist in the absence of causal conditions, how can the (so-called) nature of your mind be an (independent) Host if it disappears when it returns to its (illusory) causes?'[27]

---

[26] Primordial darkness at the beginning of existence, out of winch all things arose.

[27] This shows the second basic inversion (see p. 13), hence the Buddha used the essence of seeing to reveal the non-existence of the Seventh Consciousness before exposing the Essence of (the Eighth) Consciousness as the substance of Nirvāṇa. For the Seventh is the organ of the Sixth Consciousness and is the nature of discrimination, using the latter to perform its function. Both belong to the Perception of the Eighth Consciousness. The Seventh Consciousness is also called the Clinging Mind because it (depends on) inner and outer causes; it has no substance when external data cease to exist; hence causal externals are used to show its non-existence. The Buddha said: 'If you use your clinging mind to listen to the Dharma, this Dharma is also causal and pertains to the objective cause, or samsaric mind. Therefore, you have not realized the substance of (absolute) Dharma which is beyond words and phrases. When I teach the Dharma it is like pointing a finger at the moon to show it to others. As the finger is not the moon, you should disregard it to see the moon, but if you mistake my finger for the moon, you will lose (sight of) both the (bright) moon and the (dark) finger and will not be clear about the two states of brightness and obscurity. If you mistake (your intellect) that differentiates when you hear me preach the Dharma for your true mind, the latter should have substance in the absence of my voice. For example,

Borrowing the Essence of Perception to Pick Out Causal Externals

Ānanda asked: 'If every state of my mind can be return to its cause, why does the Buddha speak of the wondrous bright original mind which is not returnable to anywhere? Will you be compassionate enough to enlighten me?'

Setting up the essence of perception

The Buddha said: 'As you see me now, the essence of your seeing is originally clear. Although it is not the profound Bright Mind, it is like a second moon but is not a reflection of the moon (in water). Now listen attentively to my explanation of that which cannot return anywhere.

Picking out causal externals

'Ānanda, the doors and windows of this hall are wide open and face east. There is light when the sun rises in the sky and there is darkness at midnight when the moon wanes or is hidden by fog or clouds. Your seeing is unimpeded through open doors and windows but is obstructed where there are walls or houses. Where there is discrimination, you perceive the (stirring) causes and in the dull void, you only see emptiness. An unconscious condition results from confused externals whereas an awakened state leads to clear perception. Ānanda, see now how I return each of these changing states to its causal origin. What are these origi-

---

a guest stops temporarily at an inn but its host always stays there. If your differentiating mind is really your true mind, it should stay permanently; then why has it no substance where there is no voice? Thus not only does this mind lack substance, but it also cannot be found when you notice my face. This reveals the non-existence of the Sixth Consciousness.

As the Sixth depends on the Seventh Consciousness for discerning, now that the former's substance cannot be found, the latter does not exist. Not only is this differentiating illusion unreal, but even when differentiation ceases there is neither form nor voidness. The Seventh Consciousness, as inner cause, is cut off from the five outer sense data, so that it is beyond form, and the innermost is clung to as an Ego, so that it is beyond voidness. This is the dim substance of the Eighth Consciousness which is not yet True Mind and which heretics call Primordial Darkness. Even this is not yet Reality, still less is the discriminating Seventh which is the organ of the Sixth Consciousness. Therefore, when this Seventh Consciousness is cut off from external causes, it grasps at the inner Eighth Consciousness as an Ego, hence heretics call the latter the Spiritual Ego and set it up as a Master in Primordial Darkness. The twenty-five heretical schools regard it as permanent.

This exposes the Seventh and incidentally reveals the Eighth Consciousness which is clung to as an Ego but is unreal. If that which has no independent nature of its own in the absence of causal externals is held as the nature of your mind, how can it be a host when each (uprising) can be (traced back and) returned to a rising cause? This reveals the Host who (is independent and) cannot be returned to any external cause; this only is True Mind. (This is the origin of the kung an (Japanese koan): All things return to the One, to where does the One return?)

nal causes? Ānanda, of these changing conditions, light can be returned to the sun. Why? Because there is no light without the sun and since light comes from the sun, it can be returned to it (i.e. its origin). Darkness can be returned to the waning moon, clearness to open doors and windows, obstruction to walls and houses, causes to differentiation, emptiness to relative voidness, confused externals to unconsciousness and clear perception to the awakened state. Nothing in the world goes beyond these conditions. Now when the Essence of your Perception confronts these eight states, where can it be, returned to? If to brightness you will not see darkness when there is no light. Although these states such as light, darkness, etc., differ from one another, your seeing remains unchanged.

The nature of perception

'All states that can be returned to external causes are obviously not YOU, but that which cannot be returned to anywhere, if it is not YOU, what is it? Therefore, you should know that your Mind is fundamentally wonderful, bright and pure and that because of your delusion and stupidity, you have missed it and so are caught on the wheel of transmigration, sinking and floating in the samsaric sea. This is why the Tathāgata says that you are the most pitiable of men.'[28]

The (Underlying) Nature of Perception is not the Essence of Perception

Ānanda asked: 'I now understand that the nature of Perception cannot be returned to any external cause but how can I know that it is my True Nature?[29]

The capacity of perception

The Buddha said: 'Ānanda, though you have not yet reached the state beyond the stream of transmigration, you may now use the Buddha's tran-

---

[28] When Ānanda heard that all mental (states) that could be returned to external causes were not the real Host, he asked the Buddha about the non-returnable True Mind. Since it is very difficult to explain, the Buddha used the Essence of Seeing to reveal it. For seeing is mixed up with causal conditions whereas its essence, or the English Consciousness, is not. Therefore, He spoke of the Essence of Seeing which, though not the real, is a transformation of the Absolute and is close to it; hence it is like a second moon which is close to the real moon but is not a reflection of it in water. If you understand that this Essence of Perception cannot be returned to any cause, you will be able to awaken to the True Mind.

[29] Ānanda did not really understand the Teaching for his words betrayed his deluded mind. The Buddha had merely used the Essence of Perception as a temporary Host in order to pick out external causes to eliminate the discriminating seeing which vanished automatically when returned to its conditioning causes.

scendent power to behold the first dhyāna heaven[30] without obstruction, like Anirudha[31] who sees this world (Jambudvīpa) as clearly as fruit[32] held in his own hand. Bodhisattvas can see hundreds and thousands of worlds. Buddhas in the ten directions can see all the Pure Lands as countless as the dust. As to living beings, their range of sight is (sometimes) limited to inches.

Picking out causal objects

'Ānanda, as you and I see the palaces inhabited by the four heavenly kings with all that is there in water, on the ground and in the air, though there is a great variety of forms and shapes in the light and darkness, they are but hindrances resulting from your differentiation of objective phenomena. Here you should distinguish between your own Self and external objects. From what you see, I now pick out that which is your own Self and those which are but phenomena. Ānanda, if you exhaust the field of your vision, from the sun and moon to the seven mountain ranges[33] with all kinds of light, all that you see are phenomena which are not YOU. As you (shorten your range) you see passing clouds and flying birds, the wind rising and dust, trees, mountains, rivers, grass, men and animals; they are all external and are not YOU.

The essence of perception

'Ānanda, the great variety of things, far and near, when beheld by the essence of your seeing, appeared different whereas the nature of your seeing is uniform. This wondrous bright essence is really the nature of your perception.[34]

---

[30] The first of the four dhyāna regions, which is as large as one whole universe and comprises the three Brahma heavens. See also Ch'an and Zen Teaching, Third Series, Glossary, page 287, Rider & Co.

[31] One of the ten chief disciples of the Buddha.

[32] Amalā, a fruit like the betel nut.

[33] The seven concentric mountain ranges which surround Sumeru, the central mountain of a universe, each range separated from the other by a sea.

[34] This shows the Essence of Seeing which originally is clear and emanates from the Eighth Consciousness reflecting the five sense data and perceiving surrounding objects, hence it is causal seeing. When it first contacts things that are external, this is Direct Inference which belongs to the Eighth Consciousness (ālaya-vijñāna). If this first contact is followed by a thought which stirs the mind and causes it to discriminate, this is Comparative Inference which pertains to the Sixth Consciousness (mano-vijñāna).

The eightfold method of returning mental conditions to their original causes, previously dealt with, to wipe out the discriminative seeing which arises from causal externals, concerns Comparative Inference. Direct Inference is now dealt with to reveal the Essence of Seeing, the capacity of which is brought out for its elimination as well.

The Essence of Perception Mistaken for Externals

Refuting this misconception

'If seeing is an object, you should also see my seeing. If you can do so why when I do not see things, do you not see my non-seeing? (Even) if you do so it will not be real but your false seeing. If you do not see my non-seeing, it follows that your seeing and mine are not objects. If so, why cannot your seeing be YOU? Again if when you see an object you grasp at it as such, it should also see you; if so, that object and the nature of seeing will mingle you, I and the world will be in complete confusion.

True perception

'Ānanda, when you see (things), this seeing is yours and not mine, and its nature penetrates everywhere; if it is not YOU, what is it? Why do you still doubt about your real nature and ask me to confirm that it is not false?'[35]

Wiping Out the Capacity of Perception to Reveal the True Mind

The capacity of seeing

Ānanda asked: 'World Honoured One, if I am the nature of seeing, why when the Buddha and I saw the palaces of the four heavenly kings and

---

Though the saintly and the worldly differ, and the field of vision is either large or limited, all this pertains to the Direct Perception of the Eighth Consciousness. The vast variety of phenomena, such as heaven, earth and all that is therein, appears in the field of vision and shows that though appearances differ, perception is uniform and cannot be mixed with them. This unchanging bright essence is the Nature of Perception. If you recognize it, you will be able to leap over it to realize your True Nature.

[35] This checked Ānanda's deviation from the real nature of seeing. The Buddha was afraid that Ānanda might mistake his seeing for an object, so He said: 'Each thing seen is an object but not the seeing. If seeing is an object, yours and mine will be objects and you can also see my seeing. If so, when I do not see anything, why do not you see my non-seeing? Even if you do, it is your wrong seeing but not my non-seeing. If you do not see my non-seeing, it follows that your seeing and mine are not objects. Since this seeing exists independently of objects, is it not the nature of your seeing? If you cling to seeing as an object, the latter should also see you; then your seeing and the object will see each other without there being any distinction between man and object, and there will be utter confusion. The teaching on seeing independently of objects is to return perception (see page 10) to the Essence of Consciousness. If you understand this, you will gradually perceive your True Nature.'

Hence the Buddha said: 'When you see something, this is your own seeing that has nothing to do with me. Is it not your seeing that penetrates throughout your real nature? This is already quite clear; why do you doubt about this nature which is inherent in you and so fail to believe that it is the Real? Why do you still wait for me to confirm it?"

the sun and moon, did this seeing first penetrate the whole world and then return to this vihāra, then to its temple and now to this hall with its eaves and corridors? Does this seeing which first pervaded the universe now return to and fill only this hall; does its previous scale not shrink, or is cut up by the walls of this hall? I do not know where the "meaning" of all this really "lies"; will you be compassionate enough to enlighten me?'

Breaking up the capacity of seeing

The Buddha replied: 'Ānanda, all things in this world, whether large or small, inner or outer, as well as in other conditions,[36] are external; you should not say that your seeing expands and contracts. Take for instance a square box the inside of which is seen as containing a "square" of air. Now, tell me, is the air seen as "square" in the square box, really square or not? If so, it should not be round when "poured" into a round box. If not, then there should be no "square" of air in the square box. You say that you do not know where the "meaning" of all this really "lies," (but) the "meaning" being so, where do you want it to "lie"? Ānanda, if you want the air to be neither square nor round, just throw the box away. Since air has no location, you should not again insist on removing the place where it "lies." If, as you just said, when you entered this hall, your seeing shrank into a small compass, then when you look at the sun, do you lift it up to reach that sun in the sky overhead? If a wall can cut off your seeing, can you prevent it from peeping through a hole in the wall? Therefore, your contention is wrong.

Revealing the Real

'All living beings, from the time without beginning, have disregarded their own Selves by clinging to external objects, thereby missing their fundamental Minds. Thus they are being turned round by objects and perceive large and small sizes. If they can turn objects round, they will be like the Tathāgata, and their bodies and minds will be in the state of radiant perfection; from their immutable holy site,[37] the end of each of their hairs will contain all lands in the ten directions.'[38]

---

[36] The eight causal condition previously dealt with (see page 34).

[37] The Holy site, or bodhimandala, is the immutable Pure Land of the enlightened True Mind which is omnipresent. This is eradication of space.

[38] We have seen that the Eighth Consciousness has three characteristics: self-evidencing, perception and form. As the Buddha was about to wipe out falseness to reveal Reality, He first picked on form. He then used the essence of seeing to show that it is independent of all external causes. With the elimination of objective causes (or form), the subjective seeing (perception) disappears as well; this is the return of seeing to the essence of perception which then remains alone. Since the essence of perception or the Eighth Consciousness

Removing the essence of perception to wipe out the fifth aggregate and eighth consciousness

Eradicating Attachment to the Ego to Reveal the One Reality

Ānanda asked: 'If this essence of seeing is my wondrous nature, the latter should manifest before me. If seeing is my real ego, then what are my body and mind? But in fact my body and mind can discern (things) whereas that seeing cannot discern my body. If perception is my mind and causes me to see (things), then this perception is my Ego whereas my body is not; this is exactly what the Buddha previously refuted (with the argument that) objects should then see me. Will you be compassionate enough to enlighten me?'[39]

---

is not yet broken up, its direct inference can create body and the universe, thus implying a capacity which is limited and is incommensurate with the boundless realm of Dharma (Dharmadhātu); hence its inner, outer, great and small conditions which caused Ānanda to doubt about his seeing being cut up. If this capacity is destroyed, both sense organ and external objects will vanish and the True Nature will be boundless. This is what an ancient meant by saying: 'There is no need to seek Reality; it will suffice to lay down all views.'* If the capacity of seeing is eliminated, form will disappear instantly. Hence the Buddha said: 'If a man can turn objects round, he will be like the Tathāgata and his body and mind will be in the state of brightness and perfection, and from his immutable holy site, the tip of each of his hairs will contain all lands in the ten directions.'

Thus the Buddha wiped out Perception to root out the Seventh Consciousness as well as the fourth Aggregate, saṁskāra, in His partial revelation of Reality. This deals with the second basic inversion. (See page 13.)

*Quotation from the gāthā 'Have Faith in Your Mind' by Seng Ts'an, the third Chinese Patriarch of the Ch'an School.

[39] The Buddha was about to break up the ālaya's self-evidencing, thus implying the eradication of the ego to reveal the One Reality. As the Seventh is accustomed to mistake the Eighth Consciousness for an inner ego, Hinayanists mistake it lor the True Self in Nirvāṇa and heretics for the Spiritual Ego which is their all-embracing Self in the ten directions. This is why the Buddha said; 'The ālaya-vijñāna is very profound and subtle, and the seeds of its long habits have developed into an (irresistible) torrent. I have always refrained from revealing it to deluded people lest they grasp at it as an ego.' This is why the Buddha seldom mentioned it lightly.

When Ānanda said: 'If this essence of seeing is my wondrous nature, the latter (should) manifest before me,' he meant that if objects could be turned round so that he could become like the Tathāgata, then a myriad things appearing to him were all his essence of seeing. This implied that form was the ego.

When he said: 'If seeing is my real ego, then what are my body and mind?' he meant that if things were his true seeing, they (should be) his ego; if so, what were his body and mind? This implied an ego existing apart from form.

When he said: 'But in fact my body and mind can discern (things) whereas that seeing cannot discern my body,' he meant that if objects were the ego, then body and mind should

Rooting Out Ānanda's Misconception of Objects BEING and NOT BEING Perception

Misconception of objects BEING perception

The Buddha replied: Ānanda, your conception of perception being in front of you is incorrect because if it is, the essence of perception should have a position which can be shown. As you sit in Jetavana park, you see its trees and nullahs as well as this hall, with the sun or moon overhead and the Ganges in the distance. As you are now, in front of my lion-seat, moving your hand to point to the surroundings, such as the dark foliage of the wood, the blight sun, blocking walls and clear open spaces as well as grass, plants and very small things, although they are of different sizes, each of them can be pointed out. If they are really your seeing manifesting in front of you, you should be able to show which one is your seeing.

'Ānanda, you should know that if voidness is your seeing, since it has already become your perception, then how can it be empty? If an (external) thing is your seeing and has already become your perception, how can it be external? So, after dissecting all things in front of you, pick out the bright and pure principle of your perception and show it (to me) to prove that it is clearly and irrefutably identical with externals.'

Ānanda said: 'From this hall, I now see the Ganges in the distance, the sun or moon overhead and all that I can point out with my finger and see with my eyes; they are all (external) things but not one of them is my perception. World Honoured One, as the Buddha has said, not only a beginner in the śrāvaka stage, like myself, who is still in the stream of transmigration, but even a Bodhisattva, cannot dissect things and pick out the essence of seeing which has an independent nature apart from phenomena.'

The Buddha said: 'Correct, correct.'

Misconception of objects NOT BEING perception

The Buddha said: 'As you have said, there is no essence of seeing with an independent nature apart from phenomena. Now if there is no perception

not be it, but in fact body and mind could discern objects, and if the latter were the ego, why could they not discern his body? This implied a large ego and a small form, that is the ego containing form.

When he said: 'If seeing is my mind and causes me to see, then this perception is my ego whereas my body is not,' he meant that if these objects were his mind and caused him to see, then the nature of his seeing was the real ego whereas his body and mind were not. This was exactly what the Buddha had previously refuted about objects that should see him. This implied a large form and a small ego, that is form containing the ego.

Thus Ānanda's query concerned external objects mistaken for the ego because he misunderstood the Buddha's teaching on how to 'turn things round' to become equal to the Tathāgata.

in the things you point out, I now ask again: As you and the Tathāgata sit in this Jetavana park, when you see the wood and all externals including the sun or moon, if there is no essence of Seeing which can be picked out from them, tell me which one is not the seeing?'

Ānanda replied: 'Of all things seen in this Jetavana park, I do not know which one is not the seeing. Why? Because if the trees are not the seeing, why do I see them? If they are the seeing, why are they trees? If the void is not the seeing, why do I see it? If the void is the seeing, why is it empty? I too have thought carefully about all this and now conclude that each one of them is the seeing.'

The Buddha said: 'Correct, correct.'

In the assembly, all those who had not achieved the stage beyond study, were very surprised at hearing the Buddha say this. They failed to understand His meaning and were perturbed and thrown off balance. The Buddha realized their perplexity and alarm and took compassion on them, saying: 'Virtuous men, the words of the King of the Supreme Law are true, accord with Reality and are neither deceitful nor false, unlike those of the heretics whose sermons are arbitrary and aimless.[40] Now listen attentively, your faith in me shall not be in vain.'[41]

Mañjuśrī's Helpful Interposition

Thereupon, Mañjuśrī Bodhisattva, who took compassion on the four varga, rose from his seat, prostrated himself at the Buddha's feet, brought his two palms together and said: 'World Honoured One, these people do not understand the Tathāgata's twofold revelation of the reality and unreality of the essence of perception in form and voidness. They think that if causal form and voidness are the seeing, there should be an indication of it, and if they are not, there should be no seeing. They do not understand your teaching and are, therefore, surprised and bewildered, but they are not like those whose roots are frivolous and inferior.[42] May the Tathāgata be compassionate enough to enlighten them (so that they know) what objects and this essence of perception are fundamentally and that there exists neither "is" nor "is not" between them.'

---

[40] Lit. Unlike those from Maskari Gośālīputra who preaches four kinds of non-dying states arbitrarily and aimlessly.

[41] The Buddha's aim was to point directly at the One Reality which is beyond both what 'is and 'is not.' As Ananda and those who had not achieved the stage beyond study, clung to this duality of existence and non-existence, they were bewildered, perplexed and thrown off balance when their usual props were swept away. Therefore, the Buddha comforted them.

Up to here the Teaching consisted in rooting out the misconception of a real Ego.

[42] A reference to those arrogant disciples who refused to listen to the Buddha's expounding of the Lotus Sutra.

The Buddha declared to Mañjuśrī and the assembly: 'To all Tathāgatas and great Bodhisattvas of the ten directions, abiding in the state of Samādhi, seeing and its (concurrent) causes, as well as all forms imaginable, are like flowers in the sky which fundamentally do not exist. This seeing and its causes are essentially the profound, pure and bright substance of Enlightenment;[43] how can there be "is" and "is not" within it? Mañjuśrī, I now ask you this; you are already the real Mañjuśrī; can there be another Mañjuśrī who first "is" and then "is not"?'[44]

Mañjuśrī replied: 'No, World Honoured One, I am the real Mañjuśrī and there cannot be another. Why? Because if there is, then there will be two Mañjuśrīs, but my presence here does not mean that there is no Mañjuśrī, with an (arbitrary) conception of "is" and "is not" in between.'

The Buddha said: 'Likewise this clear seeing as well as the objects (seen) and the void are fundamentally the perfect, pure, true Mind of the Wonderful, Bright, Supreme Bodhi wrongly perceived as form and voidness as well as hearing and seeing, just as a second moon is perceived with the accompanying misconception of real and unreal moons. Mañjuśrī, there is only one real moon which is beyond the condition of "is" and "is not." Therefore, if you discern seeing and its objects and give rise to all kinds of (mental) creation, this is wrong thinking which will prevent you from getting out of this dual condition of "is" and "is not." (If you look into them by means of) this true, essential, wonderful, bright, and enlightened Nature, it will enable you to avoid this duality.'[45]

---

[43] The seeing and its causes spring from the fundamental substance of Enlightenment.

[44] This is the arbitrary conception of existence and non-existence.

[45] Under delusion, wisdom is transformed into consciousness, hence the wrong conception of a body and its surroundings with a vast variety of different things, all of which are created by consciousness. If consciousness is transmuted into wisdom, all external things will vanish at once. Hence the saying: 'Perception of form is consciousness and its non-perception is wisdom.' The only difference between these two states lies in a mere change. For when the substance of the One Reality is transformed into the ālaya-vijñāna, body and universe come to be. If body and mind are disentangled from within and the universe is disengaged from without, this storehouse (ālaya) consciousness is essentially the permanent True Mind of the Dharma-realm of the One Reality in the Tathāgata-garbha, in which how can there be existence and non-existence? If we rely on the wrong perception of consciousness, it will give rise to the (duality of) what is real and unreal. If we use the Great Wisdom to illumine them, we will find no such things. Therefore, Mañjuśrī who personified the Great Wisdom, asked the Buddha to explain how this essence of perception and its objects could be free from this dualism. The Buddha, while dwelling in the state of Great Samādhi, replied as in the text, specifically revealing the One Reality beside which there is nothing else.

Previously the Buddha had wiped out false seeing with the aid of the essence of perception and had said: 'Although this essence of perception is not the profound essential bright Mind, it is like a second moon but not its reflection in water.' Now as He was about

Wiping Out Ālaya's Self-Evidencing to Reveal One Reality

Ānanda's Discrimination

Ānanda said: 'World Honoured One, the King of the Law has preached the nature of causal enlightenment (Bodhi) which is always present in the ten directions[46] and which is beyond birth and death; does this differ from the concept of primordial profundity, according to the doctrine of Kapila and that of a true Ego pervading everywhere according to heterodox ascetics who cover their heads with ashes and dust? The Buddha, while on Laṅkā mountain, once said to Mahāmati: "Heretics always speak of natural existence but I preach causes and conditions[47] which are beyond the stage they have reached." Now as I look into this nature of Enlightenment, it is self existent, above birth and death and beyond all falsehood and inversion. There seem to be neither (your) causes and conditions nor their natural existence. Will you please teach us so that we shall not fall into heresies but win the bright nature of wonderful enlightened True Mind.'

Wiping Out Ānanda's Discrimination

Rooting out the self as such

The Buddha said: 'I have expediently revealed the truth to you, yet you do not awaken to it but mistake it for being the self as such. Ānanda, if it is the self as such, it should show clearly that its substance is the self. Now look into this wondrous seeing and see what is its self; do you mean that light, darkness, clarity or obstruction is its self? Ānanda, if light is its self, you should not see darkness and if the void you should not see obstruction. If darkness is its self, the nature of your seeing should cease to exist when there is light; if so, why do you still see light?'

---

to eliminate the essence of perception, He said: 'There is only one real moon,' that is, there is no second moon; this clearly shows the Buddha's skilful preaching on the rooting out of misconceptions, from the coarsest to the finest, thus gradually leading His disciples to return to Reality which would then be clear to them. If wrong thinking is used to contemplate things, they would not be able to escape from this duality of 'is' and 'is not.' But if they used the wonderful bright Enlightened Nature in their contemplation, it would enable them to avoid this duality. This reveals the nature of the One Reality, and up to here, attachment to the reality of the ego was cut off to disclose it.

[46] The nature of Bodhi follows worldly causes to appear everywhere for the salvation of living beings but without straying from its nirvanic condition.

[47] Hetupratyaya: Hetu = primary cause, e.g. a seed; pratyaya = condition or secondary cause, e.g. the earth, rain, sunshine.

Ānanda said: 'If so, the nature of this wondrous seeing is not the self as such. I now guess that it is created by cause and condition but I am still not clear about it. I pray the Tathāgata to teach me how this accords with the nature of cause and condition.

Eliminating cause and condition

The Buddha said: 'You now speak of cause and condition. Let me ask you this: When you see things, the nature of seeing manifests; does this seeing exist because of light, darkness, clarity or obstruction? Ānanda, if it exists because of light, you should not see darkness and if because of darkness, you should not see light; it is the same with clarity and obstruction. Again, is this seeing in a bright, dark, clear or obstructed condition? Ānanda, if it is clear, you should not see any obstruction and if it is obstructed you should not see that it is clear; it is the same with light and darkness.

Revealing the essential Bodhi

'Therefore, you should know that the essential Bodhi is wondrous and bright, being neither cause nor condition, neither self as such nor not self as such, neither unreality nor not unreality, and neither reality nor not reality, for it is beyond all forms and is identical with all things (dharma).[48] How can you now think of it and use the frivolous terminology of the world to express it ? This is like trying to catch or touch the void with your hand; you will only tire yourself, for how can you catch the void?'

Brushing away wrong assumptions

Ānanda asked: 'World Honoured One, if the nature of Wonderful Enlightenment has neither cause nor condition, why has the Buddha always told the bhikṣus about the nature of seeing which exists because of the four conditions of voidness, light, mind and eye; what does all this mean?'

The Buddha replied: 'I spoke of worldly cause and condition which have nothing to do with Supreme Reality.'[49]

---

[48] Which arise from this underlying principle.

[49] The Buddha broke up Ānanda's idea of the nature of Enlightenment as being self as such and as existing because of cause and condition, for such a nature as he conceived did not exist independently of external phenomena but still depended on cause and condition. He then revealed the essential Bodhi which is neither 'is' nor 'is not,' is beyond cause and condition, is not self as such and is independent of all forms and phenomena, that is the stage from which the path of words and speech is cut off and with which the mind's activities no longer connect; how can it be imagined and expressed in the conditioned language of this world? To attempt to speak of it is as futile as trying to catch the void with one's hand.

All false assumptions had now been rooted out to reveal the One Reality.

Eliminating the Essence of Perception to Reveal Inceptive Enlightenment[50]

Wiping Out Ānanda's Discrimination

'Ānanda, I now ask you this: When a worldly man says that he can[51] see things, what does he mean by "seeing" and "not seeing"?'

Ānanda replied: 'When a worldly man sees forms by the light of the sun, moon and lamps, this is called seeing but in the absence of such light, he cannot see (anything).'

(The Buddha asked:) 'Ānanda, if it is called not seeing when there is no light, he should not see darkness. If he does, this is because there is no light; how then can there be no seeing? Ānanda, in the dark, if this is called not seeing solely because he does not see the light, then when there is light, if he does not see darkness, this is again called not seeing; thus there would be no seeing in both cases. But in these two states which replace each other, the nature of your seeing does not cease for an instant. Therefore, there is (actual) seeing in both states; so how can there be no seeing?

Revealing the Inceptive Bodhi

'Therefore, Ānanda, you should know that when you see the light, your seeing is not clear; when you see the darkness, your seeing is not obscure; when you see the void, it is not empty, and when you see obstruction, it is not obstructed. After you have understood these four states, you should also know that when your (absolute) seeing perceives the Essence of Seeing, the former is not the latter which still differs from it; how can your (false) seeing reach that (absolute) seeing?[52] How can you speak of cause and condition, of the self existing as such and of the (so-called) union? You are all ignorant and narrow-minded hearers (śrāvakā) and cannot understand pure and clean Reality. I now teach you (the Truth) into which you should look carefully; so do not

---

[50] There are three kinds of Bodhi (a) basic or dormant Bodhi inherent in every living being; (b) inceptive Bodhi, resulting from the arousal of basic Bodhi by the practice of Dharma; and (c) ultimate Bodhi, or Complete Enlightenment realized when the first two unite.

[51] The word 'can' in the text is meaningful for it shows the subject that can see objects.

[52] Lit. 'When seeing (perceives) seeing, seeing is not seeing, (for) seeing strays from seeing; seeing cannot reach it.' This is a most difficult sentence to interpret and many Chinese commentators have explained it wrongly. The above accurate English rendering is made possible thanks to Master Han Shan, who wrote his commentary after his own enlightenment. This sentence was also widely discussed in Chinese Ch'an monasteries.

allow indolence and remissness to obstruct your Path to Profound Bodhi.[53]

[53] This wiped out the essence of perception to reveal inceptive Enlightenment. From the start of this discussion on seeing, the essence of perception was used to root out the discriminating seeing which arises from external causes. Then ālaya's perception was eliminated to reveal the essence of perception. For both perception and form are two characteristics of the same substance and depend on the essence of consciousness to manifest. Therefore, objects (form) and seeing (perception) intermingle and are not easy to separate. Hence Ānanda mistook either seeing (perception) for objects (form) or vice-versa, and gave rise to heterodox views. The Buddha used external objects to rebuke the disciple's discrimination.

Now that the essence of perception had been eliminated, only one True Essence remained, free from all other things and dualities. So all Ānanda's doubts about the existence of the self as such and about cause and condition were wiped out. This was the elimination of perception for its return to the essence of consciousness, which, however, was still under delusion. This is ignorance itself, called the storehouse of consciousness (ālaya-vijñāna). It is likened to a second moon, and if it is not eliminated, it will not be possible to unite with the real moon that is the true Mind of basic Enlightenment. This is why the essence of perception was wiped out to achieve the wisdom of inceptive Enlightenment.

When the Buddha was about to root out the essence of consciousness (ālaya). He probed Ānanda about the worldly conception of seeing and not seeing. This differed from His previous discussions based on causes, for it was now given in the absence of causal externals. He wanted to show this essence of perception which did not owe its existence to (external) causes and was not created by conditions - but is the one real essence which is close to the true Mind. If this ālaya consciousness is eliminated, all the five aggregates will vanish instantly; this is the wisdom of inceptive Enlightenment.

So the Buddha probed Ānanda about perception which an ordinary man speaks of when seeing things and asked him. 'What is seeing and what is not seeing?' The disciple replied that there was seeing when it was light or dark and the Buddha wiped out all this as said in the text and concluded that though light and darkness alternated, the nature of seeing was unchanged and did not cease for an instant. Therefore, the four conditions of light, darkness, clarity and obstruction are only externals whereas this essence of perception does not depend on any cause for its existence and is not created by any condition; it is essentially perception only. When all external objects had been wiped out, this essence alone remained but it still pertained to ignorance.

Therefore, the Buddha wiped out this essence of perception and said: 'When your (real) perception sees this essence of perception, it is not the latter which, though straying from it, is yet dose to it; how can your false seeing which is so far from (real) perception, ever reach it? How can you still speak of cause and condition, of the self as such and of union? This wiped out the essence of consciousness (ālaya-vijñāna). This non-discriminating true perception is the true Mind of the pure and clean Reality which you fail to realize because of your delusion and narrow mindedness. This is the wisdom of inceptive Enlightenment and only when it is realized can basic Bodhi manifest. This is the path of śamatha which I now teach you.'

After Ānanda's query about śamatha at the beginning, the Buddha had wiped out the body and mind, made of five aggregates, to reveal the unreality of man. This cut off attachment to the reality of an ego and was only (a state of) relative voidness for the attachment to things (dharma) still remained. Hence in the following text, the Buddha taught the elimination of the world to cut off this attachment to dharma.

Revealing the unreality of the two realms[54] to expose the non-existence of Dharma (things)

Ānanda said to the Buddha: 'World Honoured One, although the Buddha has taught us about cause and condition, the state of the self as such, of mingling and union and of non-mingling and non-union, our minds are still not open to the teaching. As we listened to His further instruction on seeing that is not seeing, we became more deluded and perplexed. Please be compassionate enough to open our wisdom-eye to enlighten us.' After saying this, he shed bitter tears, prostrated himself at the Buddha's feet and waited for the holy teaching.[55]

The Buddha took pity on Ānanda and the assembly and was about to teach the profound practice of the samādhis of the great Dhāraṇī when he said to Ānanda: 'Though you have tried to memorize (my Dharma), you have only broadened your hearing (or knowledge) and are still not very clear about deep insight into śamatha. Now listen with attention to what I now tell you fully (for the benefit of you) and those who are still in the stream of transmigration so that you can all win the bodhi fruit.

'Ānanda, all living beings are subject to transmigration through various worlds because of two inverted, discriminative and wrong views which, wherever they occur, cause people to be caught in the turning wheel of saṁsāra. What causes these two wrong views? They are due to their individual and collective karmas.

Individual Karma

'What is the individual karma that causes wrong views? Ānanda, it is like a man who, because his eyes are inflamed, sees at night a five-coloured circle round the light of a lamp. Is this circle the colour of the flame or that of his seeing? If it is the colour of the flame, why does only the man with bad eyes see it while others do not? If it is the colour of his seeing, since his seeing is already that colour, what do you call the circle? Moreover, Ānanda, if this circle is independent of the lamp, the man should see it when looking at nearby curtains, tables and mats; if it is independent of

[54] The realm of living beings and the real of material things.

[55] The five aggregates previously eradicated by the Buddha were mere names and terms but these seemingly real things (dharma) still remained for Ānanda had no personal experience of their non-existence. So, when he heard about 'the seeing which was not real seeing,' he became more deluded and perplexed. This was because although as a Hinayanist he was no longer attached to the reality of an ego, he still clung to the existence of the body, mind and universe. Hence his request for elucidation.

The Buddha then explained the unreality of the body, the mind and their surroundings.

the seeing, it should not be seen by the eyes, but why does the man with bad eyes see it? Therefore, you should know that this colour is revealed by the lamplight and becomes a circle when perceived by defective seeing; both the circle (form) and the seeing (perception) are due to bad eyes, but that which recognizes this disease is not sick. Thus you should not (discriminate and) say that it is either the lamp or the seeing, with the further idea of it being neither the lamp nor the seeing. It is like a second moon which is neither the real moon nor its shadow. Why? Because the sight of this second moon is an illusory creation. So wise people should not say that this illusion "is" or "is not" form or that it exists apart from seeing or non-seeing. In the same way how can you prove that an illusion caused by bad eyes is (due to) the lamp or to your seeing? Still less can you establish that it is (due to) neither the lamp nor your seeing.

Collective Karma

'What is the collective karma that causes wrong views? Ānanda, this universe (Jambudvīpa) comprises, beside the great sea, 3,000 continents, with the largest at the center, containing altogether, from east to west, 2,300 countries and other small continents each consisting of 1, 2, 30, 40, 50, 200, or 300 countries. Ānanda, in a small continent there (may) be only two countries, one of which is inhabited by people who, as a result of their evil karma, may witness all sorts of evil states, while the inhabitants of the other country neither see nor even hear of them.

'Ānanda, let us compare these two karmic conditions (dealing first with wrong views caused by individual karma which are similar to those by collective karma). Ānanda, all living beings whose individual karma causes them to see wrongly, are like the man who because his eyes are inflamed, sees round the light of a lamp a circle which seems to be out there in front of him, but in fact exists because his sight is disturbed; this circle is not created by form. However the (faculty of) seeing through which he is aware of this trouble, is free from it. Similarly if you now look at mountains, rivers and the country with its inhabitants, they are all created by a disturbance in your seeing since the time without beginning. Though this seeing and its causal externals seem to be (phenomena) in front of you, they originally arise from your (subjective) awareness of that brightness (of Reality) which leads to a (wrong) perception of (objective) causal falsities. Thus awareness and perception (cause) wrong seeing, but the bright true Mind of basic Bodhi which sees clearly these causal states is free from all ills. That which realizes this awareness as faulty does not fall into delusion. This is (what I mean by true) seeing that is not (discriminative and about which you asked for elucidation). How can this be comprehended by your (discriminative) seeing, hearing, feeling and knowing? Therefore, your actual seeing of yourself, of me and of living beings of the ten types of birth is a disturbance of your seeing and certainly not that which is aware of your wrong seeing. For the basic nature of the true essence of perception is beyond all ills: hence it is not called seeing.

'Ānanda, let us now compare wrong seeing caused by collective karma with that by individual karma. The (illusion of a) circle round the light of a lamp seen by a man because his eyes are bad, and the evil condition experienced by all the inhabitants of a country because of collective karma, are both created by false seeing since the time without beginning. Thus the Jambudvīpa's 3,000 continents, the four great seas, the sahā world and samsaric countries in the ten directions as well as their inhabitants are the product of causal seeing, hearing, feeling and knowing which arise from the (subjective) awareness of the brightness of supramundane wondrous Mind, entailing mixtures and unions of concurring causes which result in their rise and fall.[56]

---

[56] Attachment to dharma (things) implies man's clinging to the inner body and mind, made of five aggregates (i.e. the realm of living beings) and to outer mountains, rivers, space and the world (i.e. the realm of material things), all of which seem to exist. Hence the Buddha spoke of 'wrong views, which *wherever* they occur, cause living beings to be caught there in the turning karmic wheel of existence.' This is the meaning of the saying: 'All (mental) stirrings cause suffering.'

Individual karma causes *direct retribution*, which affects the individual with a body and mind, and collective karma causes *dependent retribution*, which affects the material world, or the surroundings of all who share the same karma. Fundamentally these two falsities do not exist in the absolute state, but under delusion, the ālaya consciousness gives rise to *perception* which is the false mind, and *form* which is the illusory object. Hence the true Mind is likened to good eyes and lamplight; the false mind to inflamed eyes; the body and mind, to the circle round the light of a lamp; and the material world, to a flower in the sky. He who awakens to this illness of the eyes, realizes the unreality of these two falsities; hence the Buddha used an inflammation of the eyes to expose their non-existence.

Individual karma causing false seeing is man's direct retribution in the form of a body and mind which do not exist fundamentally and depend on false seeing for their seeming existence. This is likened to an inflammation of the eyes which causes the seeing of a circle round the light of a lamp. This illusion neither exists because of the lamp nor apart from it; therefore, how can it be discussed on the basis of the dual 'is' and 'is not'? Like the colour that comes from the lamp, what is false also comes from what is real. This is like a second moon which is beyond both existence and non-existence. He who understands this, awakens to the unreality of the five aggregates and wipes out all doubts about cause and condition, the self as such, mingling and union, and non-mingling and non-union.

Collective karma concerns all living beings sharing the same retribution, that is the material world which fundamentally does not exist and arises also from false seeing. It is easy to awaken to the unreality of an ego but it is very difficult to realize the non-existence of the material world. Hence the comparison of individual with collective karma and vice-

Revealing the Independent Basic Bodhi to Expose the Unfettered Absoluteness (Bhutatathatā)

'He who can avoid the (illusory) mixture and union and non-mixture and non-union of concurrent causes, will be able to destroy all causes of birth and death, thereby perfecting the transcendental nature of Enlightenment and realizing the permanent basic Bodhi of pure and clean Self-mind.

Wiping Out All Traces of the False to Enter the Abstruse to Reveal the Bhutatathatā

'Ānanda, though you have understood the profound and bright nature of basic Bodhi which is neither causal, nor conditional, nor the self as such, you are still not clear about this enlightened substance which neither mixture and union nor non-mixture and non-union can create.

'Ānanda, I must now ask you a question. Since you still hold that all false thinking mixes and unites with causes and conditions, you are in doubt and worry about (the thoughts of) a Bodhi mind arising from such mixture and union. If so, does your essence of perception mix with light, or darkness, with clarity, or obstruction? If it mixes with light, when the latter appears and you see it, where does it mix with your seeing? Since your seeing is clear, where can you find such mixture? If it is not the seeing, why do you see light? If it is the seeing, how can you see your own seeing? Since your seeing is complete by itself, how can it be mixed with the light? Since light is complete by itself, where can it contain your seeing? Therefore, seeing and light differ, and if they are mixed up, even the word "light" would cease to exist; in other words, such a mixture would suppress the light. Consequently, your concept of a mixture of seeing with light is wrong, and so is a mixture of seeing with darkness, clarity and obstruction.

'Again, Ānanda, does the essence of your perception unite with light, darkness, clarity and obstruction? If it unites with light, then when light vanishes and is replaced by darkness, the seeing should not unite with the latter, but why do you still see darkness? When you see darkness, if your seeing does not unite with it, then when it unites with light, you should not see light as well. If light is not seen, then when there is light, do you

---

versa, to explain the unreality of the realm of material things. For both the circle round the light of a lamp and the material world come from a defect in the seeing since the time without beginning, due to basic ignorance caused by the first stirring thought that resulted in (subjective) awareness of the brightness of True Mind and subsequent wrong *perception* which created phenomena (*form*).

This wiped out the two realms to reveal the unreality of dharma.

know that it is light and not darkness? Likewise, a union of the seeing with darkness, clarity and obstruction is equally false.'

Ānanda asked: 'World Honoured One, I am thinking again about this enlightened substance; does it neither mix nor unite with causal externals and with the mind's thinking and discerning?'

The Buddha replied: 'You now speak of not mixing and not uniting. Do you mean that this essence of seeing does not mix with light, darkness, clarity and obstruction? If so, then when you see the light, there should be a demarcation line between seeing and light. Now look carefully (and tell me) where are the fields of light and of your seeing, and where are their boundaries? Ānanda, if you do not see where light is, then your seeing will not reach it; if so, you will not ever know where the light is, and how can there be a border line? It is the same with darkness, clarity and obstruction.

'Again, do you mean that this essence of seeing does not unite with light, darkness, clarity and obstruction! If it does not unite with light, then both the seeing and light are in opposition, like your cars and the light which can never meet. So your seeing would not perceive anything where there is light; then how can you cause them either to unite or not? It is the same with darkness, clarity and obstruction.[57]

Direct Pointing to the One Mind

'Ānanda, you are still not clear about the illusory appearances of all passing phenomena which vanish wherever they arise. These illusions in the shape of forms spring from (their underlying nature which is) the substance of wonderful Bodhi. So also are the six entrances (organs), the twelve āyatana (six sense organs and six sense data) and the eighteen realms of senses which falsely arise from the mixture and union of causes and conditions and which falsely vanish when the same causes and conditions are disconnected. They are but creation and destruction appearing and vanishing within the permanent, wonderfully bright,

[57] The Buddha had already taught that basic Bodhi could only appear after inceptive Bodhi had been aroused, but Ānanda still thought that when inceptive Bodhi mixed and united with basic Bodhi, ultimate Enlightenment would result. Thus he thought that the True Mind of basic Enlightenment would arise when there was such mixing and uniting. Therefore the Buddha wiped out the disciple's discrimination to reveal absolute true Mind which is free from all relativities and contraries. Hence the above heading '*Wiping out all traces to enter Abstruseness*' (added by the commentator Han Shan). This wiped out the false view of Unity-with-differentiation to reveal the Absolute which is beyond monism and pluralism. (See also Ch'an and Zen Teaching, First Series, *The Diamond Sutra*, page 202.)

So far samsaric illusions have been used to distinguish the false from the real in order to reveal the true Mind of basic Bodhi. In the following text the uncreate is dealt with to return the false to the real in order to reveal the absolute Voidness of the Tathāgata womb.

immutable, all-embracing and profound Bhūtatathatā (absolute) nature of the Tathāgata store wherein neither coming nor going, neither delusion nor enlightenment, and neither birth nor death can be found.[58]

Fusing Myriads of Things with the Absolute to Reveal the Identity of Phenomenon with Noumenon

Fusing the Five Aggregates

The First Aggregate Rūpa

'Ānanda, why are the five aggregates fundamentally the wondrous nature of the Absolute of the Tathāgata store? Ananda, for instance, when a man looks at a clear sky with clear eyes, he sees only the void which contains nothing. If suddenly without any apparent reason he steadies his seeing, it will be disturbed and he will see flowers dancing and other objects moving in the sky. It is the same with the aggregate rūpa. Ānanda, these dancing flowers come neither from the void nor from his eyes. If they came from the void, they would return to it; if there was really such a coming and going of these flowers, the void would not be empty. If voidness was really not empty (i.e. if it was solid), then they could not appear and vanish in it. This is like Ānanda's (solid) body which does not allow (another) Ānanda to enter it. If these flowers come from the eyes, they should be able to return to the eyes, and because they come from (the faculty of) seeing, they should be able to see (things). Thus when they leave the eyes, they become flowers in the sky and when they return, they should see the organ of sight. If they cannot see (things), then when they

[58] This is the direct pointing at the source of the One Mind of the uncreated and unending nature of the Tathāgata store to fuse myriads of illusory phenomena into their underlying principle. For mind and seeing pertain to ālaya's *perception* and all causal objects to ālaya's *form*; this is basic ignorance, hence man's inability to realize the non-existence of all appearances. This is why the Buddha picked our causal objects to show the unreality of *form* and thereby of *perception*. Thus *perception* and *form* were returned to the essence of consciousness, that is the ālaya consciousness, which would then be broken up to reveal inceptive Bodhi for ultimate return to the One Mind. This exposed the substance of the absolute voidness of the Tathāgata store. All this was beyond the comprehension of Ānanda who was still a man of the Small Vehicle. Hence the Buddha's teaching on illusions which vanish wherever they arise, for they all spring from the True Mind of the Tathāgata store which is immutable, permanent and all-embracing. If phenomena are clung to, there seem to be birth and death, but if the true Mind is looked into, they are only illusions that rise and fall within it. (This is what the Heart Sūtra means by 'Form does not differ from the void, nor the void from form. Form is identical with the void and the void is identical with form.' So also are the remaining four aggregates in relation to the void. See Ch'an and Zen Teaching, First Series, *The Heart Sutra*.) This is direct pointing at the One Mind.

leave, they should screen the sky and when they return, they should veil the eyes; but when the man sees these flowers, his eyes are not veiled. Then why do you wait until the sky is clear (of these flowers) to say that your eyes are really clear? Therefore, you should know that the aggregate form is unreal for it is neither causal nor conditional nor self-existent.[59]

The Second Aggregate Vedanā

'Ānanda, when, for instance, a man is in good health and his limbs are in good condition, he does not feel anything. But if suddenly, without any reason, he rubs his palms together, he feels coarseness, smoothness, cold and warmth. It is the same with the second aggregate vedanā. Ānanda, these sensations come from neither the void nor his palms. If they come from the void, why are they felt by his palms only and not by his body? It should not be up to the void to choose his palms to feel them. If they come from his palms, they should not wait for the palms to be brought together to be felt. Moreover, if they really come from his palms and are felt when the latter are brought together, when they are separated, these sensations should re-enter the palms, arms, shoulders, bones and marrow which should also feel their re-entry. They should also be felt by the mind as coming in and out, as if something had moved in and out of the body. If so, there is no need to bring the two palms together to feel these sensations. Therefore, you should know that the aggregate vedanā is unreal and is neither causal nor conditional nor self-existent.

The Third Aggregate Sañjñā

'Ānanda, if someone speaks of sour plums, your mouth will water, and if you think of walking above an overhanging cliff, you will have the sensation of shivering in the soles of your feet. This is the same with the third aggregate sañjñā. Ānanda, this talk of sourness does not come from the plum, nor does it enter your mouth. If it comes from the plum, it should be spoken of by the plum itself; then why does it wait for someone to speak of it? If it enters your mouth, it should be your mouth which actually talks about it; then why does it wait until your ears hear of it? If it is your ears which alone hear it, why does not that water come out of them? This is the same with your thought of (walking above) an overhanging cliff. Therefore, you should know that the third aggregate sañjñā is neither causal nor conditional nor self-existent.

---

[59] Steadying stands for *ignorance*; troubled seeing, for false *perception*; and dancing flowers, for illusory form; this is the origin of form. The Buddha used the void and eyes to reveal the unreality of the first aggregate. Therefore, he who understands that dancing flowers come from neither the void nor the eyes, realizes the non-existence of form which is an illusion.

The Fourth Aggregate Samskara

'Ānanda, the fourth aggregate saṁskāra is like water which flows in a torrent endlessly and in good order over a fall. Ānanda, this flow does not come from the void nor is it due to the water; it is neither the water itself nor does it exist apart from the void and the water. If it is created by the void, boundless space would become an endless flow of water and the whole world would be submerged. If it is due to the water, then it should not be water and should have its own form and location which should be apparent. If it is water, then still and clear water should not be water. If it exists apart from the void and water, (this is impossible because) space (is all-embracing and) has (nothing) outside (it) and because there is no flow without water. Therefore, you should know that the fourth aggregate saṁskāra is false and is neither causal nor conditional nor self-existent.

The Fifth Aggregate Vijnañā

'Ānanda, the (fifth) aggregate consciousness is like the void in an empty pitcher with two mouths.[60] If someone blocks both mouths and carries it to another country, the void does not go from one place to another. If the void comes from somewhere, that place should lose some of its voidness, and on arrival elsewhere, when the mouths are opened and the pitcher reversed, one should see the void poured out of it. Therefore you should know that consciousness is unreal and is neither causal nor conditional nor self-existent.[61]

Fusing the Six Entrances

Entrance Through the Eyes

'Again, Ānanda, why are the six entrances (of illusions into the mind) fundamentally the absolute nature of the Tathāgata store? Ānanda, the

---

[60] A kavalinka pitcher.

[61] The pitcher stands for the body in the intermediate state after man's death; the void, for consciousness, and the two mouths, for the man's hearing and seeing. At death, his seeing and hearing cease to function, hence the two blocked spouts. His karma causes him to be reborn in another country. If consciousness is thought of as following the man to come at birth and go at death, then it should die in one country to be reborn in another, like the pitcher full of air carried from one place to another; if so, the place the man leaves should lose some of its air and the place where he arrives should gain some-new air that is poured from the pitcher. Hence we know that the void is immutable and that consciousness neither comes nor goes. Therefore, the concept of a consciousness that comes and goes to follow birth and death is groundless, because consciousness fundamentally does not exist.

The above wipes out the falseness of the five aggregates to reveal the absolute voidness of the nature of the Tathagata store.

steadying of the seeing that disturbs the sight, as well as the eyes and the disturbance itself are but trouble arising from Bodhi. Because the seeing arises between the two states of light and darkness, they are drawn into (ālaya's) perception which is called the (faculty of) seeing. This seeing has no independent substance that exists apart from the two states of light and dark. Therefore, Ānanda, you should know that this seeing comes from neither light nor darkness and from neither the organ of sight nor the void. Why? Because if it comes from light, it would cease to exist when darkness appears and would not perceive the latter. If it comes from darkness, it would be no more when there is light, and would not perceive the latter. If it comes from the organ (of sight), there would be no (objective) light and darkness; then such essence of perception would have no nature of its own. If it comes from the void, when it perceives these two states, it would also see the organ of sight. Moreover, the void would thus perceive everything of itself and have nothing to do with entrance through your eyes. Therefore, you should know that entrance through the eyes is false and is neither causal nor conditional nor self-existent.[62]

Entrance Through the Ears

'Ānanda, if a man suddenly closes his ears with two fingers, disturbance will arise in this sense organ and he will hear sounds in his head. (This closing of the ears) as well as the ears and the disturbance experienced are trouble that comes from Bodhi. Since this hearing arises between the two states of stillness and motion, they are drawn into (ālaya's) perception which is called hearing. This hearing has no substance independent of stillness and motion. Ānanda, you should know that this hearing comes from neither stillness, nor motion, nor from a sense organ nor the void. Why? Because if it comes from stillness, it should cease to exist when there is motion and would not hear the latter. If it comes from motion, it should cease to exist when there is stillness and would not hear the latter. If it comes from a sense organ, there would be no (objective) stillness nor motion; then this faculty of hearing would have no nature of its own. If it comes from the void, that which can hear is (certainly) not the void. Moreover, the void would hear of itself and will have nothing to do with that entrance through your ears. Therefore, you should know that entrance through the ears is neither causal nor conditional nor self-existent.

[62] Steadying the seeing stands for ignorance, and disturbance for the sight of light and darkness; both are troubles that come from Bodhi. Bodhi is thus screened by ignorance, hence ālaya's three characteristics: self-evidencing, perception and form, which are all unreal.

Entrance Through the Nose

'Ānanda, if a man suddenly holds his breath, his nostrils will feel cold. Because of this feeling, he can distinguish clearance (ventilation) from obstruction (suffocation) and emptiness from fullness and can smell fragrant and offensive odours. This restraint of breath as well as the nose and its feeling are trouble that comes from Bodhi. Since feeling arises between the two false conditions of clearance and obstruction, sensations are drawn into (ālaya's) perception which is called smell. This smell has no substance independent of clearance and obstruction. You should know that it comes neither from these two states nor from the nose nor the void. Why? Because if it comes from the clearance, it will cease to exist when there is obstruction; but why does it feel the latter? If it comes from obstruction, it will cease to be clear; but why does it come into contact with fragrance and stench? If it comes from a sense organ, there would be no (objective) clearance and obstruction; then this faculty of smelling would have no nature of its own. If it comes from the void, it should be able to smell your own nose; if so, the void itself would smell and would have nothing to do with that entrance through your nose. Therefore, you should know that that entrance is neither causal nor conditional nor self-existent.

Entrance Through the Tongue

'Ānanda, if, for instance, a man licks his lips again and again, he will have trouble (with his sense of taste); if he is ill he will experience a bitter taste, and if he is healthy, a (somewhat) sweet one. Thus bitterness and sweetness reveal this sense which is always tasteless in the absence of stirring (feelings) and which, together with the tongue and the trouble (caused by the taste) are but illusion which comes from Bodhi. This illusion is due to false externals (such as) bitterness and sweetness and is drawn into (ālaya's) perception which is called taste. This taste has no independent substance apart from flavours (such as) sweetness and bitterness, and tastelessness. Ānanda, you should know that this perception of taste comes neither from the flavours (such as) sweetness and bitterness nor tastelessness, nor from a sense organ nor the void. Why? Because if it comes from sweetness and bitterness, it will vanish in the state of tastelessness; but why does it feel the latter? If it comes from tastelessness, it will disappear when in touch with sweets; but why does it still feel sweet and bitter tastes? If it comes from the tongue, the latter originally is neither tasteless nor sweet nor bitter; hence we know that the organ of taste has no nature of its own. If it comes from the void, the latter not being your mouth, would taste by itself; then what has it to do with that entrance through your tongue? Therefore, you should know that this entrance is unreal and is neither causal nor conditional nor self-existent.

Entrance Through the Body

Ānanda, for instance, when a man touches his warm hand with his cold one, if the coldness exceeds the warmth, the warm hand will become cold and if the warmth exceeds the coldness, the cold hand will become warm. This touch is revealed when the two hands meet and then separate. This contact causes the feeling of touch which, together with his body and the illusion experienced, are but trouble which comes from Bodhi. This trouble occurs where there are two false conditions of contact and separation, and is drawn into (ālaya's) perception which is called touch. This touch has no independent nature apart from contact and separation and from pleasant and disagreeable conditions. Ānanda, you should know that this perception of touch comes neither from contact nor separation, nor from pleasant nor disagreeable conditions, nor from a sense organ nor the void. Why? Because if it comes from contact, it should vanish in the state of separation; but why does it feel the latter? It is the same with pleasant and disagreeable conditions. If it comes from a sense organ, it would be free from contact and separation and from pleasant and disagreeable conditions; then your body that feels them would have no nature of its own. If it comes from the void, the latter will feel the touch by itself; then what has it to do with your entrance through the body? Therefore, you should know that this entrance is false and is neither causal nor conditional nor self-existent.

Entrance Through the Intellect

'Ānanda, when for instance, a man is tired, he sleeps soundly; then he awakes and when he sees objects, he remembers and after a time forgets all about them. This is the inverted condition of birth, stay, change and death which is continuously drawn into the inner intellect; hence the organ of manas, which, together with the intellect and the trouble (experienced) are an illness arising in Bodhi. This illness comes from perceiving the two false conditions of birth and death, a perception which covers all inner data that cannot be reached by seeing and hearing; hence it is called knowing. This knowing has no substance of its own apart from the waking and sleeping states and from the conditions of birth and death. Thus, Ānanda, you should know that the organ of knowing comes neither from the waking and sleeping states, nor from the conditions of birth and death, and neither from a sense organ nor the void. Why? Because if it comes from the waking state, it should cease to exist in the sleeping state; then why does one sleep? If it comes from birth, it should be void at death; then who will die? If it comes from death, it would cease at birth; then who is living? If it comes from a sense organ, then while the body experiences the two states of waking and sleeping, the knowing has no nature of its own apart from these two states and will be like a flower in the sky. If it comes from the void, the latter will know everything and will have nothing to do with your entrance through the intellect. Therefore, this entrance is neither causal nor conditional nor self-existent.[63]

Fusing the Twelve Āyatana (Six Sense Organs and Six Sense Data)

Eyes and Form

'Again, Ānanda, the twelve āyatana are fundamentally (the same as) the Absolute of the Tathāgata store. Ānanda, just look at the grove and stream in Jetavana park. Is it form that creates the eyes' seeing or vice versa? If the organ of sight creates form, when you see the void which is not form, form would vanish, which means that nothing would exist. Then if form is no more, what can be used to reveal the void?[64] It is the same with the void. If form produces the eyes' seeing, when you see the void which is not form, your seeing would vanish, which means that nothing would exist; then who distinguishes the void from form? Therefore, you should know that neither seeing nor form nor the void has a place of abode, and that form and seeing are false and are neither causal nor conditional nor self-existent.

Ears and Sound

'Ānanda, in Jetavana park when you hear a drum beat to announce a meal and a bell rung to summon the bhikṣus, these sounds succeed one another; do they come to the ears or do the ears go to them? Ānanda, if they come to the ears, it is like when I go to Śrāvastī to beg for food and am absent from Jetavana park. If these sounds come to Ānanda's ears, Maudgalaputra and Kāśyapa should not hear them. Then why do all the 1,250 bhikṣus,

[63] Sleep causes forgetfulness and wakefulness produces remembrance. Remembrance stands for life and forgetfulness for death. This shows that objects (presented to) the intellect do not come from outside, but are Illusions arising from the inner consciousness. The first five senses gather only causal phenomena which cannot reach the intellect as the latter collects inner data which are the shadows of outer objects that rise and fall without interruption. Hence birth and death are caused by this non-existent intellect.

[64] Form and voidness are the two extremes of a duality; if form vanishes, how can the void remain?

when they hear the bell, go together to the eating hall? If your ears go to the sound, it is like when I return to Jetavana park and am not in Śrāvastī. Then when you hear the drum, if your ears go to it, you should not hear the bell which rings at the same time, nor the sound of elephants, horses, buffaloes and sheep (in this park). If there is no such coming and going, there would be no hearing. Therefore, you should know that hearing and sound have no location and that both are false, being neither causal nor conditional nor self-existent.[65]

Nose and Smell

'Ānanda, just smell the smoke of sandalwood in this burner. The quantity burnt is small but its fragrance spreads to Śrāvastī and the neighbourhood.[66] Do you think that this perfume comes from the sandalwood, from your nose, or from the void? Ānanda, if it comes from your nose it should be produced by and spread from it, but since your nose is not sandalwood, how can there be this fragrance there? If you say that you smell perfume, it should be inhaled into your nose, but since it emanates from it (as aforesaid), it is wrong to say that you smell it. If it comes from the void, the latter being permanent, this fragrance should be so as well and there would be no need to burn dry sandalwood. If it comes from the sandalwood, its fragrant substance has become smoke by burning, and if your nose smells this perfume, your nose should be full of smoke; as smoke rises in the air, how can it be smelt in distant places even before it reaches them? Therefore, you should know that odour, nose and smelling have no fixed location and that smelling and odour are false being neither causal nor conditional nor self-existent.

Tongue and Taste

'Ānanda, twice a day you go out to beg for food and occasionally are given butter and cream which are tasty delicacies. Do you think that this taste comes from the void, your tongue or the food? Ānanda, if it comes from your tongue, the latter has already become butter, and since you have only one tongue, how can you then taste honey? If you do not, this means that your taste does not change, then how can it be called tasting? If it changes and since your tongue is of one substance how can this single tongue know various tastes? If it comes from the food, the latter cannot know, then how can it taste itself? Assuming that it knows itself, it and other food will have nothing to do with your tasting. If it comes

[65] If hearing is disengaged from sound, all differentiation will cease and the Tathāgata store will be exposed.

[66] Lit. Śrāvastī town and places forty miles around it.

from the void, when you "bite" the air what does it taste like? Assuming that it comes from the void, when the latter tastes salt, as your tongue is salty, your face should be so too; if so all men would be like fish in the sea. If you are salty, you will not know what is tasteless. If you do not know what is tasteless, and do not taste salt, you will have no taste; then how can there be taste? Therefore, you should know that neither taste nor tongue nor tasting has location and that tasting and taste are false being neither causal nor conditional nor self-existent.

Body and Touch

'Ānanda, you are accustomed to rub your head with your hand every day early in the morning. When feeling this rub do you know whether that which rubs is your hand or your head? If it is your hand, then your head (an object) should not feel that it is being rubbed; if so how can there be touch? If it is your head, there would be no need for your hand to rub it; then how can you call it touch? If both hand and head are subjects, then you, Ānanda, should have two bodies. If it comes from the contact of your hand with your head, then both your hand and head should be one, and one thing cannot contact itself. If it is two (i.e. hand and head), from which does it arise, for subject and object differ? Neither can there be touch when your head comes into contact with the void. Therefore, you should know that neither the feeling of touch nor your body has location and that they are false, being neither causal nor conditional nor self-existent.

Intellect and Dharma

'Ānanda, because of good, evil and neutral causes, your intellect (manas) always gives rise to dharma. Are these dharma created by the mind or do they exist apart from it and have their own place? Ānanda, if they are the same as the mind, they cannot be its objects for they are not its causal phenomena; then how can they have a place (of their own)? If they exist apart from the mind and have their own place, do they possess (the faculty of) knowing or not? If they do, they are merely the mind; but since they have (the faculty of) knowing and differ from you, they should not be your dharma but should belong to someone else's mind. If they have (the faculty of) knowing and are your dharma (at the same time) they are merely your mind; then how can you have another mind as well as your own? If they differ from you and do not have (the faculty of) knowing, where are they, since they are not (inanimate phenomena such as) form, sound, smell and flavour, nor cold and warmth due to contact or separation, as well as to the void? Since they cannot be shown in either form or the void, there should not be in the universe another voidness outside the void.

Assuming that there is another outer voidness, they cannot be the mind's causal phenomena; then where are they? Therefore, you should know that neither dharma nor mind has location and that intellect and dharma are both false, being neither causal nor conditional nor self-existent.

Fusing the Eighteen Fields or Realms of the Senses

The Field of Sight-Perception

'Again, Ānanda, why are the eighteen fields or realms of the senses (the same as) the Absolute (in the Tathāgata store)?

'Ānanda, as you (already) know, eyes and form are causes that beget sight-perception. Is this sight-perception created and conditioned by the eyes or by form? Ānanda, if it is created by the eyes, in the absence of both form and the void, there will be nothing to be differentiated; then what is the use of this perception even if you own it? In this instance what you see will be neither blue, yellow, red nor white; where then can you show its boundary? If it is created by form, when you see the void, which means that form is absent, your perception should cease to exist; then why do you still distinguish the void? When form changes, you notice it but your perception is unchanging; then where can its boundary be? If perception follows the change of form to undergo its own change, there would be no boundary. If it is unchanging, it should be permanent; then (as it is created by form) it should not perceive the void. If it is created by both the eyes and form, these two are separate when (you think that they are) united and unite (when you think that they are) separate; if so, both intermingle; then how can there be the realm of the eyes and that of form?[67] Therefore, you should know that both causal eyes and form as well as the (so-called) created perception do not exist, and that the eyes, form and the realm of form are neither causal nor conditional nor self-existent.[68]

The Field of Sound-Perception

'Ānanda, as you (already) know, ears and sound are causes that beget perception of sound. Is this perception created and conditioned by the ears or

---

[67] The organ of sight and form are opposites; if you think they can unite, they cannot actually reach each other and so are separate. If you think that they are separate, when you open your eyes, you see that they are in contact with each other. If both create sight-perception, they intermingle and where then is the realm of the eyes and that of form?

[68] This is direct pointing to the Uncreate. The Mādhyamika Śāstra says: 'All phenomena are neither self-created, nor created by an originator, nor by the union of components and they do not arise without cause.' These four forms of creation are wiped out in the text to reveal the Uncreate; hence the nature of the Uncreate which is identical with the Tathāgata Store.

by sound? If it is created by the ears, this organ, in the absence of both disturbance and stillness, does not discern anything and is, therefore, devoid of objects; if it cannot discern, how can it create perception? Assuming that hearing (begets) perception by the ears, since no hearing occurs in the absence of both disturbance and stillness, how can the ears (which are) form unite with external objects to produce perception and where can the latter's field be? If it is created by sound, that is if it depends (solely) on sound, then it should have no relation to your hearing. But if hearing ceases, there will be no sound. Now assuming that it is really created by sound and that sound exists because of hearing, then your hearing of sound should be perceived by the ears. If this sound is not perceived, it would have no relation with the realm of ear-perception. (On the other hand) if it is heard, it is already sound, and since it is hearing's object, (it cannot discern anything); then who knows the perception? If there is no such knower, you will be like grass and plants. There cannot be a mixing of sound and hearing to create between them an intermediate realm (of perception by the ear) for such a realm cannot be at the center, in the inner organ, or in the outer sound, Therefore neither ears nor sound exist as causes, nor perception by the car (as effect) and ears, sound and its field are neither causal nor conditional, nor self-existent.

The Field of Smell-Perception

'Ānanda, as you (already) know, the nose and smell are causes that beget the perception of smell. Is this perception created and conditioned by the nose or by smell? If so, Ānanda, what is this nose? Is it that hooked and fleshy part of your face with which you sniff? But this piece of flesh belongs to the body and the body's perception is called touch; the body is not the nose and touch is its object. If the nose cannot be named, where is it? If it perceives smell, where is that perception in your mind? If perception comes from a part of the face, it is touch and has nothing to do with the nose. If it comes from the void, it should be known by the latter instead of being felt by the flesh; if so, the void should be you and your body would feel nothing. Then, there would be no Ānanda anywhere at the moment.

'If smell is the knower, it should know itself and would have nothing to do with you. If good and bad smells create your nose, they should not produce sandalwood and fetid herbs. Without the latter, smell your own nose and see if it is fragrant or offensive. Since fragrance cannot stink and stench cannot be fragrant, if you can smell both, you should have two noses, and now as you ask me about the Dharma, there should be two Ānandas; then which Ānanda are you? If there is only one nose and if fragrance and stench are not two different smells, they can be mistaken for each other, which proves that neither exist; if so where can the field of smell-perception be established? If it is created by smell and if perception exists because of smell, it is like your eyes which can see things, but not themselves; so that perception which exists because of smell should not scent it. If it does, it cannot be created by smell, and if it does not, it is deprived of that perception. Since smell does not depend on perception, it has no field. If perception cannot smell, its field cannot be established on the basis of smell. Since there is no intermediate perception (between nose and smell), there would be neither inner (organ) nor outer (object). Thus smell-perception is false. Therefore, neither nose nor smell, as causes, nor the field of smell-perception, as their creation, exist, while nose, smell and its field are neither causal, nor conditional, nor self-existent.

The Field of Taste-Perception

'Ānanda, as you (already) know, tongue and taste are causes that beget perception by the tongue. Is this perception created and conditioned by the tongue, or by taste?

'Ānanda, if it is created by the tongue, then sugar cane, sour black plums, bitter wort, rock-salt, wild spikenard, ginger and cassia would be tasteless. Taste your own tongue and see if it is sweet or bitter. If it is bitter, who is the taster? Since the tongue cannot taste itself, who experiences the taste? If it is not bitter, no taste can come from it. Then how can it be conditioned?

'If perception derives from taste, it would be taste itself but, like the tongue, it cannot taste itself. Then how can it distinguish various flavours? Again, since there are many flavours which cannot come from a single source, there should be as many (corresponding) perceptions. If there is only one, and if it is created by (different) flavours, then all salt, insipid, sweet and bitter flavours should unite and become one; then there would be no discerning. If so, there would be no perception (by the tongue). How then can the tongue, taste and perception be conditioned? The void cannot make your mind perceive. Since tongue (organ) and taste (object) cannot unite to create an intermediate (perception), where is the latter's field? Therefore, tongue and taste, as causes, and the field of taste-perception, as their creation, do not exist, while tongue, taste and their field of perception are neither causal nor conditional nor self-existent.

The Field of Touch-Perception

'Ānanda, as you (already) know, body and touch are causes that create the perception of touch. Is this created and conditioned by the body or by touch?

'Ānanda, if it is created by the body, what does the latter perceive when there is neither contact nor separation? If by touch, your body would not be needed; then who can, without a body, feel contact and separation? Ānanda, objects do not perceive touch, but the body knows and feels it. Body's perception is revealed by touch and touch through the body. Therefore, body and touch are inseparable but they are not the same and so originally they have no home. When touch contacts body, it becomes the body and when it ceases, it becomes the void. Since there are no such things as inner (body) and outer (touch), how can there be an intermediate (perception) between them? Where then is the field of body-perception? Therefore, body and touch, as causes, and body-perception, as their creation, do not exist, and all three are neither causal nor conditional nor self-existent.

The Field of the Sixth Consciousness

'Ānanda, as you (already) know, intellect (manas) and dharma (ideas) are causes that create the sixth consciousness. Is this consciousness created and conditioned by intellect, or by Dharma?

'Ānanda, if this consciousness is created by intellect, the latter (as organ) should contain dharma (as object) to reveal its own existence. In the absence of dharma, your intellect (does not exist and) cannot create anything; even if it does create consciousness, what is the latter's use if it is not confronted with causal ideas (dharma)? Moreover, both your mind (i.e. the sixth consciousness) and your thinking process (i.e. the intellect) discern ideas and things; are they the same as, or different from each other? If the same, consciousness is just intellect; then how can it be created by intellect? If different, consciousness would be "unconscious"; then how can it come from intellect? If it is also "conscious" then (tell me) what intellect and consciousness are. Therefore they are neither the same nor different, then where is the field of consciousness?

'If consciousness is created by dharma, all things in the world are inseparable from the five sense data of form, sound, smell, taste and touch, which clearly correspond with the sense organs and are not affected by the intellect. If your consciousness depends on dharma for its existence, look carefully into dharma and see what they look like, for beyond form and voidness, motion and stillness, clearness and obstruction, union and separation, and birth and death, where can dharma be found? For dharma arise simultaneously with form, voidness, etc., and vanish with them. Since there are no causes leading to their creation, what are the forms and shapes of dharma? If these do not exist, what then conditions dharma? Therefore, intellect and dharma as causes, and the field of the sixth consciousness, as their creation, do not exist and they are neither causal nor conditional nor self-existent.[69]

Fusing the Seven Elements Into the Absolute to Reveal the Free Intermingling of Phenomenon and Noumenon

Ānanda said to the Buddha: 'World Honoured One, the Tathāgata has often spoken of cause, condition and the state of the self as such and has taught us that all changes and transformations in the world are due to the mixture and fusion of the four elements. Why does he now wipe out all concepts of cause, condition and the state of the self as such? I do not understand; will He be compassionate enough to explain in full to all living beings the Mean which is beyond all sophistry?

The Buddha replied: 'You are tired of, and have sought to abandon, the Hīnayāna teaching on the śrāvaka and praryeka-buddha stages, and so wish to seek unsurpassed Bodhi. I will, therefore teach you the Supreme Truth. Why do you still restrict yourself by reasoning frivolously about false causes and conditions? Although you have listened to me a lot, you are like one who is accustomed to talk about medicines but who, when he sees them cannot pick out those which are good. This is why the Tathāgata says that you are really to be pitied. Listen with attention to what I now tell you, so that all who practise Mahāyāna in the future can attain Reality.

Ānanda kept silent, awaiting the holy teaching.

---

[69] Ever since Ānanda asked about the practice of śamatha, the Buddha first wiped out the unreal to reveal the real and then returned phenomena to Reality to deal with noumenon from its shallowness to its depth, thus covering the four periods of His teaching.

At first in His discussion of the seeing, He asked about the illusory mind to wipe out the idea of the body as real; this corresponded to His teaching of Hīnayāna during the Āgama period (of twelve years). His next elimination of perception and of the Essence of consciousness accorded with His expanded teaching during the Vaipulya (Hīnayāna-with-Mahāyāna) period (of eight years). Then His instruction on returning the three categories (of the seeming, that is) the five aggregates, twelve entrances, and eighteen fields of the senses, to the Tathāgata store to reveal their unreality, covered His sermons on wisdom (during the next twenty-two years). His next teaching on the fundamental nature of the Absolute in the Tathāgata store, showing the true nature of all phenomena that spring from Reality, corresponded with His final teaching in the Lotus period (of eight years).

In the following text which deals with how the all-embracing seven elements freely intermingled in the Dharma-realm, His teaching contained the Avataṁsaka doctrine of the free interaction of noumenon and phenomenon in the Dharmadhātu, thus revealing the perfect fusion of the three dogmas (of the void, the seeming and the mean) into the absolute Tathāgata store, the subject of the meditative study of the void.

So far, the Buddha had taught the fusion of the three categories (of the seeming, that is the five aggregates, the twelve entrances and the eighteen fields of the senses) to expose the identity of phenomenon and noumenon.

Exposing Faulty Differentiation

Ānanda, as you have said, when the four elements mix and fuse they cause all kinds of transformation in the world. But they cannot mix and unite if it is against their nature, just as the void cannot with form. On the other hand, if they so mix and fuse they are transformations and owe their existence wholly to their mutual dependence; they are thus subject to creation and destruction in endless succession, like the ring of fire caused when a torch is waved in a circle.

Pointing to the One Source

'Ānanda, this is like water which, after becoming ice, can change back into water.[70]

Instruction on the Seven Elements

The element of earth

'Look at the element of earth which ranges in size from the great earth to a tiny speck of dust. Split this speck which is near to nothing and reduce it to the finest mote on the extreme border of form. Then split it again and it becomes the void. Ānanda, if this mote can be reduced to nothing, you should know that form comes from the void.

'You now ask about material changes which you attribute to the mixing and uniting (of the four elements). Take, for instance, this mote which is nearest to the void; how much voidness should be mixed and united to produce it? But it is absurd to suppose that this can be done by uniting motes. Since a mote can be split and reduced to voidness, how many (particles of) form should be fused together to create the void? The union of form (with form) produces form but not voidness, and the union of the void (with the void) produces voidness but not form. Form can be split up but how can the void unite (with form)?

'You do not know that in the Tathāgata store both form and (its opposite) the void arise from self-nature and are identical with each other, and

[70] This was the Buddha's complete answer to Ānanda's question. The disciple clung to the idea of the four elements which mix and fuse to cause all transformations in the world, for he was not clear about the all-embracing and commingling nature of noumenon. The Buddha meant that if these elements did not mix and fuse with one another, they were like the void which can have no relation with form, and that on the other hand, if they did mix and fuse, they would be transformations in an uninterrupted succession of births and deaths. Therefore, one cannot speak of whether or not they mix and unite. However, if one understands that both the real and unreal arise from the same (underlying) substance, like water that can become ice which can change back to water, one will cease to discriminate and discern.

that the element of earth is fundamentally pure and clean, embraces all in the Dharma-realm and manifests because the minds of living beings know and distinguish (between things) in accordance with the laws of karma. Ignorant wordlings wrongly attribute this to cause, condition and the state of the self as such, because their consciousnesses differentiate and discriminate without their knowing that the language they use has no real meaning.[71]

The element of fire

'Ānanda, fire has no ego but exists because of (external) causes. When people in a town are about to prepare their meals, they use mirrors of polished metal to obtain fire from the sun.

'Ānanda, about (your idea of) mixture and union, take this community of myself and twelve hundred and fifty bhikṣus; though the group is one, each member has his own body, clan and name, like Śariputra who is a Brahman, Uruvilvā, a Kāśyapa tribesman, and you, Ānanda, who are of the Gautama clan.

'Ānanda, if fire comes from the mixture and fusion (of the elements), when a man holds a mirror to obtain fire in the sun, does this fire come from the mirror, the moxa or the sun? Ānanda, if it comes from the sun, it can burn the moxa in your hand; if so, all the trees will be scorched. If it comes from the mirror and then lights the moxa, why does it not melt the mirror and burn your hand? But if you do not even feel the heat, how can the mirror melt? If it comes from the moxa, why does the latter require the sun and the mirror to make it burn? Look at the mirror held by the hand, the sun up in the sky and the moxa which originally came from the ground; how can fire travel elsewhere before coming here? (Moreover) the sun and the mirror are a very long way apart and cannot mix and unite with each other. Finally fire cannot exist by itself.

---

[71] This points to the all-embracing element of earth, the substance of which is void, to reveal Reality as such. Now the great earth is an accumulation of dust, a speck of which can be split and reduced to a state of near voidness and finally to nothing. This shows that form arises from the void and that the element of earth fundamentally does not exist. If, as you reason, the great earth exists through the mixture and fusion of dust, how much void is needed to produce a mote from which the whole earth grew? If a mote can be reduced to nothing, how many are required to create the void? If form unites with form, it cannot produce voidness and if the void unites with itself, no form can result. You have therefore a wrong idea about the mixture and fusion of the four elements. You have not realized that the element of earth is a manifestation of karma within the Tathāgata store, and is not a product of the (so called) mixture and fusion of the four elements. If you are clear about this aspect of karma, you will awaken to the all-embracing self-natured Reality.

You do not realize that in the Tathāgata store both fire and (its opposite) the void arise from the self-nature and are identical with each other, and that the element of fire is fundamentally pure and clean, embraces all in the Dharma-realm and manifests because the minds of living beings know and distinguish (between things). Ānanda, you should know that fire is produced wherever a man holds a mirror (in the sun), and that if mirrors are held up throughout the Dharma-realm, fire will spring up everywhere in accordance with the laws of karma and not in a given place and direction. Ignorant worldlings wrongly attribute this to cause, condition and the state of the self as such without realizing that it is because their consciousnesses differentiate and discriminate and that the language they use has no real meaning.

The element of water

'Ānanda, water is unstable by nature for it either flows or is still. Great magicians in Śrāvastī, such as Kapila, Cakra, Padma and Hasta (?) obtain water to mix with their medicines by exposing a crystal ball to the full moon. Does this water come from the ball, the void or the moon? Ānanda, if it comes from the moon which is a very long way off it should pass through the trees in the forest before reaching the crystal ball to flow into the bowl. If it does not flow through the trees, this shows that it does not drop from the moon. If it comes from the crystal ball, it should flow regularly not only when the moon is full. If it comes from the void of space which is boundless, it should flow everywhere, submerging everything between earth and heaven; if so, how can there be living beings to walk on the earth, fly in the air and swim in the water? Think of all this again; the moon is in the sky, the crystal ball is in the man's hand and the bowl is in front of him; so where does this water come from to flow (into the bowl)? The moon and the ball are a very long way apart and cannot mix and unite with each other. It is absurd to say that this water does not come from any source.

'You do not know that in the Tathāgata store both water and (its opposite) the void arise from self-nature and are identical with each other, and that the element of water is fundamentally pure and clean, embraces all in the Dharma-realm, and manifests because the minds of living beings know and distinguish (between things). Thus water flows wherever crystal balls are used to collect it and if they are held up throughout the Dharma-realm, it will flow everywhere in accordance with the laws of karma and not in a given place or direction. Ignorant worldlings wrongly attribute this to cause, condition and the state of the self as such without knowing that it is because their consciousnesses differentiate and discriminate and that the language they use has no real meaning.

The element of wind

'Ānanda, the element of wind has no substance and either moves or is still. When you join a gathering and adjust your robe the hem (occasionally) brushes the person next you, disturbing the air which fans his face. Does this wind come from the hem of your robe, from the void or from that man's face?

'Ānanda, if it comes from the hem of your robe, the latter should leave your body (to brush the man's face). As I preach the Dharma here, my robe does not move; where can you find any wind in it? It has no hidden place where wind can be stored.

'If the wind comes from the void, why does it not fan (the man) when your robe is still? (Moreover) the void is permanent and so should be the wind; then without the wind there would be no void. You can feel when the wind stops fanning, but what indication can there be when the void ceases to exist? If the void can be created and destroyed, it cannot (really) be void, and if it is, how can it create the wind?

'If the wind comes from your neighbour's face, it should also fan you; then why does not your robe when brushing against him fan you back?

'Look into all this carefully. The robe which you adjust is yours, the face fanned is that of another bhikṣu and the void is still and does not move; then where does the wind come from? The wind and the void differ and can neither mix nor unite, while the wind cannot exist of itself without a cause. You do not realize that in the Tathāgata store wind and (its opposite) the void arise from self-nature and are identical with each other, that the element of wind is fundamentally pure and clean and embraces all in the Dharma-realm and manifests because the minds of living beings know and distinguish (between things). If, Ānanda, you move your robe, a light wind stirs. And if there is similar movement throughout the Dharma-realm, there will be wind all over the world in accordance with the laws of karma and not in a given place or direction. Ignorant worldlings attribute the element of wind to cause, condition and the state of the self as such because consciousnesses differentiate and discriminate without realizing the language they use has no real meaning.

The element of space

'Ānanda, space has no shape and is discernible only where there is form. As Śrāvastī is far from the river, people of different castes, such as Kṣatriya, Brahman, Vaiśya, Śūdra, Bhāradvāja and Caṇḍāla, who come to live there, dig wells to find water. Earn foot or earth is replaced by a foot of space and ten-feet of earth by ten feet of space, so that the shallowness or depth of each well corresponds with the amount of earth removed.

Does this space come from the earth, from the digging or from itself as such?

'Ānanda, if space exists of itself, why before the digging was it not unobstructed by the earth? Why was there only earth without any space being seen there?

'If space comes from the earth, it should be seen to enter the well when the earth is being dug out. If only the earth is removed without space entering the well, how can space come from the hole, both space and earth should be the same; then why is not space dug out with the earth?

'If space comes from the digging, when the former is produced by the latter, no earth should be removed. If space does not come from the digging, why when earth is being dug out, is space seen in the well?

'Think about all this and see where space comes from when a man uses his hands to dig earth to make a well. For digging and space are not in the same category and can be neither mixed nor united. And it is absurd to suppose that space exists of itself without coming from any cause. If space is perfectly all-embracing and essentially unmoving, you should know that it and the elements of earth, water, fire and wind - which together are called the five elements, intermingle naturally and are merely the uncreated and unending Tathāgata store.

'Ānanda, since your mind is deluded and you remain unaware of the real (identity of) the four elements in the Tathāgata store, you should look into space and see whether or not it comes or goes, or neither comes nor goes. You do not know that in the Tathāgata store Bodhi and (its opposite) the void arise from the self-nature and are identical with each other, because the element of space is fundamentally pure and clean, embraces all and manifests because the minds of living beings know and distinguish (between things). The ten quarters, Ānanda, are like an empty pit filled with space which in accordance with the laws of karma has no given place nor direction. Ignorant worldlings attribute this to cause, condition and the state of the self as such because their consciousnesses differentiate and discriminate without knowing that the language they use has no real meaning.

The element of perception

'Perception knows nothing by itself and only manifests through form and voidness. As you are now in Jetavana park, you see light by day and darkness in the evening. At night there is light when the moon shines and darkness when there is no moon. This light and darkness are discerned by the seeing, (but) is this seeing of the same nature as light, darkness and the void or not? Is it the same or different from them?

'Ānanda, if the seeing is of the same nature as light, darkness or the void, (we come to this:) as light and darkness alternate, and when there is one the other disappears, then if the seeing is one with darkness, it should vanish when there is light and vice versa. As the seeing disappears in both cases, why are light and darkness still seen? As they differ, it follows that the seeing is beyond creation and annihilation: if so, how can the seeing be the same as light and darkness?

'If the seeing is not of the same nature as light and darkness, try to find out what this seeing looks like apart from light, darkness and the void, without which there can be no seeing like the hair of a tortoise and the horns of a hare.

'As light, darkness and the void differ, where can the seeing be? As light and darkness are in opposition, how can the seeing equate with them? If there is no seeing without light, darkness and the void, how can it differ from them?

'If you try to separate the void from the seeing, you will not find their boundaries; if so, why are they not the same thing? When you see light and darkness, your seeing does not change; so why does it not differ from them?

'If you look closely and minutely into all this and examine it again and again, you will find that light comes from the sun, darkness from the moonless night, clearance from space and obstruction from the earth; so where is the begetter of this essence of seeing? Since the seeing can discern whereas the void cannot, they can neither mix nor unite. And we cannot say that this essence of seeing comes from nowhere.

'You should know that perception by seeing and hearing which pervades all and essentially does not change, and boundless unmoving space, as well as its moving (counterparts as such) the elements of earth, water, fire and wind - all of which are called the six elements, intermingle by nature and are the fundamental uncreated and unending Tathāgata store.

'You are infatuated by nature and do not understand that seeing, hearing, feeling and knowing fundamentally come from the Tathāgata store. You should enquire into them and see if they pertain to birth and death, if they are one or many, if they pertain neither to birth nor death and if they are neither one nor many.

'You do not know that in the Tathāgata store self-natured seeing is basically the enlightened perception which is pure and clean, embraces all in the Dharma-realm and manifests because the minds of living beings know and distinguish (between things). Like seeing which pervades the whole Dharma-realm, hearing, smelling, tasting and touching as well as the activities of body and mind have wonderful virtues which are bright and universal and so are not in a given place or direction. They manifest according to the laws of karma but ignorant worldlings think wrongly that they are causal, conditional and due to the self as such. Because of their consciousnesses they differentiate and discriminate and do not know that their language has no real meaning.[72]

The element of consciousness

'Ānanda, consciousness has no origin and is (an illusion) arising from the six organs and sense data. Look at this holy assembly and turn round to see those present; your eyes are like a mirror which cannot discern while your consciousness notices in turn the presence of Mañjuśrī, Pūrṇamaitrāyaṇīputra, Maudgalyāyana, Subhūti, Śariputra (etc.). Does this consciousness come from perception, form or the void, or does it (emerge) suddenly without any cause?

'Ānanda, if your consciousness comes from your seeing (perception), then in the absence of light, darkness, form and the void, there will be no seeing, and when there is no perception, how can it create consciousness?

'If your consciousness comes from form—that is not from perception, then, when light and darkness are not seen, there are neither form nor the void; then how can non-existing form create consciousness?

'If your consciousness comes from the void—that is neither from form nor perception, the absence of perception means also that of discernment which implies the non-perception of light, darkness, form and the void; and the absence of form is the end of all external causes; how, then, can your seeing, hearing, feeling and knowing occur? Thus without form and perception, consciousness which comes from the void simply does not exist. (On the other hand), if it exists in the absence of objects, what can it discern?

'If your consciousness suddenly emerges without any cause, why cannot it discern the moon in the daytime?

'Now look closely and minutely into all this; your seeing (perception) depends on the pupils of your eyes meeting an external object which "is" when there is form and "is not" when there is no form. These are the four causes (i.e. the seeing, eyes, form and voidness) from which consciousness arises, but which one of them creates consciousness? Since

---

72 This shows the element of Perception which is fundamentally all-embracing in the Dharma-realm. It is one of the ālaya's three characteristics (self-evidencing, perception and form) and is also called the essence of seeing. It is *unknowing* for it is essentially the bright light of wisdom, is absolute and is beyond all contraries and relativities. Under delusion, it has become false seeing and clings to illusory objects, such as form and the void. As it is fundamentally absolute, the Buddha used light, darkness and the void and the (worldly) concept of unity-with-differentiation to reveal it.

consciousness is always moving (to differentiate) whereas perception is still (for it does not discriminate), they cannot mix and fuse together. Your hearing, feeling and knowing are in the same category (as your seeing) but your consciousness should still have a source.

'If this consciousness comes from nothing, you should know that perception (by means of) seeing, hearing, feeling and knowing pervades everywhere and comes not from any source. Moreover with space, earth, water, fire and wind they are called the seven elements, the natures of which are real and intermingle (freely), being but the uncreated and unending Tathāgata store.

'Ānanda, because your mind is unsettled, you do not realize that the seeing and hearing that arouse consciousness, come fundamentally from the Tathāgata store. You should look into the consciousnesses inside the Six Entrances and see if they are the same or different, exist or not, are neither the same nor different, and neither exist nor not. For you do not realize that in the Tathāgata store self-natured consciousness is the enlightened basic Bodhi which embraces and pervades the whole Dharma-realm, is not (to be found) in a given place or direction and manifests according to the laws of karma. Ignorant worldlings think wrongly that it is causal, conditional and due to the self as such, according to the way their consciousnesses differentiate and discriminate while they do not know that the language they use has no real meaning.'[73]

Ānanda's Understanding Expressed in His Gāthā

After listening to the Buddha's profound instruction, Ānanda and the assembly realized that their bodies and minds were now free from all obstructions. Each understood that his self-mind pervaded the ten directions of space which he saw clearly like a leaf held in his own hand, and that all things were the wondrous and bright fundamental Mind of Bodhi. While his essence of Mind embraced all and contained the ten directions, he looked back at his own body given him by his parents, which was like a speck of dust dancing in the great void, sometimes visible and sometimes not, and like a bubble rising and falling aimlessly in a boundless clear ocean. After seeing all this clearly, they all realized their fundamental, profound, permanent and indestructible (self-) minds, and brought their palms together to pay reverence to the Buddha (thanking Him) for (showing them) what they had never seen before.

Thereupon, Ānanda praised the Buddha in the following gāthā:

---

[73] Up to here, the Buddha taught how to return all that is false to Reality to reveal the uncreated and unending nature of the absolute Tathāgata store.

'O thou serene, all powerful[74] and unchanging Lord,
Rare is your all-embracing supreme Śūraṅgama
Which helps me to root out wrong thoughts that have been held for untold aeons
And teaches me how to realize Dharmakāya in an instant.
May I now win the fruit and achieve enlightenment
To save living beings countless as the Ganges sands.
To myriad Buddha-lands I now offer this mind profound
To repay my debt of gratitude for the grace of the Lord.
Humbly I now implore the World Honoured One to seal
My oath to re-enter the five turbid realms[75] wherein
If even one being fails to become a Buddha,
I shall (at once) renounce all my claim to Nirvāṇa.
O Great Hero, the Mighty, the Compassionate One,
May you also destroy my last secret delusion
So that I soon attain to Bodhi Supreme,
Sitting in bodhimaṇḍalas[76] everywhere.
The void to an end may come,
But my firm mind will not flinch.[77]

---

[74] 'All powerful' is expediently used here for the Sanskrit 'Dhāraṇī' which means 'absolute control over good and evil.'

[75] See p. 104 for a full explanation of the five kalpas of turbidity.

[76] To sit in bodhimaṇḍalas is to turn the Wheel of the Law to save living beings. A bodhimaṇḍala is a sacred place where the Dharma is taught to enlighten and deliver living beings.

[77] The first line praises the Buddha's Dharmakāya which is pure and clean, and serenely meets all phenomena, hence it is serene. This essential body is the substance of all dharma and possesses three essential virtues; eternity, wisdom and sovereign liberty (enjoying complete control over good and evil), hence it is dominant. It is ever omnipresent and unchanging, hence it is immovable.

Ānanda used to cling to the Buddha's thirty-two excellent physical marks which caused him to join the Order without knowing that the Buddha which he saw was unreal; therefore, his mind was equally false. After hearing the Buddha's teaching, he awakened to his true mind and was able to discern the Buddha's Dharmakāya; hence his praise of the Buddha.

The second line shows Ānanda's awakening to the Śūrangama samādhī which revealed the One Mind; hence his praise of the Dharma.

The fifth, sixth, seventh and eighth lines show that Ānanda who had now developed the profound Mahāyāna mind, sought self-enlightenment for the welfare of all living beings, which was the only way to repay his immense debt of gratitude to the Buddha.

The ninth, tenth, eleventh and twelfth lines show that Ānanda had now taken the Bodhisattva's great vow to deliver all living beings without exception.

The last two lines show his determination in his Bodhisattva work, now that he had awakened to the powerful Śūrangama samādhi as taught by the Buddha.

So far the Buddha had taught śamatha or the meditative study of all as void (i.e. the noumenon in the Tathāgata store). In the following chapter, He taught samāpatti or the meditative study of all as unreal (i.e. the phenomenon in the Tathāgata store).

II

The Phenomenon in the Tathāgata Store

The Meditative Study of All as Unreal (Samāpatti)

The One Mind Being the Source of Both Delusion and Enlightenment

Pūrnamaitrāyaniputra, who was in the assembly, rose from his seat, uncovered his right shoulder, knelt upon his right knee, reverently joined the palms of his hands and said to the Buddha: 'O August and World Honoured One, you have revealed the Tathāgata's profound meaning so well to all living beings. The Buddha has always declared that I surpass all men in preaching the Dharma, but as I now listen to His melodious and deep Dharma voice, I am like a deaf man (striving to) hear flies and mosquitoes a hundred feet away; he cannot see, still less can he hear them. In spite of what the Buddha taught to cut off our delusion, I fail to understand its ultimate meaning which is altogether beyond me. World Honoured One, (it is reasonable that) those like Ānanda who have merely opened their minds but have not cast away their worldly habits, do not understand it, but though I (and others here) have reached the state beyond the stream of transmigration, we are still not quite clear about the Dharma (just) taught by the Tathāgata.

'World Honoured One, if all things (such as) the sense organs and data, aggregates, entrances and fields of sense are fundamentally the pure and clean Tathāgata store, why does the latter suddenly create mountains, rivers, the great world and all other forms that rise and fall in turn without interruption?

'The Tathāgata has also spoken of (the elements of) earth, water, fire and wind whose natures mix and pervade the whole Dharma realm in which they remain all the time. World Honoured One, if the element of earth was all-embracing how could it contain the element of water? If the latter was all-pervading, there would be no fire, then how can one be clear that these two elements pervade all space without destroying each other? World Honoured One, the nature of earth is obstructive while that of space is the reverse; how can both of them pervade the whole Dharma realm? I really do not understand. May the Tathāgata be compassionate enough to enlighten me and so dispel the clouds of my delusion?'

After saying this, he prostrated and eagerly awaited the holy teaching.

The Buddha said to Pūrṇamaitrāyaṇīputra and all arhats in the assembly who had reached the state beyond samsaric transmigration and beyond further study: 'The Tathāgata now expounds the highest transcendental Truth so that those hearers with settled minds[1] and arhats who have not yet realized that neither ego nor dharma exist and who seek Reality, will know the correct practice of the passionlessness of the Supreme Vehicle. Listen attentively to what I say.'

Pūrṇamaitrāyaṇīputra and the assembly kept silent awaiting with reverence the Buddha's Dharma voice.

The Buddha asked: 'Pūrṇamaitrāyaṇīputra, you now ask why that which is fundamentally pure and clean suddenly created mountains, rivers and the great earth, but have you not heard the Buddha declare that (self-) natured Bodhi is absolute and enlightened and that basic Bodhi is enlightened and absolute?'[2]

Pūrṇamaitrāyaṇīputra replied: 'Yes, World Honoured One, I have heard this?

A Probe into the Disciple's Understanding of Noumenon and Phenomenon to Reveal the Rise of Illusions

The Buddha asked: 'When you speak of Bodhi and Enlightenment, do you mean that because of its enlightened nature, you call it Bodhi, or because of its (basic) unenlightened nature, you (now) call it enlightened Bodhi?'[3]

---

[1] Whose minds are set on self-enlightenment and not on Bodhisattva development.

[2] Self-natured Bodhi stands for Substance which is essentially absolute (i.e. free from all dualities) and is, therefore, enlightened. Basic Bodhi stands for *Function* which is enlightened and is, therefore, absolute (i.e. free from all relativities and contraries).

[3] This two pronged probe was to expose the cause of rising illusions. Here a Ch'an Master would give a shout or a blow with his staff to dispel all remaining doubts in the student's mind. But in the Teaching school, the Buddha was obliged to trace all illusions back to their source in order to explain that the false arises from the Real; hence He set up the Dharma realm of One Reality which is the common source of both delusion and enlightenment. And so He repeated His previous statement about '(self-) natured Bodhi which is absolute and enlightened and basic Bodhi which is enlightened and absolute,' to probe the disciple's capability. He meant: 'Do you think that Bodhi-nature is fundamentally enlightened and needs no further enlightening to be called Bodhi? (This is the Absolute.) Or do you think that Bodhi-nature is unenlightened and needs enlightening to become enlightened Bodhi? (This is Saṁsāra.)' This was to see if the disciple gave an objective reply betraying the cause of his delusion.

The realization of Buddha-nature is due to three causes: *direct, concurrent* and *realizing*. Its absolute nature is fundamentally perfect and self-existing and needs no practice; this is the *direct cause*. It is attainable because of the teaching by enlightened masters for

The Real Missed by Cognizance of the False

Pūrṇamaitrāyaṇīputra said: 'If that which is unenlightened is called Bodhi, it is not aware of anything.'[4]

The Three Finer Conditions of Unenlightenment (Basic Ignorance: Subject and Object)

The Buddha said: 'You say that "that which is not aware of anything is not enlightened Bodhi," but that which creates an illusory object is unenlightened and that which abstains from so doing is free from (subjective) awareness. The unenlightened is (certainly) not the clean nature of Bodhi, for (self-) natured Bodhi is essentially enlightened but is mistaken for enlightened awareness. Bodhi is not (that) awareness of things for such awareness sets up objects, and the setting up of illusory objects implies an illusory subject.[5]

---

it is said that the Buddha-seed sprouts in favourable circumstances; this is the *concurrent cause*. It is attainable by means of practice and training; this is the *realizing cause*.

The statement: 'Self-natured Bodhi is absolute and enlightened' implies the direct cause of *Buddha-nature*, and 'basic Bodhi is enlightened and absolute' shows its *realizing cause*, for only after the effective realization of *inceptive Bodhi* can *basic Bodhi* be attained. Therefore, practice and training are required to realize Enlightenment.

[4] The disciple's answer betrayed the origin of his delusion because he clung to an object of which Bodhi should be aware; this was his samsaric awareness which implied a duality of subject and object.

[5] This shows the origin of the false. The Buddha began by repeating what the disciple had laid of an unenlightened Bodhi which was not aware of objects. If Bodhi was free from this awareness, it would indeed be genuine, for it would be free from all dualities. He then wiped out the disciple's misconception and declared that that which created objects was not true Bodhi and that which was free from them was certainly not false Bodhi, for that which fundamentally was not enlightened was not the clean nature of Bodhi. Self-natured Bodhi is essentially enlightened and needs no further enlightening to be so; *this was His teaching on the self-existing Buddha nature*. It was, however, mistaken for enlightened awareness, and because of this thought, the enlightened absolute self-nature was missed; *this was His teaching on delusion*. Awareness of an object is faulty and pertains to ignorance, *this was His teaching on the three subtle defilements of karma* (base ignorance: subject and object).

Because of ignorance caused by this faulty awareness, the absolute True Mind is screened and replaced by the duality of subject and object. This *object* is the origin of space, the world and living beings. Hence the text says: 'Bodhi is not that awareness of things for such (subjective) awareness sets up objects,' that is the manifestation *of form*. The setting up of form results in dualities and causes the fundamental, absolute and bright wisdom-light of Nirvanic Illumination to change into the false seeing of subjective perception. Hence the text says: 'The setting up of illusory objects implies an illusory subject.' This is transformation of the Absolute into form.

The Six Coarser Conditions of Unenlightenment

'Thus from that which was beyond both identity and diversity arose all differences. When the differentiating subject confronted its differentiated objects, the resultant diversity led to identification. Identity and diversity further led to that which was neither the same nor different. These conflicting disturbances resulted in troubled (perception) which in time gave rise to objective form. Self-created confusion, caused by clinging to names, caused karmic activity and so suffering. Thus that which manifested became the (changing) world and that which was still was space. Hence space stands for identity and the world for diversity, and that which is neither the same nor different is a living being.[6]

The Law of Continuity

Continuity of the (physical) universe

'Sustained confrontation of (subjective) awareness with (objective) dim voidness produced vibration and movement; hence the wheel of wind[7] in constant motion in the universe. Awareness so shaken by the void,

---

[6] This further shows the origin of the false to reveal the six coarser conditions of unenlightenment (which are: knowledge, continuous responsiveness, attachment arising from the last, naming objects, karmic deeds, and the suffering that results therefrom).

The permanent True Mind in the Dharma realm of One Reality is beyond both identity and diversity. The first thought that stirred the self-nature gave rise to delusion, thereby changing it into the unenlightened ālaya consciousness. Hence the three finer conditions of unenlightenment, the forerunner of its coarser conditions, resulting in the manifestation of different forms, such as the world and living beings in the store consciousness.

Therefore, all kinds of difference arose from that which was beyond both identity and diversity. Thus ignorance became the differentiating subject and the world its differentiated object. That which differed from the differentiated world was space, for the world was changing whereas space did not. Hence Mañjuśrī said in his gāthā: 'Thus in delusion there appeared one-sided emptiness.' After motion and stillness had come to be, a living being was created to designate that which was neither the same nor different, for a being has form and shape and so differs from the void, and is conscious and so differs from inanimate things. Hence Mañjuśrī said in his gāthā: 'In which an imaginary world arbitrarily was built . . . while the illusory knower became a living being.'

The Buddha then explained the six coarser conditions of unenlightenment. He revealed the first condition, *knowledge*, in these words: 'These conflicting disturbances resulted in troubled perception'; the second condition, *continuous responsiveness*, in: '. . . which, in time, gave rise to objective form'; the third and fourth conditions, *attachment and names*, in: 'self-created confusion caused by clinging to names'; and the fifth and sixth conditions, *karmic deeds and suffering, in*: '. . . caused karmic activity and so suffering.' That which is neither the changing world nor unchanging space is the living being who is subject to birth and death.

[7] The four wheels on which the world rests: wind, water, metal and space.

was benumbed by it and hardened into the (element of) metal; hence the wheel of metal to preserve the earth. When the movement caused by awareness produced wind and hardened into metal, the friction between wind and metal flashed fire, the nature of which was transformative. Fire sprang up and melted metal; hence the wheel of water pervades all the worlds in the ten directions. The meeting of rising fire with falling water formed wet oceans and dry continents. This is why fire (sometimes) rises from the bottom of the seas, and streams and rivers flow over continents. Excess of water over fire resulted in (the formation of) high mountains; hence rock sparks when struck and melts when submitted to great enough heat. An excess of earth over water resulted in the growth of vegetation; hence a forest fire reduces the trees to ashes (i.e. earth) and a plant bleeds when twisted. Thus these illusory (four wheels) intermingled and became mutual seeds to ensure the continuity of the world.

Continuity of living beings

'Further, Pūrṇamaitrāyaṇīputra, this defect in awareness was caused by its subjectiveness that set up illusory objects beyond which awareness (thus circumscribed) cannot reach; hence one's hearing is limited to sound and one's seeing to form. The six illusory sense data, thus created, divided (the undivided nature) into seeing, hearing, feeling and knowing. As a result (of unenlightened) activities, similarity of karma caused affinity[8] whereas dissimilarity led to either union for embodiment[9] or parting for transformation.[10]

'When the perception of (an attractive) light reveals an (illusory) form, the clearness of the latter stimulates a keen desire for it. Opposing views cause hatred whereas concordant ones lead to love, the flow of which becomes the seed-germ which, by uniting with craving, forms a foetus. Thus sexual intercourse attracts those who share the same karma and causes the five states of a foetus.[11] Therefore, the four forms of birth derive from particular causes; birth from an egg is due to (the predominance of) thoughts; that from a womb to passions; that from humidity to responsive union; and that by transformation to parting and metamorphosis. The union and parting of thoughts and passions cause further changes and transformations which rise and fall, closely followed by living beings

---

[8] Birth from womb and eggs.

[9] Birth from humidity.

[10] Birth by transformation

[11] The five stages of the formation of a foetus are: kalala, or slippery coagulation, i.e. the human embryo during the first week; arbuda, or a mass during the second week; peśī, or a piece of soft flesh during the third week; ghana, or a solid lump during the fourth week; and praśākhā, or a foetus with organs during the fifth week.

who are thus subject to the retributive effects of their karma. Hence the continuity of (the realm of) living beings.[12]

Continuity of karmic retribution

'Pūrṇamaitrāyaṇīputra, since desire and love are tied so closely together, no disengagement is possible and the result is an endless succession of the births of parents, children and grandchildren. This comes mainly from (sexual) desire which is stimulated by love.

'Since passion cannot be destroyed, living beings born from wombs, eggs, humidity and by transformation tend to use their strength to kill each other for food. This comes mainly from their passion for killing.

'So if a man (kills a sheep to) eat its meat, the sheep will be reborn as a human being and the man, after his death, will be reborn as a sheep (to repay his former debt). Thus living beings of the ten states of birth,[13] devour each other and so form evil karma which will have no end. This comes mainly from their passion for stealing.

'Due to such causes as "you owe me my life"[14] and "I pay my debt,"[15] living beings are subject to birth and death for hundreds and thousands of aeons. Due to such causes as "you treasure my heart, I love your beauty,"[16] they continue to be tied to each other for hundreds and thousands of kalpa. Therefore, the basic causes of continuous karmic retribution are three: killing, stealing and carnality.

'Thus Pūrṇamaitrāyaṇīputra, these three evil causes succeed one another solely because of unenlightened awareness which gives rise to the perception of form and so sees falsely mountains, rivers and the great

[12] In the intermediate state after death, man's consciousness wanders in search of its former love. It is bodiless but can see from a distance of several thousand miles, always looking for its cherished object. Hence the text says: 'When the perception of (an attractive) light reveals a form . . .' When it finds its object, it rushes to it with all thoughts directed to being embodied in or through that object. Hence 'the clear sight of a form stimulates a keen desire for it.' It is attracted to sexual intercourse; if it is male, it loves the woman and hates the man and if it is female, it loves the man and hates the woman. And so: 'opposing views cause hatred whereas concordant ones lead to love.' It is thus attracted by this play of sex and is drawn by flowing love to the woman's womb wherein it becomes the seed of a foetus. Hence 'the flow of love becomes the germ.' This seed enters the couple's generative fluid, and by uniting with its craving, takes the illusory form of an ego. Hence: 'the germ by uniting with craving forms a foetus.' This is birth from the womb. The four forms of birth accord with the retributive karma of each living being.

[13] Cf. Ch'an and Zen Teaching, First Series, p. 161, for a detailed explanation of the ten states of birth.

[14] Killing as basic cause of karmic retribution.

[15] Stealing as basic cause of karmic retribution.

[16] Carnality as basic cause of karmic retribution.

earth as well as other phenomena which unfold in succession and, because of this very illusion, appear again and again, as on a turning wheel.'

The Uncreated and Unending

Pūrṇamaitrāyaṇīputra asked: 'If Bodhi, which is basically absolute and enlightened and is the same as the unchanging Tathāgata mind, can suddenly create mountains, rivers, the great earth and other phenomena, when will the Buddha, who has attained Absolute Enlightenment, again give rise to the worldly perception of mountains, rivers and the great earth?'

The Buddha said: 'Pūrṇamaitrāyaṇīputra, if a man loses his way to a village by mistaking south for north, does his error come from delusion or enlightenment?'

Pūrṇamaitrāyaṇīputra replied: 'From neither. Why? Because, since delusion has no root how can this error come from it? Since enlightenment does not beget delusion, how can it cause him to err?'

The Buddha asked: 'If this man, while erring, suddenly meets someone who shows him the right way, do you think in spite of his mistake, he will lose his way again?'

(Pūrṇamaitrāyaṇīputra replied:) 'No, World Honoured One.'

(The Buddha said:) 'Pūrṇamaitrāyaṇīputra, it is the same with all Buddhas in the ten directions. Delusion has no root for it has no self-nature. Fundamentally there has never been delusion and though there is some semblance of it, when one is awakened, it vanishes (for) Bodhi does not beget it. This is like a man suffering from an optical illusion who sees flowers in the sky; if he is cured, these flowers will disappear. But if he waits for them to appear again, do you call him stupid or intelligent?'

Pūrṇamaitrāyaṇīputra replied: 'Fundamentally space has no flowers but due to defective sight they are seen as being in the void; this is already a false attitude. If in addition, they are required to appear again, this is mere folly; how then can that man be called stupid or intelligent?'

The Buddha said: 'Since you have interpreted well the non-existence of flowers in the sky, why do you still ask me about the immaterial absolute Bodhi of all Buddhas creating mountains, rivers and the great earth? It is like ore which contains pure gold; once the latter is extracted, it cannot be mixed with the ore again. It is also like the ashes of burnt wood which cannot become wood again. It is the same with all Buddhas of the nirvanic enlightenment.

The Unhindered Intermingling of Noumenon and Phenomenon

'Pūrṇamaitrāyaṇīputra, you now ask about the elements of earth, water, fire and wind which fundamentally intermingle without hindrance in the

Dharma realm; you are in doubt about why the elements of water and fire do not destroy each other and how the elements of space and earth can contain each other.

'Pūrṇamaitrāyaṇīputra, take for instance space which differs greatly from all forms but which does not prevent them from manifesting in it. Why? Because space is radiant in the sun and dark when the sky is cloudy, it moves with the wind, is bright in a clear sky, hazy in a mist, obscure in a dust-storm and is reflected when above clear water. Do you think that these transient forms in different places are created by these conditions or that they come from space? If they come from these conditions, then, when the sun shines, there is sunlight and all the worlds in the ten directions should be identical with the sun; then why is the sun seen in the sky? If space shines, it should shine upon itself; why then at night or when there are clouds and fog, is there no light? Light therefore is neither the same as nor different from the sun and space.

'Thus when looked into, essentially there are no forms (i.e. the seven elements) for they cannot be pointed out like unreal flowers in the sky that can only produce unreal fruit; so why do you inquire about their mutual destruction? But when their (underlying) nature is looked into, it is fundamentally real for it is absolute Bodhi. Since this absolute enlightened Mind is basically neither water nor fire, why do you question their mutual hindrance? Within this true and absolute Bodhi Enlightenment, if you give rise to (the karmic illusion of) space, space will manifest. If you have (similar illusions of) earth, water, fire and wind one after another, they will manifest separately and if you give rise to them all, they will appear simultaneously. Pūrṇamaitrāyaṇīputra, what does "simultaneous appearance" mean? If two men walking in opposite directions see the sun reflected in water, each will see the reflection follow in his direction. There is no fixed standard here and you cannot query why one sun can move in opposite directions or why two suns are seen when only one appears (in the sky)[17] thereby deepening your delusion without any prop on which to hold?[18]

Expounding the Common Source of Delusion and Enlightenment to Sum Up the Intermingling of Phenomenon and Noumenon

'Pūrṇamaitrāyaṇīputra, because you cling to form and space that displace each other in the Tathāgata store, the latter in accordance with your karma,

[17] This wipes out the concept of unity-with-differentiation.

[18] This ends the Buddha's teaching on the unhindered intermingling of noumenon with phenomenon.

manifests as space and form which pervade the whole Dharma realm, and as a result, there appear within it the blowing wind, still voidness, a bright sun and dark clouds. Due to their delusion and perplexity, living beings turn their backs on Bodhi and cling to sense objects thereby giving rise to troubles (kleśa) with the resultant appearance of illusory forms.

'(As to me), my uncreated and unending profound enlightenment accords with the Tathāgata store which is absolute Bodhi, and ensures my perfect insight into the Dharma realm where the one is infinite and the infinite is one; where the large manifests in the small and vice-versa; where the immovable bodhimaṇḍala appears everywhere; where my body embraces the ten directions of inexhaustible space; where the kingdom of treasures (i.e. the Buddha land) appears on the tip of a hair; and where I sit in a speck of dust to turn the wheel of the Dharma. As I have wiped out all illusory objects of senses to accord with Bodhi, I have realized the nature of the absolute Enlightenment of the Bhūtatathatā.'[19]

---

[19] The two last paragraphs sum up the interdependence of phenomenon and noumenon and the interdependence of all phenomena (according to the Hua Yen or Avataṁsaka School). Starting on p. 84 the Buddha taught Samāpatti or the meditative study of all as unreal or transitory. In the following text he taught Dhyāna, or the meditative study of the Mean which includes both Reality and Unreality.

III

The Tathāgata Store Containing Both Noumenon and Phenomenon

Meditative Study of the Mean (Dhyāna)

Elimination of 'is' to reveal the True Mind

'The fundamental, absolute and perfect Mind of the Tathāgata store is neither mind nor the elements of space, earth, water, wind and fire; neither eye nor ear, nose, tongue, body nor intellect; neither form nor sound, smell, taste, touch nor idea (dharma); neither the field of sight-perception nor the other fields of sense including that of the intellect;[1] neither enlightenment nor unenlightenment nor the (eleven) other links in the chain of existence including old age and death; neither the end of enlightenment nor that of unenlightenment nor that of the (eleven) other links;[2] neither misery nor the accumulation of misery, extinction of passion and the path thereto;[3] neither wisdom nor gain (realization); neither charity (dāna) nor discipline (śīla), neither zeal (vīrya), patience (kṣānti), meditation (dhyāna), wisdom (prajñā) nor perfection (pāramitā);[4] and even neither Tathāgata, Arhat, Samyak-saṁbodhi, Parinirvāṇa, nor (true) Eternity, Bliss, Self and Purity.[5]

Elimination of 'is not' to reveal the True Mind

'Thus the basic enlightened Mind of the Tathāgata store, being neither mundane nor supramundane is wonderful in that it is (also) identical with

---

[1] The Tathāgata store is neither the worldly mind (which comprises subjective consciousness and perception) nor the (objective) elements of space, earth, water, wind and fire, the six organs, six sense data and six consciousnesses.

[2] Nor is it the supramundane stage of a pratyeka-buddha attainable after awakening to the twelve links in the chain of existence and their ends.

[3] Nor is it the supramundane stage of a śrāvaka attainable after awakening to the Four Noble Truths.

[4] Nor is it the supramundane stage of Bodhisattva development which comprises wisdom and gain (realization) by means of the Six Pāramitā. Cf. Ch'an and Zen Teaching, First Series, Part IV, *The Heart Sutra*, for a fuller explanation of the above notes 2, 3 and 4.

[5] Nor is it the supreme state of Buddhahood, with its highest titles of Tathāgata, Arhat and Samyak-Saṁbodhi, nor the stage of Parinirvāṇa with its four characteristics of Absolute Eternity, Absolute Bliss, Absolute Self and Absolute Purity. Thus the 'Mean' wipes out both the worldly and saintly to expose the Tathāgata store.

(worldly) mind and (the elements of) space, earth, water, wind and fire; with eye, ear, nose, tongue, body and intellect; with form, sound, smell, taste, touch and ideas; with the field of eye-perception and all other fields before and including that of intellect; with enlightenment, unenlightenment and the (eleven) other links in the chain of existence before and including old age and death; with the end of enlightenment, of unenlightenment and of the (eleven) other links; with misery and its accumulation, with the extinction of passions and the path thereto; with dāna, śīla, vīrya, kṣānti, dhyāna, prajñā and pāramitā; and also with Tathāgata, Arhat, Samyak-Saṁbodhi, Parinirvāṇa, true Eternity, Bliss, Self and Purity.

Simultaneous elimination of 'is' and 'is not' to reveal the Absolute Mind

'Thus the (underlying) principle of the absolute Enlightened Mind of the Tathāgata store, being identical with and (including) both the mundane and supramundane, is above "is" and "is not" and beyond both identity and difference.

'How therefore, can worldly beings of the three realms of existence and in the supramundane śrāvaka and pratyeka-buddha states fathom the Tathāgata's Supreme Bodhi and penetrate the Buddha-wisdom by word and speech? For instance though a lute can make sweet melody, it is useless in the absence of skilful fingers;[6] it is the same with you and all living beings for although the True Mind of precious Bodhi is complete within every man, when I press my finger on it, the Ocean Symbol[7] radiates but as soon as your mind moves, all troubles (kleśa) arise. This is due to your remissness in your search for Supreme Bodhi, in your delight in Hināyana and your contentment with the little progress which you regard as complete.'[8]

The One Mind, Sudden Awakening and Realization

Pūrṇamaitrāyaṇīputra said: 'The Buddha and I possess the true, absolute and clean Minds of Complete Enlightenment which are the same and wholly perfect, but why, after so many transmigrations due to my delu-

[6] Practice and training.

[7] The Ocean Symbol shows the vastness of the meditation of the Buddha; the vision of all things.

[8] This ends the teaching on the meditative study of the Mean. From the beginning of the sermon, the Buddha revealed the three characteristics of the Tathāgata store: the void (its substance), the non-void (its function) and the void yet non-void (which corresponds with the threefold meditative study of all as void, of all as unreal and of the Mean which includes both). Students of the Absolute Dharma should familiarize themselves with these three characteristics of the Tathāgata store and the corresponding threefold meditative study as taught in the text in order to comprehend the profundity of the Supreme Vehicle.

sion from the time without beginning and after my present attainment of the Saintly Vehicle, am I still unable to realize the Ultimate whereas the World Honoured One has eliminated all falseness and has realized absolute permanence? I beg to ask the Tathāgata what causes the delusion that screens living beings from their profound enlightenment and so subjects them to their present perdition.'

The Buddha replied: 'Although you have wiped out your troubles (kleśa), traces of your defilement still remain. I will now put some worldly questions to you. Have you not heard of (the mad man) Yajñadatta of Śrāvastī who would look into a mirror and delight in seeing his eyebrows and eyes but when one morning he failed to see them in his own head, thought himself bedevilled? Do you think there was any valid reason for such madness?'

Pūrṇamaitrāyaṇīputra replied: 'There was no valid reason.'

The Buddha said: 'The Absolute Bodhi is basically enlightened and absolute. When it is (screened and wrongly) called false, how can there be a REAL cause (of) this delusion? For if there is a REAL reason, how can it be called FALSE? All this arises from wrong thinking which develops into further wrong thinking. When one falseness is heaped on another, in spite of the teachings by Buddhas in countless former aeons, you are still unable to avoid delusion. Its causes are also under delusion, but if you realize that it has none, falseness will have no support (and will vanish). Since (delusion) was never created, what is there to destroy to realize Bodhi?

'This is like a man who, when awake, relates what he saw in a dream; he may be ingenious but what can he get from it? Still less can he benefit from a state which does not derive from any cause and does not really exist, like Yajñadatta who, without reason, took fright at not seeing his own head. If he suddenly ceased to be crazy, his head would not come from elsewhere, and even if he was still mad, it was not really lost. Pūrṇamaitrāyaṇīputra, since this is the nature of falseness where is its cause? If you will only cease to discriminate and to believe in the (three illusions that there are) the universe, karmic retribution and (the realms of) living beings, the three conditions (derived from killing, stealing and carnality) will come to an end. Without these conditions, the three causes will not arise and, as with mad Yajñadatta, the mad nature of your own mind will come to an end and when it does, that is Enlightenment (Bodhi). Thus your unexcelled, pure and enlightened Mind which essentially pervades the Dharma realm, does not come from outside; how can it be realized by toilsome and profound practice and by achievement? This is like a man with a cintāmaṇi pearl sewn in his coat who forgets all about it, thinks he is really poor and wanders about begging for food. Although he is poor, his pearl has never been lost. If a wise man suddenly tells him that it is in his coat, all his wishes will be answered and he will become very rich. He will thus realize that his wonderful gem does not come from outside.'[9]

Ānanda then came forward, prostrated himself with his head at the feet of the Buddha, stood up and asked: 'The World Honoured One now speaks of eliminating the three conditions of killing, stealing and carnality to ensure that the three basic causes do not arise and so to stop the upsurge of Yajñadatta's madness and realize Bodhi which thus does not come from outside. This without a shadow of doubt shows the causes and conditions but why does the Tathāgata throw them away completely? It is also due to causes and conditions that my mind has opened. World Honoured One, I am not the only hearer (śrāvaka) who, though still needing study and learning, has so awakened, but others in this assembly, like Mahā-maudgalyāyana, Śāriputra, Subhūti, etc., who followed the Brahmacārin,[10] heard of the Buddha's teaching on causes and conditions, then awakened to the Dharma and achieved the state beyond transmigration. If you now say that Bodhi does not depend on causes and conditions, then the self-existent as preached by the heretics in Rājagṛha, such as Maskari Gośalīputra[11] and others, would be Nirvāṇa. Will you be so compassionate enough to enlighten my delusion and perplexity?'

---

[9] The disciple's query about the cause of delusion went to the heart of the matter (i.e. the mind). Therefore, students of the Transmission should always look into this mind's daily activities and should not think wrongly that the Teaching School does not advocate the Patriarch's profound aim (i.e. the mind). This question is very difficult to answer, so the Buddha used the story of Yajñadatta to teach that falseness has no cause, like the crazy man's head which did not come from outside. For the enlightened Mind of Absolute Bodhi is fundamentally free from all falseness. If it is called false, how can *falseness* have a *real* cause? If it comes from a real cause, it should not be called false, for falseness comes from accrued false thinking and accumulated delusion. Therefore, the cause of falseness only arises from delusion which if realized as having no (inherent) cause will lose its support and will vanish. If it has never been created, how can it now be annihilated? The non-existent nature of falseness is like things seen in a dream; how can it have a real cause? Such being the nature of delusion, where can it be found? If you only cease to discriminate and to be bound by the threefold chain of the universe, karma and life, the three conditions (of killing, stealing and carnality) will come to an end and the three basic causes (the world, karma and life) will disappear. If you awaken to these three conditions, your basic ignorance will cease suddenly and your enlightened Mind of Absolute Bodhi which is essentially not deluded will appear instantaneously, like Yajñadatta's head which was never lost and did not come from elsewhere when his mad mind came to a stop.

This is the Buddha's teaching on instantaneous awakening.

[10] Brahmin ascetics with their minds set on pure living.

[11] One of the Six Heretics (Tirthikas) who denied that their present lot was due to karmic deeds in former lives.

The Buddha said: 'Ānanda, in the case of Yajñadatta, if the (so-called) cause and condition of his madness had been wiped out, his own nature which was not mad would have revealed itself, and whatever you may rationalize about cause, condition and self-existence does not go beyond this.[12]

'Ānanda, if Yajñadatta's head had basically been self-existent, it should always have been so and could not have been otherwise. What then were the cause and condition that resulted in his[13] taking fright and going mad?[14]

'If his self-existent head became mad owing to cause and condition, why was it not lost? But when he took fright and went mad, why was it still there unchanged? Thus how could cause and condition affect his head?[15]

'If his madness was self-existent, it should always have been there but before he became mad, where was it hidden?[16]

'If his madness was not self-existent and there was nothing seriously wrong with his head, why did he go mad?[17]

'If you realize that his fundamental head (was intact), you will know that (only) his Consciousness became mad and will realize that to talk of cause, condition and self-existence is frivolous.[18]

'This is why I say that if the three conditions (of killing, stealing and carnality) are eliminated, this is Bodhi Mind. (But the idea that) Bodhi Mind is created after the samsaric mind has been annihilated pertains to saṁsāra.[19]

'Even after the ideas of both creation and destruction have been abandoned, with no more thought of practice and realization, if the (least belief in) self-existence remains this shows clearly that the death of the worldly has given birth to the self-existent mind which also pertains to saṁsāra with its implied opposite, self-existence. This is like the mixture and fusion of various worldly materials into a composite compound which implies its opposite, the uncompounded. (But) the Absolute which is neither original nor unoriginal, neither mixed and united nor not mixed

[12] Both delusion and enlightenment are false.

[13] Lit. . . . resulted in his head taking fright and going mad?

[14] Head stands for the true nature. This shows that the true nature is not self-existent.

[15] This shows that the true nature does not come from cause and condition.

[16] This shows that delusion is not self-existent.

[17] This shows that delusion does not come from cause and condition.

[18] This reveals the absolute nature which is beyond cause, condition, and self-existence, and is above all sophistry.

[19] This exposes the subtle cause of defilement which implies the duality of relative enlightenment and delusion.

and not united, and neither apart nor not apart from union and separation, is above and beyond all sophistry.

'Bodhi and Nirvana are still very far away and cannot be attained without aeons of practice and experience. Even if you (succeed in) memorizing the twelve divisions of the Mahāyāna canon taught by all the Buddhas, and the profound and perfect doctrines countless as the Ganges' sands, this will only increase sophistry. Although you speak of cause, condition and self-existence as if you are very clear about them, and in spite of people calling you the first of those with a wide knowledge (of the Dharma) with its beneficial influence for aeons past, you have been unable to avoid the pit into which Mātaṅgī fell; why have you waited to be rescued from it by my Śūraṅgama mantra which caused the girl to extinguish the fire of lust completely, to realize the state of Anāgāmin and to enter the dense forest of zeal and devotion? As the river of love dried up, you were delivered from bondage.

'Therefore, Ānanda, your memorizing and remembering the Tathāgata's profound and wonderful teaching for successive aeons cannot compare with one day's practice of the Transcendental Path which has enabled you to avoid suffering from both love and hate. Mātaṅgī was a prostitute but she gave up lust and desire with the aid of the mantra, thereby becoming a Bhikṣuṇī, called Self-nature, in this assembly. Both she and Yaśodharā, the mother of (my elder son) Rāhula, awoke to sufferings caused by desire and love in their previous lives and, in a flash of thought, practised the Transcendental Way; one was freed from bonds and the other received (my) prediction of her future enlightenment. Why do you still deceive yourself by clinging to what you see and hear?'[20]

---

[20] The Buddha thus revealed the three characteristics of the Tathāgata store for the three corresponding meditative studies, and urged the assembly to practise the Dharma (instead of memorizing His words).

IV

Self-Enlightenment

Objects Contemplated in Meditative Studies

After hearing the Buddha's teaching, Ānanda and the assembly, now rid of doubt and illusion, awoke to Reality and felt a lightness of body and mind which they had never experienced before. Ānanda again wept, prostrated himself with his head at the feet of the Buddha, knelt down, brought his palms together and said: 'O peerless, compassionate and immaculate King of Treasures, you have opened my mind so well by using all kinds of expedients and encouragement to lead me out of darkness in the ocean of suffering. World Honoured One, after hearing your Dharma-voice, although I have realized that the Bright Mind of Absolute Bodhi of the Tathāgata store pervades the ten directions to bring all the lands therein to the pure and majestic kingdom of Absolute Enlightenment, the Buddha again blames my useless knowledge acquired by listening which cannot compare with true practice and training. I am like a traveller who is suddenly given by the king of heaven a splendid mansion, which now that he owns it, he should know how to enter. May the Tathāgata not forsake His great compassion and may He teach all the deluded in this assembly how to give up the Small Vehicle and how to develop their minds in order to attain to Ultimate Nirvāṇa, so that those who still need study and learning may know how to overcome their clinging to causal phenomena in order to achieve perfect control (dhāraṇī) and enter the Buddha's All-wisdom.'

After saying this, he prostrated himself and reverently awaited the holy Teaching.

Practice of Meditation for Self-Enlightenment

The Buddha took pity on the śrāvakas and pratyeka-buddhas in the assembly whose minds set on enlightenment were still not at ease and (also) on future living beings in the Dharma ending age who will want to develop their Bodhi minds and to tread the Path of the Supreme Vehicle. He said to Ānanda and the assembly: 'As you are determined to develop the Bodhi mind and practise the Tathāgata's Samādhi tirelessly, you should first ascertain the two decisive factors in the development of your mind.

What are they?

The subjective mind in the meditation

'Ānanda, as you decide to give up the state of a śrāvaka to practise with the Bodhisattva Vehicle in order to possess the Buddha's All-Wisdom, you should see clearly if the cause-ground (used as) a point of departure and its fruit-ground (i.e. realization) are compatible or not. Ānanda, if you use your worldly mind as a causal point of departure, you will fail in your search for the Buddha Vehicle which is beyond birth and death. Therefore, you should inquire into all the creations (of the mind) which in this material world are subject to change and destruction. Ānanda, which one of them does not decay? Yet you have never heard that space can perish. Why? Because it is not a created thing.

The objective phenomena in the meditation

'In your body, that which is solid is the element of earth, that which is liquid is the element of water, that which is warm is the element of fire and that which moves is the element of wind. These four restraining elements divide your pure, perfect, absolute and enlightened Bodhi into seeing, hearing, knowing and discerning: hence the five turbid conditions (kaṣāya) from the beginning to the end.

'What is turbidity? Ānanda, take for instance clear water which is so by nature, and dust, earth, ashes and sand which are obstructive by nature. If someone throws earth and dust into clear water, the former will lose their obstructive qualities and the latter its clearness: the result is dirty water which is called turbid. Your five turbid conditions are like that dirty water.[1]

'Ānanda, when you see space in the ten directions, your perception and the void are inseparable, and since the void is bodiless and your perception unenlightened, both unite into one falseness which is the first layer, called "turbid kalpa."

---

[1] This shows the origin of birth and death, hence the two decisive factors of the point of departure. The Buddha was about to teach the correct practice by means of the true Mind which is beyond birth and death, as the main cause. Therefore, He spoke first of the five conditions of turbidity in saṁsāra, meaning that birth and death can be looked into to realize the Uncreate, that is the five aggregates can be used for meditation to win the Dharmakāya. For delusion comes from the transmutation of the One Mind into karmic consciousness, of (ālaya's) perception into form and mind, and of form and mind into the five aggregates, hence the division into organs, sense data and consciousnesses. The five aggregates are, therefore, the origin of saṁsāra. Now when returning falseness to Reality, if the five aggregates that make up body and mind are not looked into, there is no other way for right practice. Hence the meditative study of the five aggregates is the gateway to Enlightenment. In the above text, the Buddha spoke of the five conditions of turbidity as the origin of birth and death, and in the following paragraphs He gave a fuller description of them.

'Your body is made of four elements which limit your mind and divide it into seeing, hearing, feeling and knowing: the union of water, fire, wind and earth with your feeling and knowing begets another falseness which is the second layer, called "turbid views."

'Your recollection and habits give rise to intellection which responds to the six sense data. This intellect has no independent form apart from the objects of sense and is devoid of nature apart from perception: it unites with sense data to become another falseness which is the third layer, called "turbid passions" (kleśa).

'In the endless rise and fall of illusions in saṁsāra your intellect is intent on staying in the world whereas your karma forces you to transmigrate from place to place: they thus unite into another falseness which is the fourth layer, called "turbid being."

'Fundamentally your seeing and hearing are by nature the same but, being limited by sense data, they degenerate into two separate (faculties): they are aware of each other within their (common) nature but differ in their functions. As a result they are (as it were) upside down and unite into another falseness which is the fifth layer, called "turbid life."[2]

---

[2] The five conditions of turbidity are created by the five aggregates. As a man under delusion transforms his basic Bodhi nature into form and mind, he becomes a human being made of five aggregates thereby polluting his True Mind: hence the five kinds of turbidity. At first, (ālaya's) perception and dull voidness united to become the first aggregate form (rūpa), just as when clear water is mixed with earth and dust it becomes turbid. This was the origin of the aggregate of form which continued for a period of time; hence the turbid kalpa (in contrast with the timeless pure Reality).

Turbid (or deteriorated) views correspond with the second aggregate vedanā, or the responsiveness of the (first) five consciousnesses which cling to the body made of four elements, which does not exist fundamentally but divides the True Mind into seeing, hearing, feeling and knowing. The *unknowing* Bodhi Mind is thus transformed into the *knowing* ego; hence the turbid views which rise and fall without interruption.

Turbid passion (kleśa) corresponds to the third aggregate sañjñā, which is the sixth consciousness that thinks wrongly. Although kleśa has no nature of its own and wrong thinking is essentially non-existent, your recollection and habits give rise to thoughts of previously seen and known objects; hence the manifestation of the six sense data which cannot be found in the True Mind.

Turbid being corresponds with the fourth aggregate saṁskāra. Fundamentally a living being is illusory and non-existent but your wrong thinking is endless and never stops; hence your desire to stay in this illusory world wherein your continued karmic activities cause you to transmigrate through all realms of existence.

Turbid life corresponds with the fifth aggregate vijñāna. Life does not really exist but your true nature is divided by the four elements into seeing, hearing, feeling and knowing which arise from a single underlying substance but function separately. This vijñāna clings to form and mind as the basis of its existence; hence turbid life.

These five turbid conditions do not exist in the Bodhi Mind which is polluted by the five aggregates; hence the five turbidities which are the origin of delusion.

The point of departure

'Ānanda, if you wish to bring your seeing, hearing, feeling and knowing into line with the Tathāgata's absolute Eternity, BLISS, Self and Purity, you should first pick out the root of birth and death, and turn its worldly falseness back to its unworldly profound nature until it is subdued and reverts to Basic Bodhi, and then use this pure nature as the causal mind-ground (i.e. as the point of departure) to perfect your practice and realization of the fruit-ground.[3]

'This is like purifying muddy water in a clean container; left unshaken in complete calmness, the sand and mud will sink to the bottom. When the clear water appears, this is called the first suppression of the intruding evil element of passion. When the mud has been removed leaving behind only the clear water, this is called the permanent cutting off of basic ignorance. Enlightenment is (pure and) unmixed, and its manifestations are not of the nature of kleśa, but are in accord with the immaculate virtues of Nirvāṇa.

Looking into the roots of klesa to find the sense organ suitable for meditation

'What is the second decisive factor? In your determination to develop the Bodhi Mind and to advance boldly along the Bodhisattva Path by relinquishing everything worldly, you should look closely into the origin of kleśa, caused by your basic ignorance and developing discrimination, and see who creates and endures them. Ānanda, in your cultivation of Bodhi, if you do not inquire into the root of kleśa, you will never know (how and) where the organs and sense data are turned upside down. If you fail to understand this, how can you overcome them to win the Tathāgata stage?

'Ānanda, if a man who is good at untying knots, does not see them, how can he undo them? And you have never heard that the void can be unfastened for it has neither form nor shape and is not like a knot that can be untied. But your eyes, ears, nose and tongue as well as your body and mind, are the six decoys which a thief uses to steal the treasures of your house. For this reason, since the time without beginning, living beings and this world have always been interlocked (in time and space) hence you are unable to leap beyond the material world.

'Ānanda, what is (this) realm of time and space?[4] Time means duration and space location. You know that the ten directions are in space and that

[3] This accords well with the Ch'an technique which consists in banishing all thoughts and then using the thoughtless moment to look into one's fundamental face.

[4] The Chinese equivalent of the Western word 'World' is Shih Chieh, lit. Time-Boundary, or realm of time and space.

the past, present and future are in time. There are ten directions (of space) and three (aspects of) time. All living beings owe their bodies to illusory time and space which are interwoven within them and continue to affect them. Although there are ten directions, the worldly man recognizes only the east, west, south and north as cardinal points but disregards the intermediate ones and the zenith and nadir which he considers as unimportant.

'The entanglement of the three times with the four cardinal points (3 × 4) or of the four cardinal points with the three times (4 × 3) results in the constant twelve. Allowing for the change and transformation of discriminative thoughts occurring thrice (to cover the past, present and future), this constant is increased from 1 to 10,100 and 1,000 to cover the whole field of activity of each of the six sense organs, its maximum sum of merits (i.e. its potential function) being represented by the number 1,200.[5]

'Ānanda, now measure the potentiality (for merit) of each organ. For instance, your eyes can see things in front and on both sides but nothing behind you. Its incomplete field of activity represents only two thirds of the maximum, that is only 800 merits.

'As to your ears, their field of activity includes all the ten directions: a sound is heard whether near or distant while silence is registered as being boundless. Hence this organ earns the full 1,200 merits.

'The function of your nose relies on in and out breaths which lack a common point of contact: hence it earns only 800 merits.

'When your tongue propagates mundane and supramundane wisdoms, though language is restricted, the meaning is inexhaustible. Hence this organ registers all the 1,200 merits.

'When your body feels that it is touched, this feeling exists when there is touch but vanishes in its absence. Hence your body has only 800 merits.

'As intellect embraces both the mundane and supramundane of the past, present and future in the ten directions, including all the worldly

[5] This shows the suitability and unsuitability of any of the six sense organs used for the meditative study. It was explained earlier that since living beings and the realm of time and space were so interwoven that they were unable to leap beyond the material world. Time is represented by the flow of thoughts, and space by the body with its surroundings conditioned by the four cardinal points. Thus with the rise of the first thought, either time is involved in the four directions of space, (that is 3 × 4) or space in the three times, (that is 4 × 3) and the constant is 12. This is the constant for the first thought arising from nothingness, symbolized by the digit 1. Each thought lasts 90 moments (kṣaṇa) each of which involves 900 births and deaths (but for simplicity sake) the numbers 10, 100 and 1,000 are used to stand for all change and transformation when the first thought arises. When the second thought replaces the first one, each cardinal point involves 3 aspects of time which, multiplied by 10 for the change, give 30, or 120 for all the four cardinal points involved in the change. A third thought will involve another change, or 120 × 10 = 1,200 which is a maximum number which is adequate to measure the potentiality of each of the six organs.

and saintly without limits, you should know that this organ earns the full 1,200 merits.

'Ānanda, as you now wish to go against the samsaric current of desire, you should revert to the very organ (from which it flows) until you reach the state beyond birth and death. (Therefore,) you should look into the six functioning organs and see which one is consistent or not, is deep or shallow and is all-penetrating or deficient. If you find the all-pervading organ, you should turn back its karmic flow so that it accords with its penetrating quality: the difference between realization by means of this penetrating organ and that through a deficient one is comparable to that between a day and an aeon. I have now revealed to you the six organs (arising from) your True Mind and their respective potentialities so that you can choose the one most suitable to you and advance in your practice.

'All the Tathāgatas practised self-cultivation through the eighteen realms of sense to realize Supreme Bodhi; to them all these eighteen objects of meditation were suitable for their practice, but your quality is inferior and you are unable to use them to win Supreme Wisdom. This is why I now teach you to choose a suitable organ for your deep meditation: once you have entered it and freed yourself from illusion, all your six organs will become pure and clean simultaneously.'

Ānanda asked: 'World Honoured One, how can one by going against the samsaric current, enter deep into a single sense organ so as to ensure that all the six senses become pure and clean simultaneously?'

The Buddha replied: 'Although you have realized the state of stream entry (śrota-āpanna) and wiped out worldly views, you are still not yet clear about the inner thoughts that have accumulated since the time without beginning, the elimination of which can be made only by practice and training. Still less are you clear about the inner illusions of birth, stay, change and death to be wiped out during the successive stages (of Bodhisattva development).

'Now look at your six organs: are they one or six? Ānanda, if they are one, why cannot you see with your ears, hear with your eyes, walk with your head and speak with your feet? If they are six, then as I expound the profound Dharma, which one of them receives my instruction?'

Ānanda said: 'I use my ears to listen to it.'

The Buddha said: 'If so your ears should have no relation with your body and mouth when your mouth asks for its meaning and your body stands up to receive it reverently. Therefore, they are neither one ending in six nor six ending in one: in other words, basically your sense organs are neither one nor six.

'Ānanda, you should realize that your organs are neither one nor six and that because you have seen everything upside down since the time without beginning, (the illusion of) one and six have arisen from that which is perfect and clean. Although your attainment of the state of śrota-āpanna has wiped out the (illusory concept of) six. you still retain (that of) one.

'This is like the void (contained) in different vessels and called by different names according to the shapes of the containers: if you throw away the vessels and look at the void, you will say that it is one. But how can the void follow your discrimination to become one or many? Still less can it become one or none. So your fix active organs are like the void (in different containers).

'Because of light and darkness which (alternate with) and reveal each other, their adhesion to the wondrous perfect (mind) results in perception, the essence of which reflects forms and unites with them to become a sense organ. This organ originally comes from the four fine elements (of earth, water, fire and wind) and is called an eye which is shaped like a grape. Hence this organ of perception[6] is in constant search of forms.

'Because the conditions of disturbance and stillness contrast with each other, their adhesion to the wondrous perfect (mind) results in hearing, the essence of which echoes with sound and unites with it to become a sense organ. This organ originally comes from the four fine elements and is called an ear which is shaped like a young rolled leaf. Hence this organ of perception is in constant search of sound.

'Because of the two (alternating) conditions of clearance and obstruction, their adhesion to the wondrous perfect (mind) results in smelling, the essence of which responds to odour and absorbs it to become a sense organ. This organ originally comes from the four fine elements and is called a nose which is shaped like the claw (end of a hammer). Hence this organ of perception is in constant search of smell.

Because of changing and unchanged conditions, their adhesion to the wondrous perfect (mind) results in tasting, the essence of which responds to flavour and absorbs it to become a sense organ. This organ originally comes from the four fine elements and is called a tongue which is shaped like a crescent moon. Hence this organ of perception is in constant search of taste.

Because of the alternate conditions of contact and separation, their adhesion to the wondrous perfect (mind) results in feeling, the essence of which responds to touch and unites with it to become a sense organ. This organ originally comes from the four fine elements and is called a body which is shaped like a trunk narrow in the centre. Hence this organ of perception is in constant search of touch.

[6] In contrast with the faculty of perception which is behind the ordinary organ of perception.

'Because of the two successive states of creation and destruction, their adhesion to the wondrous perfect (mind) results in knowing, the essence of which clings to dharma and unites with them to become a sense organ. This organ originally comes from the four fine elements and is called an intellect which is like perception hidden in a dark room?[7] Hence this organ of perception is in constant search of dharma.

'Thus, Ananda, these six sense organs cause the enlightened Bodhi to become subjective awareness so that it misses its essence by clinging to falseness. This is why there is no substance of seeing in the absence of both light and darkness: no substance of hearing without both stillness and disturbance: no nature of smelling in the absence of clearance and obstruction: no taste without changing and unchanged conditions: no feeling of touch beyond contact and separation and no prop for knowing in the absence of creation and destruction.

'You have only not to follow the states of stillness and disturbance, of contact and separation, of changing and unchanged conditions, of clearance and obstruction, of creation and destruction and of light and darkness, and from these twelve worldly conditions, just root out any one of your six sense organs to disengage it from both inner and outer adhesion. As soon as it is subdued and brought back to the real, the latter's light will appear. When the bright nature manifests, the other five adhesions will be completely rooted out and you will be free from wrong views created by the sense data.

'This light does not follow the sense organs but manifests through them and so all the six organs function through each other. Ānanda, do not you see in this assembly Aniruddha who is blind but sees, Upānanda who is deaf but hears, the Goddess of the Ganges who is noseless but smells, Gavāṁpati who does not taste with his tongue and the God of Śūnyatā who has no body but feels touch. This God of the void appears temporarily in the Tathāgata-light; since his body is (like) air and does not exist materially, he has realized stillness (dhyāna) derived from the elimination of the second and third aggregates, thereby achieving the peace of the śrāvaka stage. And Mahākāśyapa, who is here, succeeded long ago in rooting out the organ of intellect thereby realizing perfect knowledge which does not derive from the thinking process.

'Ānanda, if all your sense organs are rooted out, your inner light will appear, all transient sense data as well as the changing conditions of the material world will vanish, like ice melted by boiling water, and you will realize Supreme Bodhi instantly. Ānanda, if a man who sees with his eyes suddenly closes them, darkness will appear before him screening all his

[7] The intellect is imperceptible from without but perceives things outside.

six sense organs including his head and feet. If he then feels his body with his hands, he will discern his head and feet although he does not see them. This shows that his knowing is the same whether he sees something in the light or nothing in the dark. That which does not rely on the light to manifest is not affected by darkness. After all organs and sense data have vanished, why cannot you realize the perfect and absolute enlightened Bodhi?'

Expedient Instruction on the One Mind

Ānanda said: 'World Honoured One, as the Buddha has said, the causal ground used as the point of departure in quest of Reality should be compatible with the fruit-ground. World Honoured One, though realization of the fruit-ground is called by seven different names: Bodhi, Nirvāṇa, the Absolute, Buddha-nature, Immaculate Knowledge (Amalavijñāna), Immaterial Tathāgata Store, the Great Mirror Wisdom, it is pure, clean and perfect, and its substance does not change, like the royal diamond which is permanent and indestructible. Now the faculties of seeing and hearing have no independent nature in the absence of brightness and darkness, stillness and motion, and clearance and obstruction, and are like the thinking mind which ceases to exist in the absence of sense data. How can they be used as the point of departure in the search for the Tathāgata's seven permanent fruits? World Honoured One, seeing ceases to exist in the absence of light and darkness, like the thinking mind which comes to an end when there are no external phenomena. As I look into all this, I search in vain for my mind and its objects: what then should I set up as the cause in my quest of Supreme Bodhi? Does the Tathāgata's previous teaching on (the nature of) seeing which is profound, pure, perfect and permanent, contradict your "true words" and become sophistry (as well)? Will you please be compassionate enough to clear away my delusion and perplexity?'

The Buddha said: 'You have widened your knowledge by hearing but have failed to get out of the stream of transmigration completely. Though you know the cause of your upset, yet when you find yourself in the presence of that cause, you fail to recognize it. Lest your trustfulness remain incomplete, I will now do something to clear away your doubt and suspicion.'

The Buddha then ordered Rāhula to ring the bell and asked Ānanda: 'Do you hear it?' Ānanda and the others in the assembly replied that they did. When the bell was no more heard, the Buddha asked again: 'Do you still hear it?' They all replied that they did not. Rāhula again rang the bell and the Buddha asked: 'Do you hear it?' They replied that they did. The Buddha then asked Ānanda: 'What do you mean by hearing and not hearing?' Ānanda and the others replied: 'If the bell is rung, we call it hearing and when the sound and its echo stop, we call it not hearing.'

The Buddha again ordered Rāhula to ring the bell and asked Ānanda: 'Is there any sound?' Ānanda and the others replied that there was a sound of the bell. A little later when it could no longer be heard, the Buddha asked again: 'Is there any sound?' They all replied that there was none. Then Rāhula rang the bell again and the Buddha asked: 'Is there any sound?' They all replied in the affirmative. The Buddha then asked Ānanda: 'What do you mean by sound and no sound?' Ānanda and the others replied that if the bell was rung, there was sound and when both the sound and its echo stopped, this was called no sound.

The Buddha said: 'Why did you talk so wildly?' Ānanda and the others asked: 'Why do you say that we talked wildly?' The Buddha said: 'When I asked you about hearing, you spoke of hearing and when I asked you about the sound, you spoke of it. So merely about hearing and sound, your answers were ambiguous; how could they not be called wild? Ānanda, when both the sound and its echo ceased, you said there was no hearing: if there really was no hearing, its nature would have died and would be like a withered log, but when the bell was rung again, how did you hear it? Existence and non-existence concern only the sound which may be present or not, but how can the nature of your hearing follow your discrimination to exist or not? If it really ceased, who then knew there was no sound?

'Therefore, Ānanda, in your hearing, the sound may exist or not, but this does not mean that the sound, whether heard or not, (can) cause your hearing to exist or not. In your delusion you mistake the sound for your hearing and so regard the permanent as transient. You should not say that hearing has no nature when it exists apart from (the conditions of) disturbance, stillness, obstruction and clearance.

'For instance, when a man sleeps soundly, if people pound rice, he may hear the beating of a drum or the ringing of a bell. So when asleep he may find it strange that the bell is like the beating of a (piece of) wood or stone, but if he suddenly wakes up and hears the pestle, he will tell his family about his mistake when asleep. Ānanda, does that man remember in his sleep (the conditions of) stillness, disturbance, clearance and obstruction? Although his body rests, the nature of his hearing is present.

'Even when your body perishes and your life comes to an end, how can this nature vanish? For since the time without beginning all living beings have followed forms and sounds and pursued the flow of their thoughts without awakening to their pure, profound and permanent nature. By straying from the permanent and by following birth and death, they have been contaminated with defilements in successive lives. If you (only) keep away from saṁsāra and dwell in real permanence, your eternal Light will appear thereby causing your organs, sense data, consciousness and (mad) mind to vanish simultaneously. The objects of your thinking process are (polluting) dust and the feelings that arise from your consciousness are impurities; if both are kept away, your Dharma eye will appear pure and bright instantly. Why then cannot you realize Supreme Bodhi?'

Main Instruction on the Three Meditative Studies of the One Mind

Ānanda said: 'World Honoured One, although the Tathāgata has taught the second decisive point (in the development of the mind), I think that if the man good at untying knots does not know how they came to be tied, he will be unable to undo them. In this assembly I and those who need to study and learn more, are in the same case. Since the time without beginning we and our delusions have both been subject to birth and death, and although we have cultivated good qualities that have enabled us to widen our knowledge by hearing (about it all) and so are called leavers of homes, we are like a person suffering from malaria which recurs every other day. Will you take pity on us and save us from drowning? Will you tell us which of our bodies and minds are in a knot and how to untie it so that all suffering beings can escape from saṁsāra and avoid falling (again) into the three realms of existence?'

After saying this, he and all the assembly prostrated themselves, shed bitter tears and eagerly awaited the Buddha's supreme revelation.

The Buddha took pity on Ānanda and those in the assembly who still needed to study and learn as well as on future living beings. In order to enable them to sow the cause of their future appearance in the world (as teachers) and so become the eye (of wisdom) to guide coming generations. He extended His shining golden-hued hand to touch Ānanda's head (and comfort him).

Thereupon all Buddha lands in the ten directions shook six times[8] and Tathāgatas, countless as motes of dust, sent out, from the tops of their heads, radiant rays of light which reached Jetavana to shine upon the Buddha's head. This had not been seen before by the assembly. Then Ānanda and all those present heard countless Buddhas declare with one voice: 'Excellent, Ānanda, if you want to know about the innate ignorance that causes you to transmigrate in saṁsāra, (you should know that) the roots of your birth and death are your six sense organs. If you want to know about Supreme Bodhi, it is these six organs that will enable you speedily to realize happiness in liberation and permanence in Nirvāṇa.'

---

[8] Bodhi which shook all the six sense organs, the root of unenlightenment.

Although Ānanda had heard these Dharma voices, he was still not clear about their (profound) meaning. So he bowed and asked the Buddha : 'How can the same six organs cause me to transmigrate in saṁsāra and be happy in absolute Nirvāṇa?'

The Buddha said: 'Ānanda, both organs and their objects spring from the same source, bondage and liberation are not two different things. Consciousness is illusory, like a flower in the sky. Ānanda, your knowing originates from each phenomenon which takes on form because of your sense organs. Both form and seeing are mutually dependent, like two bundles of rushes that stand by leaning against each other. Therefore, if your intellect acts as the knower, this is the root of your ignorance (but) if it is free from seeing, it will be Nirvāṇa which is transcendental and pure. How then can the latter allow foreign elements to intrude?'

To repeat His instruction, the Buddha read the following gāthā:

True Nature[9] is free from all phenomena[10]
Which are illusions by causes created.[11]
Noumena neither rise nor fall, but all
Phenomena are flowers in the sky.[12]
The unreal reveals the real
But both are but illusions.[13]
Since there is nothing real nor unreal
How can there be a subject and an object?[14]
For between the two there is no true nature like
The point where two rush bundles meet when set uptight.[15]
Tying and untying from the same cause arise,[16]
While the saintly and the worldly are not dual.[17]
Consider underlying nature at the point
Of meeting where both 'is' and 'is not' cannot be.[18]

---

[9] True Nature, or the One Mind, should be the point of departure in the threefold meditative study.

[10] Śamatha, or meditative study of all as void.

[11] Samāpatti, or meditative study of all as unreal.

[12] Dhyāna, or meditative study of the 'Mean' which is inclusive of both unchanged noumenon and changing phenomenon.

[13] Both the real and unreal are relative and should be wiped out so that the absolute can manifest.

[14] Elimination of both organs and sense data to wipe out the illusion of ignorance.

[15] Ignorance comes from the organs and sense data, symbolized by two bundles of rushes leaning against each other to stand upright, but is empty like their point of intersection.

[16] Both tying (delusion) and untying (liberation) come from the same cause, or the mind.

[17] Both the saintly and the worldly come from the same mind and, therefore, are non-dual.

[18] If you look into the underlying nature, you will find that it is beyond all dualities.

If you disregard it you are in delusion,
If you awaken to it you are free at once.[19]
Six knots are untied one after the other;
When six are undone one vanishes as well.[20]
Choose an organ that is all penetrating
To enter the holy stream and attain Bodhi.
Old habits flow like torrents in
Ālaya's subtle consciousness.
Since the real yet unreal can create confusion
I have refrained from revealing it to you.[21]
If mind be set on searching for the mind, that which
At heart is not illusion becomes illusory.[22]
If you stop all grasping then there is nothing real:[23]
If what is not illusion ceases
To arise, where can illusion be?[24]
This is the profound Lotus Dharma (Law),[25]
The precious Bodhi of the royal gem,[26]
The Samādhi of seeing all things as illusion[27]
Which in a finger-snap leads to the state beyond
All study. The unsurpassed Doctrine[28] was followed
By all Bhagavats in all directions
On the One Path that to Nirvāṇa leads.[29]

---

[19] You are deluded because you are confused about this underlying nature, but if you cognize it, you will be enlightened instantly.

[20] All the six organs come from the mind and when you are free from the former the latter also vanishes. This is an appropriate answer to the kung an (koan): 'All things are returnable to One, to where does One return?'

[21] Ālaya, or basic ignorance, is the object to be wiped out by the subjective threefold meditative study. This consciousness is very profound and subtle and changes according to the seeds of old habits accumulated in it since the time without beginning. It comprises both reality and falsehood, hence 'the real yet unreal' which can create confusion in the minds of beginners. For this reason the Buddha did not disclose it to His disciples.

[22] If the true Mind which is basically not an illusion is dung to, it will become one because of your clinging. Then the duality of noumenon and phenomenon is created and screens the true nature.

[23] If you only stop clinging, even the true mind cannot be found.

[24] This is total elimination of both reality and falsehood to expose the Absolute.

[25] The Sūrangama Samādhi is pure and cannot be sullied like the lotus flower.

[26] It is indestructible like the royal diamond and can destroy the darkness of ignorance.

[27] It looks into all phenomena and realizes their illusory and transient nature.

[28] Abhidharma.

[29] This gāthā deals with the profound teaching of the all-embracing Śūrangama Sūtra and answers Ānanda's request for instruction at the beginning of the meeting.

How to Untie the Six Knots

Thus Ānanda and the assembly listened to the compassionate Buddha's unsurpassed sermon and gāthā whose profound meanings were so enlightening and penetrating, that their mental eyes were opened; they praised what they had never seen before. Ānanda then brought his palms together, prostrated and said: 'I have today listened to the Buddha's compassionate teaching which revealed the pure, subtle and permanent Reality of the (self-) nature, but I am still not clear about how to untie the (six) knots one after the other and what you meant by "when the six knots are undone the one also vanishes." Will you again take pity on this assembly and future generations and teach us in order to wash our defilements away?'

The Buddha who was on his lion-seat,[30] adjusted his inner garments and outer robe and took from the teapoy a piece of beautiful cloth which the Yama deva[31] had given Him. Then in the presence of the assembly, He tied a knot and showed it to Ānanda, asking: 'What is this?' Ānanda and the others replied: 'It is a knot.' The Buddha then tied another knot and asked: 'What is this?' They all replied: 'This also is a knot.' The Buddha tied four more knots, showing each to Ānanda and asking 'What is this?' They all replied that each was a knot.

The Buddha said to Ānanda 'When I first tied this cloth, you called it a knot. There is only one piece of cloth but why did you call the second and third ties also knots?' Ānanda replied: 'World Honoured One, although there is only one piece of cloth, if you tie it once, there will be a knot and if you tie it a hundred times, there will be a hundred knots. But this cloth has only six knots because you only tied it six times. Why do you agree to my calling the first tie a knot and disagree to the second and third ones also being called knots?'

The Buddha said: 'Ānanda, originally there was only one piece of cloth but when I tied it six times, there were six knots. As you see it, the length of cloth was the same before but is now different with its six knots. The first knot I tied was called the first one and altogether I tied six of them, do you think that the sixth one can be called the first knot?' Ānanda replied: 'No, World Honoured One, so long as there are six knots, the last one is the sixth and cannot be called the first. Even if I discuss this for the rest of my life, how can I number these six knots in the wrong order?'

The Buddha said: 'It is so; these six knots are different but come from one length of cloth and you cannot reverse their order. It is the same with your six sense organs which, though coming from the same (source),

[30] Siṁhāsana: a lion throne, or couch, a Buddha seat, where the Buddha sits, even when on the bare ground.

[31] A king of the third devaloka, where the times, or seasons, are always good.

are manifestly different. Ānanda, clearly you object to the six knots and prefer one (piece of cloth) but how can you obtain it?' Ānanda replied: 'If these six knots remain, concepts of right and wrong will arise in great confusion, with (such things as) this knot is not that one and that knot is not this one. World Honoured One, if all the knots were untied, there would remain nothing, with complete elimination of thisness and thatness; then in the absence of even one, how can there be six?'

The Buddha said: 'Likewise, when the six knots are untied, the one also vanishes. It is because of confusion in your mad mind since the time without beginning that your intellect gives rise to illusions, the unceasing creation of which disturbs your seeing and causes it to perceive objects in the same way that troubled eyes see dancing flowers. Hence in the clear and bright (Reality) arise without any cause all worldly phenomena such as mountains, rivers, the great earth, saṁsāra and nirvāṇa which are but dancing flowers (created by) confusion, trouble (passions) and inversion.'

Ānanda asked: 'How can one untie these knots created by trouble and contusion?'

Then the Buddha held (up) the piece of cloth, pulled its left end and asked: 'Can it be untied in this way?' Ānanda replied: 'No, World Honoured One.' The Buddha then pulled the right end and asked: 'Can it be untied in this way?' Ānanda replied: 'No, World Honoured One.' The Buddha said: 'I have pulled both ends of the cloth but have been unable to untie the knots. What will you do now?' Ānanda replied: 'World Honoured One, (each) knot should be untied in its center (heart).' The Buddha said: 'Correct, Ānanda, correct. A knot should be untied from its heart. Ānanda, the Buddha Dharma which I expound manifests due to causes and is beyond those coarse forms that come from worldly (concepts of) mixtures and unions. When the Buddha reveals the mundane and supramundane, He knows their chief causes and concurrent conditions. He is even clear about the number of drops of rain in a place as many miles away from here as there are sand grains in the Ganges, as well as why pine trees are straight and brambles crooked, geese white and crows black. Therefore, Ānanda, choose one organ from the six, and if its knot is untied, all objects of sense will vanish of themselves. When all illusions disappear, if this is not Reality, what more do you expect? Ānanda, tell me now if the six knots of this cloth can be untied simultaneously.'

Ānanda replied: 'No, World Honoured One, because they were originally tied one after the other and should be untied in the same order. Although they are in the same piece of cloth, they were not tied simultaneously; how can they now be untied all at once?'

The Buddha said: 'Your six organs should be disengaged in the same way. When you begin to disentangle them, you will realize that the ego is void. When this voidness is perfectly clear, you will realize that all dharma (phenomena) are void. When you are disengaged from dharma, the voidness (of ego and dharma) will vanish.[32] This is called the Patient Endurance of the Uncreate achieved by means of Samādhi in the Bodhisattva stage.'

After Ānanda and the assembly had heard the Buddha's teaching, their understanding was clear and free from doubt and suspicion. Ānanda brought his palms together, prostrated himself and said: 'Today our bodies and minds are clear, at ease and unhindered. Though I have understood what you mean by the disappearance of (both) one and six, I am still unable to perfect my sense organs. World Honoured One, I am like a lonely wanderer and a hapless orphan. How fortunate have I been to meet the Buddha and to be His relative, like a hungry baby who suddenly meets its suckling mother. This gives me a chance to attain the holy goal, but although I have listened to His profound words, I am still unawakened as if I had not heard them. Will you please reveal to me the Ultimate Approach (by means of the appropriate organ)?'

After saying this, he prostrated himself and concentrated on his inner potentiality to receive the profound instruction.

Thereat the World Honoured One said to the great Bodhisattvas and chief Arhats in the assembly: 'I want to ask you, Bodhisattvas and Arhats who have practised my Dharma and have reached the state beyond study, this question: "When you developed your minds to awaken to the eighteen fields of sense, which one did you regard as the best means of perfection and by what methods did you enter the state of Samādhi?"'

Meditation on the six sense data

Kauṇḍinya, (one of) the first five bhiksus, rose from his seat, prostrated himself with his head at the feet of the Buddha and declared: 'When, soon after His enlightenment, we met the Tathāgata in the Mṛgadāva and Kukkuṭa parks, I heard His voice, understood His teaching and awakened to the Four Noble Truths. When questioned by the Buddha, I interpreted them correctly and the Tathāgata sealed my awakening by naming me Ājñāta (Thorough Knowledge). As His wonderful voice was mysteriously all-embracing, I attained arhatship by means of sound. As the Buddha now asks about the best means of perfection, to me sound is the best according to my personal experience.'

---

[32] The six knots stand for the six sense organs, and also for the six illusions of (a) the inborn and (b) discriminative Ego, (c) the inborn and (d) differentiated dharma, and the non-existence of (e) Ego and (f) dharma; all these six illusions should be wiped out before the Absolute is attained. (Cf. Ch'an and Zen Teaching, Third Series, Part III, page 181, *The Sutra of Complete Enlightenment.*)

Upaniṣad then rose from his seat, prostrated himself with his head at the feet of the Buddha and declared: 'I also met the Buddha soon after His enlightenment. After meditating on impurity which I found repulsive and from which I kept, I awakened to the underlying nature of all forms I realized that (even our) bleached bones that came from impurity would be reduced to dust and would finally return to the void. As both form and the void were perceived as non-existent, I achieved the state beyond study. The Tathāgata sealed my understanding and named me Niṣad. After eradicating the (relative) form, wonderful form (surūpa) appeared mysteriously all-embracing. Thus I attained arhatship through meditation on form. As the Buddha now asks about the best means of perfection, to me form is the best according to my personal experience.'

A Bodhisattva named 'Fragrance-adorned' then rose from his seat, prostrated himself with his head at the feet of the Buddha and declared: 'After the Tathāgata had taught me to look into all worldly phenomena, I left Him and retired to set my mind at rest. While observing the rules of pure living, I saw the bhikṣus burn sandal incense. In the stillness, its fragrance entered my nostrils. I inquired into this smell which was neither sandalwood nor voidness, and neither smoke nor fire and which had neither whence to come nor whither to go; thereby my intellect vanished and I achieved the state beyond the stream of transmigration. The Tathāgata sealed my awakening and named me "Fragrance-adorned." After the sudden elimination of (relative) smell, the wonderful fragrance became mysteriously all-embracing. Thus I attained arhatship by means of smell. As the Buddha now asks about the best means of perfection, to me smell is the best according to my personal experience.'

The two Bodhisattvas called Bhaiṣajya-rāja and Bhaiṣajya-samudgata who were present with five hundred Brahmadevas, then rose from their seats, prostrated themselves with their heads at the feet of the Buddha and declared: 'Since the time without beginning we have been skilful physicians in the world and have tasted with our own mouths herbs, plants and all kinds of mineral and stone found in the world (sahā), numbering 108,000 in all. As a result we know perfectly their tastes, whether bitter or sour, salt, insipid, sweet, acrid, etc., their natural, changing or harmonizing properties, and whether they are cooling, heating, poisonous or wholesome. We received instruction from the Tathāgata and knew clearly that taste was neither existing nor non-existent, was neither body nor mind and did not exist apart from them. Since we could discern the cause of taste, we achieved our awakening which was sealed by the Buddha who then named us Bhaiṣajya-rāja and Bhaiṣajya-samudgata. We are now ranked among the "sons of the Dharma king" in this assembly and because of our awakening by means of taste, we have attained the Bodhisattva stage. As the Buddha now asks about the best means of perfection, to us taste is the best according to our personal experience.'

Bhadrapāla who was with sixteen companions who were all great Bodhisattvas, rose from his seat, prostrated himself with his head at the feet of the Buddha and declared: 'When the Buddha with an awe-inspiring voice (Bhīśma-garjita-ghoṣa-svara-rāja) appeared in the world, I heard of the Dharma and left home. At the time of bathing, I followed the rules and entered the bathroom. Suddenly I awakened to the causal water which cleansed neither dirt nor body; thereby I felt at case and realized the state of nothingness. As I had not forgotten my former practice, when I left home to follow the Buddha in my present life, I achieved the state beyond study. That Buddha named me Bhadrapāla because of my awakening to wonderful touch and my realization of the rank of a son of Buddha. As the Buddha asks now about the best means of perfection, to me touch is the best according to my personal experience.'

Mahākāśyapa who was present with the bhikṣuṇī 'Golden Light' and others (of his group), then rose from his seat, prostrated himself with his head at the feet of the Buddha and declared: 'In a former aeon, when Candra-sūrya-pradīpa Buddha appeared in this world, I had a chance of following him and of hearing the Dharma which I practised. After he had passed away, I revered his relics, lit lamps to perpetuate his light and decorated his statue with pure gold powder. Since then, in every subsequent reincarnation, my body has been radiant with perfect golden light. This bhikṣuṇī "Golden Light" and the others who are with her, are my retinue because we developed the same mind at the same time. I looked into the six changing sense data which can be reduced to complete extinction only through the state of nirvāṇa. Thus my body and mind were able to pass through hundreds and thousands of aeons in a finger-snap. By eradicating all dharma (things and ideas), I realized arhatship and the World Honoured One declared that I was the foremost disciplinarian. I awakened to the wonderful dharma, thereby putting an end to the stream of transmigration. As the Buddha now asks about the best means of perfection, to me dharma are the best according to my personal experience.'

Meditation on the five sense organs

Aniruddha then rose from his seat, prostrated himself with his head at the feet of the Buddha and declared: 'After I left home, I was always very fond of sleep and the Tathāgata scolded me, saying that I was like an animal. After this severe reprimand, I wept bitterly and blamed myself. Because of my sadness, I did not sleep for seven successive nights and went completely blind. Then the World Honoured One taught me how to take delight in the Enlightening Vajra Samādhi which enabled me to perceive, not with my eyes (but my mind), the Pure Truth pervading the ten directions, very clearly perceptible, as easy to see as a mango held in my own hand. The Tathāgata sealed my attainment of arhatship. As He now asks about the best means of perfection, to me seeing is, according to my personal experience, the best which is made possible by turning the organ of sight back to its source.'

Kṣudrapanthaka then rose from his seat, prostrated himself with his head at the feet of the Buddha and declared: 'I did not know much (about the Dharma) for want of reading and reciting (the Scriptures). When I first met the Buddha, I heard of the Dharma and then left home. I tried to memorize a line of His gāthā but failed for a hundred days because as soon as I could retain its first words, I forgot the last ones, and when I could remember the last words, I forgot the first ones. The Buddha took pity on my stupidity and taught me how to live in a quiet retreat and to regularize my breathing. At the time I looked exhaustively into each in and out breath and realized that its rise, stay, change and end lasted only an instant (kṣaṇa); thereby my mind became clear and unhindered until I stepped out of the stream of transmigration and finally attained arhatship. I came to stay with the Buddha who sealed my realization of the state beyond study. As He now asks about the best means of perfection, to me breathing is the best according to my personal experience in turning the breath back to the condition of nothingness.'

Gavāṁpati then rose from his seat, prostrated himself with his head at the feet of the Buddha and declared: 'Because of my verbal sin when I trifled with monks in a former aeon, in every succeeding reincarnation I have been born with a mouth that always chews the cud like a cow. The Tathāgata taught me the pure and clean doctrine of One Mind which enabled me to eliminate the conception of mind for my entry into the state of Samādhi. I looked into tasting, realized that it was neither (a subjective) substance nor (an objective) thing and leaped beyond the stream of transmigration; I thereby disengaged myself from both the inner body and mind and the outer universe and was released from the three worlds of existence. I was like a bird escaping from its cage, thus avoiding impurities and defilements. With my Dharma eye now pure and clean, I attained arhatship and the Tathāgata personally sealed my realization of the stage beyond study. As the Buddha now asks about the best means of perfection, to me the turning of taste back to its knower is the best according to my personal experience.'

Pilindavatsa then rose from his seat, prostrated himself with his head at the feet of the Buddha and declared: 'When I first followed the Buddha to enter upon the Path, very often I heard the Tathāgata speak about the worldly which could not give joy and happiness. (One day) I went to town to beg for food, and as I was thinking about His teaching, I stepped inadvertently on a poisonous thorn that pierced my foot and caused me to feel pain all over my body. I thought of my body which knew and felt this great pain. Although there was this feeling, I looked into my pure and clean mind which no pain could affect. I also thought, "How can this one body of mine have two sorts of feeling?" and after a short (mental) concentration on this, all of a sudden, my body and mind seemed to be non-existent and three weeks later I achieved the stage beyond the stream of transmigration and thereby attained arhatship. The Buddha personally sealed my realization of the stage beyond study. As He now asks about the best means of perfection, to me the pure awareness that wipes out the (conception of) body is the best according to my personal experience.'

Subhūti then rose from his seat, prostrated himself with his head at the feet of the Buddha and declared: 'As my mind was already free from all hindrances in former aeons, I can now remember my previous reincarnations as countless as the sands in the Ganges. Even when I was a foetus in my mother's womb, I had already awakened to the condition of still voidness which subsequently expanded to fill all the ten directions and which enabled me to teach living beings how to awaken to their absolute nature. Thanks to the Tathāgata, I realized the absolute voidness of self-natured awareness, and with the perfection of my unmaterial nature, I attained arhatship, thereby entering suddenly into the Tathāgata's Precious Brightness which was as immense as space and the ocean, wherein I (partially) achieved Buddha knowledge. The Buddha sealed my attainment of the stage beyond study; I am, therefore, regarded as the foremost disciple because of my understanding of immaterial self-nature. As the Buddha now asks about the best means of perfection, according to my personal experience, the best consists in perceiving the unreality of all phenomena, with the elimination of even this unreality, in order to reduce all things to nothingness.'

Meditation on the six consciousnesses

Śāriputra then rose from his seat, prostrated himself with his head at the feet of the Buddha and declared: 'In former aeons, the sight-perception of my mind was already pure and clean, and in my subsequent incarnations as countless as the sands in the Ganges, I could see without hindrance through all things either on a worldly or supramundane plane. (One day), I met on the road the two brothers Kāśyapa who were both preaching the doctrine of causality, and after listening to them, my mind awakened to the Truth and thereby became extensive and boundless. I then left home to follow the Buddha and achieved perfect sight perception thereby acquiring fearlessness, attaining arhatship and qualifying as the Buddha's

Elder Son - born from the Buddha's mouth and by transformation of the Dharma. As the Buddha now asks about the best means of perfection, according to my personal experience, the best consists in realizing the most illuminating knowledge by means of the mind's radiant sight-perception.'

Samantabhadra Bodhisattva then rose from his seat, prostrated himself with his head at the feet of the Buddha and declared: 'I was already a son of the Dharma king when formerly I was with the Tathāgatas who were countless as the sands in the Ganges. All the Buddhas in the ten directions who teach their disciples to plant Bodhisattva roots, urge them to practise Samantabhadra deeds which are called after my name. World Honoured One, I always use my mind to listen in order to distinguish the variety of views held by living beings. If in a place, separated from here by a number of worlds as countless as the sands in the Ganges, a living being practises Samantabhadra deeds, I mount at once a six tusked elephant and reproduce myself in a hundred and a thousand apparitions to come to his aid. Even if he is unable to see me because of his great karmic obstruction, I secretly lay my hand on his head to protect and comfort him so that he can succeed. As the Buddha now asks about the best means of perfection, according to my personal experience, the best consists in hearing with the mind, which leads to non-discriminative discernment.'

Sundarananda then rose from his seat, prostrated himself with his head at the feet of the Buddha and declared: 'When I left home to follow the Buddha, although fully ordained, I failed to realize the state of Samādhi because my mind was always unsettled; I was, therefore, unable to reach the condition beyond the stream of transmigration. The World Honoured One then taught me and Kauṣṭhila to fix the mind on the tip of the nose. I started this meditation and some three weeks later, I saw that the breath that went in and out of my nostrils was like smoke; inwardly both body and mind were clear and I looked through the (external) world which became a pure emptiness like crystal everywhere. The smoke gradually disappeared and my breath became white. As my mind opened, I achieved the state beyond the stream of transmigration. Both my in and out breaths, now bright, illumined the ten directions so that I attained the arhat stage. The World Honoured One prophesied that I would win enlightenment. As He now asks about the best means of perfection, according to my personal experience, the best is to eliminate breath which will then turn radiant, ensuring the attainment of the stage of perfection beyond the stream of transmigration?

Pūrṇamaitrāyaṇīputra then rose from his seat, prostrated himself with his head at the feet of the Buddha and declared: 'In former aeons, my power of speech was unhindered and I preached the (doctrine of) misery and unreality, thereby penetrating deep into the absolute Reality. I (also) expounded in the assembly the Tathāgata's Dharma doors to enlightenment as uncountable as the sands in the Ganges, and thereby won fearlessness. The World Honoured One knew that I had acquired the great power of speech and taught me how to perform the Buddha work by preaching. There, in his presence, I assisted Him in turning the Wheel of the Law and since I could give the lion's roar, I attained arhatship. He sealed my unexcelled skill in expounding the Dharma. As He now asks about the best means of perfection, according to my opinion, the best consists in employing the Dharma voice to subdue the enmity of Māra and to stop the stream of transmigration.'

Upāli then rose from his seat, prostrated himself with his head at the feet of the Buddha and declared: 'I personally accompanied the Buddha and we climbed the city wall to flee from home. With my own eyes, I saw how He endured hardship in His practice during the first six years of ascetic life, subdued all demons, overcame heretics and freed Himself from worldly desires and all impure efflux (āsrava) from the mind. He personally taught me discipline, including the three thousand regulations and eighty thousand lines of conduct which purified all my innate and conventional subtle karmas.[33] As my body and mind were in the nirvanic state, I attained arhatship and the Tathāgata sealed my mind because of my strict observance of discipline and control of body. I am now a pillar of discipline in this assembly and am regarded as the foremost disciple. As the Buddha now asks about the best means of perfection, in my opinion, the best consists in disciplining the body so that it can free itself from all restraints and then in disciplining the mind so that it can be all-pervading, which results in the freedom of both body and mind.'

Mahā-Maudgalyāyana then rose from his seat, prostrated himself with his head at the feet of the Buddha and declared: 'One day as I was begging for food in the street, I met the three Kāśyapa brothers, Uruvilvā, Gayā and Nadī, who preached the profound doctrine of causality taught by the Tathāgata. Suddenly my mind opened and became all-pervading. Then the Tathāgata gave me a monk's robe and when I wore it, my hair and beard fell out. I rambled in the ten directions and met no obstruction. I thus acquired transcendental power which proved the foremost and led to my attainment of arhatship. Not only the World Honoured One, but all the Tathāgatas in the ten directions praised my super-natural powers which were perfect, pure, sovereign and fearless. As the Buddha now asks about the best means of perfection, in my opinion the best consists of returning

[33] Karma against natural law, e.g. stealing, and karma against conventional rules, e.g. for a monk to eat meat.

to stillness to allow the light of the mind to appear just as muddy water by settling becomes pure and clean as crystal.'

Meditation on the seven elements[34]

Usschuṣma then came forward in front of the Tathāgata, joined the palms of his two hands, prostrated himself with his head at the feet of the Buddha and declared: 'I can still remember that in a very remote aeon, I was filled with sensual desire. At the time a Buddha called "The King of Immateriality" appeared in the world. According to him, those with lustful desires increased their own hell fires. He then taught me to meditate on the bones in my body, on my four limbs and on my warm and cold breaths. So by turning inwardly the spiritual light for pointed concentration, my lustful mind turned into the fire of wisdom. Since then, I was called "Fire Head" by all the Buddhas. Because of my powerful Fire Light Samādhi, I attained arhatship. Then I took my great vow to become a demigod (vīra) so that when all Buddhas were about to attain enlightenment, I would personally help them to overcome the enmity of Māra. As the Buddha now asks about the best means of perfection, according to my opinion, the best consists in looking into the non-existent heat in my body and mind in order to remove all hindrances thereto and to put an end to the stream of transmigration so that the great Precious Light can appear and lead to the realization of Supreme Bodhi.'

Dharaṇimdhara Bodhisattva then rose from his seat, prostrated himself with his head at the feet of the Buddha and declared: 'I still remember that formerly when the Buddha of Universal Light appeared in the World, I was a bhikṣu who used to level all obstacles, build bridges and carry sand and earth to improve the main roads, ferries, rice-fields and dangerous passes which were in bad condition or impassable to horses and carts. Thus I continued to toil for a long time in which an uncountable number of Buddhas appeared in the World. If someone made a purchase at the market-place and required another to carry it home for him, I did it without charge. When Viśvabhū Buddha[35] appeared in the world and famine was frequent, I became a carrier charging only one coin no matter whether the distance was long or short. If an ox cart could not move in a bog, I used my supernatural power to push its wheels free. One day the king invited that Buddha to a feast: as the road was bad, I levelled it for him. The Tathāgata Viśvabhū placed his hand on my head and said: "You should level your mind-ground, then all things in the world will be on the same

[34] The seven elements are: fire, earth, water, wind, space, consciousness and perception.

[35] The third of the seven Buddhas of antiquity. Cf. Ch'an and Zen Teaching, Second Series, page 28.

level," (Upon hearing this), my mind opened and I perceived that the molecules of my body did not differ from those of which the world is made. These molecules were such that they did not touch one another and could not be touched even by sharp weapons. I then awakened to the patient endurance of the uncreate and thereby attained arhatship. Then by turning my mind inwards, I realized the Bodhisattva stage and when I heard the Tathāgatas expound the Buddha's Universal Knowledge in the profound Lotus Sutra, I was the first listener to be awakened to it and was made a leader of the assembly. As the Buddha now asks about the best means of perfection, in my opinion, the best consists in looking into the sameness of body and universe which are created by infection from falsehood arising from the Tathāgata store, until this defilement vanishes and is replaced by perfect wisdom, which then leads to the realization of Supreme Bodhi.'

Candraprabha Bodhisattva then rose from his seat, prostrated himself with his head at the feet of the Buddha and declared: 'I still remember that in the remotest of aeons countless as the sands in the Ganges, there was a Buddha, called Varuṇa, who appeared in the world and taught Bodhisattvas to contemplate the element of water in order to enter into the state of Samādhi.

'This method consists in looking into the body wherein all watery elements do not by nature suppress one another, using as subjects of meditation-first tears and snot, and then saliva, secretion, blood, urine and excrement, and then reversing the order, thereby perceiving that this element of water in the body does not differ from that of the fragrant oceans that surround the Pure Lands of Buddhas, situated beyond our world.

'When I achieved this contemplation, I succeeded in realizing only the sameness of the element of water (everywhere) but failed to relinquish (my view of) the body. I was then a bhikṣu practicing dhyāna and when my disciple peeped into the room, he saw that it was filled entirely with clear water, without anything else. As he was an ignorant boy, he picked up a broken tile, threw it into the water with a splash, gazed curiously and left. When I came out of my dhyāna state, I suddenly felt pain in my heart as if I had the same trouble which Śariputra had with a wicked demon. I thought, "Since I have realized arhatship, I should be free from all causal ailments. Why today, all of a sudden, have I pain in my heart; is it not a sign of my backsliding?" When the boy returned and related what he had seen and done during my meditation, I said: "When next you see water in my room, open the door, enter the water and take away the broken tile." The boy obeyed, for when I again entered the dhyāna state, he saw the same broken tile in the water; he then opened the door and removed the tile. When I came out of dhyāna, my pain had vanished. Later, I met countless Buddhas before I encountered Sāgara-varadhara-buddhi-vikrīḍita-bhijña Buddha (under whose instruction) I succeeded in relinquishing (the conception of) body, thereby realizing perfect union of this body and the fragrant oceans in the ten directions with absolute voidness, without any further differentiation. This is why I was called "a son of a Buddha" and was qualified to attend all Bodhisattva meetings.

'As the Buddha now asks about the best means of perfection, in my opinion the best consists in achieving the unhindered universalizing pervasion of the element water, thereby realizing the patient endurance of the uncreate which ensures Complete Enlightenment.'

The Bodhisattva of Crystal Light then rose from his seat, prostrated himself with his head at the feet of the Buddha and declared: 'I still remember that once, in the remotest of aeons countless as the sands in the Ganges, there was a Buddha called "Infinite Voice" who appeared in the world to reveal to Bodhisattvas the profoundly enlightened fundamental awareness which, by looking into this world and the bodily forms of all living beings, could perceive that all were created by the power of the wind arising from illusory concurrent causes. At the time, I inquired into the (illusory) setting up of the world, changing time, bodily motion and motionlessness, stirring of mind, in other words all kinds of movement which were fundamentally the same and did not differ from one another. I then realized that these movements had neither whence to come nor whither to go and that all living beings in the ten directions, as uncountable as the dust, came from the same falsehood. Likewise, all living beings in every small world of the great chiliocosm were like mosquitoes in a trap in which they hummed aimlessly and created a mad tumult. Soon after meeting that Buddha, I realized the patient endurance of the uncreate. As my mind opened, I perceived the land of the Imperturbable Buddha in the eastern region where I was admitted as a son of the Dharma king, serving all the Buddhas in the ten directions. My body and mind gave out rays of light that illumined all the worlds without obstruction.

'As the Buddha now asks about the best means of perfection, in my opinion the best consists in looking into the power of the element of wind which has nothing (real) on which to rely, thereby awakening to the Bodhi mind so as to enter Samādhi and (then) to unite with the profound One Mind expounded by the Buddhas in the ten directions.'

Ākaśagarbha Bodhisattva then rose from his seat, prostrated himself with his head at the feet of the Buddha and declared: 'When the Tathāgata and I were with Dīpaṁkara Buddha and realized our boundless bodies, I held in my hands four big precious gems[36] which illumined all Buddha

[36] This Bodhisattva had then succeeded in his meditation on the four elements of earth, water, fire and wind, which he could perceive as identical with the underlying principle, thus transmuting them into four precious gems.

lands in the ten directions, as uncountable as dust, and transmuted them into the (absolute) void. Then my own mind appeared like a great mirror emitting ten kinds of mysterious precious light[37] which penetrated the ten directions, reaching the boundaries of space and causing all pure lands of Buddhas to enter the mirror and then to intermingle freely with my own body which was just like unobstructive space. (Then) my body could enter perfectly as many (samsaric) countries as there are grains of dust to carry out far and wide the Buddha works (of salvation) so that universality could prevail (everywhere). This great transcendental power derived from my close inquiry into the four elements which had nothing real to rely upon and into false thinking that rose and fell (alternately and ended in nothingness). I realized the non-duality of space and the sameness of the Buddha's (pure lands) and samsaric worlds, thereby achieving the patient endurance of the uncreate.

'As the Buddha now asks about the best means of perfection, according to my own experience, the best consists in the close examination into boundless space, leading to entry into Samādhi and perfecting thereby the mysterious spiritual power.

Maitreya Bodhisattva then rose from his seat, prostrated himself with his head at the feet of the Buddha and declared: 'I still remember that in the remotest of aeons as uncountable as the dust, there was a Buddha called Candra-sūrya-pradīpa who appeared in the world (to convert others). I followed him to leave home. However, I (still) cherished worldly fame and liked to mix with noble clans. Then the Tathāgata taught me how to practise dhyāna meditation on the mind's consciousness[38] in order to realize the state of Samādhi. Ever since the following aeons, I have used this Samādhi to serve Buddhas as many as the sands in the Ganges, thereby eliminating completely my (previous) mind set on worldly fame. When Dīpaṁkara Buddha appeared in the world, (under his instruction) I realized the consciousness-perfecting supreme Samādhi of the mind which enabled me to perceive that all Tathāgata (stores) and samsaric worlds, purity and impurity and existence and non-existence were but appearances caused by my own mind's transformations. World Honoured One, because of my clear understanding that only the mind's consciousness was the cause (of all externals, I perceived) an unlimited number of Tathāgatas coming out of the nature of consciousness, hence (the Buddha's) prophecy that I shall be His successor.

---

[37] To perceive the fundamental sameness in the ten dharmadhātus, i.e. the six samsaric worlds and the four saintly realms.

[38] Mind only, the doctrine that nothing exists apart from mind, that the three worlds of existence (of desire, form and beyond form) come from the *mind only* and that all dharma (things) are created by *consciousness* only.

'As the Buddha now asks about the best means of perfection, my opinion is that the best consists of close examination into all appearances which are created by consciousness only, in order to perfect the conscious mind, thereby realizing complete reality and ensuring non-reliance on externals and the breaking of all attachments caused by discrimination, thereby achieving the patient endurance of the uncreate.'

Mahāsthāma, a son of the Dharma king, who was the head of a group of fifty-two Bodhisattvas, rose from his seat, prostrated himself with his head at the feet of the Buddha and declared: 'I still remember that in the remotest of aeons countless as the sands in the Ganges, there was a Buddha called Amitābha who was succeeded by eleven other Tathāgatas in that kalpa. The last one was called the "Buddha Whose Light Surpassed that of the Sun and Moon"; he taught me how to realize the state of Samādhi by thinking exclusively of (Amitābha) Buddha. By way of illustration, if a man concentrates his mind on someone else while the latter always forgets him, both may meet and see, but without recognizing, each other. However, if both are keen on thinking of each other, their keenness will grow from one incarnation to another until they become inseparable like a body and its shadow. The Tathāgatas in the ten directions have compassion for all living beings and always think of them, like a mother who never ceases thinking of her son. If the son runs away, her thoughts of him will not help. But if he also thinks of her with the same keenness, they will not be separated in spite of the passing of transmigrations. If a living being remembers and thinks of the Buddha, he is bound to behold Him in his present or future incarnation. He will not be far from the Buddha and thus without the aid of any other expedient, his mind will be opened. He is like a man whose body, perfumed by incense, gives out fragrance; hence his name "One Glorified by (Buddha's) Fragrance and Light." From my fundamental cause-ground and with all my thoughts concentrated on the Buddha, I achieved the patient endurance of the uncreate. (This is why) I help all living beings of this world to control their thoughts by repeating the Buddha's name so that they can reach the Pure Land. As the Buddha now asks about the best means of perfection, I hold that nothing can surpass the perfect control of the six senses with continuous pure thoughts in order to realize Samādhi.'

Meditation on the organ of hearing

Thereupon Avalokiteśvara Bodhisattva rose from his seat, prostrated himself with his head at the feet of the Buddha and declared: 'I still remember that long before numbers of aeons countless as the sand grains in the Ganges, a Buddha called Avalokiteśvara appeared in the world. When I was with Him, I developed the Bodhi Mind and, for my entry into

Samādhi, I was instructed by Him to practise meditation by means of the organ of hearing.

'At first by directing the organ of hearing into the stream of meditation, this organ was detached from its object, and by wiping out (the concept of) both sound and stream-entry, both disturbance and stillness became clearly non-existent. Thus advancing step by step both hearing and its object ceased completely, but I did not stop where they ended. When the awareness' of this state and this state itself were realized as non-existent, both subject and object merged into the void, the awareness of which became all-embracing. With further elimination of the void and its object both creation and annihilation vanished giving way to the state of Nirvāṇa which then manifested.

'Suddenly I leaped over both the mundane and supramundane, thereby realizing an all-embracing brightness pervading the ten directions, and acquired two unsurpassed (merits). The first was in accord with the fundamental Profound Enlightened Mind of all the Buddhas high up in the ten directions and possessed the same merciful power as the Tathāgata. The second was in sympathy with all living beings in the six realms of existence here below in the ten directions and shared with them the same plea for compassion.

'World Honoured One, as I (followed and) made offerings to the Tathāgata Avalokiteśvara. He taught me to use my illusory hearing and sublimate it to realize the Diamond (Vajra) Samādhi which gave me the same power of mercy of all Buddhas and enabled me to transform myself into thirty-two bodily forms for the purpose of visiting all countries in saṁsāra (to convert and liberate living beings).

'World Honoured One, it there are Bodhisattvas who practice Samādhi to attain the transcendental (Mean), when there is a chance for them to realize absolute Wisdom, I will appear as a Buddha to teach them the Dharma to liberate them.

'If there are solitary students seeking (only) self-enlightenment, who practise the stillness of Nirvāṇa, when there is a chance for them to realize it, I will appear as a teacher of self-enlightenment to teach them the Dharma to liberate them.

'If there are students of the Four Noble Truths who, after realizing the unreality of suffering and its accumulation, tread the Path leading to the extinction of passions, when there is a chance for them to achieve this, I will appear as a hearer (śrāvaka) to teach them the Dharma to liberate them.

If there are living beings who realize (the harmfulness of) desire in the mind and abstain from all worldly cravings to achieve purity of body, I will appear as Brahmā to teach them the Dharma to liberate them.

'If there are living beings who desire to be lords of devas to rule over the realms of the gods, I will appear as Śakra to teach them the Dharma so that they reach their goals.

'If there are living beings who wish to roam freely in the ten directions, I will appear as Iśvaradeva to teach them the Dharma so that they reach their goals.

'If there are living beings who wish to fly freely in empty space, I will appear as Maheśvara to teach them the Dharma so that they reach their goals.

'If there are living beings who wish to be lords of ghosts and spirits to protect their countries, I will appear as a great warrior to teach them the Dharma so that they reach their goals.

'If there are living beings who wish to rule over the world to protect all its inhabitants, I will appear as a deva king of the four quarters to teach them the Dharma so that they reach their goals.

'If there are living beings who wish to be reborn in the palace of devas to command ghosts and spirits, I will appear as a son of the deva king of the four quarters to teach them the Dharma so that they reach their goals.

'If there are living beings who wish to be kings of human beings, I will appear as a king to teach them the Dharma so that they reach their goals.

'If there are living beings who wish to be heads of clans to enjoy the respects of their clansmen, I will appear as a respectable elder (gṛhapati) to teach them the Dharma so that they reach their goals.

'If there are living beings who enjoy discussing well-known sayings and practise pure living, I will appear as a respectable scholar to teach them the Dharma so that they reach their goals.

'If there are living beings who wish to govern cities and towns, I will appear as a magistrate to teach them the Dharma so that they reach their goals.

'If there are living beings who delight in practising mysticism for self-welfare, I will appear as a Brahmin to teach them the Dharma so that they reach their goals.

'If there are men who are keen on study and learning and leave home to practise the rules of morality and discipline, I will appear as a bhikṣu to teach them the Dharma so that they reach their goals.

'If there are women who are eager to study and learn and leave home to observe the precepts, I will appear as a bhikṣuṇī to teach them the Dharma so that they reach their goals.

'If there are men who observe the five precepts, I will appear as a upāsaka to teach them the Dharma so that they reach their goals.

'If there are women who observe the five precepts, I will appear as a upāsikā to teach them the Dharma so that they reach their goals.

If there are women who are keen to fulfil their home duties thereby setting a good example to other families and the whole country, I will appear as a queen, a princess or a noble lady to teach them the Dharma so that they reach their goals.

'If there are young men who are chaste, I will appear as a celibate youth to teach them the Dharma so that they reach their goals.

'If there are young women who are keen to avoid carnality in order to preserve their virginity, I will appear as a maiden to teach them the Dharma so that they reach their goals.

'If there are gods who wish to be freed from bondage in their realms, I will appear as a deva to teach them the Dharma so that they reach their goals.

'If there are dragons (nāgas) who wish to be freed from bondage in their realms, I will appear as a nāga to teach them the Dharma so that they reach their goals.

'If there are yakṣas who wish to be freed from bondage in their realms, I will appear as a yakṣa to teach them the Dharma so that they reach their goals.

'If there are gandharvas who wish to be freed from bondage in their realms, I will appear as a gandharva to teach them the Dharma so that they reach their goals.

'If there are asuras who wish to be freed from bondage in their realms, I will appear as an asura to teach them the Dharma so that they reach their goals.

'If there are garuḍas who wish to be freed from bondage in their realms, I will appear as a garuḍa to teach them the Dharma so that they reach their goals.

'If there are kinnaras who wish to be freed from bondage in their realms, I will appear as a kinnara to teach them the Dharma so that they reach their goals.

'If there are mahoragas who wish to be freed from bondage in their realms, I will appear as a mahoraga to teach them the Dharma so that they reach their goals.

'If there are living beings who wish to be reborn as human beings, I will appear in human form to teach them the Dharma so that they reach their goals.

If there are non-human beings with or without forms and either thoughtful or thoughtless, who wish to be freed from bondage in their realms, I will appear as one of them to teach them the Dharma so that they reach their goals.

'These are my thirty-two transformation-bodies in response to (the needs of) all countries in saṁsāra, achieved by means of the uncreated sovereign power of Samādhi realized in my practice of sublimating the faculty of hearing.

'World Honoured One, I also use this uncreated sovereign power of Diamond Samādhi, derived from sublimating hearing, to share with all living beings in the six realms in the ten directions the same plea for compassion, and to bestow upon them fourteen kinds of fearlessness which emanate from my body and mind.

1. 'Since I myself do not meditate on sound but on the meditator, I cause all suffering beings to look into the sound of their voices in order to obtain liberation.[39]
2. 'By returning (discriminative) intellect to its (absolute) source, I cause them to avoid being burned when they find themselves in a great fire.
3. 'By returning hearing to its source, I cause them to avoid drowning when they are adrift on the sea.
4. 'By stopping wrong thinking and thereby cleansing their minds of harmfulness, I lead them to safety when they wander in the realm of evil ghosts.
5. 'By sublimating their (wrong) hearing to restore its absolute condition, thereby purifying all six organs and perfecting their functions, I cause them, when in danger, to be immune from sharp weapons which become blunt and useless like water that cannot be cut and daylight that cannot be blown away, because their (underlying) nature does not change.
6. 'By perfecting the sublimation of their hearing, its bright light pervades the whole Dharma realm to destroy the darkness (of ignorance) thereby dazzling evil beings such as yakṣa, rakṣa, kumbhāṇḍa, piśācī, pūtana, etc., who cannot see them when meeting them.
7. 'When hearing is reversed so that sound vanishes completely, all illusory objects of sense disappear so that (practisers) are freed from fetters which can no longer restrain them.
8. 'The elimination of sound to perfect hearing results in universal compassion so that they can pass through regions infested with robbers and bandits who cannot plunder them.

[39] This is a very profound meditation which readers should not let pass without careful study if they wish to know why Avalokiteśvara is so popular in Far Eastern countries where he is the merciful patron saint. By discarding the sound to look into the meditator himself, that is into the nature of hearing, he disengages himself from both organs and sense data and thereby realizes his all-embracing Buddha nature which contains all living beings. By developing their pure faith in him and by calling his name, or concentrating on him, they achieve singleness of mind that mingles with his Bodhi substance and become one with him; hence their liberation from sufferings which do not exist in the absolute state.

9. 'The sublimation of hearing disengages them from the objects of sense and makes them immune from (attractive) forms, thereby enabling lustful beings to get rid of desires and cravings.
10. 'The sublimation of sound eliminates all sense data and results in the perfect mingling of each organ with its objects and the total eradication of subject and object, thereby enabling all vindictive brings to bury anger and hate.
11. 'After the elimination of sense data and the return to the bright (Reality), both inner body and mind and outer phenomena become crystal clear and free from all hindrances, so that dull and ignorant unbelievers (icchantika) can get rid of the darkness of ignorance.
12. 'When their bodies are in harmony with the nature of hearing, they can, from their immutable state of enlightenment (bodhimaṇḍala), re-enter the world (to liberate others) without harming the worldly, and can go anywhere to make offerings to Buddhas countless as dust, serving every Tathāgata in the capacity of a son of the King of the Law and having the power to give male heirs with blessed virtues and wisdom to childless people who want boys.
13. 'The perfecting of the six organs unifies their divided functions so that they become all-embracing, thus revealing the Great Mirror (Wisdom) and immaterial Tathāgata womb compatible with all Dharma doors taught by Buddhas as uncountable as dust. They can bestow upright, blessed, gracious, and respect-inspiring girls on childless parents who want daughters.
14. 'In this great chiliocosm which contains a hundred lacs of suns and moons, there are now Bodhisattvas countless as sand grains in sixty-two[40] Ganges rivers. They practise the Dharma to set a good cxample to all living beings by befriending, teaching and converting them; in their wisdom their expedient methods differ. Because I used one penetrating organ which led to my realization through the faculty of hearing, my body and mind embrace the whole Dharma-realm in which I teach all living beings to concentrate their minds on calling my name. The merits that follow are the same as those derived from calling on the names of all these Bodhisattvas. World Honoured One, my single name does not differ from those uncountable ones, because of my practice and training which led to my true enlightenment. These are the fourteen fearless (powers) which I bestow upon living beings.

[40] The digit 6 stands for the sixth consciousness, or mad mind, which creates the duality of ego and dharma, symbolized by the digit 2. The duty of every Bodhisattva is to liberate living beings deceived by the illusions thus created.

'World Honoured One, because of my Perfect Understanding which led to my attainment of the Supreme Path, I acquired four inconceivable absolute virtues.

1. 'When I first realized the hearing mind which was most profound, the Essence of Mind (i.e. the Tathāgata store) disengaged itself from hearing and could no longer be divided by seeing, hearing, feeling and knowing, and so became one pure and clean all-pervading precious Bodhi. This is why I can take on different wonderful forms and master a countless number of esoteric mantras. I can appear with one, three, five, seven, nine, eleven and up to 108, 1,000, 10,000 and 84,000 sovereign (cakra) faces; with two, four, six, eight, ten, twelve, fourteen, sixteen, eighteen, twenty, twenty-four and up to 108, 1,000, 10,000 and 84,000 arms making various gestures (mudrās); and with two, three, four, nine up to 108, 1,000, 10,000 and 84,000 clean and pure precious eyes, either merciful or wrathful, and in a state either of still imperturbability (dhyāna-samādhi) or of absolute wisdom (prajñā) to save and protect living beings so that they can enjoy great freedom.
2. 'Because of my mediation by means of the (organ of) hearing, which resulted in my disengagement from the six sense data, like a sound going through a wall without hindrance, I can, with each appearance and with the aid of each mantra, bestow fearlessness upon (suffering) beings in countries as countless as dust in the ten directions in which I am regarded as the Giver of Dauntlessness.
3. 'Because of the perfection which I won by sublimating the appropriate organ, living beings in countries which I visit (lay down their desires and attachments and) offer their bodies and treasures to implore my compassion.
4. 'As I have realized the Buddha mind and attained Ultimate (Reality) I can make offerings to the Tathāgatas in ten directions and satisfy living beings in the six worlds who seek (virtuous) wives, (good) sons, samādhi, long life and even parinirvāṇa.

'As the Buddha now asks about the best means of perfection, my method which consists in regulating the organ of hearing so as to quiet the mind for its entry into the stream of mediation leading to the state of Samādhi and attainment of Enlightenment is the best.

'World Honoured One, that Buddha praised my excellent method of perfection and gave me, in the presence of the assembly, the name of Avalokitcśvara. Because of my all-embracing (absolute function of) hearing, my name is known everywhere.'

Thereupon, the Buddha, from His lion-seat, sent out from the five members of His body, rays of light which reached and shone on the heads of the Tathāgatas and Bodhisattvas countless as dust in the ten directions. In return countless Tathāgatas sent back rays of light which shone on the heads of the Buddha, great Bodhisattvas and Arhats in the assembly, causing the groves and streams to intone the Dharma and uncountable rays of light to interlace in precious nets, a spectacle never seen before. As a result, all (the Bodhisattvas and Arhats in the assembly) realized the Diamond Samādhi. At the same time showers of green, yellow, red and white lotus blossoms turned the whole of space into a seven coloured expanse and caused mountains, rivers and the great earth to disappear and all the countless other realms to merge into one universe filled with songs and recitations.[41]

Thereupon, the Tathāgata said to Mañjuśri: 'Son of the Dharma king, these twenty-five Bodhisattvas and Arhats who no longer need to study and learn, have related the expedient methods used by them at the start of their practice for their realization of Bodhi. In reality each of these methods does not differ from, and is neither superior nor inferior to the others. Tell me which one of them is suitable to Ānanda so that he can awaken to it and which one is easy of achievement, for the benefit of living beings who, after my nirvāṇa, wish to practise with the Bodhisattva vehicle in their search for Supreme Bodhi.'

Mañjuśrī's Gāthā Teaching the Appropriate Method for Human Beings

As commanded, Mañjuśrī rose from his seat, prostrated himself with his head at the feet of the Buddha and reverently chanted the following gāthā:

Perfect and clear by nature is the Bodhi ocean,
Pure and faultless Bodhi is in essence wonderful.
Its fundamental brightness shone, so by chance creating
An object which then obscured its radiant nature.
Thus in delusion there appeared one-sided emptiness
In which an imaginary world arbitrarily was built.
Steadying itself, the thinking process made the continents
While the (illusory) knower became a living being.
The voidness so created within Bodhi
Is but a bubble in the ocean. Worldly

---

[41] This reveals the blissful realm of Avalokiteśvara's reward-body (sambhoga-kāya) wherein all dualities and contraries are replaced by a uniform state of Sublime Majesty.

Realms, countless as the dust, arose
In this (relative) emptiness.
When the bubble bursts, the void's unreality
Is exposed: how much more so is that of the three realms?
Though all return to One Nature at the source,
There are many expedient methods for the purpose.
Though holy nature pervades all, direct
Or inverse methods are expedients;
Hence newly initiated minds of different
Aptitudes are quick or slow to enter Samādhi.
Form which from thought crystallizes
Is too difficult to look through.
How can perfection be achieved
Through this impenetrable form?
Sound, voice, word and speech are each
Confined to specific definition
Which by itself is not all embracing.
How can they help perfection to achieve?
Smell, perceived when in contact with the nose,
Without that contact is non-existent.
How can that which is not always present
Be a means to achieve perfection?
Taste exists not of itself, but is
Perceived when flavour's present.
Since sense of taste is ever varied
How can it to perfection lead?
Touch exists when there's an object touched;
Without an object touch is naught.
Since contact and its absence are not constant,
How can touch help to achieve perfection?
Dharma is inner defilement called;
Reliance thereon implies an object.
Since subject and object are not all embracing,
How can dharma lead one to perfection?
The organ of sight, although perceiving clearly,
Sees things in front but cannot see behind.
How can partial (sight of) the four quarters
Help one to achieve perfection?
The inward and the outward breath
Have no link uniting them.
How can they, thus unconnected,
Be used to achieve perfection?

The tongue is useless touching nothing;
When flavour is present, there is taste
Which vanishes when flavour's absent.
How can this help to achieve perfection?
Body must be conditioned to the object touched;
Both cannot be used for all embracing meditation
Which is beyond both subject and object with their limits.
How can this serve to achieve perfection?
The tumult of thinking with the mind disturbs
The serenity of right perception.
Since stirring thoughts are most hard to eradicate
How can intellect serve to achieve perfection?
Union of consciousness with eye and sight
Has three components that are not settled.
How can that which is devoid of substance
Be used as a means to win perfection?
The hearing mind which reaches into space
Needs a great cause for its development;
But untrained men cannot realize it.
How can this help to achieve perfection?
Meditation on the nose is only an expedient
Means to control the mind by fixing it for the moment.
But wrong dwelling can create an illusory abode.
How can this be used to achieve perfection?
Preaching the Dharma plays upon voice and words,
But awakening occurred during practice long ago,
Words and speeches never going beyond the worldly stream.
How can this be a means to achieve perfection?
Observance of rules of discipline controls
The body but never that which is beyond it.
Since control of body is not all embracing
How can this serve to achieve perfection?
Transcendental powers come from a former cause;
How can they derive from discriminating consciousness?
Since thinking from externals cannot stray,
How can it serve to achieve perfection?
If the element of earth be used for contemplation,
It is solid and cannot be penetrated;
Belonging to the worldly it lacks spirituality.
How can it be used to achieve perfection?
If meditation be on the element of water.
The thoughts that then arise have no reality.

Beyond feeling and seeing is the absolute;
How then can water help to achieve perfection?
If for meditation the element of fire be used,
Dislike of desire is not complete renunciation;
'Tis no expedient for newly initiated minds.
How then can fire become a means to achieve perfection?
If meditation is on the element of wind,
Motion and stillness are a false duality
From which Supreme Bodhi cannot develop.
How can wind serve to achieve perfection?
If the element of space be used for meditation,
Its dimness and dullness cannot be enlightenment.
Since whate'er is unenlightened differs much from Bodhi,
How can the element of space help to achieve perfection?
If on the element of consciousness you meditate,
It changes and is not permanent.
The mind fixed on it being false
How can that element then help you to achieve perfection?
Phenomena are all impermanent;
Thinking originally comes and goes.
Since cause will ever differ from effect,
How can the element of perception achieve perfection?
I now submit to the World Honoured One
That all Buddhas in this world appear
To teach the most appropriate method
Which consists in using pervasive sound.
The state of Samādhi can be
Realized by means of hearing.
Thus was Avalokiteśvara freed from suffering.
Hail to the Regarder of sound
Who, during aeons countless as Ganges' sand,
Entered as many Buddha lands to win
The power and comfort of his independence[42]
And bestow fearlessness upon all living beings.[43]
O you who (have achieved) the sound profound,[44]
The seer of sound,[45] of sound the purifier,[46]

---

[42] The Bodhisattva's power to take on thirty-two transformation-bodies.

[43] His power to bestow fourteen kinds of fearlessness upon all living beings.

[44] His meditation on sound leading to elimination of ego.

[45] His meditation on worldly sound to realize two unsurpassed merits.

[46] His immunization from all attachments by means of meditation on sound.

Who, unfailing as the sound of ocean tides,[47] saves all beings in the world make
Them secure, ensure their liberation and attainment of eternity.
Reverently I declare to the Tathāgata
What Avalokiteśvara said:
When one dwells in quietude,
Rolls of drums from ten directions
Simultaneously are heard,
So hearing is complete and perfect.
The eyes cannot pierce a screen,
But neither can mouth nor nose,
Body only feels when it is touched.
Mind's thoughts are confused and unconnected,
(But) voice whether near or far
At all times can be heard.
The five other organs are not perfect,
But hearing really is pervasive.
The presence or absence of sound and voice
Is registered by ear as 'is' or 'is not'.
Absence of sound means nothing heard,
Not hearing devoid of nature.
Absence of sound is not the end of hearing,
And sound when present is not its beginning.
The faculty of hearing, beyond creation
And annihilation, truly is permanent.
Even when isolated thoughts in a dream arise,
Though the thinking process stops, hearing does not end,
For the faculty of hearing is beyond
All thought, beyond both mind and body.
In this Sahā world
Teaching is by voice.
Living beings who cognize not hearing's nature,
Follow sound to continue transmigrating.
Though Ānanda memorized all that he had
Heard, he could not avoid perverted thoughts.
This is to fall into saṁsāra by clinging to sound;
Whilst reality is won against the worldly stream.
Listen, Ānanda, listen closely,

[47] His realization of universality that causes him always to respond to the needs of others like the tide that never fails to rise and fall.

In the name of Buddha I proclaim
The Vajra King of Enlightenment,
The inconceivable understanding that illusions
Are unreal, the true Samādhi that begets all Buddhas.
You may hear of esoteric methods
From Buddhas countless as the dust,
But if you cannot eradicate
Desire, to hear much causes errors.
To hear your very Self, why not turn backward
That faculty employed to hear Buddha's words?
Hearing is not of itself,
But owes its name to sound.
Freed from sound by turning hearing backwards,
What do you call that which is disengaged?
When one sense organ has to its source returned,
All the six senses thereby are liberated.
Seeing and hearing are like optical illusions,
Just as all three worlds resemble flowers in the sky.
With hearing disengaged, the illusory organ vanishes;
With objects eradicated, perfectly pure is Bodhi.
In utter purity, the bright light pervades all,
With its shining stillness enfolding the great void.
All worldly things, when closely looked at,
Are but illusions seen in dreams.
Dream-like was the Mātaṅgī maiden:
How could she keep your body with her?
Like a clever showman
Presenting a puppet play,
Though movements are many,
There is but one controller.
When that control is stopped,
Figures show no nature.
Likewise are the six organs,
Derived from one ālaya
Which divides into six unions.
If one of these returns to source,
All six functions are ended.
With all infection ended,
Bodhi is then realized.
Any defiling remnant requires further study
Whereas full enlightenment is the Tathāgata.

Ānanda and all you who listen here
Should inward turn your faculty
Of hearing to hear your own nature
Which alone achieves Supreme Bodhi.
That is how enlightenment is won.
Buddhas as many as the Ganges' sand
Entered this one gateway to Nirvāṇa.
All past Tathāgatas
Have achieved this method.
All Bodhisattvas now
Enter this perfection.
All who practise in the future
On this Dharma should rely.
Avalokiteśvara did not practise
It alone, because through it I also passed.
The Enlightened and World Honoured One
Has asked about the best expedients
For those in the Dharma ending age
Who wish from saṁsāra to escape
In their search for Nirvāṇa's heart.
It is best to contemplate on worldly sound:
All other methods are expedients
Used by Buddha in particular cases
To keep disciples from occasional trouble.
They are not good for indiscriminate practice
By men of different types.
I salute the Tathāgata Store
Which is beyond the worldly stream.
Blessed be coming generations
So that they have (abiding) faith
In this easy expedient.
'Tis good for teaching Ānanda
And those of the Dharma ending age
Who should use the hearing organ
Which surpasses all others
And with the True Mind accords.

(After hearing this) Ānanda and the assembly (felt) their bodies and minds to be in tune with the profound teaching. To them the Buddha's Bodhi and Parinirvāṇa were like the way home which a traveller should know well before returning from a long journey abroad. Others present, such as the eight classes of non-human beings,[48] students of Hinayāna and Bodhisattvas who had just developed the Bodhi Mind and whose number was countless as the sand in ten Ganges rivers, awakened to their fundamental minds, avoided defilement and won the pure Dharma eye. After hearing the gāthā, Bhikṣuṇī Self-Nature realized arhatship and an uncountable number of living beings developed the unsurpassed Samyak Sambodhi mind.

---

[48] Cf. Chan and Zen Teaching, Third Series, p. 278, note 3, for a description of the eight classes of spirits who always came when the Buddha preached the Dharma.

V

The Enlightenment of Others

Ānanda adjusted his robe, brought his palms together and prostrated himself with his head at the feet of the Buddha. He rejoiced at his good understanding of the mind and, for the benefit of coming generations, bowed again and said: 'O great Compassionate and World Honoured One, I have now awakened to the Dharma gateway to Buddhahood by means of right practice about which I have no more doubt. I have always heard the Buddha speak of Bodhisattvas who, before their own liberation, set their minds on freeing others, and of Buddhas who, after their own complete enlightenment, appeared in the world to enlighten others. Though I am not yet liberated, I now vow to deliver all living beings in the Dharma ending age.

'World Honoured One, future generations will gradually move farther away from the Buddha and (will meet) heretics as many as the sand grains in the Ganges. In order to control their minds for entry into Samādhi, what should they do to set up seats of study and learning (bodhimaṇḍala) to keep the demon away and avoid failure (in their cultivation) of the mind set on enlightenment?'

The Buddha praised Ānanda and said: 'Excellent, Ananda, excellent, (it is good that) you ask about the setting up of bodhimaṇḍalas for the protection of living beings against failure in the Dharma ending age. Listen attentively to what I now tell you.'

Ānanda and the assembly reverently awaited the (holy) teaching.

Discipline and Its Three Decisive Steps: Śila, Dhyāna, and Prajñā

The Buddha said: 'Ānanda, you have always heard me teach about discipline (vinaya) which consists in the practice of three decisive steps, the control of mind, called śīla which leads to stillness (dhyāna) and thence to wisdom (prajñā). This is called the threefold study of the supramundane way.

Prohibition against carnality

'Ānanda, why is control of mind called śīla? If all living beings in the six worlds of existence abstain from sexual desire, they will not be subject to the continual round of births and deaths. Your practice of Samādhi should free you from defilements but they cannot be eliminated if your lustful mind is not wiped out. Even after you have acquired such wisdom, if you fail to kill sensuality, then when dhyāna manifests,[1] you will fall into the way of demons in which their king takes the high, his male subjects the middle and his female subjects the low rank. These demons have their following and boast of having attained the Supreme Path. After my nirvāṇa, in the Dharma ending age, these subjects of Māra will be found everywhere, will encourage sensuality and will disguise themselves as men of good counsel (kalyāṇamitras) and cause living beings to fall into the pit of lust thereby missing the Bodhi path.

'You should teach worldly men who practise Samādhi to cut off their lustful minds at the very start. This is called the Buddha's profound teaching of the first decisive deed. Therefore, Ānanda, if carnality is not wiped out, the practice of dhyāna is like cooking gravel to make rice; even if it is boiled for hundreds and thousands of aeons, it will be only hot gravel. Why? Because instead of rice grains it contains only stones. If you set your lustful mind on seeking the profound fruit of Buddhahood, whatever you may realize will be carnal by nature. If your root is lustful, you will have to transmigrate through three unhappy ways (to the hells of fire, blood and swords) from which you will not escape. How then can you find the way to cultivate the Tathāgata's nirvāṇa? You should cut off both the sensual body and mind until even the very idea of doing so ceases; only then can you hope to seek the Buddha's Enlightenment. This teaching of mine is that of the Buddha whereas any other one is that of evil demons (pāpiyān).

Prohibition against killing

Ānanda, if living beings in the six worlds of existence cease to kill they will not be subject to the continual round of births and deaths. Your practice of Samādhi should free you from defilements but if your murderous mind is not cut off, they cannot be eliminated. You may acquire much wisdom but if you fail to stop killing, when dhyāna manifests, you will fall into the way of spirits, in which the high rank is attained by the mighty ghost (preta), the middle one by flying yakṣas and chief ghosts, and the low one by earth-bound rākṣasas. These have followers and boast that they have attained the Supreme Path. After my nirvāṇa, in the Dharma ending age, these ghosts will be found throughout in the world, and will boast of how they feed on flesh which leads them to realize Bodhi. Ānanda, I

[1] This is the worldly dhyāna. Cf. Ch'an and Zen Teaching, Third Series, p. 44, note 1, for the three kinds of dhyāna.

permit the bhikṣus to eat only the five kinds of pure flesh[2] which are the product of my transcendental power of transformation and not of animal slaughter. You, Brahman, live in a country where vegetables do not grow because it is too damp and hot and because of all the gravel and rock. I use my spiritual power of compassion to provide you with illusory meat to satisfy your appetite. How then, after my nirvāṇa, can you eat the flesh of living beings and so pretend to be my disciple? You should know that those who eat meat, though their minds may open and realize a semblance of Samādhi, are but great rākṣasas who, after this life, will sink back into the bitter ocean of saṁsāra and cannot be my disciples. They will kill and devour one another ceaselessly, how then can they escape from the three worlds of existence?

'In addition you should teach worldly men who practise Samādhi not to kill. This is called the Buddha's profound teaching of the second decisive deed. Therefore, Ānanda, if killing is not stopped, the practice of dhyāna-samādhi is like shutting one's ears while crying in the hope that people will not hear one's voice, or like trying to hide something that is already exposed to full view. All bhikṣus who live purely and all Bodhisattvas always refrain even from walking on the grass; how can they agree to uproot it? How then can those who practise great compassion feed on the flesh and blood of living beings? If bhikṣus do not wear garments made of (Chinese) silk, boots of local leather and furs, and refrain from consuming milk, cream and butter, they will really be liberated from the worldly; after paying their former debts, they will not transmigrate in the three realms of existence. Why? Because by using animal products, one creates causes (which are always followed by effects), just like a man who eats cereals grown in the soil and whose feet cannot leave the ground. If a man can (control) his body and mind and thereby refrains from eating animal flesh and wearing animal products, I say he will really be liberated. This teaching of mine is that of the Buddha whereas any other is that of evil demons.

Prohibition against stealing

'Further, Ānanda, if living beings in the six worlds of existence cease to steal, they will not be subject to the continual round of births and deaths. Your practice of Samādhi should free you from defilements, but if your robber's mind is not wiped out, they cannot be eliminated. You may acquire much wisdom but if you do not stop stealing, when dhyāna mani-

[2] The five kinds of pure flesh which may be eaten by a beginner who does not see, hear of, or doubt about the animal having been killed purposely for him to eat, but is certain that it either died naturally or that its flesh had been abandoned by birds of prey.

fests, you will foil into the way of devils in which the high rank is attained by cunning spirits, the intermediate one by evil spirits and the low one by bedevilled men. These devils have their following and boast that they attain Supreme Bodhi. After my nirvāṇa, in the Dharma ending age, these devils will be found everywhere in the world. They will hide their perfidy, pose as men of good counsel and declare that they have won the Superior Dharma to deceive the ignorant who will thus lose their minds; wherever they pass, they will cause untold miseries to their believers.

'This is why I teach the bhikṣus to beg for food so that they can overcome cupidity and realize Bodhi. They do not cook themselves and pass their remaining years as transitory travellers in the three realms of existence to prove their last transmigration without incarnating again. How can thieves who wear the Saṅgha robe, act as Tathāgata-mongers[3] and commit karmic deeds, claim that they all preach the Buddha Dharma? They are not (true) leavers of home and are not ordained Hīnayāna bhikṣus. They deceive an incalculable number of living beings causing them to fall into the realm of unintermittent hells.

'After my nirvāṇa, if there is a bhikṣu who, in token of his determination to practise Samādhi, lights in front of an image of the Tathāgata a torch (planted in his body) or burns a bone of his finger or an incense stick inserted in his flesh, I say he will thus repay all his karmic debts since the time without beginning, will leave the worldly way for ever and will escape from the stream of transmigration, for although he has not yet attained Supreme Bodhi, his mind is already set decisively on the Dharma. However, without these small sacrifices, even if he realizes something, he will be reborn as a human being and will have to repay his former debts, as I did when I had to eat the grain fed to horses.[4]

'Then you should teach worldly men who practise Samādhi not to steal. This is called the Buddha's profound teaching of the third decisive deed. Ānanda, if stealing is not stopped, the practice of dhyāna-samādhi is like pouring water into a vessel which will never hold it in spite of the passing of aeons countless as dust. If this bhikṣu does not keep garments in excess of what he needs, gives to others all food in excess of his requirement, joins his two palms to salute the community and regards as praise abuse and blows - that is if he is ready to give away his own flesh, bones and blood, and if he does not pose as an expert interpreter of the

---

[3] This term is frequently found in Buddhist Scriptures and means an unscrupulous person who knows nothing about the Dharma but posts as an expert in Mahāyāna to win fame and make money.

[4] The Buddha's food when he spent three months with the Brahmin ruler Agnidatta with five hundred monks; one of his ten sufferings.

expedient incomplete doctrine and does not teach it to beginners in order not to mislead them,[5] the Buddha will seal his realization of Samādhi. This teaching of mine is that of the Buddha, whereas any other is that of evil demons.

Prohibition against lying

'Ānanda, if living beings in the six worlds of existence, after cleansing their bodies and minds from killing, stealing and carnality, continue to lie, they will fail to realize Samādhi and will become demons (filled with) pride and prejudice. As a result, they will lose the Tathāgata seed and, in their search for worldly fame, will claim that they have achieved and realized what really they have not. They boast of their realization of the states of śrota-āpanna, sakṛdāgāmin, anāgāmin, arhat and pratyeka-buddha and the ten stages of Bodhisattva development, in order to attract believers who will make offerings to them for the atonement of sins. These unbelievers (icchantika) will destroy the Buddha seed as easily as cutting into the trunk of a palm with a sharp chopper (to stop it from growing). The Buddha predicts that these people will destroy their excellent roots, will not regain common sense, will sink into the three oceans (realms) of suffering and will never achieve Samādhi.

'I now command Bodhisattvas and Arhats to appear, in the Dharma ending age after my nirvāṇa, in all appropriate transformation bodies to save those caught in the wheel of saṁsāra. They should come as monks, lay disciples, princes, ministers, boys, girls, and even as prostitutes, widows, rogues, thieves, butchers, pedlars, etc., to keep company with them and praise the Buddha Dharma in their presence so as to convert them and urge them to practise it. In so doing they should not disclose that they are true Bodhisattvas and Arhats. They will not reveal to beginners the Buddha's esoteric cause but when they are about to die, they will secretly show some proof of their enlightenment (to increase their disciples' faith in the Dharma). How then can such persons deceive living beings by telling deliberate lies?

'You should teach worldly men who practise Samādhi not to lie. This is called the Buddha's profound teaching of the fourth decisive deed. Ānanda, if lying is not stopped, the practice of dhyāna-samādhi is like copying in excrement a sandalwood statue and expecting it to be fragrant, which is impossible. I teach the bhikṣus to develop a straightforward mind which is the temple of enlightenment (bodhimaṇḍala) and to be righteous in their common acts of daily life, while walking, stand-

[5] Hīnayāna should never be taught to those who are responsive only to Mahāyāna and vice-versa.

ing, sitting and reclining. How can a liar pretend that he has realized the Supreme Dharma? This is like a poor man proclaiming himself a king; he will only invite trouble and misfortune. Still less can he usurp the (throne of the) King of the Law. If the causal ground is false, its fruit will be distorted, and the quest of Buddha's Enlightenment will become impossible.

'If a bhikṣu (develops) a mind as straight as a lute-string and is truthful under all circumstances, he will avoid, in his practice of Samādhi, all troubles caused by the demon. I will seal his realization of the Bodhisattva's Supreme Bodhi. This teaching of mine is that of the Buddha whereas any other one is that of evil demons.'

VI

Bodhisattva Development into Buddhahood

Ānanda rose from his seat, prostrated himself with his head at the feet of the Buddha and said: 'We were ignorant and sought only (knowledge by) listening; this is why we failed to forsake the worldly mind. Now after we have heard with great benefit the Buddha's compassionate instruction on the right practice of sublimation, our bodies and minds experience great comfort. World Honoured One, in this practice of Buddha Samādhi and before attaining Nirvāṇa, what are the progressive steps from the manifestation of dry (i.e. unfertilized) wisdom, through the forty-four stages of Bodhisattva development, to the realization of Universal Enlightenment?'

After saying this, he prostrated himself and together with the whole assembly reverently stared at the Buddha and awaited His compassionate voice.

The Buddha praised Ānanda and said: 'Excellent, excellent! It is good that, on behalf of this assembly and of all living beings in the Dharma ending age who will practise Samādhi in their quest of Mahāyāna, you can ask for my instruction on the unsurpassed Path from the worldly condition to (transcendental) Parinirvāṇa. Listen attentively to what I now tell you.'

Ānanda and the assembly brought their palms together and concentrated their minds to receive the Teaching.

The Tathāgata Store from Which Arise Both Samsāra and Nirvāna

The Buddha said: 'Ānanda, you should know that the absolute nature is completely enlightened; it is beyond name and form and is fundamentally free from either the world or living beings. Because of ignorance, there arises birth which is followed by death. So birth and death are unreal and the wiping out of the unreal brings about the real which is called Supreme Bodhi and Parinirvāṇa. Hence these terms, imply the twofold transmutation (of kleśa and saṁsāra into Bodhi and Nirvāṇa). Ānanda, if you now wish to achieve the state of Samādhi in order directly to reach the Tathāgata's Parinirvāṇa, you should know first the two inverted causes which lead to the existence of living beings and the world. The non-rising of these inversions is the Tathāgata's true state of Samādhi.

The Origin of Living Beings and the World

'Ānanda, what are these two inversions? Because of the mind's (arbitrary) awareness of the (underlying) bright nature, the latter which is fundamentally enlightened becomes an objective (form) as opposed to a false (perception). Thus from fundamental nothingness arises actual phenomenon. (Therefore), the existence (of ignorance) and its creation (of the world and living beings), the causeless cause of subjective (ignorance) and its objective creation, and subjective (living beings) dwelling in their objective abode (the world) have no real basis. From (Reality) which does not abide anywhere spring the world and living beings.

The Inverted Cause of the Existence of Living Beings

'(What is the inverted cause of the seeming existence of living beings?) The faulty awareness of completely enlightened nature creates a falsehood which has neither nature nor basis. If you wish to restore the real, this very wish (pertains to the samsaric mind and) is not related to absolute nature. If the unreal mind is used to recover real nature, the latter will be unreal and of necessity there follow illusory birth and existence as well as unreal mind and dharma which will unfold endlessly and will gain in intensity thereby creating (new) karma and so responses from those sharing the same karma. This karmic responsiveness leads to the interdependence of births and deaths. Hence the inverted cause of the seeming existence of living beings

The Inverted Cause of the Existence of the World

'Ānanda, what is the inverted cause of the world (i.e. the realm of space and time)? Because of the illusory existence (of ignorance) and its creation (of the world and living beings) there arises the mortal lot clinging to space. Because of the causeless cause of subjective (ignorance) and its objective creation and because of subjective (living beings) dwelling in their objective abode, all unfolding continuously and transitorily, time arises. Thus the three aspects of time and the four cardinal points of space intermingle and combine to produce the twelve (3×4) categories of beings.

The Twelve Types of Transformation

'Therefore, in the world, movement leads to sound, sound to form, form to smell, smell to touch, touch to taste, and taste to thoughts (dharma). These six illusions contribute to the formation of karma which causes the division into twelve (i.e. six illusions each for body and mind) different types of change. Hence the wheel turning in saṁsāra wherein these illusory sense data end in twelve different transformations in each rotation (i.e. each false thought turns the wheel and contributes to these twelve types of births).

The Twelve Groups of Living Beings

'Such inversion that turns the wheel of saṁsāra, creates (twelve groups of) species born of eggs, wombs, humidity, and by transformation, having forms, being beyond form, thoughtful or thoughtless, having neither form nor no form and being neither thoughtful nor thoughtless.

'Ānanda, because of the turning wheel of illusion in (objective) saṁsāra as a result of inversion caused by (subjective) stirring minds, both subject and object are in harmony and combine to produce favourable conditions for 84,000 rising and sinking confused thoughts which form the embryos (kalala) in eggs for incarnation as fishes, birds, turtles, snakes, etc.: they are found in plenty all over the world. (This is birth from eggs.)

'Because of the turning wheel of moral infection in (objective) saṁsāra as a result of inversion caused by (subjective) sensual minds, both subject and object sustain each other and combine to produce favourable conditions for 84,000 confusing divergent thoughts which become foetusses (arbuda) in the wombs for incarnation as men, animals, dragons, immortal beings, etc.; they are found in plenty all over the world. (This is birth from wombs.)

'Because of the turning wheel of attachment in (objective) saṁsāra as a result of inversion caused by (subjective) craving minds, both subject and object inflame each other and combine to produce favourable conditions for 84,000 vacillating confused thoughts which become damp embryos (peśī) in humidity for incarnation as crawling insects and wriggling worms; they are found in plenty all over the world. (This is birth from humidity.)

'Because of the turning wheel of change in (objective) saṁsāra as a result of inversion caused by (subjective) deceitful minds, both subject and object stimulate each other and combine to produce favourable conditions for 84,000 changing confused thoughts taking the shape of solid lumps (ghana) for incarnation as beings which shed their skins, change their forms and fly; they are found in plenty all over the world. (This is birth by transformation.)

'Because of the turning wheel of stiff dispositions in (objective) saṁsāra as a result of inversion caused by (subjective) hindering minds, both subject and object adhere and combine to produce favourable conditions for 84,000 mystical, translucent and confused thoughts which take solid form to incarnate as people whose luminous quality forebodes good and evil; they are found in plenty all over the world. (These are heretics and mystics having forms.)

'Because of the turning wheel of dissipating dispositions in (objective) saṁsāra as a result of inversion caused by (subjective) deluded minds, both subject and object unite with dullness and combine to produce favourable conditions for 84,000 confusing mysterious thoughts for formless rebirth as beings (whose bodies and minds) are dissolved in the great emptiness; they are found in plenty all over the world. (These are formless beings.)

'Because of the turning wheel of fanciful dispositions in (objective) saṁsāra as a result of inversion caused by (subjective) imaginative minds, both subject and object unite with recollection and combine to produce favourable conditions for 84,000 latent and firmly confused thoughts to be reborn as ghosts or spirits of thoughtful beings; they are found in plenty all over the world. (These are thoughtful beings.)

'Because of the turning wheel of dull dispositions in (objective) saṁsāra as a result of inversion caused by (subjective) stupid minds, both subject and object cling to intractableness and combine to produce favourable conditions for 84,000 confusing lifeless thoughts for rebirth as spirits dwelling in earth, trees, metals and stones;[1] they are thoughtless beings that are found in plenty all over the world. (These are thoughtless beings.)

'Because of the turning wheel of parasitic dispositions in (objective) saṁsāra as a result of inversion caused by (subjective) guileful minds, subject and object infect each other and combine to produce favourable conditions for 84,000 confusing commensal thoughts for rebirth as beings who are formless, yet have form, such as jelly-fish which use shrimps as their eyes; they are found in plenty all over the world. (These are beings which are beyond, yet have, form.)

'Because of the turning wheel of seductive dispositions in (objective) saṁsāra as a result of inversion caused by (subjective) artful minds, both subject and object rely on (magic and) spells and combine to produce favourable conditions for 84,000 entreating confused thoughts for rebirth as beings with form, yet formless, who grow weary of witchcraft; they are found in plenty all over the world. (These are beings with form, yet beyond form.)

'Because of the turning wheel of deceitful dispositions in (objective) saṁsāra as a result of inversion caused by (subjective) tricky minds, both

[1] e.g. bronze and stone statues.

subject and object combine to produce favourable conditions for 84,000 interchanging confused thoughts to be reborn as thoughtful yet thoughtless beings, such as wasps which mistake larvae of other insects for their own; they are found in plenty all over the world. (These are thoughtful, yet thoughtless beings.)

'Because of the turning wheel of revengeful dispositions in (objective) saṁsāra as a result of inversion caused by (subjective) murderous minds, both subject and object unite in whimsy and combine to produce favourable conditions for 84,000 fantastic thoughts of parricide and matricide to be reborn as beings who are thoughtless, yet thoughtful, such as certain owls and tigers which respectively devour their mothers and fathers; they are found in plenty all over the world. (These are thoughtless, yet thoughtful, beings.)

Transmutation of Samsāra into Nirvāna

'Thus, Ānanda, each of these species has its twelve kinds of inversion which, like dancing flowers seen when one rubs one's Enlightened Mind and cause wrong thinking. As you now practise the Buddha-Samādhi, you should take three gradual steps to deal with the basic causes of stirring thoughts in order to wipe them out. This is like removing poisonous honey from a pot by using hot water mixed with ashes to cleanse the container; only when the latter is completely clean can it be used to hold ambrosia.

The Three Gradual Steps to Wipe Out Samsāra

'What are these three gradual steps? (They are:) the contributory practice to remove all accessory causes; the main practice to obliterate the basic causes and the progressive practice to stop the growth of karma.

'What are the accessory causes? Ānanda, these twelve species in the world owe their existence to four ways of feeding: by eating,[2] touching,[3] thinking about[4] and being conscious of food.[5] Therefore, the Buddha says that all living beings depend on feeding for their stay (in saṁsāra).

'Ānanda, all beings live if they eat wholesome food and die if they take poison. In their search for Samādhi, they should abstain from eating five kinds of pungent roots (i.e. garlic, the three kinds of onions and leeks); if eaten cooked, they are aphrodisiac and if raw, they cause irrita-

[2] e.g. in the world of desire where men actually eat food.

[3] e.g. in the world of ghosts and spirits who only smell the odour of food to satisfy their hunger.

[4] e.g. in the dhyāna heavens where the mere thought of food satisfies hunger.

[5] e.g. in the formless realm where the mere consciousness of feeding satisfies hunger.

bility. Although those who eat them may read the twelve divisions of the Mahāyāna canon, they drive away seers (ṛṣi) in the ten directions who abhor the bad odour, and attract hungry ghosts who lick their lips. They are always surrounded by ghosts, and their good fortune will fade away day by day to their own detriment. When these eaters of pungent roots practice Samādhi, none of the Bodhisattvas, seers and good spirits come to protect them, while the mighty king of demons takes advantage of the occasion to appear as a Buddha as if to teach them the Dharma, defaming and breaking the precepts and praising carnality, anger and stupidity; at their death, they will join his retinue, and at the end of their time in his realm, they will fall into the unintermittent hell. Ānanda, practisers of Samādhi should never eat these five pungent roots. This is the first step of gradual practice.

'What are the basic causes? Ānanda, those practisers who wish to enter the state of Samādhi should first observe strictly the rules of pure living to cut lust from the mind by abstaining from meat and wine and by taking cooked, instead of raw food. Ānanda, if they do not abstain from carnality and killing, they will never escape from the three worlds of existence. They should consider lust as dangerous as a poisonous snake and a deadly foe. They should begin by strictly observing the Hīnayāna's four prohibitions for monks and eight for nuns[6] to regulate the body, and then adhere to the Bodhisattva discipline to ensure the non-stirring of mind. If they observe these precepts, they will wipe out for ever the karma that leads to birth and killing. If in addition they cease to steal, they will owe nothing to others and will not have debts to repay. Those who keep the rules of pure living in their practice of Samādhi, will be able to see with their own eyes, without the aid of deva sight, all the worlds in the ten directions. They will behold the Buddha preaching the Dharma, will personally receive the holy teaching, will win the transcendental power which enables them to roam freely in all worlds and will acquire the Buddha-knowledge of all forms of their own and others' previous existences, and so will be immune from all calamities. This is the second step of gradual practice.

'What happens when karma (no longer) grows? The minds of these practisers who observe the prohibitions, now free from sensual desire, will not wander outside in search of sense data, but return to the inner (mind). For lack of causal sense data, their organs, thus disengaged from

[6] The Hināyāna's four prohibitions against carnality, stealing, killing and lying for monks, and its eight prohibitions for nuns against the above four offences, plus lustful contact with a male, eight sorts of improper association with him leading to carnality, concealing the misconduct of a member of the order, and improper dealings with him or her.

externals, turn back to the (undivided) one to which, since the six functions have ceased to discriminate, all countries will appear pure and clean. This is like a crystal ball with a bright moon inside it.[7] Their bodies and minds will experience joy and great comfort in the state of absolute and perfect impartiality in which the esoteric perfection and pure absoluteness of all Tathāgatas appear. They will then achieve the great patience of the uncreate and will continue their progress towards sainthood. This is the third step of gradual practice.

Progressive Advance in Bodhisattva Development

The Stage of Dry Wisdom

'Ānanda, these virtuous men will dry up their sensual desire and disengage their organs from sense data; this withering of causes stops the growth of karma. The clinging mind is now empty and clear, being but unmixed wisdom which is perfect and bright by nature, illumining all worlds in the ten directions. This realization of wisdom is called the stage of dry wisdom because they have cut off their sensual habits but have not yet entered the Tathāgata's Dharma stream.

The Ten Stages of Bodhisattva Faith

1. '(After realizing the dry wisdom, if) they use their (progressive) mind to look into the innermost depth, the perfect and profound (essence of mind) will manifest. This state of absolute perfection leads to that of true absoluteness, resulting in the permanence of absolute faith and the total eradication of all false thinking. This is the Mean in its true purity and is called the stage of Bodhisattva faith.
2. 'Their faith, thus genuinely achieved, ensures their complete understanding which is no more hindered by the (five) aggregates, (twelve) entrances (āyatana) and (eighteen) fields of senses (dhātu) and thereby embraces the past, present and future. Thus are exposed the vicious habits which led to their countless incarnations in the past, the smallest details of which they can now remember. This is called the stage of remembrance (or unforgetfulness).
3. 'This absolute perfection in its purity causes the essential (wisdom) to turn all vicious habits contracted since the time without beginning into one bright essence which continues to advance towards the real and the pure.[8] This is called the stage of zealous progress.

[7] The crystal ball stands for wisdom which wipes out all defilements and the bright moon for enlightened mind.

[8] This is the Hīnayāna's Nirvāṇa.

4. 'The essence of mind which now manifests is the wisdom (that destroys the darkness of ignorance). This is called the stage of wisdom.
5. 'This bright wisdom now shines upon its own substance in stillness and profundity, thus ensuring the permanent union (of function and substance). This is called the stage of dhyāna.
6. 'The light of dhyāna becomes brighter; it is now more penetrating and prevents all back-sliding. This is called the stage of non-retrogression.
7. 'The mind now advancing smoothly preserves all previous achievements and is aware of all Tathāgatas in the ten directions. This is the stage of protection of the Dharma.
8. 'The brightness of wisdom, thus preserved and strengthened, can now, by means of its transcendental power, reflect the light of the Buddha's compassion and thereby abide within His (body) like two bright mirrors facing and reflecting each other to infinity. This is the stage of reflective powers.
9. 'The light of the mind then turns inwards and unites for ever with the unsurpassed absolute purity of the (inner) Buddha, thereby resting in the non-retrogressive state of transcendental non-activity (wu wei). This is called the stage of (unshaken) discipline (śīla).
10. 'A great comfort derives from this rest in discipline which enables the mind to roam at will anywhere in the ten directions. This is called the stage of the mind (of high) resolve.[9]

The Ten Practical Stages of Bodhisattva Wisdom

1. 'Ānanda, after achieving these ten stages (of Bodhisattva faith) by practical expedients, the essence of mind manifests and radiates; the intermingling of these ten functions of mind perfects the One Mind. This is called the purposive stage.[10]
2. 'The inner mind now radiates like brilliant pure gold in a globe of clear crystal. As the previous (contemplative) wisdom now reaches this mind-ground, this is called the stage of the control of the (mind-) ground.[11]
3. The cognizance of the mind-ground fully reveals both wisdom and its object as one reality in the ten directions free from all hindrance. This is called the stage of (Bodhisattva) practice.[12]
4. 'This Bodhisattva conduct is now similar to that of the Buddha which influences it. Like a dead man in the intermediate state seeking par-

---

[9] This is the perfect achievement of the One Mind.

[10] This is realization of inceptive Bodhi before basic Bodhi manifests.

[11] Clear crystal stands for the contemplating wisdom, and pure gold for the One Mind.

[12] The mind, now free from all bondage, expands and embraces the whole of space.

ents as a channel for his rebirth in the world, the advancing mind enters the Tathāgata seed.[13] This is called the stage of noble birth.

5. '(The mind) gestating in the holy womb inherits the basic Bodhi, and the foetus is formed with all its characteristics. This is called the stage of all in readiness (for enlightenment).[14]
6. 'Both form and mind are identical with those of the Buddha. This is called the stage of True Mind.[15]
7. 'The integration of body and mind becomes firmer with the passing of time. This is called the stage of non-retrogression.
8. 'The foetus is now complete with the ten aspects of the Buddha-body.[16] This is called the stage of Bodhi in its infancy (or immaturity).[17]
9. The foetus, now completely formed, is born and becomes a son of Buddha. This is called the stage of the heir to the King of the. Law.[18]
10. 'The celebration of his coming of age is like the consecration[19] ceremony held when a crown prince assumes the reins of government. This is called the stage of investiture.[20]

The Ten Lines of Bodhisattva Action

1. 'Ānanda, although these virtuous men, after attaining the rank of a son of Buddha, have acquired the Tathāgata's countless merits, they remain in harmony with all beings in the ten directions. This is called joyful service.
2. They are able to work for the welfare of all living beings. This is called beneficial activity.
3. 'Their self-enlightenment and the enlightenment of others are free from all contradiction. This activity is called non-resentful.
4. 'Their continuous appearance in countless forms in the unending future (for the welfare of others), free from the conception of time and space, is called inexhaustible activity.
5. 'Their preaching, free from all clinging, conforms to (the teaching of) non-duality of all Dharma doors and is called an activity never out of order.

---

[13] The Tathāgata seed is the basic Bodhi inherent in us all.

[14] This is the contemplating mind without which the basic Bodhi cannot manifest.

[15] The True Mind which is free from the duality of subject and object.

[16] The ten aspects of the Buddha-body are: Bodhi-body, vow-body, nir-māṇakāya, mighty body, majestic body, awe-inspiring body, body reproduced at will, blessed body, Dharmakāya and wisdom-body (jñānakāya).

[17] This is the complete basic Bodhi in its immaturity.

[18] As the meditation is successful in realizing inceptive Bodhi, basic Bodhi manifests like a baby born into the world.

[19] Consecration by sprinkling, or pouring water on the head.

[20] The union of inceptive Bodhi with basic Bodhi culminates in ultimate Bodhi as a result of the meditative study of the Mean. This is realization of the immaterial Tathāgata store.

6. 'The (noumenal) Unity reveals a vast variety of undifferentiated phenomena. This is called skilful activity to appear (at will).[21]
7. 'In this state, all the worlds in the ten directions appear in every speck of dust, with neither dust nor worlds hindering each other. This is called the non-clinging activity.
8. 'All manifestations are but the highest perfection (paramita leading to the other shore of Bodhi). This is exalting activity.
9. 'This perfect intermingling (of noumenon and phenomenon) achieves the Buddha pattern in the ten directions and is called the skilful performance of the Law.
10. 'Each line of action is but pure and transcendental non-activity (wu wei) derived from the One Reality of Thatness. This is called activity in harmony with the Truth.[22]

The Ten Acts of Dedication (Parināmanā)[23]

1. Ānanda, after these virtuous men have won transcendental powers in their performance of the Buddha-work, they attain the state of pure Reality which frees them from all hindrances. They should deliver living beings without clinging to the notion of salvation in order to turn the non-active (wu wei) mind towards the path to Nirvāṇa. This is dedication to the salvation of all living beings while avoiding the conception of (saving) them.[24]
2. The wiping out of all that is destructible while avoiding the very idea of so doing is called dedication to the indestructible.[25]

---

[21] This is the perfect intermingling of noumenon and phenomenon.

[22] These ten lines of Bodhisattva actions are the beneficial function which reveals the material or manifesting Tathāgata store.

[23] Dedication of acquired merits to one's enlightenment, to one's rebirth in the Buddha-land, or to the salvation of all living beings.

[24] In his practice a Bodhisattva should dedicate all merits to (a) his attainment of Reality, (b) his realization of Bodhi and (c) the salvation of all living beings. As his basic Bodhi now manifests he clings to neither noumenon nor phenomenon; hence *his freedom from all hindrances. He should deliver all living beings* means dedication to the salvation of all beings. *Without clinging to the notion of salvation* of living beings who are fundamentally in the state of the absolute; this is dedication to his attainment of Reality. *To turn the non-active wu wei mind towards the path of Nirvana* is dedication to the realization of Bodhi. Since he himself and all living beings are one, he devotes all his time to delivering them without clinging to the idea of their being delivered; hence *dedication to the salvation of all living beings while avoiding the conception of (saving) them.*

[25] Kleśa caused by ignorance is destructible; hence *the wiping out of all that is destructible.* While destroying kleśa, one should avoid even the idea of not thinking about its existence or destruction.

3. 'The realization that basic Bodhi is profound and equal to the Buddha's Enlightenment is called dedication to equality with all Buddhas.[26]
4. 'Manifestation of the pure Mind-ground which is identical to the state of a Buddha is called dedication to omnipresence.
5. 'The free intermingling of the worldly and the (absolute state of the) Tathāgata is called dedication to the inexhaustible store of merits.
6. 'The rising of only pure causes from the same state of Buddhahood in search of Nirvāṇa is called dedication to the excellent roots of impartiality.
7. 'The realization of impartiality in this way which reveals the identity of all living beings in the ten directions with one's fundamental nature, the perfecting of which does not exclude any one of them, is called dedication to the sameness of all beings.
8. 'The realization of the identity of all phenomena, free from all differentiation with no clinging to either sameness or difference, is called dedication to the Absolute.
9. 'The achievement of this absolute (state), free from all hindrance in the ten directions, is called dedication to unimpeded liberation.
10. 'Perfect realization of self-nature which wipes out all consideration about the realm of Dharma, is called dedication to the boundless Dharmadhātu.[27]

The Four Additional Harnessing Stages (Prayoga)

'Ānanda, these virtuous men, after achieving these forty-one stages of Bodhisattva development, should train in four additional harnessing stages.

1. The Buddha Bodhi, employed as self-mind, now seems to manifest but actually does not yet do so; this is like kindling a fire by rubbing two sticks together in order to burn them. It is called the warming stage.[28]

---

[26] The One Mind which clings to neither 'is' nor 'is not' is pure and clean and is as enlightened as the Buddha-mind.

[27] In spite of the ten acts of dedication to intensify the preceding ten lines of action in accordance with the Mean, the practiser has not yet reached the source of the One Mind. Hence the following four additional harnessing stages which wipe out the relative idea of training to merge all the forty-one previous stages of Bodhisattva development into actual ascension to the absolute Buddha stage.

[28] The mind reaches maturity when it is about to enter the Buddha stage, hence *the Buddha Bodhi now seems to manifest*, but the contemplating wisdom is still there, hence it *actually does not yet do so*.

2. 'Further, the self-mind now used as the ground for Buddha Enlightenment,[29] seems to rely on wisdom but actually does not, like a climber reaching the top of a mountain with his body in the air while his feet still touch the ground. This is called the summit stage.[30]
3. 'The realization of the sameness of Mind and Buddha leading to the perfecting of the Mean is like forbearing from something which can be neither retained nor rejected. This is called the forbearing stage.[31]
4. 'Being above all estimate and measure, the Mean which is between delusion and enlightenment, is neither the one nor the other. This is called the highest stage on the worldly plane.[32]

The Ten Highest Stages of Bodhisattva Attainment (Daśabhūmi)

1. 'Ānanda, after these virtuous men's skilful understanding of the Great Bodhi, they become aware of the Tathāgata's full state of Buddhahood. This is called the stage of joy (pramuditā) at having overcome all hindrances and so entering upon the path to Buddhahood.
2. 'They now realize that all differentiation merges into a single unity which also vanishes. This is called the stage of freedom from all defilements (vimala).
3. 'Utter purity now begets further enlightenment. This is called the stage of illumination (prabhākara).
4. 'Perfect understanding leads to Bodhi in its fullness. This is called the stage of mastery of glowing wisdom (arciṣmatī).
5. 'Realization of the condition beyond unity and differentiation is called the stage of mastery of utmost difficulties (sudurjayā).
6. 'The manifestation of non-active Bhūtatathatā is called the stage of the appearance of the Absolute (abkhimukhī).
7. 'Thorough penetration of the whole region of the Absolute is called the all-embracing stage (dūraṁgamā).
8. 'Full manifestation of the absolute One Mind is called the stage of imperturbability (acala).
9. 'Full manifestation of its absolute function is called the stage of finest wisdom (sādhumatī).

---

[29] Lit. 'now used as the ground for the Buddha to walk on.'

[30] The feet still standing on the ground are the last hindrance to the leap over the world.

[31] The contemplating wisdom is about to vanish, hence *neither retained*, but its shadow is still there, hence *nor rejected*. This requires great forbearance.

[32] The highest stage in the world, ready for the leap over it. All the above stages still pertain to the quest of relative Bhūtatathatā in the realm of relativities and contraries. The following ten stages of development belong to the absolute Nirvanic One Mind which is beyond all dualities.

'Ānanda, as these Bodhisattvas complete their practice and training with great success, this is also called the stage of successful practice.

10. 'They now realize the state in which sheltering clouds of compassion cover the ocean of Nirvāṇa; this is called the stage of Dharma-clouds (Dharmamegha).

The Universal Enlightenment

'While the Tathāgata goes against the (holy) current to appear in the world for His work of salvation, these Bodhisattvas follow that current to reach their goals. The point where the former (the fruit-ground) meets the latter (the cause-ground) is called the stage of Universal Enlightenment (Samyak-saṁbodhi).

The Absolute (or Wonderful) Enlightenment

'Ānanda, the dry wisdom in the Diamond Mind can be fully realized only after passing through the whole process of Bodhisattva development, that is from the first stage of dry wisdom up to that of Universal Enlightenment. Thus by passing through twelve stages, either singly or in groups of ten states each,[33] Absolute Enlightenment can be completely realized for the attainment of Supreme Bodhi. Throughout these different stages achieved by means of diamond insight into the ten profound illusions,[34] the Tathāgata's clear perception (vipaśyanā) is effectively used during the stilling of mind (śamatha) in gradual practice and training. Thus, Ānanda, the three gradual steps (to wipe out saṁsāra)[35] complete the fifty-five stages of Bodhisattva development on the Bodhi path.

'Such meditation is right whereas any other is heretical.

The Titles of This Sutra

Thereupon Bodhisattva Mañjuśrī rose from his seat, prostrated himself with his head at the feet of the Buddha and asked: 'What name should be given to this sūtra and how should we and living beings receive and practise it?'

---

[33] Dry Wisdom, Warming, Summit, Forbearing, Worldly Height, Universal and Absolute Enlightenment are single stages whereas Faith, Wisdom, Action, Dedication and Highest Attainment are in groups of ten states each, thus numbering in all twelve stages.

[34] The ten illusions are: (1) all karma are like an illusion; (2) all phenomena are like a flame; (3) all bodies are like the moon in water; (4) the wonderful form (of the Buddha) is like empty space; (5) the wonderful voice (of the Buddha) is like an echo; (6) all Buddha-lands are like a mirage city; (7) the Buddha's work (of salvation) is like a dream; (8) the Buddha-kāya is like a shadow; (9) the Sambhoga-kāya is like an image; and (10) the Dharma-kāya is like a transformation.

[35] See page 163.

The Buddha replied: 'This sutra is called: "The Unsurpassed Seal of the Supreme Dharma's Sitātapatra,[36] the pure and clean ocean-eye of all Tathāgatas in the ten directions."[37]

'It is also called: "The Sūtra on the Protection and Deliverance of Ānanda and Bhikṣuṇī Self-nature of this assembly so that they realize the Bodhi Mind to enter the Ocean of All Wisdom."[38]

'It is also called: "The Practice and Realization of the Whole Truth by means of the Tathāgata's Esoteric Cause."[39]

'It is also called: "The Universal Lotus King, the Dharāṇī of all Buddha-Mothers in the Ten Directions."[40]

'It is also called: "The Bodhisattva's Foremost Practice of the Śūraṅgama of the Abhiṣeka (consecration) Division."[41]

'Under these (five) names you should receive and practise this Sūtra.'

---

[36] Sitātapatra: A white canopy. *White* stands for pure, immaculate and spotless, i.e. the One Mind in the store of consciousness which is beyond all defilements. Hence the *White Canopy*, or pure mind that embraces all dharma and protects all living beings.

[37] Title in accordance with the noumenal in essence and in knowledge.

[38] Title in accordance with its function.

[39] Title in accordance with the self (the practiser) and the Dharma (this sūtra).

[40] Title in accordance with the dharāṇī, or the control of all Dharma and the benefit derived from its practice.

[41] Title in accordance with the Bodhisattva practice of this Sermon.

VII

The Six Planes of Existence Caused by Unenlightenment

The Six States of Living Beings in Samsāra

After hearing the Buddha's disclosure of the Sitātaprata's esoteric Seal, and of the Whole Truth, as the titles of this sūtra, Ānanda and the assembly instantly awakened to (the state of) dhyāna, the practice of which could lead to the holy stages and increase their understanding of the profound doctrine, so that they could wipe out all the troubles derived from (the first) six classes of delusion in the three realms of existence.[1]

Ānanda then rose from his seat, prostrated himself with his head at the feet of the Buddha, brought his palms together and said: 'O August and World Honoured One, your compassionate voice has revealed so skilfully to us the subtle delusions of all living beings for my great benefit, thereby bringing great comfort to my body and mind. World Honoured One, if this Bright and pure Absolute Mind were essentially perfect, then even the great earth, plants and trees (i.e. inanimate things) as well as wriggling worms and all beings possessing life (i.e. sentient beings) would be the fundamental Bhūtatathatā which is but the Tathāgata's real substance in the state of Buddhahood. If the Buddha's substance were true and real,

---

[1] The three realms of existence are the realm of desire (kāmadhātu), of form (rūpadhātu) and beyond form (arūpadhātu). There are one realm of desire, four realms of material forms and four of pure spirit, thus nine in all. Each has nine classes of delusions: the upper, middle and lower superior grades, the upper, middle and lower *intermediate* grades and the upper, middle and lower *inferior* grades.

He who wipes out the three *inferior* grades of the realm of desire, realizes the first stage of the Hīnayāna path, called śrota-āpanna, or entry into the holy stream. Ānanda had wiped out only the first six categories of delusion as said in the text, and thereby realized the second stage called Sakṛdāgāmin which involves only one rebirth.

If the last three categories of delusion are wiped out as well, the practiser will realize the third, or non-returning, stage called Anāgāmin.

If all the eighty-one categories of delusions in the three realms of existence are wiped out, the practiser will realize arhatship which is the fourth or highest stage of the Hīnayāna path. (See Ch'an and Zen Teaching, First Series, *The Diamond Cutter of Doubts*, pp. 170/1 for the four Hīnayāna attainments.)

how could there also be the world of hells, hungry ghosts, animals, asuras, men and devas? World Honoured One, are these worlds fundamentally self-existent or do they arise because of living beings' vicious habit of dwelling in falsehood?

'World Honoured One, let me illustrate what I mean. The Bhiksunī "Fragrance of the Precious Lotus," after receiving the rules of Bodhisattva discipline, fornicated and pretended that it was neither killing nor stealing and was, therefore, not subject to karmic retribution. As a result, after her genital organ had been slowly scorched by the flame (of passion), she fell into the unintermittent hell. King Crystal massacred men of the Gautama clan, and Bhikṣu Sanakṣatra wrongly preached the annihilation of all things (and so implied that the law of causality was invalid). Both as a result of their (evil) acts, fell into the avici hell. Are these hells really somewhere or are they self-existing for every sinner to suffer in them? Will you be compassionate enough to enlighten us so that those who observe the precepts know what they imply and do not break them?'

The Buddha said: 'It is good that you ask this question for the benefit of all living beings so that they cease to hold wrong views. Listen attentively to what I now tell you.

'Ānanda, all living beings are fundamentally pure but because of their wrong views, they have formed vicious habits, hence their inner and outer affections.

'Ānanda, inner affection concerns their inwardnesses. Because of the taint of desire, they give rise to wrong passions the accumulation of which produces the water of craving. This is why the thought of good food makes the mouth water; the thought of a predecessor whom one pities or hates fills one's eyes with tears; the craving for wealth stirs one's heart and makes saliva flow and the body sleek. When the mind gives rise to sexual desire, the generative fluid flows from the male and female organs. Ānanda, although these desires differ, their manifestations are all characterized by the secretion of water which, by nature, flows down hill instead of up. This is inner affection.

'Ānanda, outer affection concerns living beings externally. Their keen desires produce illusory thoughts which by continuous pursuit become overwhelming. Thus the mind bent on strict observance of the precepts makes the body light; the mind concentrated on incantations (mantra) and mystic gestures (mudrā) gives a virile and resolute air; the mind set on rebirth in the heaven of gods brings dreams in which the practiser seems to fly upwards; the mind concentrated on the Buddha-land causes holy realms to appear; and real devotion to a religious counsellor (kalyāṇamitra) leads to the willing sacrifice of even one's own life. Ānanda, although these thoughts differ, all these manifestations are, by nature, characterized by a lightness of body which soars up instead of sinking down so that they leap over their (present) states. This is outer affection.

'Ānanda, in the round of births and deaths in Saṁsāra, birth is caused by the habits (of passions) and death by the flow of (retributive) transformation. (This is why) at the moment of death and before the heat completely leaves the body, all good and evil deeds of a lifetime suddenly re-appear to someone who is dead but on the point of being reborn.

The realm of devas

'If his mind is wholly thoughtful, it will fly in the air and he will be reborn in heaven. If in this flight it is filled with blessedness and wisdom strongly sustained by his pure vow, it will open to let him behold the pure lands of all Buddhas in the ten directions; he will be reborn there as a result of his vow.

The realm of seers (rsi) and spirits

'If his mind is more thoughtful than passionate, it will not be light enough for him to fly to distant places; he will be reborn as a flying ṛṣi, a powerful king of ghosts, a flying yakṣa or an earth-bound rākṣasa. He will be able to roam freely in the heavens of the four deva kings. If he is good natured and has taken a vow to protect my Dharma and those who observe the precepts, repeat the mantra, meditate and realize patient endurance, he will dwell beneath the throne of the Tathāgata.

The realm of human beings

'If his thoughts and passions are in equal proportions, he will neither rise nor sink, but will be reborn in the realm of human beings where his intelligence comes from the clearness of his thoughts and his stupidity from the dullness of his passions.

The realm of animals

'If his passions exceed his thoughts, he will be reborn in the realm of animals where great passions create beasts with hair and fur and mild passions produce winged and feathered creatures.

The realm of hungry ghosts

'If his passions and thoughts are in the proportion of seven to three, he will sink into the wheel of water close to the region of fire, will endure intense heat and be reborn as a hungry ghost whose body is constantly scorched by heat and drowned in water, so that he will suffer from hunger and thirst for hundreds and thousands of aeons.

The realm of hells

'If his passions and thoughts are in the proportion of nine to one, he will sink into the wheel of fire and be reborn where wind and fire meet. He will dwell in the intermittent hell if his passions are great, in the unintermittent one if they are very strong, and in the avici hell if he is completely dominated by extremely violent ones. If in addition he slanders the Mahāyāna,[2] breaks the Buddha's precepts, distorts the Dharma when preaching it to deceive his patrons for selfish gain or for fame, and commits the five rebellious acts[3] and ten grave sins[4] he will be reborn (in turn) in all the avīci hells.

'Although the above are self-inflicted retributions resulting from individual evil deeds, all sinners endure the same kinds of suffering which originate from (the same) concurrent causes.

The Ten Causes and Six Effects in the Realm of Hells

The Ten Karmic Causes of the Realm of Hells

'Ānanda, these (retributions) come from the karmic acts of living beings who create ten karmic causes by their vicious habits and so suffer from six kinds of retribution.

The habit of sexual desire

'Ānanda, what are these ten causes? Lust grows into a habit because of sexual intercourse in which two people caress each other thereby producing heat that in turn stimulates desire. This is like the heat caused by rubbing the hands together. The two habits from karma and lust stimulate each other and cause visions of hot iron beds on hot copper supports.[5] Hence all Buddhas regard sexual intercourse as a burning fire of desire and all Bodhisattvas avoid carnality as if it was a fiery pit.

The habit of craving

'Craving grows into a habit because of grasping which is a kind of suction, which in time creates the illusion of cold, frost, chill and shivering.

---

[2] Modern commentators who do not understand the Mahāyāna and Ch'an transmission are sincerely urged to think twice before foolishly vilifying or damning the holy teaching.

[3] The five rebellious acts (pañcānantarya): parricide, matricide, killing an arhat, shedding the blood of a Buddha, and destroying the harmony of the order.

[4] The ten grave sins (pārājika): killing, stealing, carnality, lying, dealing in spirits, talking of a monk's misdeeds, self-praise for degrading others, meanness, anger at rebuke and vilifying the Buddha, Dharma and Sangha.

[5] The bed stands for sexual desire and its supports for the partner on whom the sinner depends to stimulate his sexual appetite.

This is like the cold sensation felt when one breathes in through pursed lips. The combination of karma and craving leads to retribution in the form of suffering expressed by crying out against biting cold and shown by (the skin turning) blue, red or white. Hence all Buddhas regard craving as the water of greed and all Bodhisattvas avoid it as they would a sea of pestilential vapour.

The habit of arrogance

'Arrogance grows into a habit because of abuse which manifests by the oppression (of others), which in time creates the (illusion of) restless waves which build up a volume of water. This is like licking one's mouth to make it water. The two habits from karma and arrogance stimulate each other and create (visions of) rivers of blood, (hot) ashes, burning sand, poisonous seas and molten copper poured on the sinner's tongue. And so all Buddhas regard self-importance as the water of stupidity and all Bodhisattvas avoid it as they would drowning.

The habit of anger

'Anger grows into a habit because of irritation which manifests as stubbornness which in time inflames the heart whose heat turns the vital breath into metal; hence the illusions of hills of knives, iron posts, trees and wheels of swords, axes, halberds, spears and saws. This is like a man pushed by his obstinacy to avenge a wrong. The two habits from karma and anger stimulate each other and create visions of castration, hacking, beheading, chopping, wounding, mutilating, bludgeoning and striking. This is like a man flying into a rage and ready to kill to redress a wrong. Hence all Buddhas regard hatred as a sharp sword and all Bodhisattvas flee from it as from their own execution.

The habit of deceitfulness

'Deceitfulness grows into a habit because of enticement which manifests as deceit which in time creates (illusions of) cords, sticks, ropes and cangues that restrain the sinner. This is like a field flooded for growing grass and plants. The two habits from karma and deception sustain each other and create more and more evil deeds that deserve punishment with fetters, locks, whips, staves, birches and cudgels. And so, all Buddhas regard deceitfulness as harmful as calumny and all Bodhisattvas avoid it as they would a wolf.

The habit of lying

'Lying grows into a habit because of beguilement which manifests as fraud, which in time ends in treachery. This creates (illusions of) filth such as dust, excrement and urine. This is like dust blown by the wind which screens everything. The two habits from karma and lies intensify each other and end in suffering from drowning, tossing, flying, dropping, drifting and sinking. Hence all Buddhas regard lying as harmful as plundering and killing and all Bodhisattvas avoid it as they would stepping on venomous snakes.

The habit of resentment

'Resentment grows into a habit because of aversion which manifests as malice. This creates (illusions of) being stoned, catapulted, shut in a prison van, trapped, bagged and struck. This is like a mischief-maker always with evil designs. The two habits from karma and resentment combine and result in punishment by being tossed and hurled about, seized, apprehended, struck and shot. And so all Buddhas regard resentment as an evil spirit and all Bodhisattvas avoid it as they would poisoned wine.

The habit of wrong views

'Wrong views grow into habit because of misinterpretation which covers (the five misconceptions from) the reality of the ego and objects down to rigorous ascetic prohibitions.[6] This causes the misunderstanding of karmic effects due to rejection of the real and attachment to the unreal. Hence the (illusion of) judgement with proofs of evidence (which cannot be denied), as when two people coming from opposite directions cannot avoid meeting on the same road. The two habits from karma and wrong views combine to cause (visions of) questioning, cross-examination, judicial investigation, enquiry, interrogation and the unveiling of right and wrong in court while good and bad counsel produce the documents and argue about them. Hence all Buddhas regard wrong views as an abyss of perversion and all Bodhisattvas avoid them as they would a ravine full of poison.

The habit of unfairness

'Unfairness grows into a habit because of false accusation which manifests in slander. This creates (illusions of) hills and rocks which close in from all sides to crush, break, score and grind the dinner. It is like abusing the innocent. Both habits from karma and injustice combine to bring

[6] The five wrong views: (1) satkāyaṛṣti, the reality of an ego and its objects; (2) antargrāha, dual views, e.g. permanence and annihilation; (3) mithyā, denial of the law of causality; (4) dṛṣtiparāmarśa, obstinate views which imply wrong inference, e.g. mistaking the state of thoughtlessness for Nirvāṇa; and (5) śīla-vrata-parāmarśa, rigid views in favour of rigorous austerities, e g. covering oneself with ashes to obtain rebirth in heaven.

about (illusions of) apprehension, pressure, beating, repression, coercion and restraint of the sinner by the law. Hence all Buddhas regard defamation as harmful as a tiger and all Bodhisattvas flee from it as from a clap of thunder.

The habit of disputation

'Disputing grows into a habit because of much talk which manifests in concealing (one's shortcomings). This creates (illusions of) secrets being exposed by being reflected in a mirror or by a lamp being lit, like objects that cannot be hidden in broad daylight. The two habits from karma and disputation end in the exposure (of sins); for the mirror and lamp reveal former karmic deeds for (final) judgement. Hence all Buddhas regard concealment as a secret enemy and all Bodhisattvas consider it as dangerous as carrying a hill on the head or walking into the ocean.

The Six Retributive Effects in the Realm of Hells

'What are the six retributive effects? Ānanda, all living beings whose six consciousnesses cause them to commit karmic acts suffer from evil effects through the six sense organs.

Retributive effects of wrong seeing

'What are the evil effects suffered through the six sense organs? When karma ripens at the time of death, the evil effects of wrong seeing cause one to see a raging fire that fills the ten directions. His spirit will follow the smoke and, in a flash, will fall into the unintermittent hell where he will experience both light which reveals all sorts of evil things everywhere which give rise to boundless dread, and silent darkness which hides everything and causes infinite fear. So the flame of wrong seeing scorches the organ of hearing and transforms it into (purgatories of) cauldrons of boiling water and seas of molten copper; the organ of smell into black smoke and purple flame; the organ of taste into hot pills and molten iron; the organ of touch into hot ashes and burning charcoal; and the organ of intellect into scattered sparks that disturb the whole of space.

Retributive effects of wrong hearing

'When karma ripens at the time of death, the evil effects of wrong hearing cause one to see rising waves that submerge heaven and earth. His spirit then follows them to fall into the unintermittent hell where he will experience both unbearable noises that confuse and disturb him and dead silence that makes him dispirited. So these waves flow into the organ of hearing to transform it into rebuke and interrogation; into the organ of sight to turn it into thunder, roars (of animals) and jets of poisonous gas;

into the organ of smell to change it into rain, fog and showers of venomous insects that cover his whole body; into the organ of taste to transform it into pus, blood and all sorts of filth; into the organ of touch to turn it into animals, ghosts, excrement and urine; and into the organ of intellect to change it into lightning and hail that strike and break up his spirits.

Retributive effects of wrong smelling

'When karma ripens at the time of death, the evil effects of wrong smelling cause one to see (clouds of) poisonous gas everywhere. His spirit will leap from the earth to fall into the unintermittent hell where he will experience both the state of free breathing that draws in all sorts of foul fumes that infect and upset his heart (mind), and of blocked breathing that chokes him until he swoons and drops to the ground. Thus these foul airs enter the organ of smell to clear and obstruct his nostrils; the organ of sight to transform it into a flame or (lighted) torch; the organ of hearing to turn it into (the sounds made by) plunging into water, by drowning and by never ceasing waves; the organ of taste into rotten and stinking fish; the organ of touch into a ripped and decomposed (corpse) and a great hill of flesh with hundreds and thousands of eyes to see itself being devoured by countless beasts; and the organ of thinking into dust, miasmas and flying pebbles that strike and break his body.

Retributive effects of wrong tasting

'When karma ripens at the time of death, the evil effects of wrong tasting cause the person concerned to see an iron net and a great blaze of fire that cover the whole world. His spirit will then rise to drop upside down into the net with his head caught in its meshes and he will then be drawn into the unintermittent hell where he will both feel that his in-breath is transformed into bitter cold that bites his body and his out-breath turned into fierce fire that scorches his bones and marrow. Thus this wrong tasting enters the organ of taste to transform it into great hardships; the organ of sight into molten metal and rock; the organ of hearing into sharp weapons; the organ of smell into a huge iron cage that covers the whole country; the organ of touch into long-bows and arrows and into cross-bows and bolts; and the organ of thinking into iron (hail) that rains down.

Retributive effects of wrong touching

'When karma ripens at the time of death, the evil effects of wrong touch cause one to see great mountains closing in from all the four quarters with no way to escape. His spirit will see an iron walled town, fiery snakes and dogs, tigers, wolves and lions, jailers with ox-heads and rākṣasas with horse-heads holding spears and lances who chase him into the town and force him into the unintermittent hell where he will experience both the embrace of mountains (contact) that close in to crush his body into a mess of bones, flesh and blood, and (the pain of) being cut up (separation) when sharp swords slay his body and rip open his heart and liver. Thus this wrong touch enters its own organ to transform it into the road (to hell) and the abode (of Yama) with hall and (judgement) seat; the organ of sight into heat and burning; the organ of hearing into knocking, striking, stabbing and shooting; the organ of smell into apprehending, bagging, judging and roping; the organ of taste into ploughing, nipping, beheading, and cutting; and the organ of intellect into flying, falling, frying and roasting.

Retributive effects of wrong thinking

'When karma ripens at the time of death, the evil effects of wrong thinking cause one to see evil winds blow through and destroy the country. His spirit will be blown up into space and then dropped down to be carried into the unintermittent hell where he will suffer from both the utter confusion that obscures all his senses and frightens him into ceaseless running about, and from the perfect clarity in which all his senses function in good order to feel unbearable pain when he is being fried and scorched. Thus this wrong thinking enters his faculty of thought to transform it into a receptacle; the organ of seeing into scrutinizing and evidencing; the organ of hearing into a rock, (its warmth) into ice and frost, and (its clearness) into dust and fog; the organ of smell into a great fiery chariot, vessel and cage; the organ of taste into cries, screams, lamentation and weeping; the organ of touch into a large or small (body) subject in a single day to tens of thousands of births and deaths.

'Ānanda, these are the ten causes and six effects of the realm of hells which are all created by living beings through their own delusion and falseness.

Degrees of Perversity in Relation to Suffering in the Hells

'If at all times a living being creates these three karmic causes of retributive effects to be suffered by all six sense organs, he will fall into the avīci hell where he will endure untold miseries for countless aeons.

'If at times he creates individual karmic causes of retributive effects to be suffered by his sense organs separately, he will fall into the eight unintermittent hells.

'If he kills, steals, and is carnal in body, mouth and mind, he will fall into the eighteen lesser hells.

'If he does not commit these three evil deeds which involve body, mouth and mind but occasionally kills or steals, he will fall into the thirty-six lesser hells.

'If he commits only one of them with a single sense organ, he will fall into the 108 minor hells.

'Thus all living beings, though creating their own causes of retributive effects, have to endure the same corresponding sufferings in the same hells which are the products of their wrong thinking and which fundamentally do not exist.

The Ten Categories in the Realm of Hungry Ghosts

'Further, Ānanda, if living beings violate the precepts, break the rules of Bodhisattva discipline, destroy belief in the (self-possessed) Buddha-nature and create the (above-mentioned ten) karmic causes, after being scorched in the hells for successive aeons, they will have paid for all the wrong they have done and will be reborn in the realm of hungry ghosts.

1. If craving be the cause of their misdeeds, they will, after paying for their sins, take the form of whatever they meet (ON leaving the hells) to become Strange Ghosts.
2. 'If lust be the cause of their misdeeds, they will, after paying for their sins, take form when blown by the wind (on leaving the hells) to become Drought Ghosts.
3. 'If deceitfulness be the cause of their misdeeds, they will, after paying for their sins, take form when meeting animals to become Animal Ghosts.
4. 'If hate be the cause of their misdeeds, they will, after paying for their sins, take form when meeting worms and insects to become Noxious Ghosts.
5. 'If revengefulness be the cause of their misdeeds, they will, after paying for their sins, take form in the midst of misfortune and calamity to become Cruel Ghosts.
6. 'If arrogance be the cause of their misdeeds, they will, after paying for their sins, take form when meeting oppressed people to become Starved Ghosts.
7. 'If fraud be the cause of their misdeeds, they will, after paying for their sins, take form when finding themselves in dark places to become Nightmarish Ghosts.
8. 'If wrong views be the cause of their misdeeds, they will, after paying for their sins, take form when meeting sprites to become Naiads.
9. 'If unfairness be the cause of their misdeeds, they will, after paying for their sins, take form when seeing the light to become Servant Ghosts.
10. 'If disputation be the cause of their misdeeds, they will, after paying for their sins, take form when meeting mediums to become Messenger Ghosts (to relay the news from the dead).

'Ānanda, these beings are completely dominated by their passions which cause their fall into the realm of hells where they are scorched dry by the flame of passion and from which they will emerge as hungry ghosts. These states are the products of karma created by wrong thinking. If they awaken to Bodhi, they will find that fundamentally these karmic states cannot be found in the profound, perfect and bright mind.

The Ten Categories of Animals (Birds, Etc.)

'Further, Ānanda, when all karmic effects have been completely endured in the realm of hungry ghosts, that is after the consequences of passions and thoughts have ended, they will be reborn as animals (birds, etc.) who meet their former creditors to repay outstanding debts.

1. 'Strange Ghosts, after expiating their misdeeds in their realms, are mostly reborn as owls.
2. 'Drought Ghosts, after expiating their misdeeds in their realm, are mostly reborn as unlucky creatures (who foretell misfortunes and calamities).
3. 'Animal Ghosts, after expiating their misdeeds in their realm, are mostly reborn as foxes.
4. 'Noxious Ghosts, after expiating their misdeeds in their realm, are mostly reborn as venomous creatures.
5. 'Cruel Ghosts, after expiating their misdeeds in their realm, are mostly reborn as tapeworms.
6. 'Starved Ghosts, after expiating their misdeeds in their realm, are mostly reborn as creatures good for food.
7. 'Nightmarish Ghosts, after expiating their misdeeds in their realm, are mostly reborn as creatures who provide materials for clothing.
8. 'Naiads, after expiating their misdeeds in their realm, are mostly reborn as creatures through whom the future can be foretold.
9. 'Servant Ghosts, after expiating their misdeeds in their realm, are mostly reborn as auspicious creatures.
10. 'Messenger Ghosts, after expiating their misdeeds in their realm, are mostly reborn as domestic animals.

'Ānanda, these hungry ghosts, after withering because of the scorching effect of the flame of their passions to repay their former debts, are thus reborn as animals (birds, etc.). These states are caused by their karmic misdeeds but if they awaken to the Bodhi mind, they will find that the causes of falsehood fundamentally do not exist. You have mentioned Bhikṣuṇī Fragrance of Precious Lotus, King Crystal and hikṣu Sanakṣatra, but (you should know that) their evil karmas came from neither heaven nor earth; nor were they imposed on them by others. Since their evil deeds were self-made, they had to suffer from the consequences which were the congealation of passing false thoughts in the Bodhi mind.

'Further, Ānanda, if these creatures, while paying their former debts, are made to repay more than is just, they will be reborn as men to reclaim the difference. If the creditors are men of good virtue and can repay the outstanding balance, they will keep their human state while doing so, but if they are men of little virtue, they will be reborn as animals to make good the amount received in excess.

Ānanda, you should know that if the indebtedness consists of money and labour, it will be cancelled as soon as it has been reimbursed. But if in addition to recovering it, the creatures concerned are killed to provide food (for the creditors), this will start, between debtors and creditors, an endless round of mutual killing and eating which can be brought to an end only by (the practice of) Śamatha or when a Buddha appears in the world (to teach them the Dharma).

The Ten Categories in the Realm of Human Beings

1. 'You should know that owls, after repaying their former debts, are reborn as wayward men in the realm of human beings.
2. 'Inauspicious creatures, after repaying their former debts, are reborn as men with animal habits.
3. 'Foxes, after repaying their former debts, are reborn as vulgar men.
4. 'Venomous creatures, after repaying their former debts, are reborn as savages.
5. 'Tapeworms, after repaying their former debts, are reborn as vile men.
6. 'Creatures good for food, after repaying their former debts, are reborn as cowards.
7. 'Animals providing materials for wearing apparel, after repaying their former debts, are reborn as servile men.
8. Creatures through whom the future can be foretold, after repaying their former debts, are reborn as literary men.
9. Auspicious creatures, after repaying their former debts, are reborn as intelligent men.
10. 'Domestic animals, after repaying their former debts, are reborn as men versed in the ways of the world.

'Ānanda, these living beings, after repaying their debts, are reborn in the realm of human beings because since the time without beginning, they have, on account of their karma and perversion, killed one another and have not met the Buddha or heard the right Dharma, hence their transmigration according to the law of saṁsāra; they are most pitiable.

The Ten Categories in the Realm of Seers (Rsis)

'Ānanda, there are men who, instead of cultivating the Samādhi of right Bodhi, practise (immortality) wrongly according to their false thoughts, thus preserving their thinking and bodies; they are fond of living in mountains, groves and uninhabitable places. There are ten classes of them.

1. 'Ānanda, those men who diet (specially) to preserve their bodies and thereby live long through dieting, are called earth-bound seers.
2. 'Those who take herbs and fruits to preserve their bodies and thereby live long through taking medicine, are called flying seers.
3. 'Those who take mineral products to preserve their bodies and thereby live long by means of alchemy, are called unhindered roaming seers.
4. 'Those who regulate their (organic) functions to preserve their bodies and thereby live long by means of proper breathing, are called immaterial seers.'
5. 'Those who make good use of controlling their saliva to preserve their bodies and thereby live long by means of their glowing spirituality, are called heavenly seers.
6. 'Those who feed on the vital principle of nature to preserve the essence of form, and thereby live long by absorbing natural purity, are called all-entering seers.
7. Those who use incantations to preserve their bodies and thereby live long by means of occultism, are called seers of the (lesser) Tao.
8. 'Those who concentrate on their thoughts to preserve their bodics and thereby live long by means of mental concentration are called illuminating seers.
9. 'Those who practise the integration of (the positive and negative) principles to preserve their bodies and thereby live long by means of the spiritual harnessing power (of yoga) are called Spiritual seers.
10. 'Those who practise sublimation of their bodies and thereby live long by means of spiritual awareness are seers of the highest order.

'Ānanda, these men regulate their minds but do not practise the right Bodhi, and live for perhaps a thousand and ten thousand years; they live on high mountains or (desert) islands and cut off all worldly connections. Their states still belong to the samsaric stream of wrong thoughts, and since they do not practise Samādhi, when they have enjoyed their conditioned blessing, they will have to return to the (lower) planes of existence.

The Realm of the Gods (Devaloka)

The Six Heavens of the Realm of Desire (Kāmadhātu)

1. 'Ānanda, there are men who do not seek the permanent because they cannot relinquish their love for their wives. They, however, do not commit adultery, and so their minds are clear and bright. After their death, they will be reborn in the regions near the sun and the moon, called the four heavens of the four deva-kings (catur-mahārāja-kāyika).[7]
2. 'There are men who, though living with their wives, are lukewarm about love and sexual desire. Their chastity is, therefore, not perfect and so, after their death, they will be reborn in the regions above the sun and the moon and on the top of the world, called the Trayastrimśā heavens.[8]
3. 'Those whose sexual indulgence is only incidental[9] and is then always forgotten,[10] and who prefer tranquillity to disturbance, will, after their death, be reborn in space where they will dwell in brightness which eclipses the light of the sun and moon because of their luminous bodies.[11] This is the Suyāma heaven.
4. 'Those who live in tranquillity at all times but are still not yet immune to disturbance, will after their death, be reborn in the subtle region which is beyond the reach of men and lower devas and which remains unaffected by the three calamities (of fire, water and wind) during the kalpa of world-destruction. This is the Tuṣita heaven.[12]
5. 'Those who have relinquished all sexual desires but are prepared to satisfy those of their wives and who feel as if they chew (tasteless) wax during the intercourse, will, after their death, be reborn in the region attainable by leaps and bounds (direct from the realm of human beings).[13] This is the Nirmāṇarati heaven.[14]

---

[7] They are Indra's four external 'generals' who dwell each on a side of mount Sumeru: the east deva is called Dhṛtarāṣtra, the south deva, Virūḍhaka, the west deva, Virūpākṣa, and the north deva, Vaiśramaṇa. They are guardians of the world and their statues are inside the entrance door of every monastery in China.

[8] They are the heavens of the thirty-three devas, the heaven of Indra on mount Sumeru.

[9] They still belong to the world of desire.

[10] They have relinquished love.

[11] Their sexual indulgence consists of embracing, without intercourse.

[12] This is the heaven of contentment which has an inner court, the Pure Land of Maitreya who will descend to earth as the next Buddha. Most Buddhists who take the vow to liberate all living beings after their own enlightenment, will be reborn there and will follow Maitreya, as assistants, to teach human beings after the present Dharma-ending age.

[13] Without passing through the four lower heavens.

[14] Where every form of joy is attainable at will and where mere smiles satisfy sexual desires.

6. 'Those who have cut off their worldly minds and are thus free from earthly prejudices when dealing with worldlings will, after their death, be reborn in the region beyond those where joy is attainable[15] and unattainable[16] at will. This is the Paranirmita-vaśavartin heaven.[17]

'Ānanda, though these six realms of heavens are free from (mental) disturbances, they still retain the conception of mind; hence they are called realms of desires.

The Four Regions of the Dhyāna Heavens of the Realm of Form (Rupadhātu)

The first region of the three dhyana heavens

1. 'Ānanda, all worldly men who do not practise dhyāna in their cultivation of the Mind, cannot achieve Wisdom. If they only abstain from sexual desires of which they do not even think in their daily activities, they will not be contaminated by love and will leave the realm of desires. They will be reborn, as they wish, as people (Brahmā-pāriṣadya) in the heaven called Brahma-kāyika.[18]
2. 'Those who relinquish their habits of desire and so realize minds free from lust, are able to keep the rules of morality and discipline and to live purely whatever they do. They will be reborn as ministers of Brahmā in the heaven called Brahma-purohitas.[19]
3. 'Those whose bodies and minds are profound and perfect, whose deportment and pure living are irreproachable and who thereby achieve clear understanding, are qualified to rule over the Brahmādevas as their lords (Mahābrahmā-deva-rāja). This is the Mahabrahmā heaven.

'Ānanda, these three heavens are free from all worldly troubles which cannot reach them. Although these gods do not practise the right Samādhi, their minds are still and free from all disturbances. This is the first region of the dhyāna heavens.

The second region of the three dhyana heavens

1. 'Ānanda, next comes the heaven of Brahmā who reigns over his people and perfects the rules of pure living and whose unperturbed mind is still and shining. This is the heaven of Minor Light (Parīttābha).

---

[15] The Nirmāṇarati heaven where joy is attainable at will.

[16] The first four lower heavens where joy cannot be attained at will.

[17] The abode of Maheśvara (i.e. Śiva) and of Māra, where the devas avail themselves of the merits of others for their own pleasures, and where they look at the opposite sex to satisfy their sexual desires.

[18] The retinue of Brahmā.

[19] The ministers of Brahmā.

2. The above light grows brighter and illumines all the worlds in the ten directions thereby changing everything into clear crystal. This is the heaven of Infinite Light (Apramāṇābha).
3. 'The preservation of this Infinite Light now becomes the theme of the teaching voice that preaches purity and cleanness to all who can respond. This is the Ābhāsvara heaven.[20]

'Ānanda, these three heavens are beyond all worldly troubles and although their devas do not practise the right Samādhi, their pure and clean minds are free from all the coarse characteristics of saṁsāra. This is the second region of the dhyāna heavens.

The third region of the three dhyana heavens

1. 'Ānanda, thus these devas transmute this perfect light into the theme of the voice which reveals the wonderful (state) and thereby gives rise to pure conduct that unites with dhyāna by wiping out (all former feelings of) joy. This is the heaven of Minor Purity (Parīttaśubha).
2. 'Pure voidness now manifests in its boundless immensity causing both body and mind to experience comfortable weightlessness and nirvanic bliss. This is the heaven of Infinite Purity (Apramāṇaśubha).
3. 'Body, mind and universe are now in the state of perfect purity, which reveals clearly a supramundane abode full of nirvanic bliss. This is the heaven of Universal Purity (Śubhakṛtsna).

'Ānanda, these three heavens accord with the (state of) perfect dhyāna in which body and mind are at rest and enjoy boundless bliss. Although their devas have not achieved the right Samādhi, their still minds are full of happiness. This is the third region of the dhyāna heavens.

The fourth region of the four dhyana heavens

1. 'Further, Ānanda, these devas whose bodies and minds are beyond all sufferings the causes of which have been completely wiped out, realize that bliss is not permanent and will in time inevitably come to an end. They, therefore, relinquish completely the dual concept of suffering and happiness and, as they wipe out the coarse characteristics of both conditions, the state of felicity manifests in all its purity. This is the heaven of felicitous birth (Puṇyaprasava).
2. 'The elimination (of the above duality) results in their complete liberation from this hindrance and enables them to enjoy the full measure

[20] The heaven in which the inhabitants converse by light instead of words.

of felicity as long as they stay in this heaven. This is the heaven of felicitous delight, or cloudless felicity (Anabhraka).

3. 'Ānanda, the (above) heaven now divides into two paths, one of which is attainable by those who, in the light of boundless purity, achieve the perfection of felicity as their abode. This is the heaven of Abundant Fruit (Bṛhatphala).
4. '(On the other hand) if they wipe out both suffering and happiness thereby developing a renouncing mind, which in time ensures their complete renunciation, both their bodies and minds will be eliminated and with them all mental troubles. But because their practice is based on the samsaric idea (of birth and death) as a point of departure, they will not, for five hundred aeons, realize their permanent nature. The reason is that in every kalpa they can only succeed during its first half in wiping out all their thoughts which, however, will recur during its second half (because of the wrong starting point). This is the heaven of thoughtless devas (Asañjñisattva).

'Ānanda, these four heavens are beyond all wordly suffering and happiness which can no more stir them. But they have not yet reached the true state of transcendental (wu wei) immutability because they (still) preserve the notion of achievement. For this efficient achievement, they are called the fourth region of the dhyāna heavens.

The five heavens from which there is no return

'Further, Ānanda, above the fourth region of the dhyāna heavens there are five heavens from which there is no return,[21] whose devas have completely cut off all habits contracted through the nine types of delusion of each of the lower heavens.[22] They are thus beyond suffering[23] and happiness[24] and dwell no more in these inferior heavens. Hence their present abodes set up by their achievement of renunciation. (They are):

1. 'Ānanda, with the complete elimination of both suffering and happiness, the struggling mind ceases to arise in this heaven which is free from trouble and is called Avṛha.
2. 'There remains now the solitary renouncing mind that no longer confronts objects in this heaven which is free from the heat (of minor trouble) and is called Atapa.

[21] The devas of these five heavens will not return to the realm of desire or to the four first dhyāna heavens of the realm of form.

[22] See p. 175, note 1, for a full description of the nine classes of delusion.

[23] Suffering in the realm of desire.

[24] Happiness in the first dhyana heavens.

3. 'All the worlds in the ten directions are now clearly perceived as perfectly still without even a speck of impurity in this heaven of excellent perception, called Sudarśana.
4. 'The essence of seeing now manifests and dissolves all (subtle) hindrances in this heaven of excellent manifestations called Sudṛśa.
5. 'The utmost subtlety of form leads to its extreme limit where starts boundless space in this ultimate heaven of (finest) form, called Akaniṣṭha.

'Ānanda, these (five) heavens from which there is no return are imperceptible to the deva kings of the four dhyāna heavens who only hear of their existence but cannot see them. They are like those holy sites (bodhimaṇḍalas) situated deep in the mountains, which are the abodes of Arhats and which no worldling can see.

'Ānanda, the above are the eighteen heavens of form whose devas are solitaries beyond all desires, but are still hindered by their forms. These heavens are, therefore, in the realm of form.

The Four Heavens of the Formless Realm of Pure Spirit (Arūpadhātu)

The state of the Great Arhat

'Further, Ānanda, the region above the top of the realm of form is divided into two paths. If the renouncing minds of these devas create (transcendental) wisdom, the light of which is perfectly penetrating, they will leap over saṁsāra to become Arhats (later) to enter the Bodhisattva state. They are called Great Arhats whose minds are turned towards Mahāyāna.

The four heavens beyond form

1. 'On the other hand, if after acquiring a renouncing mind, they relinquish this achievement and feel that their bodies are no longer obstructive, they will remove all obstacles to enter the void. This is the heaven of boundless emptiness (Ākāśānantyāyatana).
2. 'If after wiping out all obstruction, they keep away from boundless voidness, they will retain only the subtle half of (kliṣṭa-) manovijñāna[25] in the ālaya. This is the heaven of boundless consciousness (Vijñānānantyāyatana).
3. 'With the elimination of both form and voidness and the additional eradication of consciousness, all the ten directions will be com-

[25] The coarse half of the seventh consciousness is form which was wiped out earlier and its subtle half is ālaya's subjective perception, or Ego.

pletely still, merging into nothingness. This heaven is called Akiñcanyāyatana.[26]

4. 'Consciousness now becomes immovable awareness, thus ending all further exhaustive search. As a result, the inexhaustible reveals the exhaustible which seems to, yet does not, stay and which seems to, yet does not, end. This is the heaven of devas who are neither thoughtful nor thoughtless (Naivasaṁjñānasaṁjñāyatana).

The Anagamin stage

'Though the devas of the four heavens beyond form succeed in looking exhaustively into the void, they fail to realize the absolute voidness of (immaterial) noumenon. They all come from the five heavens of form from which there is no return and if they do not stray from the holy Way, they are called (Anāgāmins of) Arhatship whose dull minds are not turned towards Mahāyāna.

'However, if they follow thoughtless devas of the heterodox way and stay in this inexhaustible voidness, they will delight in samsaric heavens and will be deprived of the chance of hearing the Dharma; they will finally be turned back to the wheel of births and deaths.

'Ānanda, all the devas in these heavens were once worldly men whose reward caused their rebirth there, and after enjoying its fruit, they will have to return to Saṁsāra. However, their rulers (devarāja) are Bodhisattvas who, in their practice of Samādhi, appear in these heavens which they use as paths for their progressive advance towards Buddhahood.

'Ānanda, the devas in these four heavens beyond form have wiped out all traces of body and mind. As their still (dhyāna) nature has appeared, they are free from all retribution involving [(material) forms. Hence this is the region beyond form.

'All this comes from their being not clear about the profound mind of Bodhi and because of their preservation of accumulated thoughts, they create the three illusory realms of existence through the seven states;[27] hence they are living beings (pudgala)[28] in the worlds they have deserved.

The Four Classes in the Realm of Titans (Asura-Gati)

'Further, Ānanda, there are four classes of asuras in the three realms of existence.

[26] The region where nothing exists and where only consciousness in its subtlety remains. It is not the ultimate and still pertains to Saṁsāra.

[27] The seven states or gati are: hell (nārakagati), hungry ghost (preta), animal (tiryagyoni), man (manuṣya), seer (ṛṣi), god (deva), and titan (asura).

[28] Living beings subject to metempsychosis.

1. 'If a hungry ghost, while in his realm, strives to protect the Dharma and thereby uses his powerful understanding to enter the void, he will be reborn from an egg as an asura who is connected with the realm of hungry ghosts.
2. 'If a deva, because of his diminishing merits, is about to fall into the region near the sun and the moon, he will be reborn from a womb as an asura who is connected with the realm of human beings.
3. 'A king of the asuras who rules over (the ghosts and spirits in) the world, is powerful and fearless and can fight for power against Brahmā and his people, Śakra and the four kings of the four (lower) heavens. This asura is born by transformation and is connected with the realm of heavens.
4. 'Ānanda, there is another inferior class of asuras who are born in the sea on the bed of which they live in holes. They roam in space during the day and return to the sea at night. These asuras are born from humidity and are connected with the realm of animals (birds, etc.).

'Ānanda, the above seven realms of hells, hungry ghosts, animals (birds, etc.), men, seers, heavens and titans come from their own illusions of worldly forms. They are created by their wrong thinking and are like flowers in the sky within their profound, perfect, bright and non-creating fundamental minds. Essentially they are not in bondage to anything, and are (the product of) falsehood which has neither root nor clue.

'Ānanda, these living beings are unaware of their fundamental minds and so suffer from this round of births and deaths in saṁsāra. If they have passed countless aeons without realizing the true and pure (mind), it is because they have killed, stolen and been carnal the ceasing of which has caused them to be reborn where these acts are unknown.[29] Where these acts exist is called the realm of hungry ghosts and where they do not is called the realm of devas. The presence or absence of these three evils alternate and cause the wheel of Saṁsāra to turn.

'If they achieve Samādhi, they will realize the profound, eternal and still state which is free from the duality of existence and non-existence, and is also beyond this very freedom from duality.[30] In such a state where even non-killing, non-stealing and non-carnalizing cannot be found, how can there be such evils as killing, stealing and carnality?[31]

---

[29] The realm of devas.

[30] The ultimate state is neither Saṁsāra where the three evils exist nor Nirvāṇa where they do not.

[31] A pure state which is free from all dualities.

'Ānanda, if an individual does not abstain from these three evil deeds, he will suffer from evil consequences. If a group of individuals commit them, they will all endure the same suffering in the same place which cannot be said to be non-existent. However, this (place) arises from falsehood which has no cause and cannot be sought anywhere.

'As you strive to realize Bodhi, you should wipe out these three evils. If you do not, whatever supernatural power you may acquire from your practice still pertains to worldly achievement. If your (vicious) habits are not cut off, you will fall into the realm of demons, and even if you then want to wipe out falsehood, you will only increase it. Therefore, the Tathāgata says that you are most pitiable because your sufferings are self-inflicted and do not come from any defect of Bodhi.

'The above preaching is right and any other is that of the demon (Māra).'

VIII

Warning to Practisers: The Fifty False States Caused by the Five Aggregates

States of Māra Caused by the Five Aggregates

As the gathering drew to a close, the Buddha grasped the teapoy and made a move to rise from His lion seat when suddenly he changed his mind, leant back and said to Ānanda and the assembly: 'You śrāvakas and pratyeka-buddhas need to study more in your quest of Supreme Bodhi. I have taught you the method of correct cultivation but you still do not know the subtle states of Māra which appear when you practise śamatha-vipaśyanā. When they manifest, if you fail to distinguish them and if your minds are not in a right state, you will fall into the evil ways of either the demons or your five aggregates, of the heavenly Māras, of ghosts and spirits, or of mischievous sprites. If you are not clear about them, you will mistake thieves for your own sons. Further, you may regard some little progress as complete achievement, like the untutored Bhikṣu[1] who when he reached the fourth dhyāna heaven presumed that he had become a saint; after he had enjoyed his reward in heaven, all indications of his approaching fall appeared. As he vilified the arhats, he created the karma of future incarnation and then fell into the avīci hell. You should listen carefully to what I now tell you in detail.'

Ānanda rose from his seat and, with all those requiring further study, prostrated himself at the Buddha's feet and awaited His compassionate instruction.

The Buddha said: 'You should all know that the clear substance of the profound and bright basic Bodhi of all living beings of the twelve types of birth in saṁsāra is that of all Buddhas in the ten directions. It is because you think wrongly that you are not clear about the noumenon and so become stupid and full of desires which lead to your complete delusion. Hence the (relative) voidness, and as you are always deluded, the world is falsely created. All countries countless as dust are in saṁsāra because of your obstinate wrong thinking. But you should know that (relative) voidness is created in your minds, like a small cloud that is but a speck in

[1] A monk who refused to hear the Dharma because he thought that by merely stopping all thinking he had attained sainthood.

the great emptiness; how much more so is the world which is within this (relative) voidness? If you realize the real to return to the source, the void in the ten directions will vanish. Why, then, will not all the countries in that voidness shake and crack?

'When you practise dhyāna to preserve the state of samādhi, all Bodhisattvas, and all great arhats whose essence of mind is already penetrative, are unmoved, but the kings of the demons, ghosts, spirits and lower heavens are shocked to see their palaces break open without cause and the great earth shake and crack; all those on earth and in the air take fright whereas worldly men who are deluded do not feel anything, because these demons, though they have acquired five supernatural powers,[2] still fail to realize transcendental insight into the ending of the stream of transmigration[3] for they have not broken their links with saṁsāra; how can they let you destroy their dwellings? This is why they come to trouble and annoy you when you enter the state of samādhi.

'However, in spite of their rage, these demons are there in your profound state of bodhi and are like people trying in vain to blow out sunlight and to cut water with a sword, while you are like boiling water that melts solid ice. Though they rely on their super-natural powers, they are but externals and will only succeed in destroying you if you, who own the five aggregates in your minds, are deluded and let them do so. For these demons cannot harm you in your state of dhyāna if you are awakened and are not deluded. If you wipe out the (five) aggregates, you will enter the state of brightness wherein all demons are but dark vapours. Since light destroys darkness, they will perish as soon as they approach you; how then dare they disturb the state of samādhi?

'On the other hand, if you fail to awaken and are thereby deluded by the five aggregates, then, Ānanda, you will become a son of Māra and help the demons. As an illustration, Mātaṅgī who was so base, used magic to cause you to break one of the eighty thousand (minor) rules of pure living, but since your mind was pure, you were not ruined. This shows the (imminent) loss of all your precious bodhi. You were almost like a chancellor of state whose possessions are suddenly confiscated so that he is in straitened circumstances without any hope of obtaining aid.

The Ten States Affected by the First Aggregate of Form (Rūpa)

'Ānanda, when you sit in meditation, if your thoughts are wiped out, the state (of your mind), now free from them, will be clear and will not be

---

[2] The five powers to see things in the realm of form, to hear any sound anywhere, to read others' minds, to know the former existences of self and others, and to be anywhere at will.

[3] The sixth supernatural power which should be acquired before attaining bodhi.

changed by either stillness or disturbance. In this state, both remembrance and forgetfulness are one undivided whole.[4] While in it and before realizing samādhi, you are like a man whose eyes are clear but who is still in the dark, for though your mind is clear, it does not yet shine. This is the aggregate of form that conditions your meditation. If your mind radiates, you will clearly perceive all the ten directions of space. This disappearance of darkness is called the ending of rūpa and you will then leap over and 'beyond the turbid kalpa,[5] the main cause of which is your wrong thinking.

1. 'Ānanda, in this profound and clear state of your penetrating mind, the four elements cease to hinder you, and after a little, your body will be free from all hindrance. This is your clear mind spreading to its objects[6] and shows the effectiveness of your meditation, the temporary achievement of which does not mean that you are a saint. If you do not regard it as such, it is an excellent progressive stage, but if you do, you will succumb to demons.
2. 'Ānanda, in this profound and clear state of your penetrating mind, you will be able to discern everything clearly in your body and will suddenly see lively tape-worms. This is your clear mind spreading in your body and shows its effective functioning, the temporary achievement of which does not mean that you are a saint. If you do not regard it as such, it is an excellent progressive stage, but if you do, you will succumb to demons.
3. 'Further, in this state of mind which penetrates both within and without, your spirit and faculties, though not your body, will intermingle as principals (hosts) and accessories (guests) and suddenly you will hear a voice in the air preaching the Dharma or proclaiming its secret meaning in the ten directions. This is your spirit and faculties which unite with, or disengage from, one another to sow the excellent seed, the temporary realization of which does not mean that you are a saint. If you do not regard it as such, it is an excellent progressive stage but if you do, you will succumb to demons.
4. 'Further, in this clear, revealing, bright and penetrating state of mind, your inner light radiates and gilds everything in the ten directions wherein all living beings are transformed into Buddhas. Suddenly you will see Vairocana seated on a radiant throne surrounded by thousands

[4] This is singleness of mind.

[5] See page 104 for a detailed explanation of the five conditions of turbidity.

[6] See my previous book, *The Secrets of Chinese Meditation* (Rider & Co.), which explains how the mind spreads to its surroundings.

of Buddhas, with hundreds of lacs of countries and of lotus flowers, all of which appear at once. This is the effect of being awakened by your mind's spirituality, the light of which penetrates and shines on all the worlds. This temporary achievement does not mean you are a saint. If you do not regard it as such, it is an excellent progressive stage, but if you do, you will succumb to demons.

5. 'Further, if your penetrating mind, in its profound and clear state, continues to look within without pause, and so checks and stops completely all thinking, you will suddenly see space in the ten directions change into the colours of the seven or of a hundred precious gems, which fill the whole space without hindering one another. All colours such as blue, yellow, red, white, (etc.) appear in utter purity. This is hard pressed efficiency, the temporary achievement of which does not mean you are a saint. If you do not regard it as such, it is an excellent progressive stage, but if you do, you will give way to the demons.
6. 'In this clear and penetrating state of your mind when it looks within, its light appears in all its purity and at midnight you will suddenly see in your dark room all sorts of apparitions as clearly as in broad daylight, with all the other objects usually there. This is the mind, in its subtlety, refining its clear perception which enables you to see distinctly in the dark. This temporary achievement does not mean you are a saint. If you do not regard it as such, it is an excellent progressive stage, but if you do you will give way to demons.
7. 'As the mind merges with the void, suddenly your four limbs will be like grass and plants, and will feel nothing (even) if burned by fire or cut by a knife. This immunity from injury results from the amalgamation of (mind and) externals and with the elimination of the four elements as it merges with the void. This temporary achievement does not mean you are a saint, and if you do not regard it as such, it is an excellent progressive stage, but if you do, you will give way to demons.
8. 'As your mind becomes pure and clean, its uttermost purification causes you to see suddenly the great earth, mountains and riven in the ten directions change into the Buddha's (pure) land adorned with all sorts of precious gems whose radiance is all-pervading. You will again see clearly Buddhas as countless as the Ganges' sands with beautiful temple buildings filling the whole of space, with the hells underneath and deva palaces above. This is the transformation of (usually) deep-rooted thoughts of like and dislike but does not mean you are a saint. If you do not regard it as such, it is an excellent progressive stage, but if you do, you will give way to demons.
9. 'As your mind penetrates deeper, you will suddenly see at midnight far away market-places, streets and lanes, as well as members of your

family, your relatives and clansmen or hear them speak. This results from the hard-pressed mind which expands so that you see these things no matter how far away. This does not mean you are a saint, and if you do not regard it as such, it is an excellent progressive stage, but if you do, you will give way to demons.

10. 'As a result of your mind's furthest penetration, you will see men of good counsel whose bodies change without reason in all kinds of ways. This is your perverse mind which is influenced by mischievous ghosts or heavenly demons and which without reason, preaches the Dharma and comprehends its profound meaning. This does not mean you are a saint and if you do not regard it as such, Māra's influence will vanish, but if you do, you will give way to demons.

'Ānanda, these ten states of dhyāna come from the intermingling of the aggregate of form with the meditative mind. Deluded and wayward practisers do not know their own capabilities, cannot distinguish these states when they manifest, and wrongly declare that they are saints. By so doing, they break the prohibition against lying and so fall into the uninterrupted hell. After my nirvāṇa, in the Dharma ending age, you should proclaim this teaching so that the heavenly demons cannot take advantage of such states and practisers can be on their guard and realize the Supreme Tao.

The Ten States Affected by the Second Aggregate of Receptiveness (Vedānā)

'Ānanda, in the practice of śamatha to realize samādhi, when the first aggregate of form ceases to hinder, one will see the minds of all Buddhas, like reflections in the bright mirror (of the mind). One will feel as if one wins something but cannot yet make use of it.[7] It is like a sleeper troubled with a nightmare who cannot move to repulse it although his four limbs are not bound and his consciousness is clear. This is the second aggregate of receptiveness which conditions one's meditation. If the nightmare vanishes, one's mind can leave one's body to look at one's face and will be free to stay or go without further hindrance. This is the second aggregate of vedanā coming to an end and the practiser will then be able to leap over and beyond the kalpa of turbid views, the main cause of which is the seeming perspicacity of his wrong thinking.

---

[7] The Buddhas' minds are immaterial and to see them shows your mind's receptiveness of externals which thereby hinders your insight and is the cause of your inability to make use of your achievement. When this second aggregate is wiped out, your mind will be free from all hindrance; only then can you make full use of this progressive stage.

1. 'Ānanda, when the practiser reaches this stage, he will find himself in a great mass of brightness. His mind will discern (the sorry plight of living beings) and on being pressed harder, it will give rise to infinite sadness. He will even regard gadflies and mosquitoes as his own children on whom he takes pity, bursting unconsciously into tears. This results from his hard pressed (contemplation) and is harmless if he knows its cause. It is not the saintly state and if he understands it, it will in time disappear. However, if he regards it as sainthood, he will succumb to the demon of sadness who will control his mind and cause him to be miserable and to lament when meeting others; he will lose the benefit from the dhyāna so far achieved and will fall into the lower states.
2. 'Ānanda, in this state of dhyāna, as the aggregate of form vanishes and receptiveness manifests, he makes more progress and may, because of overstrain develop infinite boldness that sharpens his resolve and makes it equal to that of all Buddhas, so that he can leap over the three great aeons[8] in a moment of thought. This comes from overstrained concentration which will be harmless if he knows it (for what it is). It is not sainthood and if it is well understood, it will in time vanish. But if he regards it as saintly, the demon of wildness will control his mind and will cause him to boast (of his achievement) when he meets others. He will become proud and self-important which will blind him to the Buddha high above and to living beings here below. He will thus lose the benefit from the dhyāna so far achieved and will fall into the lower states.
3. 'In this state of dhyāna, as form vanishes and receptiveness manifests, if the practiser makes no headway but loses (sight of) his previous state when looking back, the power of his mind weakens. As it sees nothing ahead, it suddenly gives way to dryness which causes him to indulge in endless deep reflection which he may mistake for progressive advance. This is absent-mindedness which lacks wisdom and is harmless if he knows it (for what it is). This is not sainthood but if he regards it as such, he will succumb to the demon of unforgetfulness who will control his mind and confine it to a fixed place causing him to lose the benefit from the dhyāna so far achieved and to fall into the lower states.
4. 'In this still state, as form vanishes and receptiveness manifests, the practiser's wisdom may grow out of proportion and much in excess of his dhyāna, and he may wrongly think that he has achieved the

[8] The three aeons required for a Bodhisattva to develop into a Buddha: the first one to hear the Dharma, the second to practise it and the third to realize it.

highest attainment and has reached the rank of Vairocana. So he is satisfied with a little progress which he regards as complete. This is his mind losing its usual insight and being misled by his (discriminatory) knowing and seeing. If he understands this, it will be harmless, but if he regards it as sainthood, he will succumb to the inferior self-satisfied demon who will control his mind, causing him to boast that he has realized Supreme Nirvāṇa. He will thus lose all benefit from the dhyāna so far achieved and will fall into the lower states.

5. 'In this state of dhyāna, as form vanishes and receptiveness manifests, before new headway is made and after his previous experience has passed, he may find himself in a situation which seems very dreadful and full of danger, and causes him endless anxiety and perplexity. He seems to sit on a hot iron bed or to drink poisonous medicine. As a result he tires of life and seeks to end it to get rid of this torment. This is practice without the (necessary) expedient method and is harmless if he knows the cause. It is not a saintly state, but if he regards it as such, he will succumb to the demon of anxiety who will control his mind causing him to cut his own flesh with a sharp knife so that he can die or to flee to the mountains and groves in order to avoid other people. He will thus lose all benefit from the dhyāna so far achieved and will fall into the lower states.
6. 'In this state of dhyāna, as form vanishes and receptiveness manifests, the practiser may, after feeling very comfortable in the condition of purity and cleanness, suddenly experience infinite joy which becomes so intense that he cannot check it. This is delight in weightlessness which is uncontrollable for lack of wisdom and is harmless if he knows the cause. This is not a saintly state but if he regards it as such, he will succumb to the demon of joy who will control his mind so that he laughs without cause when seeing others and sings and dances in the street, boasting of his realization of unhindered liberation. He will lose all benefit from the dhyāna so far achieved and will fall into the lower states.
7. 'In this state of dhyāna, as form vanishes and receptiveness manifests, the practiser may think that he has achieved full realization. This illusion causes him suddenly, without any reason, to give rise to self-conceit so that he regards himself, though inferior, as equal to others; though equal, as superior to others and to superiors; as being a saint when he is not; and as not inferior to inferiors;[9] all these feelings occur together. Even all the Buddhas are nothing to him; still more so the less advanced śrāvakas and pratyeka-buddhas. This is an extraordi-

[9] The sevenfold conceit comprises the above six kinds and pride in one's heresy.

nary state from which he fails to extricate himself for lack of wisdom. It will be harmless if he knows that it is not a saintly state, but if he regards it as such, he will succumb to the demon of self-conceit who will control his mind and cause him to stop revering the stūpas and temples and to destroy the sūtras and statues of Buddhas. He will declare to his patrons: "Statues are but gold, bronze, clay and wood and sūtras are but palm (pattra) leaves and clothes. Instead of revering the body of flesh and blood which is really permanent, it is sheer nonsense to worship clay and wood." Those who believe him destroy the statues and sūtras and throw them on the ground; they are misled by him and so will enter the unintermittent hell. Thus he will lose all benefit from the dhyāna so far achieved and will fall into the lower states.

8. 'In this state of dhyāna, as form vanishes and receptiveness manifests, the practiser may achieve the condition of bright purity and awaken to the profound noumenon to which he conforms, thereby suddenly experiencing infinite weightlessness. He will think that he is a saint which gives him comfortable independence. This is weightless purity which is harmless if he knows that it is not a saintly state, but if he regards it as such, he will succumb to the demon of weightless purity who will control his mind causing him to be well satisfied with his (incomplete) achievement and to refrain from striving to advance further. He is like the untutored bhikṣu who misled others and then fell into the avīci hell. He will thus lose all benefit from the dhyāna so far achieved and will sink into the lower states.

9. 'In this state of dhyāna, as form vanishes and receptiveness manifests, the practiser may misconceive the appearing bright emptiness as devoid of nature, thereby giving rise to the idea of extinction which implies that the law of causality is invalid. This (relative) voidness causes him to develop an empty mind which implies annihilation. This is harmless if he knows that it is not sainthood, but if he regards it as such, he will succumb to the demon of emptiness who will control his mind and cause him to criticize those observing the rules of pure living as men of Hīnayāna and to claim that all Bodhisattvas awakened to the void can dispense with all prohibitions. Such a person usually indulges in meat and wine in the presence of his believing patrons and leads a licentious life. Because of the demon's influence, he controls them firmly and they do not suspect him. As time passes, they will all regard excrement, urine, meat and wine as empty and good for food. They will break the rules of morality and discipline and will commit all sorts of sins. The practiser will thus lose all benefit from the dhyāna so far achieved and will fall into the lower states.

10. 'In this state of dhyāna, as form vanishes and receptiveness manifests, the practiser may cling to the empty brightness which will then penetrate his mind and (even) his bones. Suddenly he will feel strong love (for it) which drives him mad and develops his intense desire (of it). This is a condition of still comfort which he cannot control for lack of wisdom, and which misleads him into all sorts of desires. It is harmless if he knows that it is not sainthood but if he regards it as such, he will succumb to the demon of desire who will control his mind and cause him to proclaim desire as the Bodhi path and to teach to laymen the practice of universal desire, saying that sexual indulgence will make them sons of the Dharma. This demon's influence will prevail in the Dharma ending age and will affect stupid people who will number as many as hundreds, thousands and tens of thousands. When the demon is weary of the practiser's misdeeds, he will leave the latter's body which will become a sorry wreck to suffer all the miseries inflicted by the royal law. For deceiving others, he will fall into the unintermittent Thus he will lose all benefit from the dhyāna so far achieved and will sink into the lower states.

'Ānanda, these ten states of dhyāna come from the intermingling of the second aggregate of receptiveness with meditative mind. Deluded and wayward practisers do not know their own capabilities cannot distinguish these states when they manifest and wrongly declare that they have attained the holy rank. By so doing, they break the rule against lying and so will fall into the uninterrupted hell. After my nirvāṇa, in the Dharma ending age, you should proclaim this teaching so that living beings will awaken to it, that the heavenly demon cannot take advantage of such states and that practisers can be on their guard and realize the Supreme Tao.

The Ten States Affected by the Third Aggregate of Conception (Sañjñā)

'Ānanda, in the cultivation of samādhi, when the second aggregate of receptiveness ceases to hinder the practiser, although he is still in the worldly stream, his mind can now escape from his body, like a bird from its cage. From his worldly state he can now achieve the sixty succeeding holy stages of Bodhisattva development into Buddhahood and thereby take any form at will, free to move anywhere without hindrance. This is like a man who talks in his sleep and though he does not know what he says, his words are in order (and comprehensible), and those who are not asleep understand him. This is the third aggregate of conception which conditions his meditation.

'If all his stirring thoughts stop, he will be rid of the thinking process and his clear mind will be (like a mirror) rubbed clean of the covering dust, and will throw light upon his (present) incarnation from birth to death. Then the third aggregate of conception ceases to function and the practiser will be able to leap above and beyond the kalpa of turbid passions, the main cause of which was the seeming pervasiveness of his wrong thinking.

1. 'Ānanda, now that the practiser is free from anxiety, after his receptiveness has vanished, he finds himself in the state of perfect dhyāna and likes its pure brightness. But he may be tempted to concentrate on the one thought of skilfully advancing, thus submitting to the heavenly demon who immediately possesses another man (to harm the meditator).[10] This man, unaware that he is possessed will, as directed, preach the Dharma of the sūtras and think that he too has realized Supreme Nirvāṇa. He will then come to the practiser's place and take the high seat (reserved for reputable monks) to teach him the Dharma. To show his skill, he will appear either as a monk, Indra, a woman or a nun, and his body will send out rays of light that illumine the dark bedroom. The practiser will mistake him for a Bodhisattva and will believe what he says; as a result, his mind will waver and he will break the rules and have desires. The man will speak of weal and woe, of a Buddha appearing at a certain place, of scorching fire in the kalpa of destruction and of future fighting and wars to frighten and ruin other people. This is the Strange Ghost who has become a demon in his old age and who now comes to trouble the practiser. When he is weary of his misdeeds, he will leave the possessed man. Then both teacher (the possessed man) and pupil (the practiser) will suffer all the miseries inflicted by the royal law. You should first be clear about this temptation to avoid returning to saṁsāra, but if you are deluded and do not recognize it, you will fall into the unintermittent hell.
2. 'Ānanda, now that the practiser is free from false anxiety after his receptiveness has vanished he finds himself in the state of perfect dhyāna. But he may be tempted to roam about (in unknown regions) and so concentrates on the one thought of gaining further experience, thus succumbing to the heavenly demon who immediately possesses another man (to harm the meditator). This man unaware that he is possessed will, as directed, preach the Dharma and think that he himself has realized Supreme Nirvāṇa. He will then come to the practiser's

[10] As the practiser's mind is free from receptiveness, the demon is unable to influence it, so he uses another man to deceive and harm him.

place and take the high seat to teach him the Dharma. Without changing his own appearance, he will cause the practiser and those present to see their own radiant golden bodies seated on precious lotus flowers. The practiser will be deceived into mistaking the man for a Bodhisattva and will believe what he says; as a result he will indulge in luxurious ease, breaking the Buddha's rules and becoming licentious. The man will speak of Buddhas appearing in the world, of a certain person at a given place, who is a Buddha in his transformation body and of someone else who is a Bodhisattva coming to convert people. The practiser is fascinated and admires what he has seen, thereby giving rise to wrong views and so destroying (his) seed of wisdom. This is the Drought Ghost who has become a demon in his old age and now comes to trouble the practiser. When he is weary of his misdeeds, he will leave the possessed man. Then both teacher and pupil will suffer the miseries inflicted by the law. You should first be clear about this temptation to avoid returning to saṁsāra but if you are deluded and do not recognize it, you will fall into the unintermittent hell.

3. 'Now that the practiser is free from false anxiety after his receptiveness has vanished he finds himself in this state of perfect dhyāna. But he may be tempted by his delight to concentrate on the one thought of uniting with it, thus succumbing to the heavenly demon who immediately possesses another man (to harm the meditator). This man unaware that he is possessed will, as directed, preach the Dharma and think that he himself has realized Supreme Nirvāṇa. He will then come to the practiser's place and take the high seat to teach him the Dharma. Without changing his own or the listeners' forms, he will cause them to open their minds which will jump about so that in turn they know all their former lives, read the minds of others, see the hells, comprehend all good and evil worldly deeds, read gāthās and recite sūtras. And so he fascinates them with such rare things. The practiser will be deceived into mistaking him for a true Bodhisattva and will be enthusiastic about all he says, thereby breaking the Buddha's rules and becoming licentious. This man will classify the Buddhas and Bodhisattvas into big and small, early and late, real and false, and male and female. The practiser believes him so that his mind is disturbed and he becomes a heretic. This is the Beast Ghost who has become a demon in his old age and who now comes to trouble the practiser. When he is weary of his misdeeds, he will leave the possessed man. Then both teacher and pupil will suffer the miseries inflicted by the law. You should first be clear about this temptation to avoid returning to saṁsāra, but if you are deluded and do not recognize it, you will fall into the unintermittent hell.

4. 'Now that the practiser is free from false anxiety after his receptiveness has vanished he finds himself in this state of perfect dhyāna. But he may be tempted by his delight in it to go to the root of all things in order to know the beginning and the end of all transformation, thereby wishing to analyse everything to solve all his doubts to his entire satisfaction. As a result, the heavenly demon immediately possesses another man (to harm the meditator). This man unaware that he is possessed will, as directed, preach the Dharma, thinking that he himself has realized Supreme Nirvāṇa. He will then come to the practiser's place where he will take the high seat to teach him the Dharma, showing his awe-inspiring authority to which the meditator willingly submits even before hearing his words. He will declare that the Buddha's nirvanic and bodhic Dharmakāya is his own body of flesh and blood which inherits the holy essence, as a son from his father, that it is the permanent spiritual body which will be transmitted forever, that what his listeners see around them is the Buddha-land, and that there is no other pure region nor another golden body. The practiser will believe this, lose his former still mind and submit to him, praising the rare revelation; he and other deluded listeners will mistake the possessed man for a true Bodhisattva, and will follow him to break the Buddha's rules by indulging in sexual desire. This man will declare that the eyes, ears, nose and tongue are pure lands and that the male and female organs are the abodes of Bodhi and Nirvāṇa, and his deluded listeners will believe his perverse preaching. This is the Noxious or Nightmarish Ghost who has become a demon in his old age and now comes to trouble the practiser. When he grows weary of his misdeeds, he will leave the possessed man. Then both teacher and pupil will suffer the miseries inflicted by the law. You should be first clear about this temptation to avoid returning to saṁsāra, but if you are deluded and do not recognize it, you will fall into the unintermittent hells.
5. 'Now that the practiser is free from false anxiety after his receptiveness has vanished he finds himself in this state of perfect dhyāna. But he may be tempted by his delight in it to seek communion (with the Buddha) and thereby feels a strong desire for spiritual intercourse, thus succumbing to the heavenly demon who will immediately possess another man (to harm the meditator). This man unaware that he is possessed will, as directed, preach the Dharma and think that he has realized Supreme Nirvāṇa. He will then come to the practiser's place and take the high seat to teach the Dharma and cause his listeners to see him as a man a hundred or a thousand years old. They will admire him, will live with and serve him and provide him with the

four necessities (of a monk) and will not tire of so doing. Since the practiser is convinced that the man was his master in a previous life, he respects and becomes attached to him, praising his rare revelation; he and other deluded listeners will mistake him for a true Bodhisattva and will follow his instruction, thereby breaking the Buddha's rules and indulging in sexual desire. The man will declare that in a previous life he delivered his wife or brother who now comes to follow him to a particular region where they will all serve a certain Buddha; or he will speak of a radiant heaven where the Buddha now dwells and where all the Tathāgatas are at rest. The practiser who is deluded will believe all this and will lose his clear mind. This is the Cruel Ghost who has become a demon in his old age and now comes to trouble the practiser; when he grows weary of his misdeeds, he will leave the possessed man. Then both teacher and pupil will suffer the miseries inflicted by the law. You should first be clear about this temptation to avoid returning to saṁsāra, but if you are deluded and do not recognize it, you will fall into the unintermittent hells.

6. 'Now that the practiser is free from false anxiety after his receptiveness has vanished he finds himself in this state of perfect dhyāna. But he may be tempted by his delight in it to strive to go deeper in his search for restfulness, and so succumb to the heavenly demon who will possess another man (to harm the meditator). This man unaware that he is possessed will, as directed, preach the Dharma and also think that he has realized Supreme Nirvāṇa. He will then come to the practiser's place and take the high seat to teach the Dharma and cause each of his listeners to know his own karma. He will tell one of them that though the latter is still living, he is already an animal, or order another to sit on the ground and then make him unable to get up. Those present will admire his supernatural powers and submit themselves to him; if one of them thinks of anything, the man knows it at once. He will order them to practise unnecessary austerities in addition to the Buddha's precepts. He will vilify the bhikṣus and curse their followers. He will reveal others' shortcomings without being afraid of ridicule. He will foretell weal and woe which later materialize. This is the Powerful Ghost who has become a demon in his old age and who now comes to trouble the practiser: when he is weary of his misdeeds, he will leave the possessed man. Then both teacher and pupil will suffer the miseries indicted by the law. You should first be clear about this temptation to avoid returning to saṁsāra, but if you are deluded and do not recognize it, you will fall into the unintermittent hells.

7. 'Now that the practiser is free from false anxiety after his receptiveness has vanished, he finds himself in this state of perfect dhyāna.

But he may be tempted by his delight in it to strive for more learning in his search for knowledge of his former lives, thereby succumbing to the heavenly demon who immediately possesses another man (to harm the meditator). This man unaware that he is possessed will, as directed, preach the Dharma and also think that he himself has realized Supreme Nirvāṇa. He will then come to the practiser's place and take the high seat to teach the Dharma and the latter suddenly finds a precious pearl (in the room). The demon will either appear as an animal with in his mouth a pearl and other precious stones, documents and registers which it gives to the man to deceive his listeners, or will hide a bright pearl in the ground to light up the whole place. His listeners will praise the miracle. The possessed man will abstain from food, eating only medicinal herbs, or will take only a hemp-seed or a grain of wheat each day, but the demon will cause him to be strong and sturdy. He will vilify the bhikṣus and curse their followers. He will reveal other people's shortcomings without being afraid of ridicule. He will reveal secret places where treasures are hidden and where saints live, and those who then go there actually meet strange persons. This is the ghost of the mountains, groves and rivers who has become a demon in his old age. His aim is to encourage others to break the Buddha's rules, to indulge in lust and give rein to the five desires (arising from the objects of the five senses). If he makes progress at the start of his practice, he will eat only herbs and plants and his actions will be uncertain. His object is to trouble the practiser and when he is weary of his misdeeds, he will leave the possessed man. Then both teacher and pupil will suffer the miseries inflicted by the law. You should first be clear about this temptation to avoid returning to saṁsāra but if you are deluded and do not recognize it, you will fall into the unintermittent hells.

8. 'Now that the practiser is free from false anxiety after his receptiveness has vanished he finds himself in this state of perfect dhyāna. But he may be tempted by his delight in it to seek and use the above supernatural powers, thus succumbing to the heavenly demon who immediately possesses another man (to trouble him). This man unaware that he is possessed will, as directed, preach the Dharma and also think that he has realized Supreme Nirvāṇa. He will then come to the practiser's place and take the high seat to preach the Dharma. He will hold a ball of fire which he divides into as many balls as there are listeners putting one on each of their heads. They will not feel the heat and will not be burned although the fireballs are several feet high. He also walks on water, sits motionless in the air, enters a bottle

or a bag and walks through the wall but he is not immune to choppers and swords.[11] He claims to be a Buddha and though he is a layman, he dares to receive reverence from the bhikṣus, cursing their disciples and vilifying the rules of discipline. He likes to disclose other people's shortcomings without being afraid of ridicule. He boasts of his supernatural powers and causes his listeners to see Buddha-lands which are false and unreal. He praises carnality and encourages licentious conduct which he uses to transmit his Dharma. This is one of those Strong Spirits of the mountains, seas, wind, rivers and earth, dwelling in grass and plants, or a Nāga or decaying seer about to die and become a ghost, whose forms are possessed by other ghosts, one of which now comes to trouble the practiser; when he grows weary of his misdeeds, he will leave the possessed man. Then both teacher and pupil will suffer the miseries inflicted by the law. You should first be clear about this temptation to avoid returning to saṁsāra, but if you are deluded and do not recognize it, you will fall into the unintermittent hells.

9. 'Now that the practiser is free from false anxiety after his receptiveness has vanished he finds himself in this state of perfect dhyāna. But he may be tempted by his delight in it to seek the extinction of suffering (in Nirvāṇa) and so searches deeply into the nature of transformation in his search for profound emptiness. As a result he succumbs to the heavenly demon who immediately possesses another man (to trouble the meditator). This man unaware that he is possessed will, as directed, preach the Dharma and also think that he has realized Supreme Nirvāṇa. He will then come to the practiser's place and take the high seat to preach the Dharma to his listeners. In their presence, he will disappear suddenly and then descend from the sky, again vanishing and re-appearing at will. His body will seem transparent as crystal and his limbs will be fragrant like sandalwood. His excrement and urine are as hard as rock-candy. He breaks the Buddha's rules and despises all monks and nuns. He preaches that the law of causality is invalid, that there is annihilation after death and no such thing as reincarnation or worldly and saintly states (after this life). Though he has realized voidness, he indulges in sexual desires and boasts that his followers also realize the void in which there is neither cause nor effect. This is one of those ghosts and spirits who live for thousands and tens of thousands of years and have become demons in their old age; he now comes to trouble the practiser and when he grows weary of these misdeeds, he will leave the possessed man. Then both teacher

[11] Because the man still possesses a physical body which can be injured.

and pupil will suffer the miseries inflicted by the law. You should first be clear about this temptation to avoid returning to saṁsāra, but if you are deluded and do not recognize it, you will fall into the unintermittent hells.

10. 'Now that the practiser is free from false anxiety after his receptiveness has vanished, he finds himself in this state of perfect dhyāna. But he may be tempted by his delight in it to seek longevity and indulge in tiresome research in his quest for eternity by relinquishing his mortal lot in exchange for immortality. Thus he succumbs to the heavenly demon who immediately possesses another man (to trouble him). This man unaware that he is possessed will, as directed, preach the Dharma and also think that he himself has realized Supreme Nirvāṇa. He will then come to the practiser's place and take the high seat to teach the Dharma to those present, declaring that he can travel to and from distant places at will; will then go thousands of miles away and return to his seat in the twinkling of an eye, bringing things back with him. Or he may show them that for years they will be unable to walk more than a few paces across the room. They will believe him and mistake him for a Buddha. He will then proclaim that all living beings are his children, that he is a begetter of Buddhas, that he appears in the world (to save others), that he is the primal Buddha and needs no practice to be so. This heavenly demon may be either a jealous female spirit (cāmundā) from the Isvara heaven or a consumer of vitality (piśācah) from the heaven of the four deva kings, who has not a straightforward mind and uses the practiser's wrong thinking to absorb his vitality. He may not possess another man but may appear as one with power to wield a vajra to bestow long life on the practiser or as a beautiful girl to seduce him, thereby exhausting his vitality. He is delirious and can be distinguished by his incoherent speech, but if the practiser fails to recognize him, he will make mischief. The meditator will then suffer the miseries inflicted by the law; he usually dies from exhaustion before his punishment is carried out (by the authorities). You should first be clear about this temptation to avoid returning to saṁsāra, but if you are deluded and do not recognize it, you will fall into the unintermittent hells.

'Ānanda, there is no need for you to attain Nirvāṇa now. Though you have reached the stage beyond all studies, you should fulfil your vow to re-enter this world in the Dharma ending age to develop great compassion and to deliver those living beings whose minds are set on right belief so that they will not be troubled by demons but realize right knowledge. I have delivered you from saṁsāra and by carrying out my order, you will repay your debt of gratitude to the Buddha.

'Ānanda, the above ten states of dhyāna come from the intermingling of the third aggregate of conception with meditative mind. Deluded and wayward practisers who do not know their capabilities, cannot distinguish these states when they manifest and wrongly declare that they have attained the holy rank. By so doing, they break the prohibition against lying and, will fall into the unintermittent hells. After my nirvāṇa in the Dharma ending age, you should proclaim this teaching so that living beings will awaken to it, that heavenly demons cannot take advantage of such states and that all practisers can be on their guard and realize the Supreme Tao.

The Ten States Affected By the Fourth Aggregate of Discrimination (Samskāra)

'Ānanda, in his cultivation of samādhi, when the third aggregate of conception ends, the practiser will be free from the usual delusive thinking and will achieve the still and bright state of mind which is like the clear sky and is always the same whether waking or sleeping, and devoid of the shadows of coarse sense data. To him the mountains, rivers, great earth and universe are reflections in a bright mirror, appearing and vanishing without leaving a trace behind; thus his mind only reflects externals without being affected by them. This is the one essence (ālaya) in which the fourth aggregate now manifests. The practiser will perceive all living beings of the twelve types of birth in the ten directions and though he does not know the true cause of their existence, to him they are all in the same state of life. This functioning of mind (saṁskāra) is like a twinkling mirage that disturbs the clear (horizon) and is the chief cause of the illusion of the sense organs and data. This is the fourth aggregate which conditions the practiser's meditation.

'If this sparkling disturbance returns to its serene source (ālaya), like ripples that settle to become calm and clear water, the aggregate samskāra will come to an end, and the practiser will leap above and beyond the kalpa of turbid being, the main cause of which is the undetected subtlety of his wrong thinking.

1. 'Ānanda, you should know that when the practiser, as a result of pointed concentration (after the third aggregate has vanished), acquires correct knowledge in his practice of śamatha, his mind is settled and clear and can no more be troubled by the ten classes of demons. Only now can he look exhaustively into the origin of living

beings. In his discovery of the subtle disturbance (which is not easily detectable), if he begins to differentiate he will fall into error because of the (following) two heterodox conceptions of the non-existence of cause.

‘i. He finds no anterior cause (of existence) in his investigation. Why? Because he has wiped out the mechanism of life and can now, by means of the 800 merits of his organ of sight, look into the 80,000 kalpas in which all living beings transmigrate from place to place and beyond which he can see nothing. He then concludes that all living beings exist of themselves without any cause during these 80,000 aeons and, because of this differentiation, he will miss the Buddha’s universal knowledge thereby falling into heresy which will screen his Bodhi nature.

‘ii. He finds no posterior cause (of existence) in his investigation. Why? Because he has seen the root of life and concludes that, as always, men beget men and birds birds, that crows are black and storks-white, that men and devas are upright and animals slanting, that their white colour does not come from washing nor their black colour from dyes, and that all this has been and will be so throughout these 80,000 aeons. Since he never saw Bodhi before, how can he realize it now? He will now conclude that all things come from no cause; so he will miss the Buddha’s universal knowledge and will fall into heresy which will screen his Bodhi nature.

‘The above pertain to the first state of heterodox discrimination (saṁskāra) which postulates the non-existence of cause.

2. ‘Ānanda, in his cultivation of samādhi, as a result of pointed concentration, the practiser’s mind is now settled and can no more be troubled by demons. He can look exhaustively into the origin of all living beings, and in his discovery of the subtle disturbance which continues endlessly, if he begins to differentiate, he will fall into error because of the (following) four heterodox conceptions of universal permanence.

‘i. By looking exhaustively into the mind and its object, he finds that both are causeless, and since his meditative study enables him to know that in 20,000 aeons all living beings are subject to the endless round of births and deaths without being annihilated, he gives rise to the wrong concept of the permanence (of mind and its object).

‘ii. By looking exhaustively into the four elements, he finds that they exist permanently, and since his meditative study enables him to know that in 40,000 aeons all living beings preserve their forms which are not destroyed in spite of their births and deaths, he gives rise to the wrong concept of the permanence of the four elements.

'iii. By looking exhaustively into the six organs and the seventh and eighth consciousnesses, he finds that the origin of mind, intellect and consciousness is permanent. Thus his meditative study enables him to know that in 80,000 kalpas all living beings always preserve this origin and that it always remains, thereby giving rise to the concept of the permanence (of the eighth consciousness).

'iv. As the practiser has wiped out the third aggregate completely, he (wrongly) thinks that life has ceased to flow and that since his thinking mind (sañjñā) has ended, that which now remains (i.e. saṁskāra) is permanent, thus giving rise to the concept of the permanence (of the fourth aggregate).

'Because of his wrong conception of true permanence, he misses the Buddha's universal knowledge and falls into heresy which screens his Bodhi nature. The above pertains to the second state of heterodox discrimination (saṁskāra) which postulates wrong permanence.

3. 'Further, in his cultivation of samādhi which, as a result of his pointed concentration of mind, can no more be troubled by demons, if he looks exhaustively into the origin of living beings and begins to differentiate as he contemplates the continuous subtle disturbance in this clear state, he will fall into error because of the (following) four perverse views of the duality of permanence and impermanence.[12]

'i. The practiser looks into the profound bright mind which pervades everywhere and regards it as his spiritual ego; he finds that his ego which is bright and unchanging, embraces all the ten directions and that all living beings are born and die by themselves in his mind, thereby concluding that it is permanent and all those subject to birth and death are impermanent.

'ii. The practiser, instead of looking into his own mind, contemplates countries which are countless as the Ganges' sands, and thereby regards as impermanent those regions which are annihilated in the kalpa of destruction[13] and as permanent those unaffected by it.[14]

---

[12] This is the seventh consciousness clinging to ālaya's perception which is regarded as an ego.

[13] The third dhyāna heaven and the worlds below it.

[14] The fourth dhyāna heaven and those above it.

'iii. The practiser looks into his mind which, to him, is subtle and mysterious like molecules which penetrate everywhere and whose nature is unchanged, and can subject his body to birth and death simultaneously in every flash of thought. He regards that which does not decay as his permanent ego and that which is subject to birth and death and flows from his ego as impermanent.

'iv. The practiser who knows that after the third aggregate has vanished, the fourth one flows continuously, will regard the latter as permanent and the first three aggregates which have already ended as impermanent.

'By so differentiating between permanence and impermanence, he falls into heresy which screens his Bodhi nature. The above pertain to the third state of heterodox discrimination (saṁskāra) which postulates the duality of permanence and impermanence.

4. 'Further, in his cultivation of samādhi which, as a result of pointed concentration of mind, can no more be troubled by demons, if the practiser looks exhaustively into the origin of living beings and begins to differentiate as he contemplates the continuous disturbance in this clear state, he will fall into error because of the following four dual views of the finite and infinite.

'i. He looks into the origin of life which flows endlessly and concludes that the past and the future which he does not see are finite and that his present mind which does not stop is infinite.

'ii. He looks into 80,000 kalpas and sees living beings in this long period of time but when looking into the time prior even to that, he sees and hears nothing; he then concludes that the region where he sees and hears nothing is infinite and the one where there are living beings is finite.

'iii. The practiser finds that his knowledge reaches everywhere and concludes that since all living beings appear therein (i.e. in his knowing mind), his nature is infinite. As their knowledge (i.e. their minds) do not appear in his, he reasons that their minds are finite as well as their nature.

'iv. As the practiser looks exhaustively into the fourth aggregate and finds that it ends in emptiness, (he reasons that its end is annihilation and its manifestation is creation and so) infers that each living being partly exists and partly does not and so concludes that all things in the world are half finite and half infinite.

'By so discriminating between the finite and the infinite, he falls into heresy which screens his Bodhi nature. The above pertain to the fourth state of heterodox discrimination (saṁskāra) which postulates the duality of the finite and the infinite.

5. 'Further, in his cultivation of samādhi which, as a result of his pointed concentration of mind, can no more be troubled by demons, if the practiser looks exhaustively into the origin of living beings and begins to differentiate between views when contemplating the continuous subtle disturbance in this clear state, he will fall into error because of the (following) four confused views about the undying heaven.[15]
   'i. As he investigates the origin of transformation, he may call changing that which varies, unchanging that which continues, born that which is visible, annihilated that which is no more seen, increasing that which preserves its nature in the process of transformation, decreasing that whose nature is interrupted in the changing process, existing that which is created and non-existent that which disappears; this is the result of his differentiation of the (eight states) seen as he contemplates the manifestations of the fourth aggregate. If seekers of the truth call on him for instruction, he will declare: "I now both live and die, both exist and do not, both increase and decrease," thus talking wildly to mislead them.
   'ii. As the practiser looks exhaustively into his mind, he finds that each thought ceases to exist in a flash and concludes that they are non-existent. If people ask for instruction, his answer consists of the one word "Nothing," beyond which he says nothing else.
   'iii. As the practiser looks exhaustively into his mind, he sees the rise of his thoughts and concludes that they exist. If people ask for instruction, his answer consists of the one word "Something," beyond which he says nothing else.[16]
   'iv. The practiser sees both existence and non-existence and finds that such states are so complicated that they confuse him. If people ask for instruction, he will say: "The existing comprises the non-existent but the non-existent do-not comprise the exist-

[15] Heretics believe that heaven is undying and that he who does not mislead others when teaching them, will be reborn there. Hence, in their answers to their students' questions, they use abstruse terms and abstain from giving complete and specific replies which the Buddha denounces as wild talk.

[16] He sees not only the rise, but also the fall, of thoughts; hence his ambiguous reply: 'Something' without daring to speak specifically of their existence in order not to be in the wrong.

ing,"[17] in such a perfunctory manner as to prevent exhaustive inquiries.

'By so discriminating, he causes confusion and so falls into heresy which screens his Bodhi nature. The above pertain to the fifth state of heterodox discrimination (saṁskāra) which postulates confused views about the undying.

6. 'Further, in his cultivation of samādhi which, as a result of his pointed concentration of mind, can no more be troubled by demons, if the practiser looks exhaustively into the origin of living beings and begins to differentiate as he contemplates the endless flow (of the fourth aggregate), he will fall into error because of his wrong view of the continued existence of form after death[18] arising from his upset mind.

'So he clings firmly to his body and believes that form is ego; he sees that his mind embraces all countries everywhere and believes that form is within ego; he sees that form is now restored to follow his ego, and believes that ego exists apart from form; and he sees that his ego continues to exist in the flow of saṁskāra and believes that it is within form.

'These are (the four kinds of) discrimination arising from the belief that form continues to exist after death. Thus there are sixteen kinds of such discrimination due to wrong contemplation of the first four aggregates (rūpa, vedanā, sañjñā and saṁskāra).

'From then on the practiser discriminates between fundamental troubles (kleśa) and fundamental Bodhi as existing side by side without contradicting each other. For this wrong view that form continues after death, he will fall into heresy that screens his Bodhi nature.

'The above pertain to the sixth state of heterodox discrimination (saṁskāra) which postulates the wrong view that form exists after death.

7. 'Further, in his cultivation of samādhi which, as a result of his pointed concentration of mind, can no more be troubled by demons, if the practiser looks into the origin of living beings and begins to differentiate as he contemplates the fourth aggregate (saṁskāra) which will vanish in the same way the first three (rūpa, vedanā and sañjñā) did before, he will fall into error because of his wrong view of the non-existence of form after death arising from his upset mind.

[17] For he dares not say definitely that something exists in the non-existent.

[18] For he mistakes the fourth aggregate for his ego.

'He saw that form was causeless when rūpa vanished, that his mind was free from bondage when sañjñā ended and that all links were broken when vedanā stopped. He now concludes that once the aggregates are no more, life deprived of vedanā and sañjñā is like grass and plants. Even rūpa does not exist in life, how can there be form after death? So his investigation reveals the non-existence of form after death with the ensuing eightfold absence of form.[19] Hence his belief that Nirvāṇa has neither cause nor effect and that all things are void, have only (empty) names and are fundamentally subject to annihilation.

'For this wrong view of annihilation after death, he falls into heresy that screens his Bodhi nature. This is the seventh state of heterodox discrimination (saṁskāra) which postulates the wrong view of annihilation (ucchedadarśana).

8. 'Further, in his cultivation of samādhi which, as a result of his pointed concentration of mind, can no more be troubled by demons, if the practiser looks into the origin of living beings and begins to differentiate as he contemplates the fourth aggregate which now manifests whereas (rūpa), vedanā and sañjñā have vanished, he will fall into error because of the wrong dual view of existence and non-existence which is self-contradictory and which implies the negation of both after death.[20]

'Thus rūpa, vedanā and sañjñā, previously seen to exist now do not. If saṁskāra which now manifests is likewise not to exist it is (in fact) not non-existent. If these four aggregates are likewise looked into, the conclusion is the eightfold negative view of form in life and after death. Thus each of them when investigated can be said to be neither existing nor non-existent after death.

'Further, since the fourth aggregate is (always) changing, he reasons that both its existence and non-existence are invalid for it is neither real nor unreal (in life). So he infers that nothing can be said of it in the dark and obscure condition after death.

'For holding the above views, he will fall into heresy that screens his Bodhi nature. They pertain to the eighth state of heterodox discrimina-

[19] Each of the first four aggregates is devoid of cause-form and effect-form.

[20] He reasons that since the first three aggregates have vanished, the fourth will follow them sooner or later, and so infers that all four are non-existent. He then reasons that the fourth aggregate manifests now in spite of the disappearance of the first three, and so infers that all four are not non-existent. Thus he concludes that since the four aggregates are neither existing nor non-existent in life, they will be so after death; hence the eightfold negative view.

tion (saṁskāra) which postulates the invalidity of both the existence and non-existence of the five aggregates after death.

9. 'Further, in his cultivation of samādhi which, as a result of his pointed concentration of mind, can no more be troubled by demons, if the practiser looks into the origin of living beings to differentiate as he contemplates the fourth aggregate which is subject to annihilation after its rise and fall in every flash of thought, he will fall into error because of his wrong conception of either one of the seven states where body, desire, suffering, joy, and indifference[21] are destroyed and where nothing exists after their annihilation which is final.

'For this wrong view of annihilation after death, he will fall into heresy which screens his Bodhi nature. This is the ninth state of heterodox discrimination which arises from the upset mind and which postulates the annihilation of the five aggregates after the present life.

10. 'Further, in his cultivation of samādhi which, as a result of his pointed concentration of mind, can be no more troubled by demons, if the practiser looks into the origin of living beings and begins to differentiate as he contemplates the fourth aggregate which will recur after its annihilation (after death), he will fall into error because of his misconception of the five false conditions of Nirvāṇa.

'In his contemplation of the condition of perfect clearness which now manifests, he is tempted to transmute into Nirvāṇa either (a) the heaven of desire because of his delight in that condition; (b) the first dhyāna heaven because it is free from trouble and anxiety; (c) the second dhyāna heaven because it is free from suffering; (d) the third dhyāna heaven because it is foil of joy; or (e) the fourth dhyāna heaven which is free from both suffering and joy and is beyond birth and death in saṁsāra. Thus he will mistake samsaric heavens for the (fundamental) wu wei state and cling to (either one of) these five states as an ultimate abode offering peace and security. Because of this differentiation, he will fall into heresy which will screen his Bodhi nature. This is the tenth state of heterodox discrimination (saṁskāra) which postulates five conditions of Nirvāṇa, arising from the five aggregates.

---

[21] Annihilation of body in the realms of men and devas; of desire in the first dhyāna heaven; of suffering in the second; of joy in the third and of indifference in the fourth dhyāna heaven and the formless world.

'Ānanda, these ten kinds of wild interpretation of dhyāna come from the intermingling of the fourth aggregate of discrimination with meditative mind. Deluded and wayward practisers who do not know their own capabilities, cannot distinguish these states when they manifest and wrongly declare that they have attained the holy rank. By so doing, they will break the rule against lying and so fall into the unintermittent hells. After my nirvāṇa, in the Dharma ending age, you should proclaim this teaching so that living beings will awaken to it, that the demons of their minds will not lead them to self-inflicted calamities, and that all practisers can be on their guard and wipe out heterodox views. You should teach them how to discipline their bodies and minds so that they awaken to Reality and avoid straying from the Supreme Path, and to refrain from wishful thinking and from mistaking some little progress for complete realization. You should act as their guide to Supreme Enlightenment.

The Ten States Affected by the Fifth Aggregate of Consciousness (Vijñāna)

'Ānanda, in the cultivation of samādhi, when the fourth aggregate of discrimination (saṁskāra) comes to an end, the subtle disturbance in the state of clearness, (that is the functioning of samsaric mind), which is the mechanism of birth and death, suddenly explodes and exposes an outlook completely different from that of the profound karma of pudgala (i.e. all beings subject to transmigration). This is the moment when Nirvāṇa is about to dawn, like the cock-crow that heralds the first light of the day in the east, when the six senses are void and still and no more wander outside. Within and without there is only a profound brightness reaching the root of life of all beings of the twelve forms of birth in the ten directions of space wherein there is nothing that can be further penetrated. This contemplation of the essence of basic clinging (i.e. the fifth aggregate of consciousness) releases the practiser from all attraction (by old habits and new karma) and immunizes him from further transmigration in saṁsāra for he has realized the identity of mind with its self-created externals everywhere. As the nature of consciousness now manifests clearly, he will discover its hidden depth. This is the fifth aggregate of consciousness which conditions the practiser's meditation.

'As the practiser is immune against external attractions and realizes the identity of mind and objects, the separateness arising from the six different sense organs ceases and the mind functions uniformally with seeing and hearing in regard to a single function which is pure and clean. In this state, all the worlds in the ten directions, together with his body and mind, are clear and transparent like crystal both within and without.

This is the end of the aggregate of consciousness which enables the practiser to leap over and beyond the kalpa of turbid life, the main cause of which is the (first) seeming shadow of his wrong thinking.[22]

1. 'Ānanda, you should know that, as the practiser looks exhaustively into the fourth aggregate (saṁskāra), it will return to its source, that is (the fifth aggregate) consciousness. Though he wipes out birth and death, he does not yet achieve the pure and profound state of Nirvāṇa. He can now unify the different functions of the sense organs, and so is aware that all beings are created by consciousness. Thus he can enter the source of perfection but if, on his return to it, he wrongly sets it up as the cause of true permanence, and regards this as correct, he will fall into error and will become an adherent of the Kapila doctrine which postulates primordial darkness, thereby screening his Bodhi nature and missing the Buddha-knowledge.

'This is the first state of the aggregate of consciousness which sets up the mind thus realized as ultimate attainment so straying far from Complete Enlightenment and standing opposite to Nirvāṇa, thus sowing the seed of heresy.

2. 'Ānanda, as the practiser looks exhaustively into saṁskāra which now becomes void, he will wipe out birth and death but will not yet achieve Nirvāṇa. If he regards consciousness as his substance and insists that he is right in thinking that all living beings of the twelve types of birth in boundless space spring from his body, he will err because of his wrong conception of a subjective creator and will become an adherent of Maheśvara who appears in a body which has no limit; it will screen his Bodhi nature and will cause him to miss the Buddha-knowledge.

'This is the second state of the aggregate of consciousness which sets up the mind-creator as ultimate attainment, thus straying far from Complete Enlightenment and standing opposite to Nirvāṇa, thereby sowing the seed of great pride in an omnipresent divine ego.

3. 'As the practiser looks exhaustively into saṁskāra which now becomes void, he will wipe out birth and death but will not yet achieve Nirvāṇa. If he clings to consciousness as his refuge, he will interpret that his body and mind as well as the whole of space spring from that refuge, thereby wrongly inferring that this source is true Reality, free from

[22] i.e. the first thought that stirred the mind since the time without beginning.

birth and death. Because of his misinterpretation of vijñana (consciousness) as permanent, he will understand neither the Uncreate nor (the created) birth and death. For his delight in this deluded state, he will fall into error because he mistakes impermanence for permanence and will thus become an adherent of Iśvaradeva, (the divine ego who creates all things), thereby screening his Bodhi nature and missing the Buddha-knowledge.

'This is the third state of the aggregate of consciousness which sets up the causal mind as ultimate attainment, thus straying far from Complete Enlightenment and standing opposite to Nirvāṇa and so sowing the seed of perfection's opposite.

4. 'As the practiser looks exhaustively into saṁskāra which becomes void, he will wipe out birth and death but will not yet achieve Nirvāṇa. If he clings to his knowledge of his all-embracing consciousness (ālaya) and so sets up his own interpretation that all grass and plants are sentient and do not differ from men and that after death men will become grass and plants. If he delights in such misconception, he will fall into error because of wrong knowing and will become an adherent of the doctrine of Vasiṣṭha[23] and Śani, thus screening his Bodhi nature and missing the Buddha-knowledge.

'This is the fourth state of the aggregate of consciousness which sets up the knowing mind as ultimate attainment, thus straying far from Complete Enlightenment and standing opposite to Nirvāṇa, thereby sowing the seed of inverted knowing.

5. 'As the practiser looks exhaustively into saṁskāra which now ends, he wipes out birth and death but does not yet achieve Nirvāṇa. If he awakens to the uniformity of the (six) sense organs, as he contemplates the original transformation (of the four elements), he may be tempted to worship the brightness of fire, the purity of water, the freedom of wind and the creativeness of earth. He will regard them as fundamental causes of creation and as permanent Reality, thereby falling into error because of his wrong view of creation. He will follow the teaching of Kaśyapa[24] and other Brahmans and will, in his quest of immortality, offer his body and mind to serve and worship fire and water, thereby screening his Bodhi nature and missing the Buddha-knowledge.

---

[23] A Brahman who is said to have denied the permanence of Nirvāṇa and maintained that plants had lives and sentience.

[24] Who sets up a Creator of gods, demons, men and animals.

'This is the fifth state of the aggregate of consciousness which postulates the worship (of the elements) thus throwing away the mind to pursue its objects and wrongly seeking the causes of fruition; he will thus stray far from Complete Enlightenment and will stand opposite to Nirvāṇa, thereby sowing the seed of inverted transformation.

6. 'As the practiser looks exhaustively into saṁskāra which now ends, he wipes out birth and death but does not yet achieve Nirvāṇa. In this state of bright and empty consciousness, he may be tempted to believe that voidness destroys all things and will cling to annihilation as his last refuge. He will fall into error because he clings to nothingness and so will think that devas without thought are void thereby screening his Bodhi nature and missing the Buddha-knowledge.

'This is the sixth 'state of the aggregate of consciousness which is completely void and mindless leading to empty fruition; the practiser will stray far from Complete Enlightenment and will stand opposite to Nirvāṇa, thereby sowing the seed of annihilation

7. As the practiser looks exhaustively into saṁskāra which now ends, he wipes out birth and death but does not yet achieve Nirvāṇa. In this continued state of consciousness, he may be tempted by its seeming permanence to try and make his own body deathless and free it from mortality. Such misconception will cause him to fall into error because of his wrong desire and to follow the teaching of Asita-ṛṣi who postulates longevity, thereby screening his Bodhi nature and missing the Buddha-knowledge.

'This is the seventh state of the aggregate of consciousness which clings to long life and sets up the false cause of preservation in the search for permanent fruition; the practiser will thus stray far from Complete Enlightenment and will stand opposite to Nirvāṇa, thereby sowing the seed of false prolongation of life.

8. 'As the practiser looks exhaustively into saṁskāra which now ends, he wipes out birth and death but does not yet realize Nirvāṇa. In his contemplation of the aggregate of consciousness from which springs life, he may be apprehensive that its end will cause the total annihilation of the worldly; he will by means of the power of transformation (of ālaya), sit in a lotus palace and exhibit the seven treasures and beautiful girls to give rein to his mind. He will thus fall into error because of his indulgence in falsehood and will follow the heavenly

demon, thereby screening his Bodhi nature and missing the Buddha-knowledge.

'This is the eighth state of the aggregate of consciousness which gives rise to the cause of worldly fruition; the practiser will thus stray far from Complete Enlightenment by standing opposite to Nirvāṇa, thereby sowing the seed of heavenly demons.

9. 'Further, as the practiser looks exhaustively into saṁskāra which now ends, he wipes out birth and death but does not yet achieve Nirvāṇa. As he contemplates his bright consciousness, if he begins to differentiate between its fine[25] and coarse[26] characteristics, thus implying the duality of reality and falsehood in his search for the truth, he will stray from the pure and clean Path; he will look into suffering, the cutting of its cause, its destruction and the way thereto, and will stop at its annihilation without striving to advance further. By so doing, he will follow those whose minds are fixed on the śrāvaka stage, those devas of the four dhyāna heavens and those who refuse to hear further about the Dharma, and so develop self-conceit, thereby screening his Bodhi nature and missing the Buddha-knowledge.

'This is the ninth state of the aggregate of consciousness which unites with its essence for nirvanic fruition; the practiser will thus stray far from Complete Enlightenment by standing opposite to Nirvāna, thereby sowing the seed of obstructive voidness.

10. 'Further, as the practiser looks exhaustively into saṁskāra which now ends, he is free from birth and death but does not yet achieve Nirvāna. As he contemplates the bright and pure essence of consciousness, if he looks deeper into its depth, he may regard the latter as Nirvāna and will not strive to advance further. He will be one of those whose minds are set on pratyeka Buddhahood and who live apart from others to seek self-enlightenment, thereby screening his Bodhi nature and missing the Buddha-knowledge.

'This is the tenth state of the aggregate of consciousness which is the union of mind with pure awareness culminating in clear fruition; the practiser will thus stray far from Complete Enlightenment by standing opposite to Nirvāna thereby sowing the seed of incomplete enlightenment.

---

[25] Ālaya itself.

[26] Ālaya's objects.

'Ānanda, these are the ten states of dhyāna leading to wild speculations because the practiser relies on delusion and regards inadequate achievement as full realization. They are due to the intermingling of the fifth aggregate of consciousness with meditative mind. Deluded and wayward people who do not know their own capabilities, rest their minds infatuated by former habits on these states which now manifest and which they regard as their ultimate abodes. They will wrongly declare that they have realized Supreme Bodhi and will thus break the rule against lying, thereby forming the evil karma of heretics and evil demons which will send them down to the unintermittent hells. As to śrāvakas and pratyeka-buddhas (whose minds are fixed), they will not make further progress.

'After my Nirvāṇa, in the Dharma ending age, you should all proclaim this teaching so that living beings will awaken to it, that the demons of their false perception cannot cause them self-inflicted calamities and that all practisers can be on their guard and wipe out heterodox views. You should teach them how to discipline their bodies and minds so that they achieve the Buddha-knowledge by not going the wrong way from the start of their practice. This Dharma-door was followed in past aeons countless as the Ganges' sands by Tathāgatas numberless as dust, who thereby opened their minds and won the Supreme Tao.

'If the aggregate of Consciousness comes to an end, all your sense organs will intermingle for uniform functioning and you will enter the indestructible state of dry wisdom in which your enlightened essence of mind will manifest, like pure crystal with the precious moon within. You will then leap over the ten stages of Bodhisattva faith, the ten stages each of a Bodhisattva's wisdom, activities and dedication, the four stages of intensified efforts, the ten indestructible Bodhisattva positions (Daśabhūmi) and the state of Universal Enlightenment to enter the Tathāgata's majestic ocean of Wonderful Enlightenment, thus perfecting Bodhi to return to where nothing can be won.

'The above are very fine states of Māra discerned by past Buddhas while abiding in the condition of vipaśyanā when they practiced śamatha. If you know beforehand these māra states, you will be able to rub off the dust of your mind and will avoid wrong views; the demons of the five aggregates will vanish; the heavenly demons will be crushed; the powerful ghosts and spirits will take fright and run away; the spirits of the rivers and the hills will not come to trouble you until you achieve Bodhi. You will thus begin your practice from inferior states of mind and then progress toward great Nirvāṇa with a mind free from delusion and perplexity.'

The Falsehood of the Five Aggregates

After hearing the Buddha's instruction, Ānanda rose from his seat and prostrated himself with his head at His feet. Since he had received the teaching which he could now remember well, he said: 'As the Buddha has said, the five kinds of falsehood arising from the five aggregates are due to the thinking mind but we have not heard your explanation in detail. Further, should the five aggregates be wiped out simultaneously or separately one after another? What are their boundaries? Will you be compassionate enough to teach us so that everyone here can cleanse his mind-eye and be the future guiding eye for living beings in the Dharma ending age?'

The Buddha said: 'Ānanda, pure Reality is profound Enlightenment, and basic Enlightenment is perfect and pure, containing neither birth and death nor any impurities nor even voidness, all of which spring from false thinking. From the profound enlightened true essence of basic Enlightenment arises the illusion of a material universe in the same way that Yajñadatta deceived himself into believing in the image of his head. Fundamentally falsehood has no cause but false thinking sets it up and deluded people (further) mistake it for being the self as such. Even voidness is but an illusion, (how much more so are) cause and the self as such which are the product of discrimination arising in the false mind of living beings. Ānanda, if you know where falsehood arises, you can speak of cause, but if fundamentally there is no falsehood, how can you speak of cause? Still less can you speak of the self as such. Therefore, the Tathāgata reveals to you that the basic cause of the five aggregates is false thinking.

Falseness of the first aggregate of form (rūpa)

'Your body owes its existence first to your parents' thought of giving birth but had you not thought (of being born), there would have been no chance for your incarnation in their thought. As I said earlier, when you think of vinegar, your mouth waters and when you think of scaling a high cliff, you feel distress in the soles of your feet. But there is neither vinegar nor cliff and if your body is not of the same (illusory) nature as falsehood, how can water come to your mouth when you think of vinegar? Therefore, you should know that your physical body (rūpakāya) is the first state of congealation of your false thinking.

Falseness of the second aggregate of receptiveness (vedanā)

'We have spoken of the thought of scaling a cliff which can cause your body to feel distress. This is the aggregate of receptiveness affecting your physical body which is thus moved by favourable or adverse feelings. This is the second state of empty reflection of your false thinking.

Falseness of the third aggregate of conception (sañjña)

'Your thought can make your body move but if both are not akin how can body obey thought's order to act? Therefore, when mind stirs, body obeys and both act in perfect unison. When you are awake, your thinking mind works but when you sleep, dreams take the place of thoughts.[27] Therefore, you should know that your thoughts stir your false feelings. This is the third state of pervasiveness of your false thinking.

Falseness of the fourth aggregate of discrimination (saṁskāra)

'Transformation never stops and changes imperceptibly every instant, as shown by the growth of hair and nails, and the loss of vitality in old age as revealed by the wrinkles on one's face. This change occurs day and night but we do not notice it. Ānanda, if this is not you, why does your body change? (On the other hand) if it is you, why do you not notice the change? Therefore, you should know that every discrimination does not stop in a flash of thought. This is the fourth state of concealment of your false thinking.

Falseness of the fifth aggregate of consciousness (vijñāna)

If your pure, bright, profound and subtle (consciousness) is permanent, why (is it conditioned by and) does not go beyond your body's seeing, hearing, feeling and knowing? If it is the real, it should not allow itself to be affected by your false habits. Very long ago you saw unusual things but you then forgot all about them. Why do you remember them so vividly when you now see them again? This shows that the contamination of your clear and still consciousness continues, instant after instant, in unbroken continuity; how can you ascertain this? Ānanda, you should know that this still (Consciousness) is not Reality and is like a river which flows swiftly but seems to be still; if you do not see it flow, this does not mean that it stops. If consciousness is not the source of false thinking, how can it be influenced by wrong habits? If you fail to (wipe out separateness and) achieve the uniform functioning of all your six sense organs, your false thinking cannot be brought to an end. Therefore, behind your seeing, hearing, feeling and knowing, there is chain of subtle worldly habits and within your still consciousness there is something which seems not to but does exist and which is the fifth subtle state of your false thinking.

'Ānanda, all the five aggregates are created by this fivefold false thinking. As to their boundaries about which you wish to know, form and voidness are the boundaries of the aggregate of rūpa; receptiveness and

[27] This is probably why the late Prof. C. G. Jung studied dreams in his research into what he called the unconscious.

non-receptiveness of vedanā; remembrance and forgetfulness of sañjñā; rise and fall of saṁskāra; and the return of consciousness to, and its union with, its substance are those of vijñāna.

'The five aggregates arise by piling themselves upon one another. They originate from consciousness (mind) and should be eliminated beginning with form (matter). In principle, they all vanish the moment one is instantaneously awakened, but in practice, they are wiped out gradually due to the force of habit. I have shown you how to untie the six knots in a cloth and all this should have been clear to you; why do you still ask me (about it)?

'You should awaken to the source of false thinking and open your mind, and then teach practisers in the Dharma ending age so that they know its falsehood and reject it, become aware of the existence of Nirvāṇa, and so stop hankering after the three worlds.

'Ānanda, if a man fills space in the ten directions with the seven treasures and then offers them to Buddhas uncountable as dust, with his mind set on serving them faultlessly, what do you think of his merits from such a good cause?'

Ānanda replied: 'Space is boundless and the treasures that fill it cannot be counted. Once a man only offered seven coins to (seven) Buddhas and his merit led to his rebirth as a heavenly ruler of the world; how much more so is the unlimited merit derived from offering treasures that fill Buddha-lands in boundless space?'

The Buddha said: 'Ānanda, the words of Buddhas are not deceitful. If another man, after committing the four[28] and ten[29] sins (pārājikas) and after falling into the avīci hells, can, in a flash, think of teaching this Dharma door to living beings in the Dharma ending age, his evil sins will vanish and his hells of suffering will change into happy places for his merit surpasses that of the giver of treasures, because the latter's cannot be even a hundredth, a thousandth, a hundred thousandth of the former's, in fact no comparison can be made between the two. Ānanda, if someone reads (and practises) this sūtra, the whole aeon will pass long before his merits can be enumerated in full. He who follows and practises my teaching will be free from all the obstructions of Māra and will realize Bodhi.'

After the Buddha had expounded this sūtra, all the monks, nuns, male and female devotees, devas, men, Bodhisattvas, śrāvakas, praryeka-buddhas, ṛṣis and newly initiated ghosts and spirits were filled with joy, paid revenue to Him and left.

---

[28] The four sins are: killing, stealing, carnality and lying.

[29] The ten sins are: killing, stealing, carnality, lying, selling wine, talking of a monk's misdeeds, self-praise for degrading others, meanness, anger at rebuke and vilifying the Triratna.

Glossary

Ābhāsvara: The third dhyāna heaven of the second region where infinite light is the theme of the teaching voice that preaches purity and cleanness to all who can respond.

Abhimukhī: The stage of the appearance of the absolute; the sixth of the ten highest stages of Bodhisattva attainment.

Abhisecana: Consecration by sprinkling, or pouring water on the head.

Acala: Stage of imperturbability; the eighth of the ten highest stages of Bodhisattva attainment.

Ajñāta-kauṇḍinya: A disciple of the Buddha who attained arhatship by means of meditation on the sound.

Akaniṣṭha: The last of the five heavens from which there is no return.

Ākāśagarbha: A Bodhisattva who realized enlightenment by means of meditation on the element of space.

Ākāśanantyāyatana: The heaven of boundless emptiness, the first of the four heavens beyond form.

Akiñcanyāyatana: The heaven of nothingness; the third of the four heavens beyond form.

Ālaya: The store of consciousness, also called the eighth consciousness.

Amitābha: The Buddha of Infinite Light of the Western Paradise of Bliss, with Avalokiteśvara on his left and Mahāsthāmaprāpta on his right.

Anabhraka: the heaven of felicitous delight, the second of the four dhyāna heavens of the fourth region.

Anāgāmin: A non-coming or non-returning arhat who will not be reborn; the third stage of the path.

Ānanda: A cousin of the Buddha. He was noted as the most learned disciple, and famed for hearing and remembering His teaching. He was a compiler of sūtras and the Second Patriarch of the Ch'an sect.

Aniruddha: A disciple of the Buddha who realized enlightenment by turning the organ of sight back to its source.

Anutpattika-dharma-kṣānti: The patient endurance of create, or rest in the imperturbable reality which is beyond birth and death and requires a very patient endurance. The Prajñapāramitā-śāstra defines it as the unflinching faith and unperturbed abiding in the underlying reality of all things, which is beyond creation and destruction. It must be realized before attainment of Buddhahood.

Apramāṇābha: The heaven of infinite light; the second of the three dhyāna heavens of the second region.

Apramāṇaśubha: The heaven of infinite purity; the second of the three dhyāna heavens of the third region.

Arbuda: Or a mass, during the second week of formation of a foetus.

Arciṣmatī: The state of glowing wisdom; the fourth of the ten highest stages of Bodhisattva attainment.

Arhat: A saintly man, the highest type or ideal in Hīnayāna in contrast with a Bodhisattva as the saint in Mahāyāna.

Arūpadhātu: The realm beyond form.

Asañjñisattva: The heaven of thoughtless devas; the last of the four dhyāna heavens of the fourth region.

Āsrava: Worldly or impure efflux from the mind, as contrasted with anāsrava, i.e. outside the passion-stream.

Asura: Titanic demons, enemies of the gods, with whom, especially Indra, they wage constant war.

Atapa: a heaven free from the heat of minor trouble; the second of the five heavens from which there is no return.

Avalokiteśvara: Kuan Yin or Goddess of Mercy in China, so called because of his appearance as a benevolent lady. He attained enlightenment by means of the faculty of hearing.

Avīci: The last and deepest of the eight hells, where sinners suffer, die and are instantly reborn to suffer without interruption.

Avṛha: A heaven free from trouble; the first of the five heavens from which there is no return.

Āyatana, The twelve: Six sense organs and six sense data.

Bhadrapāla: A Bodhisattva who realized enlightenment by means of meditation on touch.

Bhaiśajya-rāja: The elder of the two brothers, who was the first to decide on his career as Bodhisattva of healing and led his younger brother to adopt the same course.

Bhaiśajya-samudgata: The Bodhisattva of healing whose office is to heal the sick; younger brother of Bhaiśajya-rāja.

Bhikṣu, bhikṣuni: Buddhist monk and nun.

Bhīśma-garjita-ghoṣa-svara-rāja: The king with awe-inspiring voice, the name of countless Buddhas successively appearing during the kalpa or aeon called 'the kalpa free from the calamities of decadence, famine, epidemics, etc.'

Bhūtatathatā: Bhūta is substance, that which exists; tathatā is suchness, thusness, i.e. such is its nature. It means the real, thus always, or eternally so; i.e. reality as contrasted with unreality, or appearance; and the unchanging or immutable as contrasted with form and phenomena.

Bodhi: Enlightenment.

Bodhimaṇḍala: Holy site, place of enlightenment; the place where the Buddha attained enlightenment or where He expounded the Dharma; a monastery.

Bodhisattva: A Mahayanist seeking enlightenment to enlighten others; he is devoid of egoism and devoted to helping all living beings.

Buddha: The Enlightened One; the first of the Triple Gem, the second being Dharma (Doctrine) and the third, Saṅgha (Order).

Buddha Dharma: The doctrine or teaching of the Buddha.

Brahmā: The father of all living beings; the first person of the Brahminical Trimūrti (trinity): Brahmā, Viṣṇu and Śiva, recognized by Buddhism as devas but as inferior to a Buddha, or enlightened man.

Brahmacārin: A Brahman ascetic with his mind set on pure living.

Brahmakāyika: Assembly of brahma-devas.

Brahmapurohitas: Retinue of Brahmā.

Bṛhatphala: The heaven of Abundant Fruit; the third of the four dhyāna heavens of the fourth region.

Candraprabha: A Bodhisattva who realized enlightenment by means of meditation on the element of water.

Candra-sūrya-pradīpa: The title of 20,000 Buddhas who succeeded each other preaching the Lotus Sūtra.

Catur-mahārāja-kāyika: The four heavens of the four deva-kings; the first of the six heavens of the realm of desire.

Ch'an: Name of mind; ch'an being name and mind being substance; wrongly interpreted as meditation, abstraction, or dhyāna in Sanskrit.

Dāna: Charity, almsgiving, i.e. of money, goods or doctrine.

Dānapāramitā: the first of the six pāramitās, consisting in the perfect exercise of almsgiving for the purpose of crossing over from this shore of mortality, or saṁsāra to the other shore, or Nirvāṇa. The five other pāramitās are: śīla, moral conduct; kṣānti, patient endurance; vīrya, zeal and devotion; dhyāna, abstract meditation and prajñā, wisdom.

Daśabhūmi: The ten highest stages of Bodhisattva attainment.

Devas: The gods; the highest incarnations of the six worlds of existence.

Devaloka: The realm of gods.

Dhāraṇī: Or mantra; an incantation, spell, oath; mystical formulae employed in yoga to control the mind so that it cannot be affected by external influence.

Dharaṇimdhara: Or 'Ruler of the Earth'; a Bodhisattva who realized Bodhi by means of meditation on the element of earth.

Dharma: The truth, law or doctrine; a thing, all things, anything great or small, visible or invisible, real or unreal, concrete thing or abstract idea. It connotes Buddhism as the perfect religion and has the second place in the triratna, or Triple Gem.

Dharmadhātu: (a) A name for things in general, noumenal or phenomenal; for the physical universe, or any part of it. (b) The unifying underlying spiritual reality regarded as the ground or cause of all things, the absolute from which all proceeds, (c) One of the eighteen dhātus, or realms of senses. There are categories of three, four, five and ten dharmadhātus. The ten are the realms of (1) Buddhas, (2) Bodhisattvas, (3) pratyeka-buddhas, (4) śrāvakas, (5) devas, (6) men, (7) asuras, or titans, (8) animals, (9) hungry ghosts and (10) hells. The four are: (1) the phenomenal realm, with differentiation; (2) the noumenal realm, with unity; (3) the realm of both the noumenal and phenomenal which are interdependent and (4) the realm of phenomena which are also interdependent. The three are the above four minus the phenomenal realm, i.e. (1) the noumenal realm, (2) the realm of both noumenal and phenomenal which are interdependent, and (3) the realm of phenomena which are also interdependent. The five are: (1) the worldly, or the above 'phenomenal' realm; (2) the transcendental, or the above 'noumenal'; (3) the realm of both the worldly and transcendental, or the above 'noumenal and phenomenal which are interdependent'; (4) neither the worldly nor the transcendental or the above 'noumenal and phenomenal which are interdependent'; and (5) the unhindered realm, or the above 'phenomena which are also interdependent'.

Dharmakāya: Body in its essential nature, or that of the Buddha as such; it is perceptible to Buddhas only.

Dharmamegha: The stage of Dharma-clouds in which sheltering clouds of compassion cover the ocean of Nirvāṇa; the last of the ten highest stages of Bodhisattva attainment.

Dhyāna: Meditation, abstract contemplation; meditative study of the 'mean' which is inclusive of both unchanged noumenon and changing phenomena.

Dhyāna-pāramitā: The fifth of the six pāramitās, consisting in the perfect meditation for the purpose of crossing over from this shore of mortality, or saṁsāra to the other shore, or Nirvāṇa.

Dīpaṁkara Buddha: The twenty-fourth predecessor of Śākyamuni, who predicted the latter's attainment of Buddhahood.

Dūraṁgamā: The all-embracing stage, the seventh of the tert highest stages of Bodhisattva attainment.

Gandharvas: Spirits on the fragrant mountain so called because they do not eat meat or drink wine, but feed on incense and give off fragrant odours.

Garuḍa: A mythical bird, the queen of the feathered race, enemy of the serpent race; vehicle of Viṣṇu.

Gāthā: Stanza, poem or chant; one of the twelve divisions of the Mahāyāna canon.

Gavāṁpati: A disciple of the Buddha, who attained arhatship by means of meditation on the organ of taste.

Ghana: A solid lump during the fourth week of formation of a foetus.

Han Shan: 'Silly Mountain', a name adopted by Ch'an matter Te Ch'ing who was responsible for the revival of the Ch'an Sect in China in the Ming dynasty. Born in 1546 and died in 1623.

Hetupratyaya: Hetu, primary cause, e.g. a seed; pratayaya, condition or secondary cause, e.g. the earth, rain, sunshine. Translated as cause and condition.

Hīnayāna: 'Small Vehicle', also called 'half-word', preliminary teaching given by the Buddha to His disciples who were still not qualified for receiving His Mahāyāna doctrines, called 'whole-word.'

Hsu Yun: Also called Te Ch'ing, a Ch'an master regarded as the right Dharma Eye of the present generation, 1840-1959.

Jambudvīpa: Our earth.

Jetavana park: A park near Śrāvasti, said to have been obtained from Prince Jetā by the elder Anāthapiṇḍada, in which monastic buildings were erected. It was the favourite resort of the Buddha.

Jñānakāya: Wisdom-body of the Buddha.

Kakuda Kātyāyana: An Indian philosopher who said that when the body died, its annihilation was Nirvāṇa.

Kalala: A slippery coagulation, the human embryo during the first week of formation of a foetus.

Kalpa: Aeon. The period of time between the creation, destruction and recreation of a world or universe.

Kalyāṇamitra: A man of good counsel, or one who is ready to teach the Dharma to others.

Kamādhātu: The realm of desire.

Karma: Moral action causing future retribution, and either good or evil transmigration.

Kaṣāya: A period of turbidity, impurity or chaos, i.e. of decay.

Kātyāyana: Also called Mahākātyāyana and Mahākātyāyaniputra, one of the ten noted disciples of the Buddha.

Kauṣṭhila: also called Mahākauṣṭhila, an arhat, maternal uncle of Śāriputra, who became an eminent disciple of the Buddha.

Kinnara: The musicians of Kuvera (the god of riches) with men's bodies and horses' heads.

Kleśa: Worry, anxiety, trouble, distress and whatever causes them.

Kliṣṭa-mano-vijñāna: The seventh consciousness; it is the discriminating and constructive sense, more than the intellectually perceptive, it is the cause of all egoism and individualizing, i.e. of men and things.

Kṣaṇa: The shortest measure of time; 60 kṣaṇa equal one finger-snap, 90 a thought, 4,500 a minute.

Kṣāntipāramitā: The third pāramitā consisting in the practice of patient endurance to cross over from this shore of mortality, or saṁsāra to the other shore, or Nirvāṇa.

Kṣudrapanthaka: A disciple of the Buddha who realized arhatship by means of meditation on the organ of smell.

Kukkuṭa park: Cook's Foot mountain in Magadha, on which Kāśyapa entered into Samādhi but where he is still supposed to be living.

Mādhyamika: The Middle School, founded by Nāgārjuna.

Mahābrahmā heaven: The last of the three dhyāna heavens of the first region.

Mahākāśyapa: A Brahmin of Magadha, disciple of the Buddha, to whom was handed down the Mind Dharma, outside of Scriptures; the First Patriarch of the Ch'an sect; accredited with supervising the first compilation of the Buddha's sermons.

Mahā-Maudgalyāyana: Also called Maudgalaputra, one of the ten chief disciples of the Buddha, specially noted for his transcendental powers.

Mahāsthāma: Also called Mahāsthāmaprāpta, a Bodhisattva representing the Buddha-wisdom of Amitābha. He is on Amitābha's right with Avalokiteśvara on the left. They are called the Three Holy Ones of the Western Paradise of Bliss.

Mahāyāna: The Great Vehicle which indicates universalism, or salvation for all, for all are Buddhas and will attain enlightenment. (See Hīnayāna.)

Mahoraga: A class of demons shaped like the boa.

Maitreya: The Buddhist Messiah, or next Buddha, now in Tuṣita heaven, who is to come 5,000 years after the Nirvāṇa of Śakyamuni Buddha.

Mañjuśri: A Bodhisattva who is the symbol of wisdom and is placed on the Buddha's left with Samantabhadra on the right. His bodhimaṇḍala is on the Five-Peaked mountain (Wu T'ai Shan) in China.

Mano-vijñāna: The faculty of mind, usually called the sixth consciousness.

Mantra: See Dhāraṇī.

Manuṣya: A man.

Marā: A demon.

Maskari Gośālīputra: One of the six Heretics who denied that the present lot was due to karmic deeds in former lives.

Mātaṅgī: a low-caste woman who inveigled Ānanda.

Mṛgadāva park: A deer park north-east of Vārāṇaśī, a favourite resort of the Buddha.

Mudrā: Manual gestures used in yoga which stands for deed (body) while the repetition of mantra for word (mouth) and meditation for thought (intellect). The three are necessary to disengage the mind from externals in the practice of dhyāna.

Nāga: A dragon.

Naivasaṁjñānā-saṁjñāyatana: The heaven of devas who are neither thoughtful nor thoughtless; the last of the four heavens beyond form.

Nārakagati: The realm of hells.

Nirmāṇakāya: Transformation body of a Buddha, that of power to transform himself at will into any form for the omnipresent salvation of those needing him. It is perceptible to men and devas.

Nirmāṇarati: A heaven where joy is attainable at will.

Niṣad: See Upaniṣad.

Pañcānantarya: The five rebellious acts: parricide, matricide, killing an aehat, shedding the blood of a Buddha, and destroying the harmony of the Order.

Pārājika: The ten grave sins: killing, stealing, carnality, lying, dealing in spirits, talking of a monk's misdeeds, self-praise for degrading others, meanness, anger at rebuke and vilifying the Buddha, Dharma and Saṅgha.

Pāpīyān, pāpīyas. A very wicked demon, the Evil One, Devil.

Pāramitā: Crossing over from this shore of births and deaths to the other shore, or Nirvāṇa.

Pāramiti: An Indian monk from Central North India who came to China to translate the Śūraṅgama Sūtra.

Paranirmata-vaśavartin: The last of the six heavens of the realm of desire.

Pariṇāmanā: Dedicating merits acquired by oneself to further progress in Bodhi, or to others so that they succeed in their practice of the Dharma.

Parinirvāṇa: Final extinction of samsaric existence with complete end of its concommitant suffering for entry into the transcendental realm of true permanence, bliss, self and purity as described in the Mahāparinirvāṇa Sūtra.

Parīttābha: The heaven of Minor Light, the first of the three dhyana heavens of the second region.

Parīttaśubha: The heaven of Minor Purity, the first of the three dhyāna heavens of the third region.

Peśī: A piece of soft flesh during the third week of formation of a foetus.

Pilindavatsa: A disciple of the Buddha who attained arhatship by means of meditation on the body.

Prabhākara: The stage of illumination, the third of the ten highest stages of Bodhisattva attainment.

Prajñā: Wisdom.

Prajña-pāramitā: The last of the six pāramitās consisting in the perfect arousal and exercise of inner wisdom for the purpose of crossing over from this shore of mortality, or saṁsāra to the other shore, or Nirvāṇa.

Pramuditā: The stage of joy; the first of the ten highest stages of Bodhisattva attainment.

Praśākhā: A foetus with organs during its fifth week of formation.

Prasenajit: Kings of Śrāvastī, contemporary of the Buddha.

Pratyeka-buddha: One who lives apart from others and attains enlightenment alone, or for himself, in contrast with the altruism of the Bodhisattva principle.

Preta: A hungry ghost.

Puṇyaprasava: The heaven of felicious birth; the first of the four dnyāna heavens of the fourth region.

Pūrṇamaitrāyaṇīputra: A disciple of the Buddha who realised arhatship by means of meditation on tongue perception.

Rāhula: The eldest son of Śākyamuni and Yaśodharā.

Rākṣasa: A female demon.

Rṣi: A seer, an immortal.

Rūpa: The first aggregate; form, matter, the physical form related to the five sense organs.

Rūpadhātu: The realm of form.

Sādhumatī: The stage of finest wisdom; the ninth of the ten highest stages of Bodhisattva attainment.

Sāgara-varadhara-buddhi-vikrīḍitābhijña Buddha: The Buddha who taught Candraprabha to wipe out the conception of body in order to realize Bodhi.

Sahā: Our world of birth and death.

Sakṛdāgāmin: Once more to come, or be reborn; the second stage of Hīnayāna path involving only one rebirth.

Samādhi: Internal state of imperturbability, exempt from all external sensation; this state precedes the attainment of Buddhahood.

Samantabhadra: A Bodhisattva, symbol of the fundamental law, dhyāna and the practice of all Buddhas. He is the right-hand assistant of the Buddha and Mañjuśrī is His left-hand assistant. Mount O-Mei in Szechuan, China, is his bodhimaṇḍala, and devotees go there to see myriad Buddha lamps in the sky at night.

Samāpatti: Holding the mind in equilibrium or holding oneself in equanimity; abstract meditation preparatory to the final attainment of Samādhi.

Śamatha: Rest, peace, power to end passion, etc.; interpreted by the T'ien T'ai (Tendai) School as 'Chih' which stops the wandering mind, silences or puts to rest the active mind; the mind steadily fixed on one place, or in one position; getting rid of distraction for moral ends; it is abstraction and is complemented by 'Kuan' which observes, contemplates, sifts evidence.

Śamatha-Vipaśyanā: Interpreted as 'Chih' and 'Kuan' in Chinese. Chih is silencing the active mind and Kuan is developing an insight into the still mind. The chief object is the concentration of the mind by special methods for the purpose of clear insight into the truth and to be rid of illusion.

Sambhoga-kayā: Reward body of a Buddha, that of bliss or enjoyment of the fruits of his past saving labours. It is perceptible to Bodhisattvas only.

Saṁsāra: The realm of births and deaths.

Saṁskāra: Action, activity, conception, disposition.

Samyak-saṁbodhi: Abbreviation for Anuttara-samyak-saṁbodhi: unexcelled complete enlightenment, an attribute of every Buddha Translated into Chinese: the highest, correct and complete or universal knowledge or awareness, the perfect wisdom of a Buddha Omniscience.

Saṅgha: The Buddhist Order, the last of the Triple Gem.

Sañjñā: The third aggregate; conception or discerning; the functioning of mind in discerning.

Śariputra: A disciple of the Buddha, noted for his wisdom.

Sauvastika: A reverse Svastika with its arms turned to the left; an auspicious sign in the centre of the chest of the Buddha.

Śīla: Precept, prohibition, command, discipline, rule, morality.

Śīlapāramitā: the second of the six pāramitās, consisting in the perfect observance of precepts and discipline for the purpose of crossing over from this shore of mortality or samsāra to the other shore or Nirvāṇa.

Siṁhāsana: A bon throne, or couch, a Buddha seat, where the Buddha sits, even when on the bare ground.

Sitātaprata: A white canopy. White stands for pure, immaculate and spotless, i.e. the One Mind in the store of consciousness which is beyond all defilements. Hence the 'white canopy' or pure mind that embraces all things and protects all living beings.

Skandhas, The five: Pañcaskandha in Sanskrit, the five aggregates: form, feeling, ideation, reaction and consciousness.

Śrāvaka: A hearer, disciple of the Buddha who understands the Four Noble Truths, rids himself of the unreality of the phenomenal and enters the incomplete Nirvāṇa.

Śravastī: "The famous City' near which was Jetavana park, the favourite resort of the Buddha.

Śrota-āpanna: One who has entered the stream of holy living, the first stage of the Hīnayāna path.

Śubhakṛtsna: The heaven of universal purity; the last of the three dhyāna heavens of the third region.

Subhūti: A senior disciple of the Buddha who realized arhatship by means of mediation on the intellect.

Sudarśana: The heaven of excellent perception; the third of the five heavens from which there is no return.

Sudṛṣa: The heaven of excellent manifestations; the fourth of the five heavens from which there is no return.

Sudurjayā: the stage of mastery of utmost difficulties; the fifth of the ten highest stages of Bodhisattva attainment.

Sunakṣatra: One of the three sons of the Buddha. After reading the sūtras, he succeeded in keeping from troubles (kleśa) in the world of desire and in achieving the mental concentration of the fourth dhyāna heaven which he mistook for the real Nirvāṇa. Later, he followed heterodox teachers, backslid and did not believe in the doctrine of Nirvāṇa and the law of causality. He became hostile to the Buddha and was reborn in the world of hells. Hence he was called the "Unbelieving bhikṣu'.

Sundarananda: A disciple of the Buddha who attained arhatship by means of meditation on smell perception.

Śūnya: Empty, void, vacant, non-existent.

Śūnyatā: Voidness, emptiness, non-existence, immateriality, unreality, the illusory nature of all existence, the seeming which is unreal.

Surūpa: The wonderful form or body, i.e. of a Buddha's sambhoga-kāya and his Pure Land. When form or rūpa is successfully looked into as identical with the underlying principle from which it springs, it becomes surūpa or wonderful form.

Sūtra: The Buddha's sermons; one of the twelve divisions of the Mahāyāna canon.

Suyāma heaven: The heaven the brightness of which eclipses the light of sun and moon; the third of the six heavens of the realm of desire.

Tao: Road, way, path, doctrine, truth, reality, self-nature, the absolute.

Tathāgata: He who came as did all Buddhas; who took the absolute way of cause and effect, and attained to perfect wisdom; one of the highest titles of a Buddha.

Tathāgata-garbha: Tathāgata store or womb, the absolute in the midst of delusion of desires and passions.

Tirthika: Or Tirtyas, the heretics in India.

Tiryagoni: Animals.

Tiryagoni-gati: The realm of animals.

Trayastriṁśa: the heavens of the thirty-three devas; the heaven of Indra on mount Sumeru; the second of the six heavens of the realm of desire.

Tuṣita: The fourth of the six heavens of the realm of desire; the heaven of contentment which has an inner court, the Pure Land of Maitreya who will descend to earth as the next Buddha.

Ucchuṣma: 'The Fire-head,' an arhat who attained enlightenment by means of meditation on the element of fire.

Upāli: A disciple of the Buddha who attained arhatship by means of meditation on the perception of the abject of touch.

Upananda: A disciple of the Buddha.

Upaniṣad: A disciple of the Buddha who attained arhatship by means of meditation on form. See also Niṣad.

Uruvilvā Kāśyapa: One of the chief disciples of the Buddha, so-called because he practised asceticism in the Uruvilvā forest.

Vairātīputra, Sañjaya Vairātīputra: An Indian heretic who taught that there is no need to seek the right path, as when the necessary aeons have passed, mortality ends and Nirvāṇa naturally follows; a teacher of naturalism.

Vajra: The thunderbolt.

Varuṇa: A Buddha who controlled the waters and taught Bodhisattvas to meditate on the element of water in order to realize Samādhi.

Vedanā: The second aggregate; reception, sensation, feeling, the functioning of mind and senses in connection with affairs and things. Also the seventh of the twelve links in the chain of existence.

Vihāra: A garden, park, monastery, temple.

Vijñāna: The fifth aggregate; mental faculty in regard to perception and cognition, discriminative of affairs and things. Consciousness. Also the third of the twelve links in the chain of existence.

Vijñānānantyāyatana: The heaven of boundless consciousness; the second of the four heavens beyond form.

Vimala: The stage of freedom from all defilement; the second of the ten highest stages of Bodhisattva attainment.

Vira: A demigod.

Virya-pāramitā: The fourth of the six pāramitās, consisting in the perfect exercise of zeal and progress for the purpose of crossing over from this shore of mortality, or saṁsāra to the other shore of Nirvāṇa.

Viśvabhū: The 1000th Buddha of the Glorious Aeon who taught Dharaṇiṁdhara Bodhisattva to meditate on the element of earth in order to realize enlightenment.

Wu Wei: Or Asaṁskṛta, anything not subject to cause, condition or dependence; out of time, eternal, inactive, transcendental.

Yajñadatta: A mad man of Śrāvasti who thought himself bedevilled when one morning he failed to see his head while looking into a mirror.

Yakṣa: Demons in the earth, air or lower heavens.

Yaśodharā: Wife of the Buddha before his enlightenment and mother of Rāhula.

Index

Absolute, The, 44-45, 51, 95, 140-41
Absoluteness, Unfettered, 4
Abstruse, The, 43-44
Adhesions, Five, 89-90
Affections, Inner and outer, 145
Āgama period of teaching, 58
Aggregates, Fifth, 47, 85
  Fifty false states caused by five, 165
  First, 3, 45-46, 85; Fourth, 46-47, 85
  Fusing the five, 45
  Second, 3, 46, 85; The five, 3, 40-41, 43, 45, 84, 136; Third, 47, 85
  Wiping out the fifth, 32; first two, 3; fourth, 25, 32; third, 9, 15, 30
Ājñāta-kauṇḍinya, 18, 98
Ākāśagarbha Bodhisattva, 107
Ālaya's Consciousness, 40, 43, 45, 71, 94, 161
  Form, 45, 85
  Perception, 45, 47-49; 85
  Self-evidencing, 36
  Three Characteristics, 17, 48
Amitābha Buddha, 109
Anāgāmin, 82, 144
Ānanda's weakness, 2
Animals, 145
Anirudha, 29, 90
Annihilation, 145, 170, 179, 184, 187, 191
Approach, Ultimate, 98
Arhat, Arhatship, 3, 98, 100-107, 115, 123, 129, 144, 161, 164
Ascetic life, Six years of, 104
Asita-ṛṣi, 192
Asura, 112, 146
Attachment and names, 71
Avalokiteśvara Bodhisattva, 109, 115, 119-120, 122
  four inconceivable virtues, 114
  Fourteen kinds of fearlessness, 113-14
  Thirty-two transformation-bodies, 112-115
Avataṁsaka doctrine, 58
Awakening, Instantaneous, 80
Awareness, Enlightened, fundamental, 70, 107
  Subjective, 41, 90
  Unenlightened or faulty, 73, 131
Āyatana, The twelve, 44, 51

Behaviour Inverted, 22
Beings, Human, 112
  Non-human, 112, 122
  Twelve categories of, 132
Bhadrapāla, 100
Bhaiṣajya-rāja, Bhaiṣajya-Samudgata, 99
Bhikṣu, The Untutored, 165, 172
Bhikṣuṇī Self-nature, 82, 123, 143
Bhūtatathatā, 43, 45, 76, 141, 143
Birth, Twelve types of, 131
Bodhi, Absolute, 92-94, 97-99, 102-103
  Basic or Dormant, 38, 40, 42-44, 66, 70, 85, 137-139, 165, 195
  Essential, 36; -fruit, 40; Great, 141; Inceptive, 38-40, 44-45, 69, 138; -nature, 69-70, 183-184, 186-192; Perfect, 83, 91; Precious, 114; Pure, 83, 121; Self-natured, 68-70
  Supreme, 3, 78, 88, 90-91, 93, 105-106, 116, 119, 122, 126-127, 130, 142, 165, 193
  Ultimate, 38, 44, 138; Unsurpassed, 58; Wonderful, 113, 124, 160
Bodhimaṇḍala, 114, 124, 161
Bodhisattva, 1, 98, 105, 107, 115, 122, 128, 145
  action, Ten lines of, 138, 189
  attainments, Ten highest stages of, 138, 189
  dedication, Ten acts of, 139, 189
  development into Buddhahood, 88, 128, 130, 142
  faith, Ten stages of, 136, 194

Bodhisattva (*Contd.*)
harnessing stages, Four additional, 140, 189
vehicle, 116
wisdom, Ten stages of, 137, 189
Body, Boundless, 108
Bondabe and liberation, 93
Brahmā, Brahman, 99, 110, 125, 158, 162, 191
Brahmacārin, 80
Buddha bodhi, 140
body, Ten aspects of, 138
Buddha Dharma, 97; hood, 124, 140; Imperturbable, 107; knowledge, 102, 136, 189-192
land, 76, 119, 174; light, 19; mind, 116, 139; nature, 69, 90, 182; seed, 69, 128; Transformation, 2
with an awe-inspiring voice, 100; work, 103, 108, 139

Cakra, 61
Candraprabha Bodhisattva, 106
Candra-sūrya-pradīpa Buddha, 100, 108
Carnality, 125, 134
Causal conditions, 20; externals, 27-28, 40, 43
objects, 28; phenomena, 23, seeing, hearing, feeling and knowing, 42
Causality, Doctrine or law of, 104, 179
Causes and conditions, 80-82
condition and the self as such, 36-38, 195
Direct, concurrent and realizing, 69
Illusory, 25
Chain of the universe, karma and life, The Threefold, 80
Characteristics, Thirty-two excellent, 2
Chiliocosm, Great, 107, 114
Cintāmaṇi pearl, 79
Clearance and obstruction, 89-91, 93
Compassion, Suddha's, 136
Universal, 2, 113
Conditions, changing and unchanged, 89
of killing, stealing and carnality, The three, 79-80
Consciousness(es), Essence of, 11, 40
Store of, 39
The Eighth, 26, 28, 32, 40
The first five, 3
The seventh, 14-15, 25-26, 32;
The sixth, 13
Constant 9, The, 87
Contact and separation, 89-90
Continuity, The Law of, 71
of karmic retribution, 73
of the physical universe, 71-72
of the realm of living beings, 72-73
Control, Perfect (dhāraṇi), 83
Creation, 130, 184, 191
and destruction, 44, 58, 81, 90
Illusory, 41

Decoys, The six, 86
Defilement, Inner, 117, 125-126
Delusion, Origin of, 85
Six classes of, 144
Demigod (vira), 105
Demon, 124, 126-127, 132
Deva, 111-112, 144; Realm of, 145; sight, 136
Dhāraṇi of the great samādhi, 2
Dharaṇirhdhara, 105
Dharma banner, 16; clouds, 141; dhātu, Boundless, 140; eye, 92, 101, 123; kāya, 85, 138, 175
Reality of, 40; realm, 74; stream, 135; voice, 4, 104; Wonderful, 100
Dhyana, 3, 76-77, 91, 94, 106, 108, 124-127, 136, 144, 158-159, 163, 165-166, 170-180, 189, 193
heaven, 29
-samādhi, 114, 125, 127
Seven states of, 15
Differentiation, Faulty, 58
Dipaṁkara Buddha, 107-108
Discriminating seeing, hearing, feeling and knowing, 42
Disturbance (motion) and stillness, 89, 91, 93
Doctrine, Unsurpassed, 95
Dragon (nāga) 112
Duality of Ego and dharma, 16
Existence and Non-existence, 20
mortality and immortality, 20
reality and unreality, 20
Dust, Defiling, 22; Foreign, 18

Ego, Spiritual, 32
Unreality of, 3, 42

Elements, The four, 58, 83-85, 89, 108
The seven, 57, 59-60, 118-119
Enlightenment (Bodhi), Absolute or Wonderful, 73, 76, 139-140, 189
Complete, 107; Inceptive, 37, 39; Nature of, 43; Nirvanic, 11, 74; of Others, 124
Profound, 195; Self-, 83-84; Supreme, 11, 189; Temple of, 128; Ultimate, 44; Universal, 107, 130, 141
Entrances, Fusing the six, 47-48
The Six, 44
The Twelve, 136
Esoteric causes, 143
seal, 144
Externals, Causal, 41
Eyes, Lotus-blue, 3
Mental, 95
Tao, 15

Falseness of both sense organs and consciousness, 26
Feeding, Four ways of, 134
Finger pointing at the moon, 25
Foetus, Five states of a, 72, 131
Form, 25, 41, 42, 51, 59, 98, 116
and mind, 23
and seeing, 94
Relative, 99
Wonderful, 99
Fragrance-adorned Bodhisattva, 99
Function and substance, 137

Gandharva, 112
Garuḍa, 112
Gāthā, 99, 116, 122, 175
Gautama clan, 60
Gavāṁpati, 90
Ghosts, 135, 144-145, 152
Animal, Cruel, Drought, Messenger, Naiad, Nightmarish, Noxious, Servant, Starved and Strange, 153
Giver of Dauntlessness, 115
God of Śūnyatā, 90
Goddess of the Ganges, 89
Golden Light Bhikṣuṇī, 100
Ground, Cause, 83, 90, 141
Fruit, 83, 86, 90, 141

Habit of anger, 148; arrogance and craving, 147; deceitfulness, 148; disputation, 150; lying, 148; resentment, 149; sexual desire, 147; unfairness and wrong views, 149
Hasta, 61
Hearing, Nature of, 92
with the mind, 103
Heavens from which there is no return, The five, 160; Undying, 185
Hall(s), 144
Avīci, 147, 152, 165, 172, 196
Unintermittent, 127, 135, 144, 150, 152, 169, 171-180, 188, 193
The 8 unintermittent, The 15, 29 and 87 lesser, 152
Hīnayāna, 123, 144, 170
Holy fruit, 15

Identity and diversity, 70-71
Ignorance, Haste, 11, 43, 45, 70, 80, 86, 94
Fertilized, 11; Innate, 94
Illusions, Ten profound, 142
of one and six, 88
of universe, karma and living beings, The three, 79
Impartiality, Perfect, 135
Impure efflux from the mind, 103
Indra, 157, 174
Inference, Direct, 29; Comparative, 29
Insight, Diamond, 142
Intellect (intellection), 84; Discriminating, 26
Intermingling of noumenon and phenomenon, 74, 139
Inversion, Actual, 11; Origin of, 10; Refuting all, 16; Two basic, 10, 25
Inverted views, 18
Is, Elimination of, 77
Is not Elimination of, 78
Is and *Is not*, Simultaneous elimination of, 78
Iśvaradeva, 110, 180, 190

Jambudvīpa, 29, 41-42
Jetavana, 1, 3, 5, 93

Kapila, 61
Karma, Collective, 40-42; Evil, 73; Individual, 40-42
Innate and conventional, 104
Law of, 59, 61-62, 63-64, 66
New, 130
Karmic deads and suffering, 71, 126; responsiveness, 130; retribution, 73
Kaśyapa, 60-61, 191; brothers, 102, 105
Kātyāyana (Kakuda), 20
Kauṇḍinya, 98
Kauṣṭhila, 103
Killing, 135
King (kingdom) of treasures, 76, 83
Kinnara, 112
kleśa, 78, 86, 186
into Bodhi, Transmutation of, 130
Knots, The Six, 96
Knowledge, 71; Immaculate, 90; Universal, 105, 182-183
Kṣaṇa, 101
Kṣudrapanthaka, 100
Kuṁbhāṇḍa, 113

Law, King of the (Dharma-king), 6, 99, 102, 107-108, 113, 128, 138
Leavers of homes, 93, 127
Liberation, Unimpeded, 140
Light, A bright, 2, 15; (brightness) and darkness, 89-91
Eternal, 92; Inner, 90; Precious, 107; Wisdom, 16
Lion's roar, 104
-seat, 95, 115, 165
Lords of Ghosts and Spirits, 111
Lotus, A thousand-petalled, 2
period of teaching, 57
Sūtra, 105

Mahākāśyapa, 2, 51, 90, 99
Maha-kauṣṭhila, 1
Mahā-Maudgalyāyana (Maudgalaputra), 1, 7, 51, 65, 80, 103
Mahāsthāma Bodhisattva, 109
Mahāyāna, 58
Maheśvara, 111, 161, 190
Mahoraga, 112
Maitreya Bodhisattva, 108
Majesty, State of Sublime, 116
Man of good counsel, 124, 126
Manjuśrī, 1, 2, 65, 115-116, 141
Mantra, 115
Māra, 103, 105, 124, 157, 164-166, 169, 189, 192
Maskari Gośālīputra, 22, 80
Mataṅgī, 2, 82, 121, 166
Mean, The, 3, 58, 76-77, 79, 94, 110, 136, 138, 141
Meditation on five sense organs, 100; organ of hearing, 109; seven elements, 104; six sense data, 98
Stream of, 115
Mental condition, 23
creation, 35
Mind, Absolute, 78, 144
Bodhi (enlightened) 43, 82, 84, 86-87, 107, 109, 132, 143, 155
Bright, 16, 83, 153; Causal, 25; Clinging (thinking), 26, 90, 135; Consciousness, 108; Creations of, 83; Diamond, 142
Essence of, 114, 136-137; Eye, 195; False, 3, 25, 195; Fundamental, 16, 122, 162-163
-ground, 86, 105, 137, 140; Inner, 135; Inverted, 12
Mind, Light of, 104; Lustful, 125; Murderous, 125, 133
One, 44-45, 68, 79, 84, 90, 94, 101, 108, 140-142
Profound, 23, 153; Profound enlightened, 110; Robber's, 126
Samsaric (worldly), 26, 83, 130
Self-, 43, 66, 140; Still and permanent, 16; Subjective, 83
True, 3, 16, 41-42, 44, 71, 77, 84-85, 88, 94-95, 138, 163
Universal, 2
Molecules, 105
Monism and pluralism, 44
Moon, Real, 35-36, 41
Second, 27, 29, 36, 39, 41
Unreal, 35

Nature, Absolute, 102, 130-131; Bright, 90; Immaterial, 102; Imperishable, 19; Permanent, 92; Profound, 86, 92; True (real), 29, 94, 130; Underlying, 75

Nirvāṇa, 20, 67, 77-78, 80, 82, 86, 91, 93-94, 110, 122, 125-127, 130, 134, 139, 171, 174-180, 187-194, 197
-heart, 122; Hīnayāna's, 136; Ultimate, 83
Niṣad, 99
Non-activity (wu wei), 137, 139, 160, 189
Nothingness, 100, 102, 130, 161, 191
Noumenal unity, 139
Number 800, 87, 1200, 86-87

Objects being and not being, 33-34
of sense, 85
Ocean Symbol, 78
Omnipresence, 140
One Reality, 32

Padma, 61
Pāramitā, 139
Parinirvāṇa, 116, 122, 130-131
Passion for carnality and killing, 72; stealing, 73
Path, Bodhi, 124
Bodhisattva, 86
One, 95
Supreme, 114, 124-125, 188
Transcendental, 82
Unsurpassed, 130
Patient endurance of the uncreate, 98, 105, 107-109, 136
Perception, 33-34, 41, 43, 85
Capacity of, 29, 31
Discriminative, 16, 25
Essence of, 27, 29-30, 32, 36, 38-40, 42, 44, 47
False, 25; Inborn or natural, 16; Inverted, 15-16
Nature of, 28-29; True, 17; Wrong, 25, 43
Perfection, Absolute, 136; Radiant, 31
Permanence, Absolute, 79; Real, 92
Phenomena, Objective, 83
Pilindavatsa, 101
Piśācī, 114
Point of departure, 83, 85, 90-91, 160
Powers, Sovereign, 113
Spiritual, 109
Supernatural, 105, 165, 174, 176
Transcendental, 16, 104, 108, 125, 136-137
Practice, Right, 85
Prajñā, 124-125
Prasenajit, King, 1, 20
Pratyeka-buddha, 3, 58, 84, 128, 165, 171, 193, 198
Preta, 125
Primordial Darkness, 26
Pungent roots, Five kinds of, 134
Pure Land, 106, 108
Pūrṇamaitrāyaṇīputra, 1, 8, 65, 69-70, 78-79, 103
Pūtana, 113

Rāhula, 82
Rakṣa, 113, 139, 146, 151
Reality, 97, 189; Absolute, 103; Bright, 113; One, 69; Permanent, 95, 191; Pure, 85, 139, 195; Timeless, 85; Ultimate, 115
Realm(s) of animals, 146, 154
desire, The Six Heavens of the, 157
devas, 146; evil ghosts, 113
existence, Three, 144
of form, The four regions of dhyāna heavens of the, 158
hells, 146-147; human beings, 146, 157; hungry ghosts, 146
pure spirits, The four heavens of formless, 160
seers, 145, 157
senses, The eighteen, 44, 88
senses, Fusing the eighteen, 54
space and time, 131
titans, The four classes in the, 162
The two, 40
Regarder of Sound, 119
Responsiveness, Continuous, 71
Retribution, Dependent, 41; Direct, 41-42; Karmic, 144
Retributive effects, The six, 150
of wrong hearing and seeing, 150
wrong smelling and tasting, 151
wrong thinking and touching, 152

Sahā, 99, 120
Śakra, 111, 163
Sakṛdāgāmin, 128, 144
Samādhi, 2, 4, 10, 16, 83, 95, 98, 100-101, 103, 105-110, 113, 115-116, 119, 121, 124-132, 134-135, 154-155, 158-159, 161, 163, 165-166, 169, 173, 181-187

Samantabhadra, 103
Samāpatti, 2, 68, 76, 94
Śamatha, 2, 40-41, 58, 94, 139, 155, 169, 181, 189
Śamatha-vipaśyanā, 165
Sambhoga-kāya, 116
Sameness of all beings, 140
body and universe, 106
Saṁsāra, 84, 93, 97, 113, 122, 130, 142, 144, 146, 159, 162, 164, 166, 174-180, 189
 into Nirvana, Transmutation of, 130, 134
Samsaric current, 88; illusions, 44
Samyak-Saṁbodhi, 123, 140
Śāriputra, 1, 8, 60, 65, 80, 102, 106
Sauvastika, 15-16
Seeing, Capacity of, 30
 Defective, 41
 Essence of, 21, 26-27, 29, 44, 64, 161
 Faculty of, 41, 47
 False (wrong) and discriminative, 15-17, 25, 41-42
 hearing, knowing and discerning, 84-86
 Nature of, 17, 40
 True, 42
Seers, 135, 174
Self-nature, 71, 95, 156
Sense(s) data, The six, 85
 Eighteen fields of, 136
 organs, 17
 organs, The six, 90
 perceptions, 17
Śīla, 124-125
Smell, Relative and wonderful, 99
Sound, Profound, 119; Purifier of, 119; Seer of, 119
Source of delusion and enlightenment, Common, 75
Space, 71, 84
Spirits, 135
Śrāvaka, 58, 80, 83, 90, 110, 165, 171, 193, 197
Śravāsti, 1, 5
Śrota-āpanna, 88, 128, 144
State of Anāgāmin, 162
 great arhats, 161
 living beings, The six, 144
Steps, The three decisive, 124-125
 to wipe out Saṁsāra, The three gradual, 132
Stream, Worldly, or stream of transmigration, 101-103, 105, 118, 120, 122, 127
Study, State beyond, 99, 101-102
Subhūti, 1, 2, 8, 65, 80, 102
Subject and object, 70
Sublimation, Practice of, 130
Substance of enlightenment, 34
 Nirvāṇa, 26
Sudden awakening and realization, 78
Sundarananda, 103
Śūraṅgama mantra, 82
 Supreme, 4

Tao (Truth) Supreme, 25, 58, 169, 173, 180, 194
Taste, 100
Tathāgata, 1, 98-105, 108, 110, 114, 116, 120, 122, 127-128, 130, 136-137, 141-143, 144, 146, 174
 's absolute Eternity, Bliss, Self and Purity, 77
 light, 90
 mind, 73
 -mongers, 126
 seed, 137
 stage, 86
 store (womb) 1, 44-45, 47, 51-52, 54, 60, 62-65, 75, 77, 79, 83, 90, 108, 113, 122, 130, 138-139
 store, The noumenon in the, 1, 67
 store, The phenomenon in the, 68, 76
 store, Both noumenon and phenomenon in the, 77-81
Teaching, The Four periods of, 58
Thatness, The One Reality of, 139
Thinking, False thinking, 16
Three meditative studies of the mind, 93
Touch, 99
Transformation body, 1
Truth(s), Four Noble, 98, 110
 Whole, 143-144
Turbid conditions, The five, 83
Turning of taste back to its knower, 101
 the breath back to nothingness, 101
 the mind inwards, 106
 the organ of sight back to its source, 100

Ultimate, The, 78
Unbelievers, 113, 128
Uncreate, The, 55, 73, 84, 190
  and unending, The, 73
Unenlightenment, Six coarse conditions of, 70-71
  Three finer conditions of, 70
Unity-with-differentiation, 44
Universality, 108
Unreal, Wiping out the, 25
Upāli, 104
Upānanda, 90
Upanīṣad, 1, 98
Uruvilvā, 60
Usschuṣma, 105

Vaipulya period of teaching, 58
Vairātīputra (Sañjaya), 20
Varuṇa Buddha, 106
Vasiṣṭha and Śani, 191
Vehicle, Bodhisattva and Buddha, 83; Saintly, 78; Small, 83; Supreme, 78, 83
Views, False, 24
  Heretics' inverted, 20
  Hinayanist's inverted, 19
  of annihilation, 20
  The five wrong, 149
  The worldling's inverted, 18
  Wrong, 16
Vipaśyanā, 142, 194
Viśvabhū Buddha, 105
Voice, Infinite, 107
Void, The, 59
Voidness, Absolute, 44, 48, 107
  Relative, 166

Water and ice, 58
  of craving, 145
Way(s) of demons, 124; devils, 126; spirits, 125
  Three unhappy, 124
  Transcendental, 82
Weightlessness, 159, 170-171
Wheel of birth and death, 2, 162; fire, 146; illusions, 131; metal, 72; saṁsāra, 3, 40, 128, 132, 163; space, 72
  the Law (Dharma) 1, 76, 104; water, 72, 146; wind, 72
White Canopy, 143
Wisdom, Absolute, 110, 115; All, 83-84, 143; -body, 138
  Dry or unfertilized, 130, 135-136, 142, 189
  Essential, 136; -eye, 40, 93; Fire of, 104; Great Mirror, 90, 113
  Perfect, 106; Supreme, 88
Worlds of existence, The three, 134

Yajñadatta, 79-81, 195
Yakṣa, 112, 114, 125, 145
Yama, 96, 151
Yaśodharā, 82